# Crime o
## Mov

## The Official Anthology of the Crime Writers' Association

*stories by:*
Ann Cleeves
Mat Coward
Judith Cutler
Carol Anne Davis
Martin Edwards
Jürgen Ehlers
Kate Ellis
Michael Gilbert
Lesley Grant-Adamson
John Harvey
Reginald Hill
Edward D Hoch
Bill Kirton
Keith Miles
Stephen Murray
Amy Myers
Christine Poulson
Chris Simms
Sally Spedding
Rebecca Tope
Alison White
David Williams

# Crime on the Move

The Official Anthology of the
Crime Writers' Association
edited by

## Martin Edwards

First Published in Great Britain in 2005 by
The Do-Not Press Limited
16 The Woodlands
London SE13 6TY
www.thedonotpress.com
email: cotm@thedonotpress.com

C-format Paperback Original: ISBN 1 904316 46-8

British Library Cataloguing in Publication Data. A catalogue record
for this book is available from the British Library.

1   3   5   7   9   10   8   6   4   2

# Crime on the Move

## LIST OF CONTENTS

# Foreword
## Michael Jecks

As a boy, I used to delight in reading short stories. I was brought up on the magnificent William Brown tales, and as I grew older I progressed to Conan Doyle, then the incomparable Saki. There were so many condensed stories to read, it seemed as though it was a flourishing form of writing and I never gave a thought to the effort involved.

In the past, shorts were highly regarded. The Victorians and Edwardians had magazines which depended upon decent short stories to keep their sales up, and many a nineteenth and twentieth century writer owed his or her career to those publications.

But those magazines have disappeared. It is hard now to win a commission for a short story, especially for one which is crime-based. With the demise of the great monthlies of the past like the *Strand Magazine*, sadly a market for new writing disappeared. Now there are only a few outlets for good short stories. Thankfully, the CWA is one of them.

We are fortunate to have a member who is a keen proponent of the genre: Martin Edwards, who every year threatens, cajoles, and blackmails otherwise sensible authors into writing for him, and I would like to express my thanks for all his hard work over the year during which he has edited this anthology.

When I look at these stories, I have to say that there is something inherently attractive about them. Short stories are complete tales told well and concisely. Ideally they are entire in themselves, and with all the complexity of a novel. Which is why, although they appeal to me hugely, I find writing them very difficult.

This may seem odd. After all, when you look at the stories in these pages, for example, they seem so natural, as though the words flowed easily. One would assume that writing them must be an easy job compared with a whole novel; a short story may be as few as a couple of thousand words long, while a novel could be a hundred thousand or more. There's a great difference there in terms of length. Surely they're less work?

It is the skill of the authors that lulls the reader into that impression, because in reality, to craft a good, a really good, short story, takes a huge amount of effort.

The writer has the same need to create characters, settings, surroundings, and the vital spark that fires the whole: the plot. To invent a short story that is going to work, similar creative energy must be invested, just as though a full-length novel was being written.

Yet whereas a novelist can gradually lead up to the main themes in a book and has the luxury of many pages in which to investigate a character's motivations, with a short story there is no space for prolixity. All has to be precise and succinct. The author must set the scene, sketch out characters and describe action with brevity. These are not skills which all authors possess (myself least of all), but within the Crime Writers' Association we are blessed with many very skilful novelists who are capable of crafting excellent short stories. As you will find, reading this book.

Yes, many of the original vehicles for short stories have disappeared over the years, and many writers and readers mourn their passing. Occasionally there is a new publication which attempts to reinvigorate the short story market, but they rarely succeed. Perhaps it is the competition from television. Commuters read papers on the tubes, and when they arrive home they turn on their favourite soap, rather than immerse themselves in a magazine.

But for all that, it is proof of the enduring appeal of the short story that the CWA anthologies still sell so well.

This anthology is a truly worthy enterprise, and it is a matter of great pleasure to know that there are still many thousands of readers who enjoy picking up a book which has such a rich mix of authors.

If I had been told many years ago as I read Saki or Conan Doyle, that I would be asked to write the forward to an anthology like this, I would have laughed. It would never have occurred to me that I could be lucky enough to become the Chairman of the Crime Writers' Association, nor that I would be asked to write this Foreword.

So, as Chairman of the Crime Writers' Association, I would like to thank the writers for their efforts in creating this anthology, Martin for his efforts in editing, and you, the reader, for buying it.

I hope you take as much pleasure in reading it as me, and that you'll look forward to future CWA anthologies with as much excitement as I do myself.

*Michael Jecks, Chairman, Crime Writers' Association*

# Introduction

## Martin Edwards

Welcome to the third CWA anthology in the current series published by The Do-Not Press. Its predecessors, *Crime in the City* and *Green for Danger*, were very well-received and I am confident that *Crime on the Move* will provide mystery fans with just as much enjoyment. I hope that readers who have yet to read our earlier collections will be tempted to seek them out after sampling the delights assembled here, and also to read more books written by the authors represented.

The 'crime on the move' theme has brought out the very best in the contributors. Members of the CWA are nothing if not ingenious and this book contains a dazzling array of original stories about crimes ancient and modern, amusing and shocking, imaginative and ironic. All but three of the entries were written especially for this book by authors both well-known and relatively unsung. Contributors include not only short story specialists, but also one novelist who had never before turned her hand to the short form. Do check out the other work of those whose stories you find especially entertaining.

As for the three previously published stories, they come from luminaries of the genre. I am sure that Reginald Hill's legion of admirers will be delighted by the chance to read an excellent tale that deserves a wider audience. Ed Hoch's story is a splendid example of the 'impossible crime', while Michael Gilbert's classic mystery is a reminder of the craftsmanship of a mystery writer, born in 1912, who is as prolific as he is accomplished. It is a privilege to have the support of distinguished authors who have been stalwarts of the CWA for many years; indeed, Michael Gilbert was one of its founder members, just over half a century ago, and is a former co-editor of the CWA's annual anthology. It is also an honour to have been allowed to include a brand new story submitted by David Williams shortly before his untimely death last year.

A book such as this does not come into being without a great deal of hard work from a lot of people. As ever, I am very grateful to all the CWA members who offered stories for consideration, to Mike Jecks and the CWA committee for their enthusiastic support, to everyone at The Do-Not Press, and also to my family, for their patience over many months while this collection gradually took shape. A final word of thanks must go to you, the reader. The short story is often described, especially by publishers, as an endangered species, and it is not often a highly remunerative form for the writer. But the pleasure that readers take in these collections is in itself a reward for CWA members. As long as you keep telling us how much you enjoy our short mystery stories, you can be sure that we will keep writing them.

*Martin Edwards*

# OWL WARS

## Ann Cleeves

*Although her novels are almost invariably set in the UK, Ann Cleeves'*
*contributions to the last two CWA anthologies have been short stories*
*set in, respectively, Africa and Alaska. This time she makes effective*
*use of an unusual setting in Finland. Her early novels reflected her*
*interest in and extensive knowledge of the world of ornithology. This*
*story sees a welcome return for a key character from that much-*
*acclaimed series.*

It was eleven o'clock. At home, the pubs would be closing, the
street lights would be on and people would be preparing for bed.
Here, on the edge of the Arctic Circle, there was no night in June.
The birds still sang at three in the morning and it seemed that nobody
slept.

The small group outside the nature centre was edgy and awake.
The Finnish guide sat in the minibus, smoking a cigarette, bored. He'd
worked thirty-seven nights without a break. What did it matter to
him if they started a little late? But the group wanted to see owls. Ural
and pygmy and great grey. They'd seen hawk owl and Tengmalm's in
Kuusamo and needed to complete the list. They gathered around
Annie, expecting an explanation.

She was tempted to say, *Look, it's not my fault he's not on time.*
*You know what he's like. Go without him.* But they couldn't go without Simon. He was their leader. As soon as he turned up their restive-
ness would disappear. They'd be all smiles and understanding then.
He'd been late before and they'd always forgiven him. He was like
their surrogate son, their favourite nephew.

'Ten minutes,' Annie said. 'He might have gone to the tower to
photograph the cranes.'

She ran along the path cut through the reeds towards the orange
sun which would never quite set. She paused once to brush the

mosquitoes away from her face. When she looked back at the group, she saw that George, the oldest of them, was watching her.

The trail was made of stripped pine trunks, split in half and laid flat side up. The path was only two logs wide and uneven, so she had to watch her feet. It had been cut through birch scrub from the centre, then ran across the reed bed to the bay. Simon had brought them here earlier in the day while the sun was still hot. The watch tower was more than sixty feet high, three storeys, built of rough planks. It had steep wooden steps and was enclosed at the top by a single rail. From there they'd looked over the reed bed to the sea. They'd watched flocks of cranes coming into the marsh, and heard whooper swans. He'd pointed out, on islands of rock in the water, the huts where fishermen and hunters stayed. The space, flat and wild as far as she could see, had made her dizzy.

Now, lost in memory, she had come, quite suddenly to the base of the tower. Beyond it there was a wide ditch full of brown water. A rotting punt was tethered to a loose post. She heard a bittern wheezing, and footsteps behind her, though the reeds were too tall and thick for her to tell who it could be. Then she saw Simon. He lay, crumpled and damp as if he'd been washed up the creek by the tide. He had been the centre of her life for nine months and she could tell without touching him that he was dead.

They'd met at the British Birdwatching Fair at Rutland Water, in the main marquee, which had that English summer smell of crushed grass, tarpaulin and rope. She saw *him* first. He was sitting on a stool by a stand which advertised natural history tours, talking earnestly to a middle aged couple. No doubt he was selling, persuading, but the couple seemed not to mind. They listened, giving him their full attention, as if they were getting a story, not a sales pitch. Then he looked up and saw Annie and gave a wide, flattering smile of appreciation. In that moment she felt she knew everything about him. She knew, for instance, that he'd used that smile to get his own way since he was a baby.

And still, even knowing that, she didn't walk away. She took her time. She didn't rush over immediately to pretend an interest in

Madagascar or Morocco. She had more sense than that. She picked up the recently published *Birds New to Britain* and admired the illustrations. She filled out a form to join the British Trust for Ornithology. But from the corner of her eye she was watching him and she knew he was trying to catch her attention. She moved across the boarded floor of the marquee, a teasing minuet of approach and retreat, until she landed next to him. He wore a green polo shirt with the name of his company on the back and a badge: *Simon Webb.* He said nothing and she thought this was unusual for him. He would earn his living by talking. Talking and travelling. From a distance she had thought he was young. Younger even than she was. Now she could tell he was approaching middle age. That made him no less attractive. She saw him as a raffish and dashing adventurer, dangerous and a challenge. In the silence between them, the surrounding background noise seemed to fade.

'Will you take me to lunch?' she said.

He frowned and she wondered if she'd blown it.

'How long have you got?' he asked. 'There's nowhere decent on site.'

It was on the tip of her tongue to suggest somewhere indecent, but she was scared of frightening him off. 'All afternoon. I'm on my own. I can please myself.'

And he smiled again.

They ate in the back room of a pub. It was cool and shadowy and the other diners were finishing as they arrived. She asked for a mineral water. Best, she thought, to keep a clear head. Everything was happening quickly and she wanted to cry out, *I don't do this sort of thing. Not usually. I mean propositioning strange men. It's not me at all.* But the speed excited her too, the sense that she'd started on a journey she could no longer control.

He asked her what line of work she was in. A peculiar phrase. Slightly old fashioned.

'I teach English as a foreign language,' she said. She waited for him to ask for more details, but he just looked at her, drinking her in, and she had to continue. 'I worked abroad for a couple of years, but now I'm in a language school. Cambridge.'

Then, realising that some reciprocal information was required he began talking about his company. There was, she was told, only someone to run the office and him. 'We specialise in small groups. Sometimes just three or four people. Expert birdwatchers with very specific requirements. People who would travel independently if they had the time or expertise to arrange it. We can give them individual attention. Make sure they get the species they really need.' She raised her eyebrows and he grinned. 'OK, sorry. That was the sales pitch. Sometimes, you know, it just spills out.'

He worked out of a cottage with an overgrown garden and a slow stream choked with weed. 'Terribly impractical,' he said. 'But I just fell in love.' That afternoon, the afternoon of the Bird Fair, he took her there and led her up the uneven wooden stairs to his bedroom. His hand was resting on her head so she shouldn't hurt herself on the low doorway. He lay her on the bed and undressed her deliberately and told her that it was a willow warbler singing in the orchard and that kingfishers bred near the stream. Again she wanted to say, *I'm not this sort of woman.* But she felt the sun on her eyelids and his tongue on her skin. When she spoke again, it was dark outside and perhaps she *was* that sort of person. Certainly she was different.

They met as often as they could after that, which meant whenever he wasn't travelling. During the day she would repeat the lessons she had prepared for the students the year before. She could tell that she performed well, saw them respond to her encouragement, laugh at her jokes. There was no engagement. She knew their names – the Marias and the Mai Lis and the Berndts – but she didn't care at all what happened to them. All the time she was thinking of her next meeting with Simon, what she would wear for him, how he would respond. She knew it was a madness, an obsession. And he was obsessed too. That gave her hope and carried her on.

She decided on Northern Finland for her first trip away with him. He gave her free choice. 'Wherever you like,' he said, waving his arm expansively. They were sitting in the cottage. She had cooked for him and he'd drunk lots of the good red wine he'd brought back with him from a short break in the Cevennes. It was November, a damp and gloomy Saturday night and they'd lit the first fire of the winter. His face was flushed. He'd invited her before to go with him – once to the Coto Donana, once to Goa – but those invitations had followed last minute cancellations by punters and she hadn't been able to arrange cover for her classes. Anyway, she'd said, hot places didn't appeal.

'Are you serious?' she asked. She was sitting on the floor, her arms round her knees.

'Of course.' And he *became* suddenly serious and fetched her the brochure and maps and began making suggestions.

When she asked for Finland, she wondered at first if there might be a problem, because he seemed to be considering, then he gave that wonderful smile and said of course. Finland. Kuusamo first, then Oulu.

'I love owls,' she told him in explanation. She spoke tentatively. Wasn't it the sort of thing a teenage girl might say? Owls were so easy to love, with their thick, white feathers and huge eyes. It was as unsophisticated as saying she liked teddy bears.

But he only looked at her fondly. 'Oh, I can promise you owls. I've that side of things all sewn up with the locals. They take owls very seriously there. It brings them thousands of dollars in eco-tourism. They even have owl wars.' She did not ask what he meant. Perhaps she should have done.

There were only six of them in the group. She and Simon and four paying punters. There was a middle-aged couple called Norman and Jean, who had travelled with the company before; George, the elderly man; and a frail and beautiful young woman named Emily. Annie dismissed Norman and Jean immediately as tedious. They came from Wolverhampton and talked at length, even on the plane, about the rare birds they had seen, the distance they had travelled to see them, the cost of each twitch. Simon attended to their stories with great courtesy and she saw that it was on this ability to pretend an interest that his success must be based. There was something disturbing about the sight of his listening to them. She saw for the first time that he was a ruthless businessman and she also considered the possibility that he might lie to her if the situation demanded it.

George, it seemed, was rather a famous birdwatcher. Simon had been excited when he'd booked. 'Everyone knows he has the biggest list in the UK but he doesn't talk about it. He once found a seabird that was new to the world. Before he retired he worked in the Home Office. Something to do with the police.'

On the journey the older man was very self-contained. He read all the way on the plane and, at the transfer in Helsinki, he brusquely rejected Simon's offer of help with his bags. Annie found him intimidating. He would not be satisfied, like the couple from Wolverhampton, with smiling admiration and kind words.

She did not know what to make of Emily, who said very little and had a distracted smile. Simon usually enjoyed the company of pretty, young women and Annie wondered why he did not make more of a fuss of her. It occurred to her that Emily had been on one of his earlier trips and that perhaps there had been a brief romance, which he now preferred to forget. Certainly in Annie's presence. In their hotel room in Kuusamo, she couldn't quite bring herself to enquire if he had met Emily before. She hardly recognised Simon in work mode. Besides, the hotel itself cast a sinister gloss over everything and she did not trust her judgement in this setting.

It was a massive building constructed in a Soviet brutalist style. Everything was solid and dark. There was a huge desk at reception and the wood panelled walls had a varnish which was almost black. Yet there were touches of kitsch which were playful and unsettling. Lava lamps on the bar. Two stuffed bears in the dining room. Red plush upholstery in the lounge which made her think of a Victorian bordello. Everywhere – in the lifts and the saunas and the long straight corridors – lush arrangements of Burt Bacharach filtered through an invisible sound system.

'What do you think?' Simon was lying in the bath, with a large glass of the gin he had thought to bring from home. Booze in Scandinavia was outrageously expensive, he'd said when she'd questioned the number of bottles he'd wrapped in his underpants and packed. And it was always useful as a present for the locals. An aid to negotiations when required.

'I'm not sure... '

'Isn't it crazy? You can imagine western spies lurking here during the Cold War, setting honey traps for their Soviet colleagues. The border is only twenty miles away, after all.'

'Yes,' she said. 'Yes that's just what it's like. An elaborate Cold War movie.'

And for the three days that they spent there, she felt she was an actor in the film. There were the brooding and atmospheric sets – miles of birch forest and long, grey lakes, distant mountains with patches of dirty snow. Even the weather, chill and gloomy, could have been ordered by a director. And there were incidents which seemed to have been designed only to add to the intrigue and further the plot. Simon gave them a free afternoon, to rest before the big push for owls. Annie felt she had to get away from the stifling hotel and wandered into the town. On a street corner she saw Emily, wrapped in the long fur trimmed parka she always wore, smoking a cigarette, obviously waiting for someone. It had started to rain, but still she lingered, the hood pulled low over her eyes. Annie stood in a doorway and watched. At last a young man arrived in a small, battered car. He expected Emily to get in beside him. At first she refused and there was a sharp and angry conversation. In Finnish. Then she relented and climbed in.

Back in the hotel Annie recounted the scene to Simon. 'Why didn't she tell us that she spoke the language? I mean, you'd think she'd mention it.'

'I don't know,' he said, but she couldn't tell whether this was news to him or not.

The next night, when the rest of the group went to bed early, Simon told her he couldn't sleep, that he'd go to the bar for a night cap. Sleepless herself, she dressed and followed him. He was sitting in a dark corner of the bar, drinking vodka and in earnest conversation with their local guide, a taciturn bear of a man they called Olli. When Simon saw her she thought she caught a frown of annoyance before he turned on the wonderful smile.

But she could have been mistaken. They had stayed up all the previous night to stumble through the forest for a glimpse of an owl swooping in to feed young then another perched in silhouette on a pine tree. The group had been jubilant, too wired up for real sleep. Norman and Jean had surprised her by their passion. They had the glitter of fanatics in their eyes. In the mini bus on the way back to the hotel they listed again the species they'd seen since the start of the trip. Misers counting hoarded gold. Annie thought that after only snatches of rest it was easy to make mistakes. Perhaps she saw intrigue and mystery where there was none. She was glad when they left Kuusamo and began the drive on the long straight road to Oulu.

In Oulu the sun was shining and the harbour and the beaches provided some relief from the endless birch forest and peat bog. There was warmth on their backs as they watched the cranes and the swans fly into the bay. Even Emily shed her anorak and seemed to blossom in the sun. She smiled and became more expansive. She had grown up in Finland, she said. Her father had been a businessman, had seen the possibilities at the end of the Cold War. Importing luxury goods into the new ski resorts near Kuusamo, exporting reindeer skins and handicrafts from Lapland. Now she'd taken over. She handed round her business card. The logo in the corner was a stylised owl.

They had lunch in the market place in Oulu, surrounded by elegant houses, sitting at the outside stalls, eating fried fish cooked in big flat pans shaped like dustbin lids. Annie felt for the first time that she was among friends.

But now Simon was dead and she couldn't trust these people who played themselves like actors. It came into her head that she would have to tell them that there would be no owls tonight.

She was kneeling beside Simon, when she heard footsteps behind her again. Turning, she saw Olli. She realised she must have been there for some time and that she was crying. The tears seemed to have come from nowhere. Inside she felt frozen.

But now she came to her senses and began shouting to him. Simon must have fallen from the tower. Was there anything which could be done? An ambulance? Perhaps it wasn't too late. She caught her breath, suddenly picturing Simon's plunge from the tower. Would he have felt, even for a moment, the exhilaration of a bird in flight? Like a tern, wings folded, diving into the waves? Or had there been only terror?

'It is too late,' Olli said. She had learned that Finns never waste words.

'No,' she whispered. She remembered the winter afternoons in the cottage, realised she was feeling sorry for herself and not for Simon. 'What a waste. A senseless accident.'

'Perhaps not an accident,' Olli said quietly. He had lit another cigarette and was looking over the salt marsh. 'Another victim of the Owl Wars.'

He explained in the bar of the nature centre, where they were staying that night. She had wanted to go home immediately, longed to be a child again, tucked up by her mother between cool sheets in a dimly lit room, to wait for the fever to pass and reality to return, but there were no flights. Besides, the local police had politely asked that the party should stay, at least for another day. So she sat with Olli in the bar, drinking vodka and beer, and he told her about the Owl Wars. It was very different from the bar in Kuusamo. No heavy furniture and wood panels here. This was Scandinavian minimalist, pine floor and low wooden tables, a view over the salt marsh to the viewing towers. And still full of people despite the hour. All their party were there, watching her at a discreet distance. Simon had been their favourite and they owed it to him to take care of her.

'It's big business,' Olli said. 'The tour companies bring thousands of people to birdwatch in northern Finland in the Spring. Mostly Germans and Americans, but Brits too. They pay for the certainty of seeing the owls, all species. Luck isn't involved here. They don't understand luck. To provide certainty we have to find where the birds breed. That knowledge is valuable. Do you understand?'

She nodded. She understood.

'For us, the guides, there is fierce competition. To find the nest site and then sell our skill to the highest bidder. It would be impossible for an outsider to locate the nest sites. The forests here all look the same. We don't allow maps or GPS. We do the driving. Even tour leaders who have been to the same spot three years in a row would never find their own way back there.' He stopped talking, stared into the glass, drank the shot of vodka in one go. 'It's a short season. It's how we earn our living. You understand the competition can lead to conflict, even among friends. Between the tour companies, also.' He stood up clumsily to go to the bar and she realised for the first time how drunk he was, how miserable.

'You said Simon could be another victim,' she said when he returned. 'Who was the first?'

'A young man. Pekka Kapanen. A friend of mine. But greedy. He arranged to sell his information to one tour leader then broke the contract when he was offered more money. That was an accident too. A car accident. Apparently. He drove off a mountain road near Kuusamo. The police thought another driver was involved, but he was never traced.' His face was mottled now and his words were slurred. He stared moodily into his drink.

When the bar closed Annie couldn't sleep. She followed one of the walkways at random into the marsh and sat on a bench looking over a small pool. The sun was further above the horizon and there was a breeze which made the reeds rustle and hiss like the sound of waves on shingle. The footsteps startled her. She thought Olli must have followed her. He would be drunk and slightly amorous and there would be an embarrassing encounter while she fended him off.

'I think we should talk.'

It was George. She was more irritated than if it had been Olli. She had wanted to be alone and now he stood, looking down at her and because of his age, because Simon had so admired him, she was forced to be polite.

'Of course,' she said.

'Why don't you tell me what happened?' He sat beside her. She felt the wax on his Barbour jacket, clammy on the back of her hand. She could smell the apple in his pocket.

'I'm sorry?'

'I should have realised,' he said. 'I was distracted by the others. Everyone with guilty secrets. Everyone with something to hide. Norman and Jean cheat you know. They haven't seen half the species on their lists. Hardly illegal, but they'd be mortified if anyone found out. It would kill them. And Emily. She sells native art. If she can't get an export license she smuggles it out. It's her passion. I don't think she does it for the money. Not entirely. Is that an excuse, do you think?'

'I fell in love,' Annie said. It was a confession, her guilty secret.

He frowned, as if he had guessed as much. 'Of course you did. But not with Simon.'

'I was teaching in a language school in Helsinki. There was a student from the north, Pekka.' She tried to picture him, but the image was blurred and all she had left was the story she'd repeated every night for a year, about their meeting and his death. 'He wanted better English for his work, but his first love was natural history. He worked as a guide, finding owls. He loved this landscape. Olli called him greedy, but it wasn't like that. Pekka didn't break his contract with the tour operators because he wanted more money from them. He tried to organise all the guides into a co-op. His idea was that they'd pool information...'

'And keep the prices high.'

'Why not? It was his country. He and the others did all the work. There would be no owl tours without them.'

'And then he was killed?'

'Driven off a mountain road on an afternoon in early Spring.'

'How did you know Simon was involved?'

'It was an obsession.' Like Norman and Jean with their lists. Emily and the Lapp art. 'I tracked him down. Talked to the German operators. He was in Kuusamo when it happened. The police thought he was involved but they couldn't prove anything. When I was sure, I came back to England and got a job in Cambridge, waited for the right time.'

'Did you ask him about it?'

'There, on the watch tower. Of course he denied it. If he'd told me the truth, perhaps I wouldn't have lost my temper. I wouldn't have pushed out at him.' She closed her eyes, but she couldn't shut out the scene. The two of them held on the top of the tower, space all around them, Simon's mouth open to speak words of reasonable explanation, which it would have been a betrayal to hear. The push to stop him speaking, to stop herself listening. The cracking and shattering of the wooden handrail, his body, arms outstretched, flying.

'But that was what you intended all along. To kill him. That was why you set out to meet him.' George's words brought her back to the present. She opened her eyes.

'Yes.' Only occasionally, in the cottage by the stream, she had forgotten. There were times when she believed the fiction, got so caught up in her role, that she was no longer acting.

'Simon was telling the truth,' George said. He wasn't looking at her. She couldn't tell what he was thinking. 'Simon had nothing to do with Pekka's murder. Olli killed Pekka. He didn't want to share his information with any co-op. He wanted to keep it and sell it to the tour companies himself. So he drove Pekka off the road near Kuusamo. He was drunk. You saw what he was like tonight. He was drunk and out of control. A crazy moment of rage. Simon hired me to investigate. He wanted to find out who had murdered Pekka. To put a stop to all the rumours'

Then she felt dizzy again, as she had looking out from the tower. Above her circled the cranes, carried by the morning thermals. She tipped back her head and watched them until George touched her elbow and walked with her through the reeds back to the centre.

# ONE HAND ONE BOUNCE

## Mat Coward

*Mat Coward's many short stories are so diverse in content and theme that it is not easy to analyse the secret of his success. But as this story illustrates, one of Coward's principal gifts is his ability to capture the distinctive voice of each of his protagonists. In Coward's hands, eccentric lifestyles become not merely believable, but fascinating and often poignant.*

Until I was fifteen, when I left home for good, I more or less lived in the back of a car. Various cars. You could say leaving home was easier for me than for many, since I didn't really have a home to leave. When the time came, all I did was get out of the car and not get back in. Just got out, clunked the door behind me, and that was that.

I wish.

Kathy wasn't my mother, but she was the nearest thing I had to one. It's complicated. She ended up being my mother because I went with my father when my parents split up, and my parents split up because my father was with Kathy. Then, when Kathy and Dad split up, I went with Kathy. I don't know; perhaps Dad felt that he'd done his bit when he took me with him the first time. My parents went their bitter ways a week before my second birthday. Maybe, three years later, he felt I was too old to go with him.

'You all right in the back there, Rocket?'

'I'm all right. I don't feel sick.'

'Good boy. If you feel sick, shout.'

I would. I always did, except for the first time. I was never a deep learner, but I was always quick. 'I don't feel sick.'

'All right, Rocket.' Kathy was a confident driver, provided it was summer and provided the car was small. In winter she didn't talk much because she was busy. She was busy squinting, in fog or rain, leaning so far forward her nose was almost through the windscreen. Most people didn't bother to wear seatbelts in those days, because they didn't believe it was worth it, and Kathy didn't bother wearing glasses because she didn't believe men would see her if she did.

'Looking forward to seeing your dad?' I didn't say anything to that, I just looked out of the window, watching England turn into Wales. 'He'll be glad to see you, he hasn't seen you since Easter.'

'Are we going to stop?'

She looked at me in the mirror. 'Do you want to stop?'

I nodded.

'Do you feel sick, Rocket?'

'I forgot to get a comic.' Of course I didn't feel sick. If I'd felt sick, I'd have shouted.

I never once set foot in my father's house in Wales, or any of the homes he had after that one. He'd hear the car, and he'd come out. He'd crouch down by the driver's window and whisper to Kathy, and when she'd gone, leaving me and my bags on the unmade road, he'd look at me for the first time. He'd pull my ears and make a noise with his mouth like a frog and he'd ask me how I was.

'I'm all right.'

'You all right, Trouble? Yeah? You don't feel sick?'

'I don't feel sick.'

'Good man.' He gave my duffel bag a bit of a shove with his toes. He was wearing denim boots. 'Tell you what I thought we'd do, right? I thought we'd go on a tour. In the car.' He waited for me to nod. I didn't. 'Tour round in the car, just you and me. Here and there, see what we see.' He looked over his shoulder at the windows of his house. I never once met the woman who lived there. 'You'd like that, wouldn't you?'

'All right,' I said. I didn't nod. I wanted to read my comic.

'That won't make you feel sick, will it?'

'No.'

He pulled my ears. My dad never touched my hair, which was blond; he stuck to ear-pulling and wildlife noises. 'Well done. Right then, Trouble – you pop yourself into the car, I'll just be two minutes, then we'll be off. Leave your bags, I'll do them in a minute.'

He walked back to the house, walking quickly with his hands in his pockets, the slight favouring of his left leg less obvious the faster he went. As he got to the front door he took his hands out of his pockets to open it, but it opened anyway and he hesitated and then stepped through, with his hands on his chest.

I'd needed a pee since we got there, so after half an hour I got out of Dad's car and had a pee in his bushes. The rest of the time I read my comic. I'd need another comic soon, which would have to be worked out. Dad came back eventually, wearing sunglasses.

'There we are, Trouble – we're off. Off on tour! All right?'

'All right,' I said. It was what we'd done at Easter. Where are you supposed to wash your hands when you have to pee in the bushes? You can't, so you just have to forget about it.

On a beach in West Wales, when we were playing French cricket, I saw my father punch a man in the mouth. I thought it was funny at first, and then I thought it was frightening when the man began to bleed, and then I thought it was funny again when the man said 'Don't worry, kid. Only messing about.' But not as funny as before.

As there were only ever two of us playing, we had to modify the rules slightly. In addition to the usual rule – that if the tennis ball bounced once after leaving the bat, the batsman could still be out provided the catch was taken one-handed – we allowed run-outs delivered by foot. If the fielder kicked the ball at the batsman, and it hit him on the wicket area while he was passing the bat around his legs, then that was out. In practice, all the batsman had to do was to stop running before the ball got to him – but it's funny, you get greedy I suppose, and wickets were occasionally lost to booted direct hits. My father's wickets, that is, not mine. He never caught a ball one-handed, or kicked at a run-out chance. I didn't know whether that was because of his bad leg or because he thought second chances were for kids. There were things I could ask him about and things I couldn't, and most of the things I could were to do with natural history.

The man who bled on the beach was older than my dad, probably in his forties, and he was wearing suit trousers and a white shirt. My dad was batting, holding the old bat straight in front of his legs, when the man crept up behind him. He didn't do anything, he just stood behind dad's back, his knees slightly bent, a bit like a wicketkeeper. I thought perhaps he wanted to join in, which I knew from experience my father wouldn't like. Dad must have noticed my uncertainty, because he turned around quickly.

The man winked at me and raised a finger to his lips, to tell me to keep quiet. But he only did that once Dad was looking at him, which seemed pointless.

'All right?' said the man, looking over Dad's shoulder at me. 'Having a nice holiday with your dad?' My father moved to one side, so that he was in the sightline between me and the man. But the man dodged this way and then that way and he kept calling cheerfully to me: 'I expect your holiday's nearly over, is it? You'll be back at school, soon, will you?'

Then my father put the cricket bat down on the sand, punched the man in the face, and the man fell down. Dad picked up the bat and walked over to me, and took hold of my arm. I thought it was funny and then not funny and then funny again, and the man said his thing about not worrying, still lying on the sand, and Dad led me up the beach to the car-park.

The car seat was hot. I was wearing shorts. I opened the window as far as it would go. It took ages to get away from the seafront and out of the town and out on to the main roads where we could go fast enough for the draught to cool us down.

After half an hour, my father stopped by a phone box and made a call.

'Am I going back to Kathy's?' I said, when he got back in.

'Not just presently, no.'

'Am I going to your place?' I knew I wasn't, but sometimes when I said something like that, Dad would stop to buy a comic or a lolly.

'Tell you what, Trouble – you're going to stay with your gran for a while. By the seaside. How about that?'

That was a turn up. I didn't know I'd got a gran. 'All right,' I said.

'Good man. You all right for comics, there?'

We drove to somewhere in the Midlands and we stopped in a lay-by and I got out of Dad's car and into Gran's. I was asleep when we got to the lay-by and Dad had to shake me, leaning down from outside with the door open. I tried to wake up as much as I possibly could so that I wouldn't leave anything behind; my big bag in the boot, my small bag by my feet, and my comic. In Gran's car, on the back seat, there was a packet of boiled sweets.

When we got to Gran's, which was by the sea in Yorkshire, she showed me my room which had a slanting ceiling and I asked her if she was my mum's mother or my father's mother.

'Not exactly,' she said. 'Now – would you like some ice cream?'

I said I would, please.

'Are you sure, Treacle? You're not feeling sick from the car?'

I said I wasn't.

Usually, during the days, Gran couldn't see me, so I went to the pier. Gran and I didn't talk much during the month I was with her, though she made a great effort to be kind. It was hard work. Whenever the opportunity arose, I would tongue the boiled sweets into my hand and later flush them away. They tasted like toothpaste. She was old and I was young, and really that was about all we had in common.

People drop money at the seaside and if you look for it you can find it – or some of it, anyway – so I always had a few coins in my pocket for putting in the machines. I learned quickly, though, that the machines in the amusement arcade took coins faster than I could look for them, so most of the time I just watched.

There was one machine I watched a lot. It was called the 'Whee of Fortune', and I liked it because it played whether or not anyone was playing it. There was a dial with money amounts written on, and an arrow which spun around the dial for a second or two, then stopped and pointed briefly at 1p or 10p or 2p or 5p and then went on its way again. Next to each number was a slot; the player put his penny in the slot of his choice, and if he'd correctly guessed the next destination of the arrow, he won the amount indicated plus his stake back. Every now and then, the Whee of Fortune decided to reward an invisible player with an imaginary win. It would flash, judder a little, and make a chunking noise.

Because it kept working all the time, it was a good game to play without paying. You could imagine betting on £1, and if £1 came up you could imagine watching 101p clunk into the tray. You could imagine what you were going to spend it on. A summer special comic, for instance, or some prawns.

It was because I watched the Whee of Fortune so much that I noticed its pattern. I knew I mustn't write it down because that would be cheating and the man in the tiny room who gave out change and swore at teenagers would shout at me and make me go. But if I remembered it, that wasn't cheating. That was just being good at remembering.

It was quite a complicated sequence, but what it boiled down to was this: about every twenty minutes, 1p came up immediately after a 10p and a £1. This was the only time £1 ever followed 10p, so that if you saw those two come up, you knew for certain that the next number was 1p. If, after seeing the 10p and the £1, you put a penny in the 1p slot, you were guaranteed a flash, a judder, a chunking noise, and two 1p coins.

I didn't always win. Sometimes, someone else would be playing the Whee of Fortune at the crucial moment – and would always, I noticed, pick the wrong number, usually going for 50p or £1, never for 1p. Sometimes I lost count. Sometimes I got distracted, watching children pulling their mother's jumpers and asking for things. But some days I won a lot. Once, I won 24p in a single day.

When I knew it was my last day in that town, I decided to pass on my secret. There was a boy a couple of years older than me, playing a slot machine. I went over to him and I said: 'Do you like winning money?'

'What?' He didn't look at me, so I told him the secret I had discovered of how to win on the Whee of Fortune. He made me say it again, and then he looked at his watch and his lips moved for a while. 'You're mad!' he said, and he shoved me with his hip and the side of his arm. 'Piss off – you'd have to wait around half the day to make the price of an ice cream!'

I shrugged. If he didn't want to inherit the secret, that was his business. Maybe he didn't like winning money as much as he thought he did. Anyway, there was one more thing to do.

'I know a secret about the Whee of Fortune,' I told the man in the tiny room, the one who gave out change and swore at the teenagers.

'What?' he said. He was reading a newspaper.

'There should be an "l" on it,' I said. 'It should be "Wheel".' I'd worked that out on the first day. It was no mystery as far as I was concerned; some kids had done it, I was sure, for a joke. Probably with a penknife.

'So what?' said the man in the tiny room. 'What's it got to do with you?'

I never saw Gran again after that day, and I never found out whether she was my mother's mum, or my dad's mother.

When I was twelve, I started wondering about two things. One was why I never heard anything about my mother, and the other was why I never went to school. Not that I particularly wanted to go to school, if it was anything like it was in the comics. At Bash Street, the teachers were always whacking you, and as often as not the whole school got blown up or flooded or otherwise demolished.

I knew quite a lot anyway, about vipers, and reading and writing and numbers, and being a commando against the Germans and Japs. I wasn't sure what else school could teach me, except to do with being whacked. I would have liked to know why I didn't go to school, though, to reassure me that I'd never have to.

My twelfth birthday caught me by surprise, because it was on a different date to my eleventh birthday. I was staying with Kathy at the time, above an electrical shop in a small town in Tyne & Wear, and one day, three weeks before the anniversary of my eleventh birthday, she gave me a Buster annual and a kiss and a card and said 'Happy Birthday, Rocket.' I thanked her and put the card on top of the TV, and started to read the annual. It was 1983's, and this was 1985, but I hadn't seen it before and it was very good.

'I expect your dad'll give you his present when you see him,' said Kathy. 'Rather than post it.'

'I wonder if I'll get a card from my mother,' I said. I said it to myself, mumbling more or less, so that Kathy could choose to hear it or not. Or so that I could pretend I hadn't said it, if I really needed to.

Kathy went very quiet and started to smile, the way a woman does when she's about to put her arm around a child who's got a sore throat, and then she changed her mind and slammed her coffee mug down on the table so hard that its handle broke off. 'I'll take him there myself, if that's all the bloody thanks I get,' she said, and slammed the door when she left the room.

I read my annual for a while. Kathy came back in and said that she was sorry because she knew none of it was my fault. I said it didn't matter and it didn't. I thought she'd probably had a long day, even though it was a while until lunchtime.

Dad took me to Arundel Castle in Sussex, where we almost saw an adder. I was full of questions that autumn, warm as it was. I wondered what my father did for a living, and having wondered that, I wondered what Kathy did, and then Uncle George, and various others. Not Gran, because grannies don't work. I asked my father what his job was, and he said that when it was winter he'd buy me a football and teach me how to be a goalie.

We'd bought some crisps and a bottle of fizzy orange earlier and we were walking through some woods looking for a place to sit for our picnic when a little girl screamed and said she'd been stung. She ran to her mum, but her dad got to her first. 'Jesus Christ!' he said, looking at the little girl's leg. 'She's been bitten by an adder!'

Her father had been arguing at her mother. I knew because I'd been watching them; Dad said there'd been no comics at the garage, only crisps and fizzy drinks, and he said those were three times as much as they should be and that if he could he'd go abroad and stop getting ripped off. But now, when the girl screamed, the man stopped arguing at the woman and they both became angry on the same side instead. They were angry with the adder.

One of the nearby mums was a doctor's receptionist, so she looked after the little girl who was crying, while a gang of dads picked up bits of tree branches and went off into the ferns to kill the adder. One of the men said, 'A little tot her size, a viper could bloody kill her,' and after that none of the dads said 'adder' any more – they all said 'viper'.

I was baffled. 'Why do they have to kill the adder, Dad?' Dad just shook his head. 'Is it like a man-eating lion in Tarzan, where once it's got the taste for human flesh it'll strike again and again and again?'

'Could be. That lot seem to think so, anyway.' We were sitting up against a tree eating our crisps.

'Dad? If they do kill an adder, how will they know it's the right one?'

Dad made a noise like a duck, and reached over to pull my nose. 'Good question!' He seemed very pleased. 'Good bloody question. I suppose they'll have to kill every adder in Sussex, to be on the safe side.'

'Will they?'

He stood up. 'That should keep them busy for a while, daft tossers. Come on, Trouble – let's go for a drive.'

I was fed up with driving, though nothing to do with feeling sick, so I said could we go for a row on the lake?

Dad pulled his own nose, and made a face. 'The thing about a lake,' he said, 'is it's a body of water enclosed on all sides by land. I mean, what's the point of that? That's why man invented the car.'

We went for a drive. When we stopped for a comic, I asked him why he didn't go with the other dads to kill the adder.

'It wasn't a bloody adder, Trouble, that's why.' He laughed, but he didn't pull anyone's nose. 'Bloody viper! It was a wasp.'

'Was it?'

'Bet you anything it was a wasp.'

For a while when I was very young, my greatest fear was that if I wasn't careful I'd end up in an awfulage. I have no idea where all that came from, if anywhere, so I'm not going to start apportioning blame at this late date. The only significance of the dreaded 'awfulage' is that I made certain assumptions about my status early on, some of which I didn't question until much later.

I think I was ten when my father and I were walking along a winter beach somewhere on the Kent coast, him ahead and me behind, and I asked him: 'Was that the same accident where Mum died?' There was a gale blowing, but I didn't shout.

He turned to me and for a moment did nothing but polish his teeth with his tongue. Then he said: 'What accident you on about?'

I pointed at his leg. 'Were you in the car with Mum? Did you try to pull her out but it was hopeless? Is that why you don't work?'

'What car? You know nothing about any car.'

I nodded.

'Come on,' Dad said, 'this wind's getting ridiculous. We'll turn back.'

I really didn't think the wind was my fault – though in a way it could be, for being small, because the wind didn't bother Dad – but I did wonder how my mother had died if it wasn't in a car. It wasn't in the war because she wasn't born. I hoped it wasn't in hospital.

Most things I remember are to do with my father, which seems unfair to Kathy since she had me more of the time than anyone else. Not much I can do about that now, though.

Sometimes, during the season, my father and I would go to village fetes. We'd watch the Dog With The Prettiest Eyes competition, and have a go on the tombola, and look for annuals at the book stall and eat cream teas. Dad always liked to be doing something with me, driving from one event to another. Sometimes we'd visit three or four fetes in a single day; eight or nine in a weekend. I asked him once whether we were looking for something in particular. 'God, no,' he said. He made a noise like an owl and tugged at my chin. 'Don't ever think that, Trouble. We're not looking for anything, we're just having a day out.'

At one fete we were queuing for the coconut shy when a young woman came up behind us and touched my father's sleeve. She was wearing a white blouse and a blue skirt and had earrings and make-up. Her hair was nice.

'Would you like your fortune told?'

My dad looked at her with his eyes almost closed, frowning as if the sun was in his eyes although it was quite cloudy. He looked at her hand on his sleeve. 'No, thanks,' he said.

She took her hand off Dad's sleeve and pointed at me. 'Or perhaps his fortune?'

Dad took me by the shoulder and led me to the car. I was puzzled by the fortune-teller. She looked like a businesswoman. 'Was she a witch?' I asked.

'That's a very interesting question,' Dad said. But he didn't answer it.

When we parked in a pub car-park near Birmingham hours later, and I saw who got out of the car next to ours, I was a bit disappointed. I wouldn't want that to sound the wrong way; Uncle George was always very kind to me, and he was very generous with comics and fizzy drinks, but being with him wasn't like being with Kathy, or my father. Uncle George always made sure I was all right and had what I needed, but he didn't smile often, or say much to me except to see if I was OK.

I said goodbye to Dad and got into Uncle George's car with my bags. Uncle George watched the road in his rear-view mirror for a few minutes, chewing something and never blinking, and then we drove off, southward.

'Is that bubblegum?' I asked.

'Say again, young man?'

'Is that bubblegum you're chewing?'

'No,' he said. He looked at me in his mirror. 'We can get some bubblegum if you want some. I can stop.'

'No. That's all right.'

'Sure? You all right, young man – you don't feel sick?'

'I don't feel sick. What is it, then?'

'Dill,' he said, and then a few miles later he added: 'They used to call it church seed in the old days. It's got a drug in it that stops you feeling tired or hungry. They used to give it to kids, to keep them awake during long sermons.' He got a paper bag out of his pocket. 'There you are – try a few.'

They were seeds, and I chewed some to be polite but they tasted unpleasant. If I'd had any of Gran's boiled sweets left, I'd even have sucked one of them to take the taste away. The church seed didn't make me feel any more sick or any less sick, though I knew why Uncle George had given it to me. The next time we stopped for petrol, he bought me some bubblegum. It was pink and very sweet. I got rid of it as quickly as I could. Even so, I was sick near Gloucester. Mostly I was sick on the verge, but a very small amount of sick got on Uncle George's car. He was cross, but because he was kind he tried to disguise it.

He gave me some water from a bottle and some tissues for my face and hands. He used some more tissues on the car; on the car, not in the car. There is a difference.

'Is it just me, young man, or are you sick in other people's cars too?'

I told him other people's too, because it'd be worse if it was just him. It wasn't anything to do with him, anyway, or his car. There was a reason, and it was a different reason each time. The second time it was because of the church seed and the bubblegum, neither of which I liked or actually asked for, and the first time it was because I was on the floor of his car with a blanket covering me completely and I could hardly breathe.

When we were underway again, I asked him: 'Did you used to work with my dad?'

After a bit, Uncle George said: 'Why do you ask that?'

'Because he always looks in his mirror like that, too. You haven't got a limp, though. Were you spies?'

Uncle George didn't say anything, so I told him it didn't matter. 'I was just wondering.'

We did a few more miles, then he said: 'Yes, I did. While ago, now.'

'What did you do?'

'We drove a car together,' he said. 'You finished that comic already?'

When we got where we were going – which was a camp site in Dorset – Uncle George said: 'Feeling better?'

I nodded, to say that I was, but really I was thinking. It seemed pretty obvious to me at that moment that the reason people were always passing me on was because I sometimes got carsick. I didn't make a fuss, but it seemed a bit unfair. You can't help being carsick, and I always shouted, except for that first time.

\*

In my early teens, I began referring to them – in my own thoughts, not out loud – as pop-ups; the people who popped up now and then, a few times a year, all through my childhood. Getting punched on beaches, or tugging sleeves at village fetes, or lurking somewhere beyond the scope of a rear-view mirror in a pub car-park. Pop-ups.

They were looking for us, certainly: for me, or for Dad, or for all of us. But what I couldn't understand was why, having found us, they always let us go. And on the heels of that – since they always let us go, why did we always run from them?

My main lasting impression of Aunty Jane is that when she had a shower, she used to leave the bathroom door open in such a way that she was visible from the landing via a full-length mirror. She was in her thirties, heavily freckled, and, as she told me more than once, divorced. I was fifteen, and happy to accept any favours the mirror might offer.

'If you use the shower, sweetheart, try to remember to leave the door ajar. The extractor fan's buggered,' she told me, and I admired, with a connoisseur's eye, the way she thus covered herself and at the same time allowed me an escape clause, should I want one.

The first night, she happened to catch a glimpse of me wearing only a towel. 'You've got lovely big shoulders,' she said, as she carried on down the stairs without looking back. 'You'd suit a uniform, just like your dad.'

I held my breath. It could have been any uniform, and she was almost out of earshot, so I had to guess quickly. 'No thanks,' I said. 'I don't fancy being a copper.'

She laughed as she slid the kitchen door open. 'Don't blame you, sweetheart. Who could?'

After only two days and three nights with Aunty Jane, I was handed back to Kathy for a long drive to meet up with my father. That put me in a bad mood to begin with and then, at the first hand-over, something silent passed between the two women and Kathy spent the next hour interrogating me about what had happened while I was in Aunt Jane's care. I gave no polysyllabic answers, but it seemed I didn't need to.

'Should never have left you with her,' Kathy muttered, squinting angrily at the road ahead.

'Why did you, then?'

'Last resort,' she said, without any apology in her voice. 'People take sides, Rocket. Family, friends, colleagues. You're stuck with who you get.'

'Anyway,' I said, 'there's nothing wrong with Aunty Jane. At least she talks to me, unlike—'

'Dirty old slapper,' said Kathy. 'She always was.'

'Takes one to know one,' I said, not loud but loud enough. Why was it my fault if people took sides? I hadn't done anything. Unlike some I could mention.

By the time she'd handed me over to my father, I wasn't talking to either of them. When I woke up the next morning in a bed and breakfast in Blackpool and realised I still wasn't talking to them, something occurred to me for the first time. Several things, really, occurred for the first time to my conscious mind, at least. That evening, I looked in my dad's wallet while I was supposed to be sleeping and he was downstairs having a light ale with the landlady. He always kept his wallet hidden, but of course it wasn't me he was hiding it from.

Now I knew what my father's full name was. As a bit of a bonus, I also knew mine. Armed with that information, I went into a police station directly after breakfast to turn Dad and Kathy in.

The detectives took me seriously. I hadn't been confident they would, me being a kid, my dad being an ex-cop, it being – in all fairness – quite a story.

But I suppose they have to take murder accusations seriously, no matter what their source. They gave me lunch in the canteen, asked me questions about school which I was careful not to answer, and after a couple of hours a young, thin detective with a bottle scar on his forehead told me that my mother wasn't dead. She lived in East Anglia. I asked him how he could be sure he'd got the right woman.

'Births, deaths and marriages,' he said. 'The paperwork says this woman married your father on such-and-such date, gave birth to you on such-and-such date, and is, at present date, not deceased. To make sure, I got the local police to confirm, face-to-face.' He smiled, and I tried to do likewise. 'You can have her phone number, if you like.

There's no access or custody complications, I've checked.'

Seeing me safe seemed to make Dad even more frantic than he'd evidently been while I was missing. 'My God, I thought they'd—'

'I was talking to the police,' I said. I wanted to see him blanch, even if my mother was alive. Even more if she was alive, because then why hadn't I seen her since I was two?

'The police?' He looked furious. 'Bastards! They had their go years past, and now they want a second chance? Pathetic, self-indulgent bastards! I'm sorry, Trouble, it's my fault, I never guessed for a moment that they'd actually—'

'No, Dad. I went to them.' And I told him why I'd gone. I quite enjoyed it.

He packed, and took me to the car. He drove and he gave me his statement; he never looked at me, he kept his eyes on the road and on the rear-view mirror. He was quite brief. It took less time to tell than it did to hear.

'When you were a baby, back in London, I was involved with a woman.'

'Kathy?'

He winced. 'Before Kathy. Sorry. It was just… well, anyway, she was a colleague.'

'A cop?'

'Right, but from another station. Then she was killed. In an accident, a hit-and-run. That's where—'

'Who was driving?' I asked; the sort of question you only need to ask because you already know the answer.

'They never traced the car.'

'Did they not?'

'Anyway – I took retirement on invalidity, and one of the nurses was Kathy.' He shrugged one shoulder, as if to say 'And you know the rest.' No chance.

I started with the pop-ups. 'Are they police?'

'Unofficially. This girl, the one in the accident – she was very popular. Some of her mates just can't let it go.'

'So what do they want with me?'

'With you?' A spasm of pain swept his face. 'Oh shit, son, I'm sorry – they don't want anything with you. They want me to give a statement, saying your mother was driving the car. It's just harassment, I just try to ignore it.'

I gave him a moment, to see if he'd save me having to ask the next bit. He didn't. We drove. 'So, Dad, why do they think you'd lie to protect Mum, even though you left her for another woman?'

I braced myself for a long pause. Instead, he answered straight away. 'Because she's the mother of my child. I suppose, you know, they think that's enough.'

Even so, how could I not ask the penultimate question? 'When was it that I was sick under a blanket on the floor of Uncle George's car?'

Dad sighed. 'OK. When Kathy and I broke up, your mum wanted you back. Took you back, in fact, without my consent or knowledge – one of her psycho brothers did. So... the thing is, you couldn't stay with her. She loved you, she wasn't a bad mother, but she was really too unstable to look after a kid.'

There we were; at the final question. I let him off that one. It would have been unnecessarily cruel to ask him 'Why do you say she's unstable?' when I already knew that the answer was 'Because I saw her commit murder.'

My going to the police had complicated things for a while, Dad explained, so I was going back to Kathy for a few days. I didn't care, or reply.

Not far from Bury, I asked Kathy if she could stop at the next shops. 'I want to get some bottled water, I'm not feeling great.'

'I'll get it,' said Kathy.

'Don't be daft, I'm not a kid. You wait there.'

I wonder how soon she came looking for me? Not soon enough; I was lost from view in seconds, long gone in minutes.

Two lifts and five hours later, miles away, I wondered just once more about the pop-ups. He just tried to ignore them, Dad had said, just harassment. But we didn't ignore them. They were the centre of our lives. Again, the question: if they could do us no harm, why did we run from them?

Distance, perhaps, gave me perspective. We didn't run from the pop-ups, of course. We ran from the others, the dangerous ones, the ones never quite seen in the rear-view mirrors. Kathy and Dad, they hadn't been protecting themselves, and they hadn't been protecting my mother. They'd been protecting me, from the long arm of my mother's murderous love.

I would have thanked them, if I could. Especially Kathy. Too late; I'd travelled miles, in all directions, and the only person in the world I had a phone number for was my mother.

# Revenge on the High C
## Judith Cutler

*Like her partner, Keith Miles, Judith Cutler is not only a prolific writer but a versatile one. Although fans of the crime genre would regard her primarily as a novelist, she has in recent years published a number of distinctive short stories. Her latest, an account of misadventures on a cruise ship, is characteristically entertaining.*

'Just remember, in these troubled times, that security is as important at sea as safety. Any suspicious package, any odd behaviour: report it directly to me. Any time of day or night. Twenty-four seven, as they say.' I paused for effect, looking at each of the assembled faces in turn. As they gazed up at me, I felt like a headmaster addressing his pupils in an old-fashioned school hall – any moment I'd announce I'd expel anyone caught cheating. I had to remind myself that I was in the grandiose surroundings of the theatre of the cruise liner *Tropic of Capricorn*, giving the third of some half dozen briefings to the crew. Despite the theatre's size, you couldn't accommodate them all, so they came in batches at the start of each shift. 'You don't touch anything yourself. Anything. If anyone's going to get blown up by a terrorist bomb let it be an old codger like me.'

Obligingly the laugh came, but it was a bit ragged. Not surprising. *Tropic of Capricorn* had a truly international complement – over sixty nations were represented on board. Though all the crew spoke excellent English, often with less accent than my own Devon burr, some might not have got round to learning words like codger. Many, too, had grown up in cultures where you did not mock the old. Not that I was old: at fifty-five I liked to think I was in the prime of life. Admittedly, I was drawing a pension, but that was only because so long as you put in your thirty years' service you could draw your police pension at fifty and then swan off into the sunset and do another job. In my case they were pretty glamorous sunsets, had I been able to see them all. But the job – Chief Security Officer on a vessel this size – meant I didn't get to spend much time leaning on the side-rail admiring the view. Like all those with me in the theatre, I was on board to work. When I was on deck, even at sunset, my eyes and ears were on full alert.

I continued: 'We're much more likely to get mundane incidents, such as the odd brawl when the alcohol's been flowing. Whatever it is – men getting too amorous, petty theft, anything – you report it to me. Oh, if there's a fight, stop them knocking each other senseless, but leave everything in place exactly as it was. In the police, we call it – *they* call it – preserving the scene. The scene of the crime,' I added, seeing worried frowns. 'For instance, if someone says they've had a ring stolen, you don't barge in and search their cabin, though ten to one that's where it'll be. You call me. Don't touch anything. *Preserve the scene.*' I smiled. Yes, one or two were assiduously taking notes – these'd be the ones on their first voyage. But I always insisted that everyone, whatever his or her job, came to one of my briefings – even the captain made an appearance.

He stepped forward now, his own accent – Italian – only faint. 'I'd like to confirm, ladies and gentlemen, that what Mr Taylor has said is absolutely our policy. Security and passenger safety are our number one priority. If Mr Taylor calls any unscheduled meetings, attend them: they are as vital as lifeboat drill.' Not much, but to the point.

Of course, there were one or two who tried to wag – funny how the language of school kept coming into mind. But I'd found a way to sort them out. Just like the passengers, all the crew had electronic swipe cards. They'd had to use them to get into this theatre. I could check, via the ship's computer, who'd attended and who hadn't.

Not who'd been attending to my words, unfortunately. And I knew from bitter experience that at least one of them wouldn't be. The ship's Director of Music – I wish I knew how he'd wangled such a title – was sitting in a prominent position, his mind clearly on other things. His profile tilted uncomfortably skyward, so everyone could see how artistic it was, he was swooping down with his pen from time to time to record flourishes of notes in his heavy manuscript book for his next pianoforte recital. You and I would know he was a poseur as soon as we looked at him, but many of the crew were young and impressionable and couldn't drag their admiring eyes from him. Boys and girls: yes, I'm afraid the maestro, in real life one Budd Doppler, liked to play both ends of the keyboard.

The artistes' dressing rooms backstage were best described as functional. Front of house, however, the corridor walls were covered with portraits in oil of the great composers – Bach, staring serenely into the distance, a pugnacious Beethoven, Sibelius looking like a skinhead about to head-butt someone. The paintings were augmented by photographs, signed by luminaries who might have given recitals there but clearly hadn't. I knew the names, if not the faces, from CDs. Menuhin. Oistrakh. Kennedy. I've heard them all offer their different interpretations of Beethoven's Violin Concerto. And Budd Doppler's. A pianist? Beethoven's Violin Concerto? Don't ask. Director of Music he might be: musician he wasn't.

You see, Budd doesn't so much play as give a performance.

He'll have relegated other, more talented colleagues to less frequented bars and the bijou restaurants, but as music director he'll be performing in the theatre itself. He'll time his first appearance on stage – when most musicians would be lurking in the green room – to coincide with the arrival of the audience, so they'll see everything he does. First he'll check the spotlights. There. Now, no matter how good the on-board housekeeping – and if I know anything of Mrs King's staff it will be excellent – he'll take from his music-case a large piece of silk, big as a lady's head scarf, and wipe the piano, a concert grand, of course, from stem to stern. Yes, all of it. From the glossy lid to the stool, taking in each individual key on the way. Nothing escapes from his ministrations: he even checks the music stand and the lid support. A step back. A tilt of the head. Ah! Another mote offends his eye. At last, he flits from the stage. But he returns! This perfectionist hasn't checked his microphone. A concert grand with a mike? That's Show Biz.

Only then will he reappear – to rapturous if bemused applause – and perform.

I took a moment to flick through the entertainment brochure – the ship catered for all tastes, from lectures on the ports we visited to

karaoke competitions – to find when he was playing. Yes. He was
saving his recital for the very last evening. The pinnacle of our week's
entertainment, no doubt. Although our Director of Music always
announced what he was playing as he went along, he'd decided to
splurge some of his budget on printed programmes. I took one. It
promised classical music. In much smaller print came the words, *with
a modern slant. Completely skewed,* more like – or even *skewered.*
Mozart, Brahms, Bach – what had they ever done to deserve this?
Being served up with new rhythms, in entirely alien keys? What piece
ever merited the pianist striking the last note on the piano string itself?

So, to whom would he dedicate this cruise's musical evisceration?
Oh, yes, that's what he usually did. To celebrate his latest conquest.

Although fraternisation between crew and guests was strictly
forbidden, sometimes we had to turn a blind eye – young love would
blossom, even in a short week, with the tears that parting inevitably
brought. But Budd, under that cute toupee of his, was undoubtedly
old enough to know better. And the only love he felt was cupboard
love. It was the older, richer ladies he squired tenderly round the deck,
ladies whose tear-ducts had long since been atrophied by their
cosmetic surgery but whose purses were still responsive to the crudest
blandishments. He aimed high. He'd been known to kiss most
tenderly several of our directors' wives. When we had a slight engine
problem during our last cruise, he soon consoled the Chief Engineer's
wife: I saw them myself in the most compromising position. Her
husband promised most audibly and most profanely to deal with the
little runt. I trusted he would. At least he was in a position to, unlike
the little Chinese steward, face as lovely as an unfolding chrysanthe-
mum, whom darling Budd had reduced to lovelorn tears on the same
voyage. This trip the poor lad's eyes narrowed with something like
anger, not despair, when Budd flitted by with his latest flirt.

At the end of my working day, I retired to my cabin and slapped on
my earphones. If anyone asked what I didn't like on board, I'd say not
the roll of the ship, although at times despite the most up-to-date
stabilisers it could be surprisingly violent, or the claustrophobia of the
endless corridors. It was the noise: the constant hum of the genera-
tors, the deep throb of the engines as we cruised through the night. So

I had my own little refuge – a pile of CDs. I didn't go for the grand opera the TV detective Morse was supposed to favour, though I left the police service at a rather higher rank than his and with a good deal of technical and electronic expertise that never appeared in the series. I was a middle-of-the-roads classics man, and used to be a team favourite at pub quiz nights when you had to identify a piece from a ten bar extract. Mozart; Chopin; Brahms – I was a bit of a whiz, though I say it who shouldn't. And it wasn't just a party trick: I really enjoyed music, thanks to the help of my dear wife, dead some five years now. If she'd still been with me, I'd have stayed a landlubber. Even now I only had to hear a Dvorak quartet, for instance, and I could almost feel her standing beside me, though I'd be eight thousand miles from what used to be my home.

There were dark-ringed eyes in the Mess for breakfast the first morning at sea. It was hard work, checking two thousand people and their luggage aboard, not to mention the food and fuel we needed. I doubt if the purser got to bed before dawn: he and Mrs King, the chief housekeeper, overcame huge logistical problems with admirable forward planning but that never stopped them having first night nerves, as it were. Today they were deep in conversation over their toast and coffee – we lived more frugally than our guests. As I reached for the low-fat spread, I couldn't help overhearing: it seemed one of the Italian cabin-staff had already been to visit the medical centre with a tale of woe. Could she be put ashore for the treatment she insisted she wanted? And she wouldn't name the father, though I could have offered an educated guess, having witnessed what you might call a Budding romance. 'What worries me most,' Mrs King explained, 'is that her Sicilian cousin's one of the bar staff – I hope he doesn't go in for vendetta.'

It was no laughing matter. In the confines of a ship, however large and luxurious she might be, passions had no obvious outlet. Ships' crews no longer had to bunk down in huge dormitories, crushed together in hammocks. But even in accommodation not unlike student halls of residence, four sharing a cabin with en suite facilities, there was little privacy. It was only as you climbed the promotional ladder that you got a cabin of your own, like mine.

I assured her that my plainclothes staff would keep their eyes open, and headed to my office to start the day's tasks. A lost mobile phone, a passport query – sometimes the routine was so predictable I might have got bored. Sometimes I hankered after a real crime to solve.

The week passed, each day as gentle and placid as the waters we sailed on. We landed at favourite spots, disembarking two thousand passengers to see the sights. Each one, man, woman and child, was safely re-embarked: not a single lost passport or even swipecard, without which no one was allowed aboard. They were a temperate group, our alcohol consumption being, according to Mrs King, at least ten per cent down. As far as the crew were concerned, there was no violence, apart from a scuffle involving words but not a handy meat cleaver. The Italian girl continued to weep, her cousin to glower. The Chinese lad's eyes narrowed further. As for the Chief Engineer, he used some words even my police service had never taught me.

Call it masochism, call it what you will, but on impulse I decided to pop into the theatre for the final evening's recital. The auditorium was almost full. The weather had changed, and strong winds made the decks less hospitable than usual. I took my place at the back, nursing my usual shipboard tipple, a Virgin Mary: a Bloody Mary without the alcohol. I preferred to stay alert at all times.

Budd tiptoes to the mike, smiling his most winsome smile, but not offering a dedication: he's obviously not had his usual carnal success. He tells us he would like to offer a little smidgen of Verdi to start. He sits, adjusting his piano stool to the nearest thou', as if about to embark on an epic like the *Hammerklavier* Sonata, not a trite extract from the Force of Destiny Overture. Force of Destiny, indeed!

At least he starts his evening seated.

As it progresses, he will stand for the odd bar, waving a hand as if summoning a full orchestra to aid and abet him. He will toss his hair (very careful, that operation) and sigh audibly. Liszt, Paganini, Wagner – all the great musical showmen: they'd have queued to take lessons from him. But at least they can be remembered more for their music than for their histrionics.

Dear God, now he's murdering 'Nimrod', that wonderful Elgar piece played at solemn moments of remembrance. One old guy, white handlebar moustache aquiver, stumbles out. Budd thinks he's been overcome by emotion. I'm sure he has – the emotion being fury.

Now for the *piece de resistance*. Beethoven. His 'Violin Concerto'. Budd implies he's doing the great man a favour by arranging it for piano. He clearly doesn't know that Beethoven tried it himself, but didn't like the result. Perhaps 'Old Ludwig' – nice to know they're on such friendly terms – would have done better to emulate Budd and change the key from D to C. Only Budd knows why – fewer sharps and flats to worry about, perhaps? A crescendo brings him to his feet, executing a wiggle of the hips any hula dancer would be proud of. He subsides, but only for a minute. He's playing louder and louder, rampaging up the keyboard like Attila the Hun, late for an invasion. It's a good job his technique doesn't extend to using the pedals, because he's on his feet again. He bends forward for the climax. Yes, here's his party piece! He strikes not the key but the string itself, deep in the piano's entrails.

The lid slams down.

He kicks briefly and is silent.

The audience applaud vigorously, ecstatically, thinking it part of the performance.

I despatch a barman for swipecard machines: I have to know the identity of everyone here so I can interview them later. Another fetches the doctor, though I know in my heart no one could survive a blow like that from so huge and solid a piece of wood. Soon I'm on the stage beside him, telling the guests that Mr Doppler is unwell and asking them to leave the theatre.

It's clear what has happened. The strong support holding up the piano lid has been dislodged. Well, struts like that weren't designed to be pressed sideways, especially when someone has removed the block that should have stopped it moving.

No one can accuse me of not being thorough in my investigations, as I assure the Captain. We know that the piano was in one piece at lunchtime, because some of the passengers had an impromptu hymn-singing session, and certainly no one could have touched it for at least half an hour before the performance: only Budd himself got his hands on it. So it's the late afternoon I'm interested in. I talk to the jilted Chinese steward, whose alibi is unassailable, since he was assisting in a cookery demonstration at the time to an audience of sixteen moon-struck matrons and thirty slavering West Coast gays. 'You know what, Mr Taylor? I wish I'd thought of it! He was a bad man. But someone will have a terrible job, cleaning that piano.'

Reassured that the task wouldn't fall to him, he went off, humming quietly to himself.

'You think I had time,' the Chief Engineer expostulated, 'to bother snapping the neck of that little whippersnapper? Damn it, Taylor, I'm working round the clock to persuade the sodding starboard camshaft to behave itself. And don't tell me the piano needs repairing – I don't have the blasted time, man!'

The Italian girl and her fearsome cousin were engaged in a very public row, plates and other china rocketing about the galley. 'I meant to kill! I wanted to kill!' Adriana stormed. 'I stop Guiseppe killing so I can kill the bastard. But then I find there is no baby after all and I ask the chaplain and he say it would be wrong to kill.'

I know the killer, of course, despite the apparent failure of my enquiries. As the one in charge of the scene of the crime, I do what I must to ensure justice. I can report to the police when we dock that our late and unlamented maestro brought his death upon himself, an excessive gesture coinciding with an exceptionally heavy roll of the sea. I'd warned him many a time, I'd say, each time he indulged.

It's true.

'One day you'll do this tomfoolery once too often,' I told him. 'As if breaking the hearts of the living isn't enough, you destroy the dignity of the dead. Tchaikovsky, Chopin, Rachmaninov – they'll have their revenge, you know.'

I never added, however, that they'd have a little help from me. It was easy. A security officer has access to every part of the ship. It had been a matter of seconds to remove the block stopping the lid support from slipping. Budd himself obligingly wiped any prints I hadn't. Using my master swipecard to get in, I put the missing wood and screws safely in Budd's cabin: a Music Director doesn't share.

'It is impossible to draw any other conclusion,' I wrote in my report, 'than that in his desire for dramatic effect Mr Doppler rendered the piano unsafe and brought his death upon himself.'

As I made one last tour of the vessel before the next influx of passengers, I couldn't resist a visit to the theatre. In the corridor, I'll swear that from his frame Beethoven favoured me with a conspiratorial wink.

# BETTER TO ARRIVE
## Carol Anne Davis

*Carol Anne Davis' novels, including her latest,* Kiss it Away, *are dark and disturbing, although not lacking in black humour. 'Better to Arrive' is a lighter, and highly enjoyable, work. The narrator is a memorable character – working in the same line as the heroines of Patricia Cornwell and Kathy Reichs, but very different. Like Mat Coward, Davis is always trying to do something fresh with her writing and to keep readers on their toes, never knowing quite what to expect next.*

'Have a safe journey,' my wife says. As if a driver can control his fate when the roads are over run with the inept, the drunk and over confident. Even a skilled driver risks oblivion if he's hit head on by another car.

You should see these drivers by the time I examine their remains. Or rather you shouldn't. Suffice to say that we scientists have technicolor dreams. Some of my younger colleagues in forensics can still make jokes about decapitated heads and disembodied arms – but they don't have the added pressures of newborn twins and an extremely lazy wife.

I get home from work at seven that night and let myself into the bungalow. As usual, there are no tantalising cooking smells. Indeed, the only scent is one that I'm all too familiar with, and the pile of wet nappies in the bathroom soon shows the source.

'Gina, I'm home,' I call to my wife as I wash my hands. The silence is deafening. I walk into the lounge only to find it littered with baby clothes and dirty cups. I move on to the kitchen but the only item on the table is yet another shoe box. I open it and stare down at the glossy black shoes – and at the sixty pound receipt.

She's lying on top of the bed fully dressed. Once I'd have joined her there and unbuttoned her blouse and… but that was before the arrival of the twins.

'So, Gina, what kind of a day did you have?' Not a day spent reassembling the bones from a train wreck. Two of the women were so charred that I could only identify them by their teeth.

She shrugs. I've noticed that the young shrug a lot. It's such an irritating form of non-communication.

'I see you went shopping,' I prompt her.

'Only for kitten heels,' she says defensively.

I assume she's referring to the overpriced footwear in the kitchen but I refuse to ask. I won't have conversations about such trivia, not when we used to talk about our work at such enjoyable length.

'Have you eaten?' I ask hungrily.

She shrugs again.

'Well, have you fed the twins?'

She nods. 'They're sleeping now.'

I go to the nursery and check that she's telling the truth.

I look in on Gina again but she too appears to be asleep. There are sweat stains on her blouse and her once-pretty hair lies in unwashed streaks across her forehead. Her slightly-open mouth looks both discontented and alarmingly dumb. Yet she was a vivacious twenty-five-year old when she became my PA, and, as of this year, my second wife. How can she have become this shoe-obsessed sloth, this has been, in such a short space of time?

Wearily I tiptoe into the lounge and phone my first wife, Barbara. She's almost finished preparing a chicken chasseur and assures me that there's more than enough for two. 'It'll be ready in ten minutes,' she says, and my heart starts to beat faster. Damn, that means I don't have time to walk. Once upon a time I'd have taken a taxi, but some of these cabbies drive like lunatics. Only last week I autopsied such a driver and his unfortunate passengers.

I find my Jeep's keys in the back of the writing bureau drawer and approach the garage, but can't bring myself to even open the doors. After all, I'm hungry and tired, the two main accident triggers. And there were 3,400 deaths on the road in Britain last year...

But I need to see Barbara and enjoy her delicious food and drink. She's always been such a wonderful home-maker. If only Gina hadn't tempted me away with her tight silken blouses and come-get-me smile.

Should I risk the bus? There were 12,000 people injured in bus or coach accidents last year, and 150 of them died. Others, of course, may still be dying. You can linger with a broken neck or back for an appallingly long time.

'You'll be fine,' Gina says every day as I muse over how to get to work. She always seems at her most perky when I'm leaving in the mornings. In contrast, I'm understandably anxious about the perils on the road and in the air. I've seen some terrible plane casualties in my line of work, bodies jolted so hard upon impact that every tooth flew out of their mouths and ricocheted into other passengers. Those who were catapulted out of their seats literally lost their heads. And just because you're on the ground to start with doesn't mean that you're untouchable. Oh, no, pedestrians have been killed by planes which fell on them.

'Statistically it isn't going to happen to you,' Gina says in the same patient voice that she reserves for our three-month-olds. But someone has to become a statistic – and it could be me. During some of those conversations I spend up to an hour explaining to her about baseline averages and casualty rates. Unfortunately the young have no concentration and at the end of those discussions she often goes back to bed.

Hunger drives me to the bus stop and within two minutes a bus trundles slowly along. I step on to the platform then realise that the driver is around my own age of sixty. He's also a couple of stone overweight and it's clear from his yellowing fingers that he smokes.

'Sorry,' I pat wildly at my pockets, 'I appear to have forgotten my wallet.'

'It's on me, mate,' he says, but I pretend not to hear and stumble back on to the pavement. It'll have to be a taxi after all...

I start walking slowly in the direction of Barbara's semi-detached, scanning the faces of the passing taxi drivers. When I see a healthy looking one in his thirties I flag him down.

'All right?' he asks, but how can a man with a postnatally depressed wife be all right? A man needs laundered clothes and well-aired rooms and food on the table. A man can't work with the dead all day if he knows most of the money he earns will be spent on shoes and boots. That said, if it wasn't for the footwear shop and off licence in the adjacent terrace, I don't think she'd go out at all.

The driver is looking at me expectantly. I start to sweat, wishing that he'd give his full attention to the road. 'I'm very well, thank you,' I murmur. I check again that my seat belt is fastened and keep my hands alert, ready at a seconds notice to protect my head. Not that the head is the only area that you want to protect in an accident. You also want to avoid whiplash injuries to your neck.

The driver has a healthy back of neck. Not that a good skin tone and a slender build always signifies a long life. A man can have a genetic early predisposition to a coronary or even a stroke.

Barbara was never big on stroking, but she greets me with a warm smile and a pat on the arm, serves up the chicken chasseur and urges me to help myself to the bowls of asparagus and baby potatoes. Afterwards we indulge in a chocolate mint and Turkish coffee, enjoyed in companionable silence on the settee.

'Have you lost more weight?' she asks as we put our empty cups on the little glass-top table.

'Since Monday? I doubt it.' Having dinner with Barbara has become a weekly – and sometimes twice weekly – treat.

'You've been remembering to eat? I know what you're like when you're working.'

That's true – she nagged me often about being late for meals during our shared thirty years.

'I used to lunch at my club but it's too far to walk.'

'But didn't you get the Jeep so that you could drive and still feel safe?'

'No vehicle's indestructible. I dealt with two bodies last week – one where the driver had crashed through the concrete wall on a bridge and plunged on to another vehicle. The second victim was in the car below.'

Barbara nods, smiles sympathetically and pats my hand. If only Gina could be so understanding. 'I'm going to visit the children now, but would you like another coffee to perk you up for the walk home?'

I can't face the walk home yet but I take the coffee and go to see the children – our children – with her. They share a flat just a few streets from the semi detached where Barbara still lives. They're all that I need by way of a family, two fine young men in their late-twenties. I so wish that Gina's contraception hadn't failed.

The walk home takes longer than it did on Monday because I keep especially close to the wall, putting distance between myself and the headlights. One driver can so easily dazzle another, leading to yet another pedestrian death. People don't think about the reality behind the accident stats, the collapsed lungs, ruptured spleens and ripped-open arteries. Can you imagine what it's like to drown in your own blood whilst passer-by turn pale and rush away?

By the time I get home I'm ready for bed – but Gina has put all of her shoes out on the counterpane. She's walking up and down in front of the wardrobe mirror wearing little grey ankle boots and that ugly brown maternity smock she bought late into her pregnancy.

'What are you doing?'

'I'm trying to cheer myself up,' she says, 'Do you think these stack heels make me look slimmer?'

I'm not a man who loses his temper but I show my displeasure by slowing and deepening my voice. 'You shouldn't need to be cheered up. You have a beautiful bungalow and don't have to work. I bring home a good salary. You want for nothing.'

'But the twins are always crying and...'

'That's your job, to pacify them.'

Her bottom lip trembles, the way it so often does these days. 'If we could only go out occasionally to give me a relaxing break.'

*A relaxing break?* People die on the way to the theatre and the cinema every night of the week, hit by stolen cars and motorbikes and even ambulances. You wouldn't believe the number of men and women I've seen who've had every bone broken by speeding panda cars.

'You know that there's danger on the roads when people are tired.'

She pushes her lank hair from her eyes and I notice an unbecoming rash on her forehead. 'You never used to worry this much about going out at night.'

But I didn't used to have two infants to support, used to think I'd retire in my early sixties. Now I'll have to keep working as long as the government will have me. I'll be eighty one before the twins come of age...

'I could invite Barbara over for a meal,' I suggest. 'Get in the caterers.'

I think that I'm being generous in offering to foot the bill but she simply says 'You must be mad.' Then her ringed hand sweeps over the numerous shoes. 'We used to eat out all the time but now the only place I go is the local shops for ten minutes whilst a neighbour minds the kids.'

*What's the point in eating out when you have a perfectly nice dining room at home?* I change the subject. 'You could go to the supermarket.'

'Have *you* tried shopping with two infants in tow?'

*Well of course I haven't. That's woman's work.* 'You can't keep spending money like this,' I tell her, looking at the overpriced and frankly uncomfortable footwear.

Her voice breaks. 'It's all I've got.'

'You've got me. You should be cooking the evening meal.'

'You're never home in time.'

'Well, warm it up then. Barbara always managed.'

The anger in her voice and in her face shocks me. 'Then why don't you go back to fucking Barbara and leave me in peace?'

'There's no need to be unladylike.'

'There's every need.'

'I've given you everything…'

'I have to get out of the house before I go mad.'

'Then take the twins out into the garden,' I say. She's always asking me to go for walks with her at night, but how can I protect her and myself and a double pram if a car mounts the pavement? Really, she's not thinking straight. I tell her so – which heralds yet more post natal tears – before I go off to sleep in the thankfully shoe-free spare room.

The following morning she stays in the nursery with the twins and doesn't wish me a safe journey to work. Not that her words ever acted as a talisman. It was a liar or a fool who said it's a better thing to travel than to arrive.

I arrive at my office but am immediately redirected to a hospital thirty miles away. Apparently there's been one of the worst motorway pile ups ever. They send a nerve-wracking fast car to collect me and I sweat all the way to the hospital morgue.

The first thing which hits me is the stench of blood. There must be thirty bodies – or parts of bodies – in the room and there are pools of blood on the floors, under the cadavers and congealing inside them. As I walk forward, I hear gravel crunch underfoot then realise belatedly that it's bone.

'There were fifteen cars involved,' the policeman tells me, 'But some of the vehicles went up like tinderboxes so there's limited proof of identity.'

'Leave it with me.'

I'm a human jigsaw maker for the next six hours, matching parts of limbs to equally mangled torsos. The hair, teeth and bone density all help me identify the age of the deceased whilst the width of the hipbones lets me determine the sex.

At last I allow the police to drive me home. I stagger into the bathroom to wash my hands and notice the ever-growing pile of dirty nappies. She's sitting at the kitchen table drinking what looks suspiciously like neat whisky. I can hear the twins crying in the nursery.

I set my briefcase down on the table – and it's only when it bumps against something that I notice the shoe box. Surely she can't have? I take off the cardboard lid and see the huge pointed white stiletto heels and the seventy pound receipt.

'What did I tell you yesterday?'

'That elderly road users are more likely to be killed during the daytime.'

'About buying shoes, I mean.'

'They're not for me,' she says triumphantly. 'They're a birthday present for Becky.'

It takes me a moment to realise that she's referring to her younger sister who lives in Wales.

'She phoned me today,' she slurs, and swirls her whisky around, 'She's staying at Mum's for a week so we're going clubbing. I said that you'd drive me there.'

I look out at the garage and shudder. 'It's a lovely night. Why don't you walk?'

She looks at me blankly. It's hard to remember how big and bright her eyes were last year. 'For Christ's sake, that would take hours. Oh forget it. I'll take a taxi and stay at mum's overnight.'

She prepared two bottles of formula and puts them in her little back pack.

I belatedly realise what she's up to. 'Oh no, you're not putting the twins in a cab.'

'I'll be with them.'

'But you can't protect two babies and yourself.'

'Then come with us.'

I shake my head vehemently. 'Do you have any idea how many cab drivers take ill behind the wheel?'

'No, but I'll bet you fucking do!' she yells.

I see a flash of white and feel a rush of pain. Then the room tilts and I look down at my chest and see one of the new shoes attached to it. There must be four or five inches of sharp heel buried in my flesh.

As if in slow motion, my knees give and I slump to the floor then keel on to my back. My eyelids close but I can still hear Gina and the twins crying. I can also hear the traffic outside but all too soon it starts to fade. I briefly remember the numerous transport victims I've autopsied but my last thought is something I'd previously forgotten, that most violent deaths take place in the home.

# TEST DRIVE
## Martin Edwards

*The black arts of sales and marketing have fascinated me for many years and my recent novel,* Take My Breath Away, *set in a London law firm, explored one aspect of techniques of persuasion. 'Test Drive' is such a different story, especially in terms of voice and setting, that it was only when I had completed writing it that I appreciated that in one respect it has a parallel with the book. The starting point came when an enthusiastic sales representative took me on a test drive. As he extolled the virtues of the car, I speculated about how such persuasive talents might be deployed in other aspects of a salesman's life. By the end of the test drive, we'd finished up with the perfect deal. He made the sale and I had not only a new car but also the germ of an idea for this story.*

People are like cars. Since Patrick told me this, I can't get it out of my mind. That's one of his gifts. He comes out with something that makes no sense at first, but the moment he explains, you start to see the world through new eyes. Patrick's eyes. That day in the showroom, the first time we'd met for years, he said that people are like cars. A throwaway line, but when my eyebrows lifted, he jerked a thumb towards the forecourt. Towards the executive saloons and SUVs gleaming in the sunlight, a line of vehicles as immaculate as soldiers on parade.

'You think I'm joking? Come on, Terry, you work with cars all day, every day, you must see I'm right.' He flicked a speck from the cuff of his jacket. Armani, of course. 'Take a look at that muscular roadster. A mean machine, if ever I saw one. When that beast growls, you'd better watch out.'

I laughed. Same old Patrick. People always laughed when he was around. He never needed encouragement and now he was in full flow.

'And the model with lissome lines over there? Chic and elegant, but beware. You can't put your trust in her.'

'Like Olivia Lumb,' I said, joining in. Out of the blue, our old friendship was being rekindled. 'Remember warning me off that night at the Bali, telling me I'd do better with Sarah-Jane? I wonder whatever happened to Olivia.'

Something changed in Patrick's expression, as if suddenly his skin had been stretched too tight over his cheekbones. But he kept smiling. Even as a teenager, I'd envied the whiteness of his teeth but now they shone with all the brilliance that cosmetic dentistry can bestow. When he spoke, his voice hadn't lost a degree of warmth.

'Matter of fact, Terry, I married her.'

'Oh, right.'

My face burned for a few moments, but what had I said? Olivia was beautiful, he'd fallen on his feet. As usual. Years ago, his nickname was Lucky Patrick, everyone called him that, even those who hated him. And a few kids did hate him, the sour and bitter ones who were jealous that he only had to snap his fingers and any girl would come running. Olivia Lumb, eh? After Patrick himself told me that she was bad news, the night of the leavers' disco?

Frankly, I'd always thought she was out of my league, but that night a couple of drinks emboldened me. When I confided in Patrick that I meant to ask her for a dance, he warned me she was heartless and selfish. Not that she cared so well even for herself. She went on eating binges and then made herself sick. She'd scratched at her wrists with her brother's penknife, she'd swallowed her mum's sleeping pills and been rushed into hospital to have her stomach pumped. She dosed up with Prozac because she couldn't cope, she was the ultimate mixed-up kid.

Afterwards, I spent the evening in a corner, talking non-stop and cracking jokes to cheer up Sarah-Jane, whose crush on Patrick he'd encouraged, then failed to reciprocate. Six weeks later I proposed and she said yes. I owed so much to Patrick; his words of warning, and his playing hard-to-get with Sarah-Jane had changed my life.

I mustered a man-to-man grin. 'Lucky Patrick, eh?'

'Yes,' Patrick said. 'Lucky me.'

'She was the most gorgeous girl in the class,' I said quickly. 'Obviously I never had a chance. You did me a favour, it avoided any embarrassment. So you finished up together? Well, congratulations.'

'Know something, Terry? You really haven't changed.'

'You don't think so?' I took it as a compliment, but with Patrick you could never be quite sure. Even at seventeen, at eighteen, his wit used to sting.

'Course not,' he assured me. 'A snappy mover, always smart and reliable, even if your steering is a bit erratic, lets you down every now and then.'

I wasn't offended. No point in taking umbrage with Patrick. You could never win an argument, he shifted his ground with the speed of a Ferrari. Besides, he was right. Occasionally I do try too hard, I suppose. I go over the top when I'm trying to close a difficult sale. I take corners too fast when I'm trying out a new sports car. I'm one endorsement away from losing my licence, I know I ought to take more care.

'It's great to see you again,' I said.

I meant it, and not only because he fancied buying our top-of-the-range executive saloon. The sale would guarantee enough commission to earn the award for representative of the month and win a weekend break for two in Rome, no expense spared. Just the pick-me-up Sarah-Jane needed. More even than that, I'd missed Patrick. We'd hung around together at sixth form college. Both of us were bored with the academic stuff, neither of us wanted to doss around at uni for another three years, simply to help the government massage the employment figures. We yearned to get out into the real world and start earning serious money. I learned a lot from Patrick, he was like a smart older brother, although there were only six months between us. He talked about going into sales and that's where I got the idea for my own career. But I didn't need telling that he'd climbed the greasy pole much faster. The Swiss watch and the cream, crisply tailored suit spoke louder than any words.

Fixing on his Ray-Ban Aviators, he nodded at the forecourt. 'Let's have a closer look, shall we?'

'You'll love her.'

We strolled into the sun, side by side, just like old times. Showing Patrick the features, and as he put car through its paces on the test drive, I felt confidence surging through me, revving up my engine. This was what I did, it wasn't just selling cars, it was selling dreams. I knew the brochure by heart, the phrases came spinning out as if I'd just thought of them.

The style is very emotive... good looks based on clear reasoning... touch the sports mode console button for a yet more spirited ride... sensuous curves of the door panels and dashboard... suspension, chassis and engine all operate in perfect harmony... the precise synergy... the 15-speaker premium system wraps your senses in rich, true to life, beautiful surround sound with concert hall acoustics... intelligent thermal control seat heating... ultrasonic sensors for the science of perfect parking... real-time enabled DVD-based satellite navigation... twin tail pipe baffles lend a sporting accent... potent, passionate, state-of-the-art... blending priceless power with complete control... not so much the finest car in its class as a definitive lifestyle statement.

They are the poets of the twenty-first century in my opinion, these men (or maybe women?), who script the luxury car brochures. When I borrow their words, for a few minutes I feel like an actor, declaiming Shakespeare on the stage. And guess what Shakespeare would be writing if he was alive today? Not stodgy plays about tempests or Julius Caesar, that's for sure.

'So what do you think?' I asked as we pulled back on to the fore-court. 'Isn't it simply the smoothest ride you've ever known?'

'Yeah, yeah.' Patrick's long fingers grazed the leather upholstery. For some strange reason, a picture jostled into my head, an image of him stroking Olivia's pale face while he murmured to her. 'Lovely mover. So what sort of deal are we talking for cash upfront?'

I clasped his arm. 'For you, I'm sure we can sort out something very special.'

He smiled at me in a hungry way. Like a fat man contemplating an unwrapped chocolate bar.

'You've made a good salesman, Terry, one of the best. I can picture you with other customers, teasing them like an angler with a fish on the line.'

His words cheered me as we discussed figures. I knew Patrick was a skilled negotiator and I did my best to show him how much I too had learned. Working in tandem with Bernard, my sales director, like a comic and a sad-faced straight man, I utilised every – I nearly said, 'trick in the book' – *stratagem* to avoid taking too much of a bite out of our profit margin. It wasn't exactly a success, because half an hour later we were signing up to the biggest discount I'd ever agreed. The commission was much less than I'd anticipated, but even Bernard was no match for Patrick. I could see why my old friend was no longer in sales. He'd made enough to set up his own business. Financial services. While Bernard was making a nervous call to seek head office authorisation, Patrick whispered that he could give me a fantastic opportunity with tax-efficient shelters for my investments. He'd be happy to design a personal balanced-risk strategy for me, as a sort of thank-you for my candour as well as the flexibility on the price of his car.

As we said goodbye, I joked that he'd cost Sarah-Jane and me a weekend in Rome. He smiled and asked after her.

'Lovely girl, you did well there. That cascading red hair, I remember it well. Lot of firepower under the bonnet, eh?'

His cheeky wink wasn't in the least embarrassing. Far from it: his approval of my wife sent a shiver of pleasure down my spine. For years I'd shrunk from the reflection that he'd spurned her advances in the months leading up to the leavers' disco. I hated thinking of her – or of myself, for that matter – as second best. She hadn't hidden her bitterness; that was why we hadn't kept in touch with Patrick. A reluctant sacrifice, but what choice did I have? Besides, she and I were enough for each other.

I contented myself with a smirk of satisfaction. 'Let's just say I don't have any complaints.'

'I bet you don't, you sly dog. How is she?'

'Fine, absolutely fine. Well…'

Honesty compelled me not to leave it there. I told him about the miscarriage and his face became grave. How sad, he said, and then he told me that Olivia didn't want children yet, she wasn't ready and that was fine by him. The fact he was taking me into his confidence at all was flattering; so was the way he talked about Sarah-Jane. It was as though her well-being meant more to him than I had ever realised.

'Remember me to her, now, don't forget. Tell her Lucky Patrick was asking after her.'

'I'll do that,' I said, glowing. This man was a success, he had money, status, a beautiful wife, but he hadn't lost his generosity of spirit. How much I'd missed his friendship. 'Let me give you a ring when the paperwork's sorted.'

'Thanks.' He gripped my hand. 'It's been good, Terry. I heard you'd done well, but I didn't know quite how well. We ought to keep in touch.'

'Too right.' I must have sounded as eager as a teenager, but it didn't matter. He and I went back a long way. 'Maybe we could get together again sometime.'

'The four of us? Fantastic idea, it'll be just like old times.'

It wasn't precisely what I had in mind. Olivia and Sarah-Jane as well? Not like old times at all, strictly speaking. But it was just a figure of speech, I knew what he meant. Time's a great healer.

'I don't think so,' Sarah-Jane said. 'I really don't think so.'

She was perched on a kitchen stool, wearing a grubby housecoat. I'd always liked the way she took care of herself, it's important to have pride in your appearance. But since the miscarriage, she'd become moody and irritable and didn't seem to care about anything. The dishwasher had broken down and she hadn't bothered to call out the repairman, let alone tackle the mountain of unwashed crockery in the sink.

'You mooned after him at one time,' I reminded her.

'That was then,' she said. 'Anyway, I finished up with you, didn't I?'

'Don't make it sound like a prison sentence,' I joked, wanting to lift her spirits. 'Listen, it's just one evening, all right? We're not talking a dinner party, you don't have to entertain them. We'll meet in a bar, so we're not under any obligation to ask them back here sometime. You don't have to see him again.'

'But you'll keep seeing him.'

'What's wrong with that? He's smart, he's intelligent. Most of all, he's a friend.'

She cast her eyes to the heavens. 'There's just no arguing with you, is there? OK, OK, you win.' A long sigh. 'Salesmen Reunited, huh?'

I reached for her, tried to undo the top button of the housecoat, but she flapped me away, as if swatting a fly.

'I told you last night, I need some personal space.'

Of course I didn't push my luck. During the past couple of months she'd cried so easily. Once, in a temper, she'd slapped my face over something and nothing. I needed to give her time, just like it said in the problem pages of the magazines she devoured. She read a lot about life-coaching and unlocking her personal potential. The column-writers promised to give her the key to happiness, but she was still looking for the right door to open. Fair enough, I could do 'patient and caring'. Besides, she'd agreed to see Patrick again. I could show my old friend exactly what he'd missed.

Sarah-Jane may have had mixed feelings about meeting up with Patrick and Olivia, but when it came to the crunch, she didn't let me down. For the first time in an age, we were hitting the town and she summoned up the enthusiasm to put on her make-up and wear the slinky new dress I'd bought by way of encouragement. We couldn't mourn forever, that was my philosophy. We had to move on.

The evening went even better than I'd dared to hope. Patrick was on his very best form and funny anecdotes streamed from him like spray from a fountain. In front of the girls, he congratulated me on my shrewd negotiating techniques. I thought I had the gift of the blarney, he said, but Terry knows his cars inside out, you know he can torque for England.

I hadn't seen Sarah-Jane laugh like that in a long time. As for Olivia, she'd always been silent and mysterious and nothing had changed. She spoke in enigmatic monosyllables and paid no more attention to me than when we were both eighteen. I stole a glance at her wrist and saw that it was scarred. The marks were red and recent, not the legacy of a long-ago experiment in self-harm. Hurriedly, I averted my gaze. Her own eyes locked on Patrick all night, though it didn't seem to make him feel uncomfortable. It was as if he expected nothing less.

Sarah-Jane did her best to make conversation. 'I'm longing for the day when the doctor signs me off and I can get back to work.'

'Terry tells me you work for an estate agency,' Patrick said. 'I keep trying to persuade Olivia to do a bit of secretarial work to help me out in the business since my last PA left. But it doesn't suit.'

Olivia finished her pina colada and gave a faraway smile. 'I look after the house.'

'I expect it's a mansion,' I said cheerily.

'Seven bedrooms, five reception, a cellar and a granny annexe,' Patrick said. 'Not that we've got a granny, obviously.' He mentioned the address; I knew the house, although I'd never seen it. A long curving drive wandered away between massive rhododendron bushes on its journey to the front door.

Olivia's flowing dark hair was even silkier than I remembered, though there still wasn't a spot of colour in her delicate cheeks. I couldn't help recalling how I'd worshipped her from the back of the class when I should have been listening to the teacher's words of wisdom on some writer whose name I forget. He used to say that all animals are equal, but some are more equal than others. It's the only snippet from those lessons that has stuck in my mind. Of course, it's true we don't live in a fair and just world, no sense in moping about it, you just have to do the best that you can for yourself. Beauty is like money, it isn't divided out to us all in neat proportions. How many women can match the elegance of Olivia Lumb? But I told myself I was more fortunate than Patrick. Looks matter, but a man wants more from his wife.

As Patrick might have said, Olivia was as svelte as the sportiest coupe in the dealership, but never mind. In the early years of our marriage, Sarah-Jane's handling had been tenacious, her performance superb. Of course, nothing lasts forever. It's as true of people as it is of cars. I'd hung my hopes on our starting a family, and losing the baby had devastated both of us. And then, in the course of a single evening at the bar, I saw Sarah-Jane coming back to life, like Sleeping Beauty awoken from a deep slumber. I had Patrick to thank for giving my wife back to me.

For both of us, making friends with Patrick again turned out to be a sort of elixir. He gave me plenty of inside advice on the markets. Tips that made so much sense I didn't hesitate in shifting the money my parents had left me from the building society account into the shelters he recommended. As he pointed out, even keeping cash under the floorboards was far from risk-free. After all, if you were missing out on high dividends and extra performance, you were taking an investment decision, and not a smart one.

As for Sarah-Jane, her eyes regained their sparkle, her cheeks their fresh glow. When I teased her that she hadn't even wanted to set eyes on Patrick after these years, she had to accept I'd been proved right. She was even happy for us to host a barbecue on our new patio, so that we could reciprocate after a dinner party at Patrick's lovely home. Olivia didn't cook the meal, her household management seemed to consist of hiring posh outside caterers. It didn't matter. I sat next to another of Patrick's clients and spent an enjoyable evening extolling the virtues of the 475 while Patrick entertained Sarah-Jane with tales of double-dealing in the murky world of financial services. People talk about dishonest car salesmen, and fair enough, but the money men are a hundred times worse if Patrick's gleeful anecdotes about his business competitors were to be believed.

We asked Bernard and his wife along to the barbecue and it wasn't until we'd guzzled the last hot dog that I found myself together with Olivia. As usual, she'd said little or nothing. I'd drunk a lot of strong red wine, Tesco's finest, and probably I talked too long about how difficult it had been to lay the patio flags in just the right way. She kept looking over my shoulder towards Patrick, who was sharing a joke with Sarah-Jane and our guests. Her lack of attention was worse than irritating, it was downright rude. I found myself wanting to get under her skin, to provoke her into some sort of response. Any response.

'I ought to make a confession,' I said, wiping a smear of tomato ketchup off my cheek with a paper napkin. 'Ease my conscience, you know? This has been preying on my mind for years.'

'Oh yes?' She raised a languid eyebrow.

'Yes,' I said firmly. 'It's about you and me.'

She contrived the faintest of frowns, but a frond of Virginia creeper, trailing from the pergola, seemed to cause her more concern. She flicked it out of her face and murmured, 'You and me?'

I covered my mouth to conceal a hiccup, but I'm not sure she even noticed. 'Well, I don't know whether you ever realised, when we were in the sixth form together I mean, but I had a thing about you. Quite a serious thing.'

'Oh,' she said. That was all.

I'd hoped to intrigue her. Over-optimistic, obviously. Never mind, I'd started, so I would finish. 'You're a very attractive woman, Olivia. Patrick's a lucky fellow.'

'You think so?'

I leaned towards her, stumbling for a moment, but quickly regaining my balance. 'Yes, I do think so. He thinks people are like cars. In my book, you're a high-performance model.'

She peered into my eyes, as if seeing them for the first time. 'Your wife's prettier than I remembered. I might have known.'

That was all she said. *I might have known?* I stared back at her, puzzled, but before I could ask her what she meant, a strong arm wrapped itself around my shoulder and Patrick's voice was in my ear.

'Now then, Terry. You'll be making me jealous, monopolising my lovely wife all the time.'

I could smell the alcohol on his breath, as well as a pungent aftershave. And I could hear Sarah-Jane's tinkling laughter as he spoke: 'Always did have an eye for a pretty lady, didn't you?'

The next time we got together, for a meal at an Indian restaurant a stone's throw from the showroom, Patrick offered Sarah-Jane a job as his PA. I'm not sure how it came about. One moment they were talking idly about her plans to return to work the following week, the next Patrick was waxing lyrical about how someone with her administrative skills could play a vital role in his business. He needed a right hand woman to rely on, he said, and who better than an old friend?

I glanced at Olivia. She was sitting very still, saying nothing, just twisting her napkin into tight little knots, as if it was a make-believe garrotte. Her gaze was fixed on her husband, as usual, as if the rest of us did not exist.

I assumed that Sarah-Jane would turn him down flat. In the estate agency, she was deputy to the branch manager and stood in for him when he was on holiday. There was a decent pension scheme, too. But to my amazement, she positively basked in his admiration and said she'd love to accept. It would be a challenge, she said merrily, to keep Patrick on the straight and narrow. Before I could say a word, Patrick was summoning the waiter and demanding champagne. One look at my wife's face convinced me it was a done deal. Even though nothing had been said about salary, let alone sick pay or holiday entitlements.

At least I need not have worried on those counts. Within a couple of days, Patrick hand-delivered her letter of appointment. The terms were generous; in fact, her basic rate was a tad higher than mine. When I pointed this out, Patrick was firm.

'I'm sure she's worth it, Terry. And to be honest, I'm a demanding boss. I work long hours and spend a lot of time travelling. I'll need Sarah-Jane by my side. She'll be my right hand, so I'm prepared to pay a premium.'

I shot my wife a glance. 'I don't think…'

'It'll be fine,' she said, patting me on the hand. 'A new environment, a fresh start. I can't wait.'

'But don't you think… I mean, after having so long at home… ?'

'I'm ready,' she said. 'I've gathered my strength. You're sweet to me, darling, but I don't expect to be wrapped in cotton wool for the rest of my life.'

'Don't worry,' Patrick said to me. 'I'll take good care of her.'

I can't put my finger on one single incident that caused me to believe that Patrick and Sarah-Jane were having an affair. My brain didn't suddenly crash into gear. The suspicion grew over time. Like when you begin to hear a faint knocking each time your well-loved car rounds a corner at speed. At first you don't take any notice, after a while you can't ignore the noise altogether, but you persuade yourself that it's nothing, really, that if you don't panic, sooner or later it will go away of its own accord. But it never goes away, of course, not ever.

Little things, insignificant in themselves, began to add up. She started to wear raunchy underwear again, just as she had done in those exciting days when we first got together. To begin with, I was thrilled. It was a sign she was putting the miscarriage behind her. But when I turned to her in bed at night, she continued to push me away. She was tired, she explained, the new job was taking so much out of her. It seemed fair enough, but when I suggested that it was unreasonable for Patrick to propose that she accompanied him for a week-long trip to Edinburgh, to meet people from a life company he did business with, she brushed my protests aside. The long hours came with the territory, she said. Patrick had given her a wonderful opportunity. She could not, would not let him down.

Even when she was at home, she was never off the mobile, talking to him in muffled tones while I busied myself in another room. Client business was highly confidential, she reminded me when I ventured a mild complaint. I suggested several times that the four of us might go out for another meal together, but it was never convenient. Olivia wasn't well, apparently. Although Sarah-Jane was discreet, I gathered that her old rival was seeing a psychiatrist regularly. I said that maybe Patrick would want to spend more time with his own wife, but Sarah-Jane said I didn't understand. There was a reason why my old friend buried himself in his work. He didn't need the money, it was all about having a safety valve. A means of escape from the pressures of being married to a neurotic cow.

One night Sarah-Jane announced that she would have to up at the crack of dawn the next morning to catch the early flight to Paris. Patrick thought the European market was full of opportunities and they were going to spend forty eight hours there. Putting out feelers, making contacts.

'Are you taking the camera?'

She wrinkled her nose. 'Won't have time for that. You don't realise, Terry, just what it's like. This is high-powered stuff, but it's hard work. Long meetings in offices, talking business over lunch and dinner. One hotel is much like another, it's scarcely a tourist trip.'

'Your mobile always seems to be busy or switched off when I call.'

'Exactly. It's non-stop, I can tell you. I really don't want to be disturbed. And don't fret about the phone bill, by the way. Patrick pays for everything, of course he does.'

An hour later, her mobile rang again. At one time I'd liked the *I Will Survive* ringtone, all of a sudden I hated it. While she retreated to the kitchen to take the call, closing the door behind her, I did something rather dishonourable. I crept up the stairs in my stockinged feet and opened up the suitcase she'd been packing. There were new shoes I didn't recognise, clothes with designer labels that I'd never seen before. Along with furry handcuffs, a velvet blindfold and a whip.

When at last she came off the phone, I didn't say a word about what I'd discovered. Only for a few seconds had I contemplated a confrontation. But I couldn't face it. Suppose I challenged her and she admitted everything? Said that she loved Patrick and that, compared to him, I was nothing?

How could I deny it? Lucky Patrick, he won every time.

All through their absence in Paris, I felt numb. At the showroom, I was going through the motions, scarcely caring when a customer reckoned he could beat my price by going to the dealership on the other side of town. One lunchtime, when Bernard passed me the latest copy of *What Car?* I left it unopened on the table while I nibbled at a chicken tikka sandwich and stared moodily through the glass at the drizzle spattering the windscreens of the saloons on the forecourt. Bernard asked if I was all right and my reply was a noncommittal grunt.

Of course I wasn't all right, my wife and best friend were betraying me. Worse, they were treating me like a fool. At once I saw that really, it had always been like this. Patrick used people and discarded them like he used and discarded his cars.

And I meant to do something about it.

I still hadn't decided what to do when Patrick dropped Sarah-Jane off at home that evening. I'd seen his car pulling up outside the gate and I'd wandered down the path to greet them. Good old Terry, I thought to myself as I forced a good-natured wave. Always reliable.

'Good trip?'

'Fine,' Sarah-Jane said. I don't think I'd ever seen her red hair so lustrous, her skin so delicate. 'Hard work, obviously.'

'No peace for the wicked,' Patrick confirmed with his customary grin. 'I don't know what I'd do without my trusty PA…'

'Taking things down for you?' I interrupted, with as much jocularity as I could muster.

'Absolutely.'

He roared with laughter, but out of the corner of my eye, I saw Sarah-Jane start. When she thought I wasn't looking, she shot Patrick a cautionary glance, but he wasn't fazed. The worm – I *knew* he thought this – was incapable of turning.

In bed that night, for the first time in an age, she reached for me. I sighed and said I was tired and turned away. Even though I still wanted her so much, I would not touch her again until I knew she was mine forever.

The truth dawned on me a couple of days later. I couldn't sort this on my own. I needed help, and only one person could provide it. But I'd need all my sales skills. Before I lost my nerve, I picked up the phone and rang the number of Patrick's house. I held for a full minute before someone answered.

'Hello?'

'Olivia? It's me. Terry. We need to talk.'

'What about?' Her voice was faint. I could tell she was at a low ebb.

'I think you know.'

There was a long pause before she said, 'So you finally worked it out.'

'I suppose you think I'm an idiot, a poor naïve idiot?'

I could picture her shrugging. 'Well…. '

'Like I said, we ought to talk.'

'What for? You seriously imagine I'm going to cry on your shoulder? Or let you cry on mine?'

'I want you to come here, to the showroom.' I wasn't going to be swayed by her scorn. Suddenly, I had never felt so masterful. 'We have to do something.'

Another pause. 'Do something?'

'I'll see you at reception at three o'clock. Pretend you're a customer. I'll take you on a test drive and we can decide.'

*

Looking out through the glass windows as Olivia arrived in her Fiat runabout, Bernard recognised her and shot me a sharp glance. I smiled and said, 'I finally persuaded Patrick to cough up for his wife's new car. She was ready for a change.'

He raised his eyebrows. 'Oh yes? Well, take care, young man. She's a loose cannon, that one.'

'The two of us go back years,' I said. 'I can handle her. No worries.'

Five minutes later, Olivia was at the wheel of a new fiery orange supermini. Lovely little motor, alloy wheels, sill extensions and a tiny spoiler above the tailgate, plus bags of equipment for the money. From the styling, you would never guess it was designed in Korea. But this afternoon, I wasn't interested in selling a car.

'Sarah-Jane isn't the first, is she?' I asked, as we paused at a red light.

'So you finally realised?'

'This is different from the others, isn't it?'

'What makes you think that?' Her voice was empty of emotion. I didn't have a clue what was going on in her head.

'Because I know Sarah-Jane. She lost him once, she won't let him slip away again. It's only now that I see the truth. She's been grieving for him for years. He was what she wanted, not me.'

She kept her eyes on the road. 'Perhaps you're right. Perhaps this is different.'

'You've picked up hints?'

'The others never lasted this long. I always knew he would come back to me in the end. This time... '

We moved on to the dual carriageway, picking up speed as we moved out of town.

'What can we do about it?' I asked. 'How can we stop them?'

'Is that what you want, to stop them?'

'Of course. Does that surprise you?'

'He could always twist you around his little finger, Terry. I thought – you were willing to put up with it. As long as you thought he was making money on your investments, as long as he kept flattering you, made you feel like a big man.'

It wasn't the longest speech, but then, I don't think I'd ever heard her put more than three sentences together at one time before.

'I don't care about the money,' I said hotly.

'That's just as well, because there won't be as much for you as you'd like to think. The business is going down the tube.'

'What?'

Her knuckles were white against the steering wheel. 'He's always been lazy and now he doesn't have time for anyone or anything but your wife. The creditors are pressing, Terry. Better watch out, or they'll take your money as well as his.'

I didn't speak again for a couple of minutes, I just gazed out of the window, watching the pylons in the fields, their arms out-stretched as if denying guilt. Until then, I suppose I'd had pangs of conscience. I'm not a naturally violent man. In principle, I think it's right to turn the other cheek. But there are limits, and I had raced past mine.

'You can stop him,' I said eventually. 'That's why I needed to talk to you, Olivia. Not to weep and wail. I just want an end to it.'

Ideas were shifting inside my head, even as I sat beside her. I hadn't been thinking straight. I'd thought: *what if she kills herself?* It wasn't nice, but looking at it another way, you might say it was only a question of time before Olivia stopped crying for help and finally went all the way. Imagining the headlines gave me grim satisfaction. *Faithless financier finds wife dead. Betrayed woman could not take any more.* It would finish everything between Sarah-Jane and Patrick. Their relationship would be tainted for all time. I knew enough of him to be sure he would want to get out of it, make a new beginning with someone else. Someone else's wife, most likely.

But maybe there was a different solution, leaving less to chance. Bernard's words lodged in my brain. He was no fool, he had Olivia's number. She *was* a loose cannon, they didn't come any looser. What if she was fired at Patrick himself?

Signs were scattered along the grass verge warning of police speed enforcement, pictures of so-called safety cameras and a board bragging about how many poor old motorists had been caught exceeding the limit in the past six months. None of it seemed to register with Olivia. The yellow camera wasn't hidden from view, there was no panda car lurking in the bushes, she had every chance to slow down before we reached the white lines on the road, but far from easing off the accelerator, she put her foot down. We leapt past the camera and it flashed twice in anger. I couldn't help wincing, but at the same time I felt blood rushing to my head. This was a sort of liberation. I was manoeuvring Olivia as if she was a car to be squeezed into a tight parking space. And Patrick's luck was about to run dry.

'He deserves to suffer,' she said.

'Yes.'

She tossed me a glance. It was gone in a moment, but for the first time since I'd known her, I thought she was actually *seeing* me. But I still couldn't guess what she thought about what she saw.

'Olivia loves the special edition,' I told Bernard. 'I offered her the chance to take it home, try it out for twenty four hours before she signs on the dotted line. The insurance is fine, she's not a time-waster, trust me.'

He gave me the sort of look you give delinquents on street corners, but said nothing. No way could he guess the thoughts jockeying inside my head. My voice was as calm as a priest's, yielding no hint of the excitement churning in my guts.

I had made a sale, the biggest of my career.

Olivia had told Patrick she'd be out shopping all day. She was sure he'd have seized the chance, taken Sarah-Jane home so that the two of them could romp in the comfort of the kingsize bed. She was going to drive straight home and catch them out.

What weapon she would choose? From our visit to their lovely house, I remembered the array of knives kept in a wooden block on the breakfast bar. And there was a cast-iron doorstop, a croquet mallet, the possibilities were endless.

Pictures floated through my mind as I shuffled through price lists for gadgets and accessories. Patrick's damaged face peeping from out of the covering sheet in the mortuary. Solemn policemen, shaking their heads. Sarah-Jane, pale and contrite, kissing my cheek. Whispering the question: could I ever forgive her?

Of course I could. I'm not a cruel or bitter man. I'd promise her that we would work at the marriage. Pick up the pieces.

Patrick was right about one thing, I decided. People *are* like cars. They just need the right driver.

My mobile rang. I keyed *Answer* and heard Olivia. Breathless, triumphant.

'So easy, Terry, it was so easy. They were on the drive outside the porch. Kissing, they only had eyes for each other.'

'You – did it?'

She laughed, a high, hysterical peal. 'It's like nothing else. The feeling as your wheels go over someone. Crushing out the life – *squish, squish*. The screams urge you on. I felt so empowered, so much in control. But I reversed over the body, just to make sure.'

'So... '

I heard her gasp and then another voice on the line. A voice I never wanted to hear again. Frantic, horrified.

'Terry, you put her up to this, you bastard. You jealous, murdering bastard.'

It was Patrick, lucky Patrick.

My mind stalled, useless as an old banger. I couldn't take this in, couldn't comprehend what Olivia had done. If Patrick was alive – what had happened to Sarah-Jane?

# MAN OVERBOARD
## Jürgen Ehlers

*Jürgen Ehlers, like a number of other contributors to this anthology, has a particular affinity with the short story. A number of his mysteries have been published in this country as well as in his native Germany and a couple of years ago he co-edited an anthology of short fiction,* Mord und Steinschlag. *His occasional contributions to CWA anthologies are invariably flavoursome and, to those unfamiliar with his work, 'Man Overboard' is a good introduction.*

'Gone overboard? Off the ferry?' Axel Naumann is standing in front of their cottage. He blinks into the sun, and rubs his eyes, still half asleep. The young man, who's supposed to look after the garden, has switched off the lawn mower. That's something at least. Naumann had hoped to sleep in for once. Hadn't he heard the alarm shots last night? No, he had not.

'They were out last night, with the lifeboat. Yes, somebody went overboard from the ferry. They kept searching well into the morning, but without any result.' The young man shrugs. The water is cold in October, nobody can last more than half an hour in there.

The journalist is only mildly interested. He has seen the ferry only once, from a distance. Fishguard-Rosslare. A huge white hulk on the horizon. Should be able to stay stable even in rough sea, he thinks. And last night there was no rough sea. Calm autumn weather. How could anyone manage to fall overboard?

'Either he fell or he jumped,' said the man.

'Suicide you mean?'

'Perhaps. It happens time and again.' They would know more in one or two weeks' time. At the latest. Naumann shrugs. 'I'm on holiday', he thinks. 'None of my business.' He goes into the kitchen to make tea.

Less than six hours later his holiday is over. 'Your paper's called!' Jutta looks amused. 'A certain Klaus Seedorf.'

Naumann grunts angrily. His boss. There'd been a good reason for not leaving his holiday address at his office. Let alone the telephone number! Thomas must have let on. His son.

'You're to call back at once!' Of course. Else they wouldn't have rung. Urgent, urgent! Everything is terribly urgent, even if the paper is nothing more than a local paper in Schleswig-Holstein. But he will have to call back anyway. Best right now, to get it done with. What was the country code for Germany?

'I've jotted down the number!' Jutta, the efficient one. Perhaps she should start working for the paper instead of him? True, she is older than him but far less frustrated by life's banalities.

'Naumann, that's good, calling right back!' Seedorf, dynamic as ever. 'It's a top story. Burowski has drowned, they say. In your area!'

'Burowski?'

'Come on, you know the man, Naumann, just think about it!' He doesn't know him, definitely not. 'He was in our paper, repeatedly. Appliances. In the industrial sector. *Europrecision*, you remember, don't you?'

Now it dawns on him. Hadn't the company got into the news for alleged deals with Iraq? Or had it been Libya? Who cares. They hadn't been able to prove anything, as far as he remembers. 'Precision instruments', he says.

'Exactly. In trouble for the last two years. The layoffs in February, you remember? It was on the front page.'

Should he admit that he doesn't read their own paper? Better not. 'Yes, I remember', he says curtly.

'What's the matter with you, Naumann? Lack of sleep? Hangover? – Too much sex, I bet!' Seedorf laughs. 'Whatever. I suggest that you have a look into this affair. Suicide, the police say. No wonder considering all his problems. Anyway, we'll dig up the personal background here. And you get us the details of the accident. Photograph of the ferry, interview with the witnesses, you know the stuff. E-mail us. You'll come up with something, I'm sure. – And we need it by yesterday. Needless to say. So far nobody else has got on to this!'

'Fuck,' says Naumann. But Seedor has already rung off.

Three hours later he's got the RNLI press release:
*St Davids all-weather lifeboat launched on service at 2.00 am on Sunday 5th October 2003 with Deputy 2nd Coxswain Jeffrey Thompson in command. The lifeboat was requested to search for a 56-year old passenger missing from the* Stena Europe *ferry which was on passage from Rosslare to Fishguard. The lifeboat searched an area around 10 miles north west of Strumble Head. A rescue helicopter was also involved in the search. The search terminated at 7.30am with nothing having been found. The lifeboat returned to station at 8.15am.*

Whilst Axel is after the press release, Jutta explores the splendours of their holiday resort on her own. St Davids, smallest city of the United Kingdom. A few hundred souls, but a cathedral. And the ruins of a bishop's palace. Jutta is the only visitor. The sun is shining, but it is chilly. Jutta hopes that Axel will get his task done quickly. She finds it hard to be on her own. Even more so in a foreign country, in a small town, the former greatness of which is only reflected by ruins. The former harbour, Porth Clais, nothing but a desolate inlet, some two kilometres from the town. Only used by yachts, in the summer months. A German submarine allegedly had put into Porth Clais in the Second World War, the young man with the lawnmower had said. A legend, of course. Axel had only laughed, when she'd told him. It would have been far too risky to enter this narrow inlet with its shallow water and pointed rocks.

Jutta suppresses a sigh. This then is their great holiday. Their chance to get a bit closer, at last. Not just for a few hours, under the disapproving eyes of Axel's son from his first marriage. A nice guy, in a way. A pity that he doesn't seem to like her. She sits down on the low wall at the entry. It's no good, she thinks. What am I doing wrong? Sure they'd had sex straight away, on the first evening, until they were completely exhausted. But they could have had that at home, too. Axel is as taciturn as ever. Not giving much away, until asked directly. And what she might think or dream of, he's never bothered to explore.

And she has big dreams. Dreams of having a child, perhaps even two, although she is in her forties already. And Axel, he would be all right as a father, she thinks. Even if he didn't marry her in the end. You can't force these things. Nothing can be forced. Her looks, for instance. There are prettier women, no doubt. Slimmer women. Of course, she could lose some weight. She could try, at least. But Axel is two years her junior, and, of course, there are also younger women around. And she has nothing to top that.

He's lucky, the ferry has just come in. His press card gives him access. But the captain is short with him and refuses to comment. He suggests Axel contact the Stena Line main office; they would tell him all he needed. A glossy brochure of the boat is all Naumann can get hold of. But he won't be defeated so easily. He approaches the stewards, with more success. The man who eventually talks to him looks about nervously. Nobody must see him talking to the press. He leads Naumann to the aft deck.

'It happened here', he says.

'Just like that?' Naumann finds it difficult to believe. He puts his hand on the rail.

The steward shakes his head. 'Drunk. He was dead drunk.'

Naumann looks at the man. The rail is high enough; not even a dead drunk person should be able to fall overboard by accident. 'And you saw that yourself?'

The man shakes his head, says something Naumann cannot understand.

'Slowly, please!'

The man repeats himself. Gradually it emerges, that Burowski had been throwing a big party. Some important contract signing, perhaps. Eventually a group of people had staggered out on deck. There they had had another round of champagne, and in the end Burowski in high spirits had climbed up and started to walk along the thin rail. And in the end he had lost his balance and fallen into the water.

'Any witnesses to that?'

The man nods, uses his fingers. Ten, twenty people perhaps.

'Twenty people?'

He grins uncertainly, shrugs. He doesn't really know. He shouldn't have been on deck at that time. But he had been standing there in the dark having a smoke.

When they had started to scream, that had caught his attention. Somebody had thrown a life-belt. Somebody had run to inform the bridge. And then the ferry had stopped and launched a boat. Everything had taken too long, much too long. And the other boat had not been able to help either. The man had drowned.

'What other boat?'

The man lights a cigarette. 'There'd been a boat next to us, when it happened. Had used their searchlights. But found nothing. Neither did the lifeboat from St Davids. Nor the helicopter. But by the time they'd arrived, it was too late anyway. It took much too long, everything.'

Somebody calls for the steward. Telling him to come immediately. A colleague? A superior? 'Sorry, I must go!'

'One moment, please!' Naumann grabs his shoulder, holds the man back. 'Any names you might remember? People who were present when he went overboard?'

'I don't know! – Just as I've said. Ten, twenty people, perhaps. And his wife, of course.'

Naumann is sitting on a bench not far from the ferry terminal. He has to send his report to the newspaper. Luckily he has his mobile with him. 'Well, Naumann, what have you got?' Even over hundreds of kilometres the voice has an unpleasant ring. Axel reports what he has found out so far.

'Burowski's wife had been present? How dreadful.' Naumann learns that her name is Barbara and that she is twenty-four, not even half her husband's age.

'What else have you got? Some technical details. How big is the ferry?'

As if that made any difference! But that is what they always want, these press people. Hard facts, as Seedorf would put it. The captain's name and age. And the size of the ship, of course. Naumann glances back to the *Stena Europe* which is just leaving port. '37.000 GT', he maintains.

His boss whistles through his teeth. 'That's quite a tub!'

It dawns on Naumann that he's guessed too high.

*

One call at the RNLI, and he knows. The other boat's name is the *Aslan*. Why hadn't it been mentioned in the press release? Simply because it hadn't taken part in the rescue operation. Apparently they hadn't realised that something was amiss, not having their wireless turned on. The boat is in Fishguard now. No, not in the port with the ferry terminal, but further east, beyond the hills.

Naumann drives there, sits on the harbour wall and waits. His camera and tele-lens ready beside him. Eventually a man approaches, burdened with shopping bags. A sporty type, expensive clothes. The man puts his purchase into a small dinghy. When he is about to leave and row out to one of the boats, Naumann approaches him.

'The *Aslan*? Yes, I've chartered her. Sailing in the Irish Sea. Now I've to return her. Holiday's over.'

His English is almost accent-free, or so Naumann thinks. 'Nice boat!' he says. Then he mentions the accident.

The man nods. 'Yes I was out there. Saw everything from close by. I'd been dozing, sort of, when all of a sudden that big white vessel turned up right in front of me, nearly ran me over. Gave me a real fright. I had to switch on my searchlight to get their attention. And the ferry sounded her horn. That was probably when the drunk fell overboard. Been balancing on the rail, they say. Very hazardous, that. Quite incredible.'

'And you weren't able to save him?'

The man shakes his head. 'Hadn't even realised what had happened. Not until the ferry had stopped and launched a boat. But by then I was no longer anywhere near the site of the accident. I shone the searchlight all over the area, but by then he was probably gone already. Goes pretty fast at these temperatures. Faster still, when you're drunk.' No, he hadn't bothered to wait. He'd wanted to be in Fishguard the next morning. For breakfast! He laughs.

Unpleasant chap, Naumann thinks. But perhaps he is a bit biased because he's now hungry and cold. He watches the man stow away his supplies, lots of exquisite food, and row back to his boat. It's almost too late when Naumann thinks of the pictures. He lifts his camera. Well, with the tele-lens it might still work. There is the boat, there is

the man. He looks directly into the camera. Will he get him in focus?
A tripod would be useful. He hasn't brought one. Naumann shoots a
whole series of photos.

Obviously, the man is expected. On the *Aslan* a girl is standing at
the rail. The tele-lens brings her quite close. Tall, slim, with blonde
hair. The man climbs over the rail, talks to the girl. Both look in his
direction. Another photograph. Then they disappear below deck.
That was it.

Naumann starts when someone taps on his shoulder. 'Bird watching, eh?'

Naumann nods. 'Yes, birds.' He points at his tele-lens.

The man laughs. He looks like a docker. 'Bird's name is Barbara
Burowski,' he says.

Naumann stares at him.

'Perhaps I should introduce myself. Davies, Pembrokeshire Police.
May I ask, what specific interest you take in that particular bird?'

'I'm a journalist', says Naumann.

'Then you're not from the insurance?'

'Insurance?'

'Could well be, don't you think? That they send a detective over, I
mean. In a case like this, with such a high life insurance policy signed
so shortly before one's death. One million Euros. That young woman
over there, Burowski's wife, she's the heir presumptive.'

'Not bad,' says Naumann. 'But I wonder why… '

'Why she's here now on the *Aslan* together with one Michael
Borck? That's what I'd like to know, Mr Naumann, indeed, that's
something that I'd like to know as well!'

The policeman won't reveal any more, and finally he goes. Naumann
is left behind on the beach. It's getting rather cold now. Naumann
stops to think. Why was the policeman watching the boat? He
wouldn't have needed his binoculars in order to figure out that
Barbara Burowski was on board. Could it be that he suspects somebody else might be on board? Udo Burowski, for instance? Secretly
rescued, in order to pocket the insurance money?

Suddenly Naumann sees the two leave the boat and row ashore.

Heading for some pub, probably. Naumann can hardly believe his good luck. As soon as they're gone, he emerges. But the dinghy is chained. How can he get hold of a boat now?

By the time he's found someone who'll take him over to the *Aslan* it's almost dark. When he climbs on board eventually, his palms are wet with sweat. He looks back at the harbour wall. All quiet. No, they would not be back so soon. Naumann turns to the cabin. Locked, of course. He rattles the door handle, to no avail. Nothing stirs inside. He peeps through the window. If there is anybody on board they would have seen Naumann come and would have had ample time to hide, of course. In retrospect there was no point in coming.

The man who rowed him out sits in his boat, smoking. What does he think Naumann is doing here? The reporter takes a few photos quickly. When he's about to leave, his eye is caught by a life-belt, half hidden under a coil of rope. Naumann pulls the rope aside. Is that the life-belt that was thrown from the ferry?

He's rowed back ashore. Should he go to some Internet cafe to send the latest photos to Germany? Probably he should, but it's late enough already. Jutta will grow impatient.

'You're mad', says Jutta.

'I want to find out, by any means. You don't come across that sort of chance twice.'

'Suppose you're right, they'll have worked it out so that you can't prove anything. Why don't you tell the police what you think? That should do. We're here on holiday, remember!'

'I'm sitting here together with you right now, aren't I?'

'Your mind is somewhere else ', says Jutta.

Why is the bottle of wine empty? Naumann fetches another one from the kitchen. When he comes back, Jutta has switched on the TV.

'Do we have to watch the telly?'

'You'll only think about your happy heiress anyway!' she says.

That hits home. Actually he had been thinking about the young woman from the boat. 'Happy heiress? To me she looked more like she'd been crying', he says.

*

Jutta is still asleep when Axel Naumann starts out for Fishguard. She likes to sleep in. It's not yet eight when Naumann's car rolls down the little slope to the harbour. Automatically he gropes for the camera on the seat next to him. But there is no camera. He remembers that he's left it in the cottage having shown Jutta the photos. But it's too late anyway. Too late. He is too late anyway. Not only is the little car-park empty, the bay is empty, too. The *Aslan* must have slipped out in the night.

Naumann bangs his fist on the dashboard. There he is, without the faintest way of proving anything. And obviously the police have found nothing either against Borck or the woman, otherwise they wouldn't have allowed the boat to leave. Why had he gone back to the cottage so early? He should have followed the two instead of rowing out to the boat. Perhaps he would have got a chance to talk to the woman alone. Might have slipped her a note with his address and telephone number, at least. Had he stayed in the harbour, he would have seen in which direction they left. Might have been able to track them to the next port on their route. But whatever – it's hopeless.

Jutta is fed up with waiting. 'Axel tackles this wrongly', she thinks. 'What he 'as found out so far should be sufficient. This material in the right hands – that should be enough to blow open the whole scheme. And they could turn it into money, too. Not with the *Schleswiger Morgenpost*, of course. Axel should leave there, anyway. Should go to one of the national papers. Considering his talents. She will take charge of this now. Good thing, that the cottage has a telephone. She rings the phone exchange.

'Would you, please, give me the number of *Stern* magazine, in Hamburg?'

'There are several extensions listed.'

'Editorial department, please!' Now there is no way back.

There is a knock on the door.

Naumann drives back via Porth Clais. The roads are narrow; he steers the car cautiously. There is the inlet. The tide is out. Naumann takes it all in in one glance. So late in the year, everything looks deserted. The little kiosk closed for the season. No tourists. And no U-boats. Only a single yacht lying aground in the mud, close to the shore. It is the *Aslan*.

Naumann can hardly believe it. There she is, right next to their cottage. The girl is sitting on deck in the sun. She has not yet noticed him. And not a trace of Borck. This is the chance he's been hoping for. That is his story of a lifetime. He takes his car into the car-park, pulls off his shoes and socks. He's no longer used to going barefoot, the gravel on the road pricks like nails into his soles. But then he is at the shore, wading through the mud. He doesn't sink in much. Just a thin layer of mud over solid ground.

Barbara Burowski doesn't turn round until he climbs on board. She stares at him. 'What do you want?', she says. 'Why have you come here, spying on us?' His muddy feet leave prints on the pristine deck.

'I'm sorry to intrude like this', Naumann says. 'I'm a journalist. Can we talk?' He gives her his card.

'You must be mad', she says. There is gin on her breath. She is afraid of something, he thinks. She holds his card between her fingers without actually looking at it. Then, after a moment of consideration, she tears it to pieces and throws it overboard.

'I know what happened', says Naumann. 'You and your husband – you worked this out together. Him jumping overboard, the *Aslan* picking him up. Everybody believes him to be dead, and you collect the insurance money. But Burowski is not dead. No way. He's alive. He's here on board... ' The very moment he says this, Naumann realises he's on very thin ice. He's by no means sure of his allegations. And even if he is right – the woman is taller than him and looks very fit. Should Burowski really be on board, he would be in trouble. If the two of them attacked him, he wouldn't stand a chance.

'Ridiculous', says the woman. 'My husband here on board? He's dead. Drowned.'

Naumann shakes his head.

'You don't believe me? Well, come on, I'll show you the boat!' She sounds very confident. She opens the cabin door. The cabin is empty. Where else could he be? There's not much space on a yacht, even if it is as big as this one. The blonde woman shows him everything, even the cupboards and the loo. The boat is empty. 'He's not on board. And never has been.'

'He went ashore with Borck', Naumann maintains. A mere guess. The woman shakes her head. 'He is dead', she says. 'And you – you claim to be press? Don't you ever read any papers yourself? Here – it's all in here!'

On the table lies that day's paper. And there it is: fishermen have picked up Burowski's body. No doubt about the identity.

'May I congratulate you to your inheritance, then?', Naumann says without thinking. It sounds as mean as it's meant.

Barbara Burowski stares at him. 'You swine!' she says, full of contempt. She sobs loudly. Then she starts crying, unchecked.

Naumann doesn't know what to do. 'I am sorry', he murmurs.

She doesn't react, keeps on crying. Like a child, Naumann thinks. Like a poor child, shocked to her bones. Like someone who knows there's no way out. He puts his hand on her shoulder. 'What are you afraid of?' he asks aloud. And then, on a sudden impulse: 'Afraid of Borck?'

'Afraid of everything,' she says. And: 'I wish I were dead, just like my husband.'

Naumann gently strokes her hair. With the other hand he searches for the start button of the little cassette recorder in his shoulder-bag. 'Just tell me what you're afraid of,' he says. And he thinks: The woman is right, I am a swine.

Now it all comes out. Borck, the glamorous hero. Borck, the lover. He had arranged everything. Yes, it had been agreed that Burowski should jump overboard, at a certain time, when Borck would be ready. Everything went as scheduled – only Borck didn't pick up the man. 'He had seen him', she says. 'He must have seen him, he had him directly in the beam of his searchlight, but he didn't pick him up. He would have got ten thousand for his part. But that wasn't enough. He wants everything. He wants all the money. He wants me!'

'You're an adult woman', Naumann says. 'It's your money, and it's your life, Barbara. You can do with it as you please.'

She shakes her head. 'You have no idea. You don't know Borck. Borck is dangerous. And he has evidence against me. Notes, letters. I wish my husband was dead!', that's what I once wrote. I'm afraid. I am so terribly afraid.'

'You should talk to the police,' Naumann says. Is the tape running? He can only hope that he pressed the right button. 'Where is Borck, anyway?'

That moment the boat shakes ever so slightly. Naumann doesn't need to turn around. He looks into Barbara's frightened face and he knows, Borck is back.

'Imagine, Barbara, that swine had really taken pictures of us!' Borck says. Dangling from his hand is Naumann's digital camera. Then Borck realises who else is on board, and his grin freezes.

'Help me, Barbara!' says Naumann. But Barbara doesn't help him.

When Naumann regains consciousness, he finds himself in the car-park, lying right next to his car.

'Are you all right?' An elderly lady bends over him; she has obviously roused him. Her companion stays at a distance, leaning on a walking stick, and he eyes him with distrust.

'Thanks', says Naumann. 'I must have tripped over something somehow. No, thanks a lot, but I'm quite all right.' He gets up with an effort. His head hurts like hell.

'Shall we get help?' the lady asks.

Naumann shakes his head. 'I've got my car,' he says. He glances at the harbour. It's high tide now, the inlet is deserted. Starting towards his car, he steps on his bag. It's empty, the tape recorder gone. Jutta! All of a sudden it occurs to him, that Borck must have been to the cottage. What has he done to Jutta? He grits his teeth, wedges himself behind the steering wheel. The car starts at once. Naumann races off, making the old couple jump out of the way.

The path to the cottage leads through two farms. Stop, open the gate, drive on a few yards, stop again, shut the gate and drive on. A dog barks ferociously. Sheep hurry out of the way as Naumann speeds towards them. Eventually he reaches the cottage.

Nothing seems to have happened to Jutta. She is sitting on the bench in front of the cottage, smoking. Naumann has never seen her smoke before. Her hands shake slightly. 'My God, what has happened to you?'

Naumann sits down next to her. 'Everything went wrong', he says.

'Well, that's obvious', Jutta says. 'Borck was here. He'd followed you last night, but he didn't dare do anything in the dark. So he has come back first thing this morning.'

'Did you call the police?'

Jutta nods. 'They're here already. Looking for fingerprints indoors.' She doesn't mention her attempt to call *Stern* magazine. Had Borck come a little later, they might have been witness to the assault. Pity it didn't work out that way.

Davies comes out of the cottage. The policeman raises his eyebrow as he sees Naumann's bruises. He takes an account of what happened. 'We'll get them', he says. 'A police boat's on the way.'

'What good will that do?' Naumann asks. 'Assumptions, speculations, but no witnesses, no proof. After all, the businessman wasn't killed. Borck just didn't save him, that's all. No-one can prove malicious intent.'

Davies seems very relaxed. 'That's what Herr Borck may think, but we have our ways. We'll reconstruct every step, every move the players in this game have made. Who – when – where – why? What exactly was the insurance policy? What kind of business trip had Burowski been on? Why of all people was his wife's lover on a boat near by, when Burowski went overboard? What did the *Aslan* do prior to, during and after the accident? We've got a lot of questions, Mr Naumann, and I assure you we will get some answers.'

'I'm afraid the guy is as hard as nails,' says Naumann.

'That's what many of them assume. I can tell you, most of them are wrong. And, by the way, the young woman, she'll crack, I'm sure she will.'

Naumann nods. But neither he nor Davies can know that by then Barbara is already dead. Borck has panicked and killed the only witness. Her body will never be found; the case against Borck will have to be based on circumstantial evidence alone.

# TOP DECK

## Kate Ellis

*Kate Ellis's contribution to the CWA anthology* Crime In The City, *'Les Inconnus', earned her a place on the shortlist for the CWA Dagger for the best short story of the year. The Dagger was won by Jerry Sykes, whose story also appeared in* Crime In The City, *but the recognition of Ellis's excellence as a crime writer caused me just as much delight. Her latest story is very different from 'Les Inconnus', but equally appealing. The theme of 'crime on the move' has sparked an idea centring upon a bus trip in Liverpool during the Merseybeat era, with a pleasing revelation in the very last paragraph.*

*November 1965*

At ten past six on a rainy Tuesday evening, Keith O'Dowd witnessed a murder.

Up until then it had been an ordinary Liverpool Tuesday, a day like every other. At half past five Keith had left the portals of the Liver Building and hurried across the Pier Head in the rain to catch his bus home. His boss, Mr Kelly was leaving at the same time, in the company of his secretary, Linda. Kelly had given Keith a distant nod of acknowledgement on the stairs before heading off in the direction of the car-park and his brand new Ford Cortina. Keith experienced a pang of envy. He could never afford a motor like that on the meagre wages he earned as a shipping clerk. But maybe one day things would be different. Maybe one day he would join the police force like his grandad and become a detective. Everyone has to dream. And, according to his mother, Keith dreamed more than most.

That evening it was pouring with rain and the number 80 bus was ten minutes late arriving at the terminus. When it finally turned up Keith clattered up the metal stairs to the top deck, his wet trouser legs flapping cold around his ankles, and made his way straight to the front seat, the seat with the best view on the bus. He sat down by the window and lit a cigarette, then he sat quite still for a few moments, inhaling deeply before wiping the misted up window with the sleeve of his coat. Looking out of the window was better than reading the paper. And you never knew what you might see.

The bus set off through the city centre, past stores closing up for the night. The glow from the bright shop windows reflected golden on the glistening pavements and umbrellas danced up and down the streets, their owners hidden beneath. Soon they were hurtling past the Philharmonic Hall and the Women's Hospital with its rows of brightly lit windows. Then past the faded Georgian elegance of Catherine Street where the houses of wealthy merchants and ship owners had long ago been claimed by the poor and the Bohemian, bedsit dwellers and students. Keith stared out of his lofty mobile watchtower, wiping the window from time to time to get a better view.

Keith took this bus every night, rain or shine, winter or summer, and there was nothing that Tuesday night to tell him that this journey was going to be different from any other. There had been no omens of death as in the horror films he loved so much. No howling wolves or circling ravens; no mysterious gypsies issuing cryptic warnings. It had been an normal day; a good day. He had been to NEMS in his lunch hour to buy The Beatles' latest LP, *Help*, for his girlfriend, Susan's birthday. He had bought some cigarettes too... and a packet of Durex from Boots just in case his luck changed when Susan saw the record. Keith patted the plastic record bag: Susan loved The Beatles so he felt rather pleased with his choice.

Once they were away from the bright, artificial lights of the city centre the scene outside grew darker... but then it was the beginning of November and the clocks had gone back. As they crawled down Princes Road Keith closed his eyes but he opened them again when the bus swung too fast round the bend at Princes Park gates, throwing him against the man who shared his seat. He restored his dignity by lighting a calming cigarette and the next time he looked out of the window he saw that they were passing the shadowy acres of Sefton Park heading down Ullet Road. His boss, Mr Kelly, lived on Ullet Road, so he'd heard from the office gossips. He owned flats there. Flats and a new Cortina. Mr Kelly was a lucky man.

When the bus stopped briefly in Ullet Road to let somebody off Keith found himself staring straight across into a lighted upstairs window. The curtains were wide open and two people were silhouetted behind the glass; a man and a woman who, for a split second, seemed faintly familiar. The man seemed to have both his hands raised up to the woman's throat and they were moving slowly to and fro as if the woman was trying to ward him off, trying to save her life. Just as one of the figures appeared to collapse to the floor, the bus suddenly pulled off and tore away from the bus stop at speed.

It had all been over in a matter of seconds and Keith sat there, dazed, wondering if he'd imagined the whole thing. He turned to the man sitting next to him, a thin, middle aged man in a shabby raincoat who smoked nervously. He was reading a newspaper, the *Liverpool Echo*, and appeared to be engrossed in the small ads. Keith contemplated asking him whether he'd seen the couple in the flat but he decided against it. The man would probably think he was mad.

He turned round and saw two girls sitting in the seat behind, one peroxide blonde and the other henna red, both with mini skirts that left little to the imagination. It would do no harm to ask... if he could phrase the question so that he didn't sound like a complete lunatic. 'Excuse me, love, did you see that murder back in Ullet Road?' might result in the men in white coats carting him away.

But from the way the two girls were chatting away, it was obvious that their minds were firmly fixed on gossip and there was no way they'd have seen anything out of the ordinary. And he guessed that, judging by the bored looks on the faces of his fellow passengers, nobody else had either. The blonde girl caught Keith's eye but she ignored him, pulling her mini skirt down to the middle of her thighs as she carried on pointedly chatting to her friend. But attractive girls were the last thing on Keith's mind at that moment. Some woman might be lying dead in the house they'd passed; a woman whose profile had triggered a bat squeak of recognition. But had he really seen her die?

As they stopped at the traffic lights in Smithdown Road, Keith felt a sudden urge to get off the bus, to hurry back to the spot where he'd seen the couple: he could remember the exact house and the exact window and for all he knew the woman might still be alive and in need of help. Perhaps he should tell the police. That would be what his mother would tell him to do. And Susan... she would always play things by the book. He stood up and the *Echo* reader beside him looked flustered as he juggled with lighted cigarette and open newspaper before swinging his legs out into the aisle to let Keith pass, thinking he was getting off at the next stop.

But Keith hesitated and sat down again, murmuring an apology. As the *Echo* reader mumbled, 'Make up your mind, pal,' and rearranged his newspaper, Keith sat on the edge of the seat, feeling foolish. Looking round the damp, smoky top deck he was quite sure that nobody else had seen what he had seen. He was the only witness. Or had he been watching too many Hitchcock films? Had his mind been playing tricks?

In all Keith's seventeen years, he had always possessed a streak of caution. He had never gone in for games of dare at school, never played on railway lines or played chicken with cars like some of his classmates. And in his heart of hearts he knew that there was no way he was going to investigate that flat in Ullet Road alone while there was a chance that a murderer might still be hanging about. But he still felt he should do something. Perhaps he should find a phone box when he got off the bus and call the police. Or venture into Allerton police station and report it.

He sat staring out of the window and by the time he passed Penny Lane he had managed to convince himself that he had probably imagined the whole thing. After all, if nobody else on the bus had seen it, it was likely that he was mistaken. Perhaps the couple had just been having a fight... or even dancing. If he went to the police, he might make a complete fool of himself. And besides, he wouldn't have time that night. He was taking Susan to the Odeon to see *Dr Zhivago*: she'd been on at him to take her to see it for ages but it didn't sound like Keith's cup of tea. He preferred something like *Psycho*; just the sort of film that would make Susan terrified enough to want to cling to him in the dark. As he thought of the evening ahead he told himself to forget about the upstairs window. He had imagined it. Or it had been a trick of the light.

As he predicted, Susan adored the film's exotic romance. And
when he had kissed her in the back row she had responded eagerly
and allowed his hands to explore parts of her body not previously
available to him. As he walked her home he wondered whether to
mention what he'd thought he'd seen from the top deck of the bus but
he decided against it: she would only have told him that he was imagining things and that he'd seen something quite innocent; a man
taking a speck of dirt out of a woman's eye; or a couple kissing. And
she would probably have been right. Instead Keith concentrated on a
long and passionate goodnight, one that might have held a promise of
something more if Susan's father hadn't been watching from the front
bedroom window.

But that night it wasn't Susan who featured in his dreams. Instead
he dreamed about murder. Dreamed that he was on the top deck of
the 80 bus, outside the house in Ullet Road watching a shadowy
figure stabbing a woman in a shower. Blood was spurting from the
open flat window and landing in rivulets on the windows of the bus
and Keith was wiping it away with his sleeve. He shouted but no
sound came from his mouth. Then the man in the raincoat next to him
on the bus suddenly turned, with mad staring eyes, and began to drive
a knife into his defenceless body.

Keith felt exhausted when his mother woke him up the next morning
but he hauled himself out of bed and dressed by the paraffin heater in
his bedroom. His mother nagged him to have a proper breakfast, just
as she did every morning, but Keith had no time. He grabbed a slice of
toast and took a sip of tea before hurrying out into the chilly, bright
morning, making it to the bus stop just in time.

He hopped on to the pea green bus with the Corporation coat of
arms painted on its side and made his way up the stairs, clinging to the
handrail. The fog of morning cigarette smoke hit him as he reached
the top deck and he was glad to see that his favourite seat was still free
– the seat at the front with the panoramic view. He settled himself
down and lit his first cigarette of the day, then he sat back, enjoying
the fresh rush of nicotine and trying not to think of the dull routine of
the day ahead.

As the bus chugged down Ullet Road he felt a thrill of anticipation. He had made sure he was sitting on the right hand side of the bus so that he would have the best view of the upstairs window as the bus drove past. But he wasn't sure what he expected to see. A body lying on a brightly illuminated bed, perhaps? Or a screaming woman clawing at the window? Or, more likely, nothing at all.

The bus shuddered to a halt opposite what he'd started to think of as the murder house and the diesel engine throbbed while the queue of passengers climbed on. He focussed on the window – the bay window on the first floor – but the thin cotton curtains were drawn, hiding the scene within. Keith studied the house: it was a large Victorian building: a corner house, probably divided into flats like most of its neighbours, standing at the end of a row of similar houses next to a side road. Red brick and vaguely Gothic in style, it was a house to grace any horror film. Just the sort of place to harbour a killer – or his victim. As the bus set off, Keith noticed a car parked close to the corner – a shiny blue Cortina, probably brand new. It looked exactly like his boss, Mr Kelly's car but Keith told himself that it couldn't be: Mr Kelly always arrived at work early so he would be on his way by now. There must be a lot of brand new Cortinas around: a lot of lucky bastards who didn't have to queue at the bus stop every morning.

For the remainder of the journey Keith stared out of the window, watching the city awake from its slumber under the blue autumn sky. The bus pulled in to its allotted spot at the Pier Head bus station and cut its noisy engine. Then Keith walked the short distance to the Liver Building, accompanied by a fanfare of screaming sea gulls. Another day, another dollar, as he had once heard someone say.

When he reached the office he sensed a strange undercurrent of excitement. The clerks kept their heads down but the secretaries talked in whispers, as if they were sharing forbidden secrets… secrets too juicy for general consumption. Keith sorted through the papers on his desk, watching and listening. Something was going on in that smoky shipping office. And he wanted to know what it was.

He realised that he hadn't seen Mr Kelly that morning, which was unusual: he was normally there in his glass-fronted office keeping an eye on things. Not that Kelly had much to say to the young clerks. He was old, at least thirty-five, tall with glossy black hair and a snub nose. But the girls in the office seemed to like him.

It was lunchtime before the clerks had a chance to get together. As Keith took a ham sandwich out of the lunch box his mother had packed for him first thing that morning, Mike Fry hurried over. Mike had joined the firm around the same time as Keith and he had a shock of red hair and a face that couldn't keep a secret. He perched on the corner of Keith's desk and looked around before leaning forward.

'So what do you think?' Mike begun in a whisper.

'Think of what?'

'Mr Kelly and Linda.'

Mr Kelly's secretary, Linda, was a tall, dark haired young woman, beautiful in an unconventional kind of way. Striking, Keith's mother would have called her. None of the young clerks knew Linda well. She was way above them… as distant as a goddess.

'What about them?' Keith asked innocently.

'They've not come into work. Someone rang Kelly's house and there was no answer.'

'What about Linda?'

'She's not on the phone.'

'Perhaps she's ill then… and she couldn't get to a phone box.'

Mike grinned knowingly. 'Perhaps. Funny though, them both being off at the same time. Maybe they've gone on a dirty weekend together.'

'It's Wednesday.'

But this inconvenient fact didn't deter Mike. Soon others had gathered around the desk and in due course the verdict was that Kelly and Linda were holed up in a hotel in Blackpool living off the fruits of passion. A small, fair haired typist, wise beyond her tender years, announced solemnly that they'd fancied each other for at least a year; certainly since the death of Mr Kelly's wife… or maybe even before. There's nothing like office gossip for exercising the imagination.

'Perhaps the big bosses know where Mr Kelly is,' suggested Keith. 'Perhaps they just haven't told us minions.'

Mike leaned forward. 'I saw Mr Davies before and I asked him if Mr Kelly would be in... trying to sound all innocent, like... but he didn't say anything. I reckon Kelly's gone AWOL. And so has Linda,' he added with a wink.

'Kelly lives somewhere in Ullet Road, doesn't he? Near Sefton Park?' Keith said innocently.

'That's right,' Mike piped up. 'I heard he owns some flats down there.'

'I heard that too,' said Keith. This was old news.

'Someone said they belonged to his late wife. She inherited them from an aunt or something.'

'What did his wife die of?' Keith asked. But nobody knew the answer.

The conversation ground to a halt. They'd covered the sum total of their knowledge about their boss's private life. Mike had done well to glean the information about the late wife's inheritance. He'd make a good detective, Keith thought with a slight pang of envy.

'I'm sure I saw his car parked off Ullet Road this morning,' said Keith.

But the clerks had lost interest and had turned their attention to their sandwiches and the subject of Saturday's football match.

That afternoon Keith found it difficult to concentrate on his work and he kept looking at his watch, longing for five-thirty. Longing for his homeward journey on the 80 bus. He kept thinking of Kelly and Linda. Why hadn't they turned up at work? He had to check out the house. And he was impatient to get it over with.

He would be late home, of course, and his mother would be annoyed because his tea would be spoiled. But she had refused to contemplate having a telephone put in so it couldn't be helped. He wanted to discover the truth. And the more he thought about it, the more he was convinced that the woman he saw being murdered might have been Linda. But had the man been Kelly? It had all happened too quickly to see.

The bus went out on time that night. Keith was first on and he hurried up the stairs to the top deck and headed for the seat at the front. He lit a cigarette. He needed one. He was afraid... afraid of what he might find. He sat there in the fog of smoke and crushed homeward-bound bodies, chain smoking and fidgeting with the clasp on the cheap leather briefcase his mother had bought him last Christmas. Somehow the journey seemed longer that evening. Like the journey to a place of execution.

When they reached the top of Ullet Road, Keith stood up and stubbed out his cigarette on the dirty grey floor. Grabbing the handrails, he made his way down the bus which rocked and lurched so much that he almost took a tumble down the stairs. The conductor stood on the platform, watching him with a smirk on his face. Keith jumped down on to the pavement outside the big red brick house as the smirking conductor rang the bell and the pea green bus pulled away in a cloud of diesel fumes. From now on he was on his own. There was no going back.

He stood at the bus stop for a few minutes looking up at the house. The curtains were still drawn across the upstairs bay window but the light was on, a single bulb shining through the thin cotton. And he could see a shadow moving behind the flimsy material. Somebody was at home.

Keith knew he had to check if the Cortina was still there. He had been so certain that it was Mr Kelly's car, but now he was there on the spot he began to have his doubts. What if he was leaping to conclusions? Adding two and two and making five? The road was a long one – Kelly might live anywhere. And he and Linda might both have come down with some illness or other and been unable to let the office know. He walked to the corner and looked down the side road. But there was no sign of the Cortina he had seen that morning.

Keith was beginning to feel rather stupid. His mother would tell him that he had been watching far too many Hitchcock films and maybe she was right. What did he have to go on? He knew Mr Kelly lived in that particular road and owned flats in the area. And he had seen what he believed to be his car parked next to the house where he had seen a man murdering a woman, who may or may not have born some vague, passing resemblance to Linda. And Kelly and Linda had not turned up for work that day, apparently without explanation. He had put all these facts together and come up with a scenario straight from the movies. Kelly had been having an affair with Linda and he had murdered her – for reasons unknown – in full view of the top deck of the number 80 bus before going to ground, a fugitive from justice.

It had all seemed so plausible sitting in the smoky warmth of the top deck but now, here in the cold November air, it began to seem rather far fetched and ridiculous. He made his way slowly back to the bus stop. Perhaps he should just wait for the next eighty and go home.

And yet he had seen the couple struggling... the man possibly strangling the woman. It had just been a glimpse, over too quickly and too far away for any sort of identification. But he had seen it – he was certain of that. And now the light was on in that very room. There was somebody up there.

He took a deep breath. He had come this far so he might as well check, just to satisfy his own curiosity. He would concoct a story. He would be looking for a friend called John who lived next door and he would apologise profusely when he was told he had the wrong house. He loved detective stories and he felt rather pleased with himself for thinking up this ingenious ploy.

He pushed open the wooden gate and walked slowly up the path to the front door. The house was divided into flats like so many of its neighbours and there was a row of doorbells at the side of the flaking front door. Beside the row of bells a fat spider was sitting in the centre of a large web. Keith peered at the labels, trying to make out names in the dim glow of the streetlight. There was one in the middle that stood out, however. A neatly typed label gave the name of the occupier of flat number three as Kelly. Keith's heart began to beat faster. Had his instincts been right all along? But then he told himself that there must be hundreds of Kellys in Liverpool, a city where at least half the population had Irish ancestry. The spider shifted slightly as he stared at the bell, pondering his next move.

He turned to go. It had been a stupid idea. But as he turned he came face to face with a young man, roughly the same age as himself, maybe a year or two older. The young man's hair was long, Beatles style, and he wore a donkey jacket and a Liverpool University scarf. 'How do?' he said with a grin. His accent was Yorkshire and he had an open, freckled face. 'Who are you looking for?'

The young man was obviously a student, and he hardly looked like a murderer. 'Er, I heard there was flat going. Is it this one? Kelly?' He pointed at the bell.

'No that's the landlord. Look, I don't think any of the flats are empty… unless the landlord's decided to move up in the world. He works in town and he inherited this place from his first wife so he can't be badly off. And he's just bought a brand new car so he must be in the money,' he added bluntly, extending his hand. He seemed the chatty type, which suited Keith fine. 'Jim Watts… doing medicine,' he said, looking Keith up and down, noting his jacket and tie. 'Are you a student then?'

'Er, no. I work in town. Thought it was time I got a place of my own… you know how it is.' He took Jim's hand and shook it. 'John McCartney,' he said without quite knowing why he felt so reluctant to use his real name.

His heart was beating fast: he'd been right all along. Kelly did live there. And now he had disappeared… so had Linda. And Keith had seen him kill her.

'Just ring that bell there.' Jim pointed to a bell marked 'Kelly'. 'The light's on so one of them should be in.'

'One of them?' Keith was aware that his voice was quivering with nerves. He had come too far to back out now.

'Either Mr or Mrs Kelly. Landlord or his wife. They've got the big flat on the first floor.'

'I thought you said his wife was dead.'

'That was his first wife.' Jim winked. 'He's remarried. Much younger than him. Linda her name is. Lovely legs.'

Before Keith could stop him, Jim had pressed Kelly's bell, trying to be helpful. 'I'll leave you to it, then,' said the student. 'One of 'em should be down in a minute. Good luck.'

With that he closed the front door and Keith was left standing on the doorstep, stunned. Kelly was married to Linda – or at least that's what he told his tenants. He was living with her in a flat on the first floor, a flat he owned. And she was calling herself Mrs Kelly. The situation would have provided hours of office gossip… if he hadn't murdered her. And he was upstairs now, probably getting rid of the evidence. Or disposing of the body. It was really time to go to the police. He had played detective but he felt he couldn't go it alone any more.

He turned to go. The next 80 bus should be due shortly. He'd report his discoveries at Allerton police station... on home ground. Perhaps this display of initiative would count in his favour if he ever applied to join the police force.

Keith had just reached the gate when the front door opened. He swung round and stared at the figure framed in the doorway.

'Hello, Keith. What are you doing here?'

Keith opened and closed his mouth, lost for words. This was the last thing he had expected.

'Seeing you're here, why not come in for a cup of tea. I'd no idea that you knew where I lived.'

As he walked back up the path, Linda smiled and smoothed her mini skirt down over her shapely legs. And a fly landed in the web of the fat spider by the doorbells.

*April 2003*

'I hate these bloody cold cases.' Detective Sergeant Bob Jones took a packet of cigarettes from his jacket pocket but, seeing the disapproving looks of all those around him, put it back again. It was time he gave up anyway.

'So how long does the pathologist reckon it's been under the floorboards then?' DC Burns asked, looking at the photographs of the crime scene and wrinkling his nose in disgust.

'Donkey's years. I'm surprised nobody noticed the smell. We found a receipt from a record shop by the body dated 1965. It could have fallen out of the murderer's pocket – then again it might not. Everything's been sent to Forensics anyway: there might be fingerprints, even after all these years. The clothes are quite well preserved... considering.' Jones smiled. 'Didn't half give those builders a turn when they found it.'

Jones flicked through the papers on his desk. 'In 1965 the place was owned by a Kevin Kelly, a widower who inherited various properties from his late wife who, in turn, had been left them by an aunt.

There was a bit of a question mark over the wife's death apparently but nothing was ever proved. Kelly was found dead in 1965. His brand new Ford Cortina had been driven into the Mersey with him inside it... when I say driven I mean the handbrake was left off and it was given a shove. But he was already dead when it hit the water – stabbed in the heart. And there were a number of defensive wounds: he'd put up a fight. Don't expect his killer thought he'd be found until time and tide had destroyed the evidence. Matter of luck, really.'

'So was anyone charged with Kelly's murder?' Burns asked, leaning back in his chair.

'Kelly had a mistress who lived with him in the flat where our new body was found – Linda Parker: she was his secretary but their relationship wasn't common knowledge at work. He'd recently altered his will so that she got everything and she disappeared around the time Kelly's body was discovered. It was thought at the time that she'd killed him during a domestic and did a runner – disappeared into thin air – so they never really bothered looking for anyone else.' Burns looked at the sergeant and raised his eyebrows. 'But this new development changes things a bit, doesn't it. The case'll have to be reopened.'

'Who else was living in those flats back in 1965?'

Jones looked pleased with himself. 'I managed to track down a Doctor Jim Watts; he trained at Liverpool University and he had a flat on the ground floor. He's now a GP up in North Yorkshire. Nice bloke. Very helpful. He was interviewed by the police at the time Kelly was found dead – and Linda Parker went missing. I've dug out his original statement and in it he says that a young man, aged around eighteen, called at the house the evening before Kelly's body was found and asked about vacant flats... which Doctor Watts thought was strange because they were all occupied at the time. Watts told him to ring the landlord's bell and he heard the door being answered and the boy going up to Kelly's flat. The statement mentions the name the boy gave – John McCartney. Watts had remembered it because of The Beatles – John Lennon and Paul McCartney. They were never able to trace this John McCartney at the time; not that they made much effort because Kelly's murder seemed to be an open and shut case.'

DC Burns picked up the photographs of the body found under the floorboards of the first floor flat in Ullet Road. The builders had been gutting the place in preparation for its metamorphosis into luxury apartments when they had made their grim discovery. The body had been found next to the hot water pipe and the dry heat had caused partial mummification of the remains. It was still recognisable as a human being. 'John McCartney, eh. Think he could have killed her?'

'Who knows after all this time? But it was strange that she was found with a knife clutched in her hand and the post mortem found no sign of stab wounds on the body or the clothes. The pathologist reckoned she died of an injury to the back of her skull that fitted exactly with her falling against the marble hearth in that room – it's got an unusual moulded edge.'

'So she could have gone for someone with the knife and they pushed her away so she fell backwards? And then they panicked and pulled up a few loose floorboards and hid her underneath. Case solved, sarge?'

Jones smiled. He doubted if it would be that easy. 'I'd better let the Chief Inspector see the papers… see how he wants to proceed. If he can be bothered – it's his retirement do next week.'

As his car was in for service, Keith O'Dowd perched on the front seat on the bottom deck of the 80 bus and looked out of the window at the passing urban scenery, so much smarter now than all those years ago: café bars and gentrification had taken their toll of the city. The bus still ran down Ullet Road… just as it had all those years ago. But now it had lost its pea green livery; times had changed. And these days Keith avoided this route when he drove into town. The sight of that house made him feel uncomfortable.

As the bus turned into Ullet Road Keith gave an involuntary shudder and felt a sudden longing for a cigarette. But he'd given them up years ago. Susan, his wife, wouldn't allow them in the house and the office was a no smoking zone so it was no use swimming against the tide.

Kelly's old house was a mess with skips and builder's rubble everywhere. And police crime scene tape had been festooned around the place like a Christmas garland. The time he had been dreading since 1965 had finally arrived: she had been found. And with modern forensic technology – he was sure he must have left some trace some-where – it would only be a matter of time before the truth came out.

But it had been self-defence. When Linda had come at him with the knife and he had pushed her away, he hadn't intended to kill her. They already thought that she had got rid of Kelly after he had altered his will in her favour and his statement would just confirm it... surely. He was bound to be believed.

He stared out of the window at the blur of shops and streetlights. When his involvement was discovered it would be an ignominious end to a successful career but he couldn't avoid the truth. He only hoped that Susan would understand and that all the questions could wait until after his retirement party.

When Detective Chief Inspector Keith O'Dowd reached the bus stop near his home, he climbed down stiffly from the platform, hold-ing firmly on to the rail. Then he stood and watched as the bus disap-peared down the road in a cloud of diesel fumes.

# A CASE FOR GOURMETS

## Michael Gilbert

*My introduction to the Crime Writers' Association came when, in my teens, I was given a predecessor volume of this anthology as a Christmas present. It contained this story by Michael Gilbert, a founder member of the CWA and a crime writer of great distinction. History will surely judge him as one of the finest British crime writers of the second half of the 20th century, equally adept with the novel and the short story. This classic tale of mystery underground, sometimes known as 'Mr Duckworth's Night Out', seemed ideal for inclusion in this anthology and I am very glad that Michael Gilbert agreed so readily to my request that it be reprinted for the benefit of a new generation of readers.*

The curious and involved transaction which is recorded in the annals of Gabriel Street under the title of 'Herring Jam' may be traced to its beginning in the Court of Mr Whitcomb, the South Borough Stipendiary Magistrate.

Detective-Inspector Patrick Petrella, who was there on duty, was reminded of a remark once made to him by Sergeant Drage of the British Railways Police to the effect that the travelling public were divisible into three classes. One, people who travelled without tickets; two, people who stole goods in transit; and three, people who defaced posters.

In the dock when he arrived Petrella found an apple-cheeked old lady accused of travelling from Wimbledon to Charing Cross with a threepenny ticket. Her defence, which she was conducting herself, was that she had asked for a ticket to the Kennington Oval, but the booking clerk had misheard her.

'But surely, madam,' said Mr Whitcomb with the courtesy for which he was renowned, 'it costs more than threepence to travel from Wimbledon to the Oval.'

Certainly, agreed the old lady, but since the booking clerk was clearly stone-deaf, what was more likely than that when *she* had said the Kennington Oval, *he* had thought she said Collier's Wood.

'But did it not occur to you that the fare to the Oval must be more than threepence?'

The old lady rode this one off. She said that she always paid exactly what booking clerks asked for. In her experience, sometimes they asked for more, sometimes less. She never argued with them.

'And why,' said Mr Whitcomb, who believed in leaving no avenue unexplored, 'if you had been given a ticket to Collier's Wood, in mistake for a ticket to the Oval, did you ultimately alight at Charing Cross?'

The old lady said she had mistaken it for Trafalgar Square. It took some time to get this one sorted out (absolute discharge – coupled with a severe warning) and then Ronald Duckworth was called forward. Mr Duckworth was charged with an act of wilful damage, committed on the premises of the London Passenger Transport Board, in that he, on the previous Tuesday, had attempted to tear down a poster at Borough High Street Underground Station, the property of Barleymow Breakfast Bricks Ltd, the said poster advertising their wares.

Mr Duckworth pleaded guilty, and an LPTB Inspector stated that at about five minutes past eleven on the evening before last, one of the porters at Borough High Street Station, a Mr Sampson, returning to the platform, had observed the accused, who had apparently thought he was alone, seize a loose corner of the advertisement in question and tear it sharply in an upward direction.

'Are you perhaps not fond of Barleymow's Breakfast Bricks?' inquired Mr Whitcomb with every evidence of sympathy.

Mr Duckworth said no. It wasn't that – it was just an impulse.

Mr Whitcomb said that such impulses, though understandable (he much preferred porridge himself) ought to be resisted. He ordered Mr Duckworth to pay the costs of the prosecution and bound him over conditionally on his undertaking to leave all posters, however offensive the products they advertised, alone for the next twelve months.

Mr Duckworth departed thankfully. The next case was Petrella's, and it was not one which he viewed with any enthusiasm at all.

The charge, against Albert Mundy, was one of receiving goods well knowing them to be stolen goods. The facts were simple enough. Mr Mundy. an electrician working in the Wandsborough Power Station, had purchased a television set from a man he had met in the Saloon Bar of a public house.

They had had a few drinks and the man had told Mundy a long story of a mix-up which had resulted in the man being in possession of two television sets. 'It's a brand-new set,' he said. 'I've got it outside in the car now. I'd be glad to get rid of it for half what I paid for it.'

Mr Mundy was not only an electrician. He knew quite a lot about television sets. It was, as he saw when he went out to inspect it, a brand-new one. The maker's and wholesaler's labels were still on it.

Even if (as Mr Mundy half suspected) it contained some hidden defect, he was confident that he could put it right, and it was still a staggering bargain. He hurried home, produced the money from a reserve which he kept under a loose floorboard, and clinched the deal. The set proved to be in perfect condition. It also, unfortunately, turned out to have been one of a consignment of twelve stolen in transit between Manchester and Tooley Street Goods Depot – probably at the depot itself.

There was a good deal to be said on both sides: on the side of Mr Mundy, that he was an honest citizen with a hitherto unblemished record, and that he had no positive proof that the set was a stolen one; on the side of the authorities, that Mr Mundy had himself admitted that he thought the deal a fishy one, and that people who buy television sets for half the list price from strangers in public houses must take the consequences of their actions.

There was also a third powerful, but unexpressed, argument – that several million pounds' worth of goods was being lost every year by pilfering in transport, a loss which fell on the Transport services, their insurers, and, ultimately, on the public.

It was a very close thing, and the sweat stood in beads on Mr Mundy's forehead before the Magistrate finally decided to give weight to his previously blameless record and dismiss the case.

Petrella thought that substantial justice had been done. Mr Mundy had been given a bad fright. To imprison him would have been bad

luck on Mr Mundy's family and would not have hurt the real criminals – those who stole and organised a stealing. For the losses were
now so large and so regular that they had a look of organisation
about them.

'We do what we can,' said Sergeant Drage. 'We can't watch the
men at work. To do that properly you'd need one railway policeman
for each worker. Anyway, most of them are honest enough. The few
who aren't do a disproportionate amount of damage. It's worse
towards Christmas – more stuff about and a lot of casual labour taken
on for the holiday season.'

'If you can't watch them, how do you hope to stop them?'

'Keep your eyes and ears open. Make the place as difficult as we
can to get in and out, and organise snap searches when they come off
duty.'

'I see,' said Petrella. 'The old ring-fence system. You can't stop
them taking it, but you can make it difficult for them to get away with
it.'

Superintendent Benjamin held monthly conferences at Causeway,
which the Detective-Inspectors in charge of stations attended. Petrella
from Gabriel Street, Groves from the Common, and Merriam from
Tooley Street. In October, and again in November, the first item on his
agenda, displacing even such established favourites as shoplifting and
juvenile delinquency, was thefts from the railways.

'The Insurance Companies are starting to kick,' said Benjamin.
'They're bullying the Commissioner, the Commissioner's given a
rocket to District, and the tail-end of the stick's landed on me.'

'Isn't it really a job for the Railway Police?' said Merriam.

'Surely,' said Benjamin. 'But once stuff's been stolen, it's our job
too. If they can't stop them lifting it, we must stop them disposing of
it. At least, that's the idea. We've got three big goods yards plumb in
our area: Tooley Street, Red Cross, and Bricklayers Arms. What I
suggest is—'

He went on to lay down certain principles for patrolling outside
these depots. They were sound enough, in their way, but his subordi-
nates knew as well as Benjamin did that it was like trying to watch an
acre of rabbit warren with one man and one dog.

It was in the second week in November that Mr Duckworth reappeared in Mr Whitcomb's Court. The charge this time had rather more serious elements in it.

It appeared that the staff of Southwark Underground Station had been on the point of closing down for the night. The last passenger train had gone through, and the last passenger, as they imagined, had been shepherded out into the street. Happening to come down to the platform for a final look-round, the porter had heard a suspicious noise from inside the closet where cleaning materials and other odds and ends were stored.

Being a man of discretion, he had fetched the station-master and the ticket collector before investigating, and the three of them had then returned to the platform. The closet door was open, and the accused, who must have been hiding in the cubicle, was engaged in tearing down a number of posters affixed only that morning to the wall of the station.

Mr Duckworth, who looked even more embarrassed than on the previous occasion, again pleaded guilty and said that he had again acted on impulse.

'As I said on the previous occasion,' observed Mr Whitcomb, 'it is understandable that a man might have a sudden, and perhaps overmastering, impulse to tear down a poster. But to secrete yourself in a cupboard, after the station had been closed for the night, and then come out and start systematically to pull down posters hardly seems to me to be conduct which could be properly described as impulsive.'

Mr Duckworth looked unhappy, and said that he was very sorry. Mr Whitcomb, a copy of the record of the earlier case in front of him, pondered for a few minutes, and then announced that he was far from happy about the matter. He wished further inquiries to be made (the Court Missioner sighed audibly) and he would put back Mr Duckworth's case for one week. He understood that the accused was a respectable family man. He could have bail on his own recognisances, for seven days.

Petrella, who was in Court in connection with another matter, caught the Missioner at the door and said, 'When you've finished with him, let me have a go at him.'

'Have him first if you like,' said the Missioner. 'He's daft as a coot. His mother was probably frightened by a railway poster when she was a girl.'

'I'm not sure,' said Petrella. He had, by now, a fairly extensive knowledge of the cranks, crackpots, and fanatics who took up so much police time and afforded such entertaining copy for the court reporters of the leading evening newspapers; but he was far from convinced that Mr Duckworth was a crank or crackpot.

So he took Duckworth out and bought him a cup of tea, and listened with infinite patience to the story of his life. Mr Duckworth was an interior decorator, and an amateur soldier of the late War, during which he served with credit in an Artillery Regiment, rising to the rank of Sergeant. He had a wife and three children (whose photographs Petrella inspected). He was a supporter of Charlton Athletic, and a keen darts player. And, he added, there was nothing at all wrong with his eyes.

Petrella felt that they might now be approaching the heart of the mystery. He ordered second cups of tea for both of them.

'Nothing wrong with my eyes at all,' repeated Mr Duckworth.

'Who suggested there was?' said Petrella.

'No one actually suggested it,' said Mr Duckworth crossly. 'It was just that – look here, if I tell you this story from the beginning, will you promise not to laugh at me?'

'I never laugh on duty,' said Petrella.

'No, I mean that. It's – it's quite mad. It's – it's sort of fourth dimensional. You know what I mean?'

'Science fiction?' suggested Petrella helpfully.

'That's right – that's just what I mean! You walk out of one life into another. That's why I'd rather people thought I was a crook than they thought I was cracked, if you follow me.'

'Lots of people think like that,' said Petrella. 'Just tell me about it.'

It was, in its elements, quite a simple story. Mr Duckworth had been attending a reunion at the Regimental Headquarters in North London, a function he attended annually and which was, as he put it, 'the one time in the year he really let his hair down.'

Being an old soldier, before plunging into the fray, he had carefully secured his line of retreat. The nearest station to the headquarters in question was Highgate Archway, on the Northern Line. His home station was Collier's Wood, on the same line. The last train left Highgate at ten minutes before midnight.

With these essential facts firmly engraved in his memory, Mr Duckworth had settled down to enjoy himself in congenial company, had drunk quite a few pints of beer and a couple (but, he thought, not more than a couple) of whiskies, and had caught his train at Highgate with two minutes to spare. As soon as the train started, he had gone to sleep.

An indeterminate number of minutes later he had wakened with a start and with the strong conviction that he had reached his own station and was about to be carried past it. The train, sure enough, was stationary, and the doors were open. There was not a moment to lose. Fortunately, he was sitting in a seat near to, and facing, the doors, and just as they closed he hurled himself between them.

The doors shut behind him, the train jerked into motion, and disappeared. A solitary porter, in the far distance, also disappeared, leaving Mr Duckworth still dazed from the combined effects of sleep and drink, alone on the platform.

His overmastering desire was to sit down somewhere for a few minutes and recuperate. Behind him, at the far end of the platform, was a recess which had possibly once contained a seat. It seemed to Mr Duckworth to be exactly what he wanted. He got his back comfortably against one end, his feet against the other, and settled down to a period of reflection. When he opened his eyes he was in darkness – a sort of dim-blue darkness, broken by one very bright light.

His head, he said, was comparatively clear. He had discovered earlier that no matter how much beer he drank, give him half an hour's sleep, and he'd be more or less all right.

Petrella interrupted to say, 'How long do you think you had been asleep?'

'Difficult to say,' said Mr Duckworth, but not, he thought, more than half an hour. He had then staggered to his feet and had seen that the bright light was a small floodlight at platform level. It was so placed that it lit up the platform side of the station which (he was clear-headed enough to note) was not one of the modern type, all gleaming tiles and cement, but quite an old-fashioned one with upright wooden billboards.

The light, as he observed when he reached it, was shining directly on to one of these billboards – almost as if it had been placed there purposely to illuminate it. The effect was emphasised by the fact that the billboards on both sides were blank.

'I take it,' said Petrella, 'you'd realised by this time you weren't at Collier's Wood?'

'Oh, yes. I realised I'd jumped off the train too soon and should have a long walk home. I wasn't worried about being locked up in the station. If there were lights on, there must be people still working. The next bit is something I can't remember very clearly at all. I thought I heard a noise behind me, a sort of scraping noise – and then the ceiling fell on me. Or that's what it felt like. Something hard and heavy landed on top of my head, and before I had time to feel anything else, I was falling forward and – well, the next thing I knew, I was opening my eyes. It was five o'clock of a perishing grey morning, and I was on a seat, just off the road, in the middle of South Borough Common.'

He waited, defiantly, for comment.

Petrella said, 'You might have dreamed it all, of course. Someone might have given you a lift back from the reunion and tried to find out where you lived. You were too pickled to give him your address, so he propped you up on the seat to cool off. Not very friendly, but it could have happened.'

'All right,' said Mr Duckworth. 'Then how do you account for the fact that I'd still had my ticket with me? I found it in my waistcoat pocket.'

'Then,' agreed Petrella, 'it might have happened just as you said. You butted in on something you weren't meant to see, got slugged and dumped.'

'I thought that out for myself,' said Mr Duckworth. 'Only not quite as quickly, because I had a nasty lump on the back of my head – that wasn't imaginary. It was sore as hell – and the father and mother of a hangover – and I had my wife to deal with. She'd got into a real state and gone to the police, and then when I turned up—'

'I can imagine that bit,' said Petrella.

'Yes, well, I thought about it, and I had the same idea as you. I thought I'd start by finding what station it really was.'

'That shouldn't have been too difficult,' said Petrella. 'Most of the stations on that bit of line have been modernised, and besides, you saw at least one of the advertisements – the one the light was shining on.'

'That's just it,' said Mr Duckworth.

'*Didn't* you see it?'

'Yes, I did. And I wish I hadn't. It's been getting me down. Here's where you've promised not to laugh. What I saw – and I saw it quite clearly – and if I shut my eyes I can see it now – what I saw was three lines of writing, with one word on each line. It said *GET HERRING JAM.*'

Petrella stared at him.

'Now be honest,' said Mr Duckworth. 'Isn't that where you start thinking I've got a screw loose? If you do, you're not the only one. I began to think it myself.'

Petrella said, 'You say you can visualise it? What sort of print was it, and how were the three lines arranged?'

'Ordinary capital letters. On the large side, but not enormous. The *GET* was on the top and a bit to the left. The middle line was *HERRING* – *that* ran right across. The JAM was the bottom line and a bit to the right.'

'I see,' said Petrella. 'I suppose there isn't some other advertisement rather like—'

'I've been up and down every perishing station between Waterloo and Balham twenty times and there's nothing like it at all – nothing remotely like it! Most of 'em are pictures of girls. There's some in writing, like notices telling you to buy Premium Bonds and drink somebody or other's stout.'

'But no herrings?'

'Not a fish among 'em. That's how I got the idea that it might have been an advertisement that had been covered up with another one. They change 'em about once a week. So—'

Light dawned on Petrella.

'So you started pulling off the new ones to see what the old ones said underneath.'

'It'd sort of got me by that time,' said Mr Duckworth. 'I can't explain it. But what I felt was, if I can find that advert, then perhaps I can find out what happened to me that night. If I can't – well, maybe I'm mad. I expect you think I'm mad anyway.'

'No,' said Petrella slowly. 'I don't think you're mad at all.'

He said the same thing to Mr Wetherall that evening. Mr Wetherall was headmaster of the South Borough Secondary School, and when Petrella had fallen out with two landladies in succession (in both cases over the peculiar house he kept and his excessive use of the telephone) Wetherall had suggested to Petrella that he set up house in the two empty rooms below his own in the big house in Brinkman Road. It was a bit far from Gabriel Street, but otherwise it suited Petrella perfectly. It had been great fun furnishing the rooms, and he enjoyed an occasional after-dinner gossip with Mr Wetherall.

'I don't think I'd have started trespassing and pulling down advertisements,' said Mr Wetherall. 'I'd have gone to one of the big agents who does advertising on the Underground, and asked him to find out what advertisements were showing that week.'

'You might have,' said Petrella, 'and so might I, and the agent might have told us. But not someone like Mr Duckworth.'

'Have you located the station?'

'I've had a shot at it. the trouble is that going from Highgate to Collier's Wood, Mr Duckworth could have gone one of two ways – via Charing Cross – that's the West End route – or via Bank. All the stations on the West End route are modern tile and chromium jobs. But one or two of the stations on the Bank route would fit. London Bridge, Southwark, and Borough High Street are all possibles.'

'Since you've done some work on it, I take it you don't think he made the whole thing up?'

'No, I don't,' said Petrella. 'But I couldn't explain why.' Mr Wetherall puffed his horrible pipe for a few seconds and then said: 'No, you can't, can you? I mean, you can't tell how you know when people are telling the truth, but it's a fact that you can. I've found that often with boys.' He reflected again and said, 'I think you'd better have a word with my friend, Raynor-Hasset. He'll tell you all you want to know about the London railway system. He used to be a schoolmaster, but he's retired now. He lives in one of those little houses up on the Heath. I'll give him a ring and let him know you're coming.'

Petrella knew that Mr Wetherall seldom made recommendations idly. So the following evening he called on Mr Raynor-Hasset. Mr Wetherall's friend had a cervine face and a slight stoop, as if much of his life had been spent in exploring places with low roofs.

'I don't imagine,' he said, when they had settled down in front of the fire, 'that you have ever heard of the Spurs?'

'The Spurs?'

'Not the football team,' said Mr Raynor-Hasset with a thin smile. 'The Society for the Preservation of Unused Railway lines. I have the honour to be their Secretary.'

'I'm afraid not,' said Petrella. 'What do you do?'

'Just as speleologists explore the recesses and convolutions of our caves, we delight in tracking down the railway lines which run under this great city. It is a curious fact but once a railway line has been constructed, it may be covered over – but it is hardly ever filled in again.'

'I suppose not.'

'Most people imagine, when they think about it, that our main railway lines stop well short of the centre of London. The Northern ones at Euston, Kings Cross, and St Pancras. The Southern ones at Waterloo and Victoria. It is far from true, of course. I could name you half a dozen ways of crossing London from North to South by steam train. I conducted a special trip along the Blackfriars, Holborn, Kentish Town line myself last year. And did you know that there was an old but still usable railway line, part of the original Charing Cross-Bayswater switch, which runs within a hundred yards of the Eros statue in Piccadilly? The entrance to it is through a shop...'

Petrella listened, entranced, as Mr Raynor-Hasset described and expounded to him that curious system of disused passages and tunnels, of unsuspected tracks, of forgotten stairways and phantom stations (akin to the traces in the human system of some dread but dead disease) which the private enterprise of our railway pioneers had left under the unsuspecting surface of London.

During an interval, while his host brewed cocoa for them, Petrella explained the idea which had come into his head.

Mr Raynor-Hasset cleared the table and spread on it a map of large scale. 'It's a very feasible idea,' he said. 'I think that the Tooley Street Goods Yard would be the one to start with. You have had losses from there – serious losses. Quite so. You'll note that although it is now linked to London Bridge by part of the ordinary Southern system, its previous history is far from simple. It began life as a private depot for goods coming up the river to St Saviour's Dock – a horse-drawn tramway connected it to Dockhead; or you could get at it under the river by the old subway – it's disused now – that came out at Stanton's Wharf. Plenty of possibilities there. As for the underground stations—' Mr Raynor-Hasset shook his head. 'If people had any idea what lay behind those shiny, well-lit platforms, they'd be pretty surprised.'

He consulted his chart again. 'If I had to make a guess I'd say that the connection lies between Tooley Street and Southwark. And I'll tell you why. Southwark Underground must be within a very short distance of the connecting line which the old Brighton and South Coast – who shared London Bridge with the South Eastern and Chatham – ran across to Waterloo. It was never a great success, as passengers found it just as easy to go straight through from London Bridge, and it was closed to traffic in the eighties. You can see it marked here.'

Petrella followed the spidery lines on the map and found his excitement kindling.

'I really believe,' he said, 'that you must be right.'

'There's no need to rely on guesswork. Why don't we go and see?'

Petrella looked at him.

'With your authority,' said Mr Raynor-Hasset, 'and my experience, I should anticipate no difficulty. I take it you can square it with the authorities?'

'Yes, certainly.'

'Then I suggest tomorrow night. We will meet at shall we say, eleven o'clock at Bermondsey South? The old station, on the north side of the Rotherhithe Road. Dress in your oldest clothes.'

At a few minutes after eleven the following night Petrella was following Mr Raynor-Hasset down a flight of wooden steps. At the bottom of the steps a man was waiting for them.

'I've opened her up,' he said. 'Had to use a pint of oil. Must be five years since anyone went through there.'

'Almost exactly five years,' said Mr Raynor-Hasset. 'I took a party along there myself. Thank you very much, Sam.' Some coins changed hands. 'You lock up behind. We'll probably be coming out at Waterloo.'

'I'll give 'em a ring,' said Sam. The door opened into what looked, at first sight, like a brick wall, but which was in fact the bricked-up entrance to a railway tunnel. It shut behind them with a solid thud, cutting off light, air, and sound.

'I should have asked you before we started,' said Mr Raynor-Hasset, 'whether you suffered at all from claustrophobia.'

'I don't think so,' said Petrella. 'I've never really found out.'

'One man I took with me was so severely overcome that he fell flat on his face and when I endeavoured to assist him he bit me – in the left leg. Straight ahead now.'

It was quite easy going. The rails were gone, and the old permanent way had become covered, in the course of time, by a thin deposit of dried earth mixed with soot from the tunnel roof. The only discomfort was the dust they kicked up as they walked.

'Ventilation is sometimes a problem,' said Mr Raynor-Hasset. 'It was originally quite adequate, but one or two of the shafts have become blocked with the passage of time. In a really old tunnel I have used a safety lamp, but we should be all right here.' He paused to consult the map, and a pedometer which was pinned to the front of his coat. 'There's an air shaft somewhere here. Yes – you can catch a glimpse of the sky.'

Petrella looked up a narrow opening and was pleased to see the stars winking back at him. The light of the torch shone on something white. It was a tiny heap of bones.

'A dog, I should imagine,' said Mr Raynor-Hasset. 'On we go. We've much ground to cover.'

They went on in silence. Petrella soon lost count of time and distance. His guide used his torch sparingly, and as they paced forward into the blackness, Petrella began to feel the oppression of the entombed, a consciousness of the weight of earth above him. The air grew thicker, and was there – or was it his imagination – greater difficulty in breathing?

'We must,' he said, his voice coming out in a startling croak, 'we must be nearly the other side of London by now.'

Mr Raynor-Hasset halted, clicked on his torch, and said, 'One mile and nearly one furlong. By my calculations we are just passing under Bricklayers Arms Depot We go past the north-east corner, and then we should swing through nearly a quarter turn to the right... Yes, here we are. Better keep an eye for possible entrances on our left.'

He kept his torch alight for two hundred yards, but the brick walls remained unbroken. Ahead of them pink beads winked and flushed in the light, retreating before them.

'Rats,' said Mr Raynor-Hasset. 'But a timid bunch. I carry a few Guy Fawkes squibs to throw at them, but I've never had to use them.'

They walked on in silence.

Petrella, who was gradually becoming acclimatised, calculated that they had gone forward another mile when Mr Raynor-Hasset spoke again.

'Can you feel,' he said, 'a sight dampness?'

'It's less dusty, certainly.'

'There's a water seepage here. Nothing serious – some defect in drainage. We must be almost under the old Leathermarket.'

Petrella tried to visualise the geography of that part of London.

'In that case,' he said, 'we shouldn't be far from Tooley Street.'

'About two hundred yards.'

The torch came on again. Ahead of them the surface shone, black and slimy. The smell was unspeakable. Even Mr Raynor-Hasset noticed it.

'Quite fresh, isn't it?' he said. 'We'll keep the torch on now for a bit.'

When they came to it, the side entrance was easy to see. It sloped upward, gently, to the right. Mr Raynor-Hasset took a compass bearing and marked his map.

'I should think there's no doubt at all,' he said. 'That's an old loading track and it goes straight to Tooley Street Depot. You'll probably find it comes out in a loading pit. Do you wish to follow it?'

But Petrella's eyes were on the ground. 'Could you point your torch here a moment,' he said. 'Look. That's not five years old.'

It was a cigarette carton.

'No, indeed,' said Mr Raynor-Hasset. 'And those, I think, are footprints. How very interesting!'

Clearly to be seen in the mud was a beaten track of men's boot prints that led from the mouth of the shaft and onward up the tunnel.

'Keep your torch on them,' said Petrella. 'This is going to save me a lot of trouble.'

'It looks as if an army has passed this way.'

An army of soldier-ants, thought Petrella. An army bearing burdens.

Four hundred yards, and the line of footprints turned into a track branching down to the left. Mr Raynor-Hasset again checked his position, and said, 'Southwark Underground Station, or I'm a Dutchman.'

They went sharply down for a short distance, then the track levelled out, ran along, and climbed again, finally emerging into a circular antechamber. Above their heads an iron staircase spiralled upwards into the gloom.

'Southwark,' said Mr Raynor-Hasset, 'was one of those stations which was developed forward. I mean that when they redesigned it, they put in a moving staircase at the far end, with the lifts, and closed the old emergency stair shaft altogether. That is what we have come out into.

But Petrella was not listening to him. The light of the torch had revealed, strewn around the foot of the staircase, an astonishing jumble of cartons, crates, boxes, sacks, and containers of every shape and size.

'This is where they unpack the stuff,' he said. 'I wonder where they store it. Can we get out on to the platform?'

'Certainly. I think this must be the way.'

There was a door in the boarding ahead of them, secured by three stout bolts.

'What time is it?'

'Just after two o'clock.'

'Should be all right,' said Petrella.

He slid the bolts and swung the door open. They stepped through and found themselves on the platform of Southwark Underground Station, lit only by the ghostly blue lamps which shine all night to guide the maintenance trolleys.

'What are we looking for?' said Mr Raynor-Hasset.

'There must, I think, be more storage space. Have you a knife? It would be about here, I'd guess. Hold the torch steady a moment.'

Petrella slid the blade between the boards, choosing the place with precision. He felt a latch lifting and levered strongly with the knife blade. A section of boarding hinged out towards them.

'Good gracious,' said Mr Raynor-Hasset mildly.

The deep recess contained, stacked on shelves and floor, an astonishing assortment of goods. There were piled cartons of cigarettes, wooden boxes with the stamp of a well-known whisky firm, portable typewriters, wireless and television sets, bales of textiles, a pair of sporting rifles, boxes of shoes, cases of tinned food.

'A producer-to-consumer service,' said Petrella grimly.

His mind was already busy constructing exactly the sort of police trap that would be necessary: two cars in the street above, to catch the people when they came to collect; men in the tunnel itself, beyond the opening, to seal the far end; and a very cautious reconnaissance to find out how the Tooley Street end worked.

He was standing on the platform, thinking about all this, when suddenly he started to laugh. Mr Raynor-Hasset edged perceptibly away.

'It's quite all right,' said Petrella. 'I'm not going to start biting you in the leg. Hold the torch on that wall. Now watch, while I open and shut those two doors.'

Mr Raynor-Hasset did so, and then himself gave a dry cackle. 'Very ingenious,' he said.

Two advertisements stood next to each other on the billboard. They were very close, with only a thin margin between them.

When the doors were shut, the two advertisements read:

THIS YEAR'S TARGET
BUY YOURSELF ANOTHER      RING PARK 0906
PREMIUM BOND      JAMES BOND & SONS
Everything for your car

When both doors were opened, most of the left-hand advertisement and most of the right-hand advertisement were neatly cut away; and when the cut-away parts vanished into the darkness of the opened doors, all that remained of the adjoining advertisements was:

GET
HER RING
JAM

'I couldn't help thinking,' said Petrella, 'that we have, at least, set Mr Duckworth's mind at rest.'

# 6-5 AGAINST

## Lesley Grant-Adamson

*The best crime writers are usually keen to stretch their skills, taking risks by trying out new types of story, new settings, new characters. This is true of many contributors to CWA anthologies and is certainly the case with Lesley Grant-Adamson. Although she originally made her name with a series about the journalist Rain Morgan, she has subsequently tried her hand at a wide variety of novels, together with a few short stories, and her mastery of the craft qualified her to publish an incisive teachyourself guide to crime writing. This story is by no means typical of her work, but is no less enjoyable for that.*

Nick walked on to the aft deck when the ferry was half an hour out of port. White cliffs gone, town lights merging into bleary yellow. Below him the wake chalked the cross-Channel route and was secreted away by dark water. No moon, no shine, the dullest end to a drearily overcast day, a day when nothing much appeared to be happening.

Anxious, he glanced over his shoulder. Stig was flopped on a bench near the bar, cropped head on rolled-up jacket, mouth open, lightly snoring. Nick watched him for a minute, the muscled figure lulled with the comfortable rhythm of the boat. Peculiar contrast, he thought, to the fizzing vitality that had left Nick feeling sluggish, outpaced, all day. They were the same age, thirties, but Stig appeared to spend time at the gym, tuning each muscle individually. Nick didn't. He muttered a joke to himself. 'So that's your secret, mate? Early bedtime?' Stig wasn't comical, though, he was alarming.

A chill stole over Nick. He blamed the weather rather than trepidation, although it might have been either. Back in the crowded lounge again, he skulked behind a newspaper, eyes scanning stories, hand turning pages, but too jumpy to read. His skittering thoughts raced through what he had done and what he was about to do. He kept promising himself that the odds on pulling it off were excellent; but he was no more than hopeful that he had concealed his state of mind from Stig. He had striven to show a normal interest – not too much and not too little – in the job they were doing, delivering furniture.

'It's crap.' Stig's tone had discouraged debate.

Nick pressed on anyway. 'What, you mean it's old junk?'

A jeer. 'Old? Nah, I don't reckon.'

'Repro?'

But Stig was changing down a gear, swinging the van out to overtake a lorry while there was, just arguably, room. Nick snuffed out his questions about whether the antiques dealer was expecting fakes. He clutched the door and concentrated on willing the van not to smash into the coach rounding the bend.

Unacknowledged excitement over, Nick marked Stig down as a man who usually drove either a peppy car or somebody else's van. He hugged a couple of comforting thoughts. One: Stig must be safe enough or a trader like Marcus wouldn't risk hiring him. Two: although Stig didn't know it, Nick wouldn't make the return run.

Stig's headlong dash got them to the port in good time, in spite of their late start. *His* late start. Nick was already outside the cafe for the pick-up when Stig phoned. Nick had hesitated, then opted for tea and toast. A few people might notice him inside; waiting outside, he would be on show to hundreds. No way of knowing how long it might be before this mattered.

Sitting by the window, with his butter-sodden toast, Nick had spent the only relaxing minutes of that drab Tuesday. First he thought about Karen and how her day would be, and what she might attempt to do about it. Abandon her latest diet and go on a binge, he supposed. Next he recalled Nollie from the garage, asking him to help Marcus out by doing the French run with Stig. Nick had seen Stig around, knew it was a name that cropped up when an easy job needed doing, nothing taxing. Stig cast a cold eye but he was nobody, although it stood to reason he would know of people who were on the front line. They all did.

Finally, Nick toyed with ruses for getting Stig to drop him off near

Flers. That was the only uncertainty. Otherwise it was simple: collect package and hurry away. And then everything would be different.

He sensed a pleasurable rush of excitement but it rapidly evolved into anxiety. So much could go wrong, and if he didn't grab the package in time, he might forfeit it altogether.

Nick nibbled the last corner of the toast, wishing he understood exactly where the van would be heading. Nollie had been vague and Stig had spoken only two sentences when they agreed the pick-up.

'Bloody mystery tour,' Nick muttered, wiping butter from his fingers, scrunching the paper napkin. He checked his watch. Immediately Stig appeared, he was going to start winkling information out of him.

An unmarked white van slewed off the road and jerked to a halt. Stig stretched out a tattooed arm to shove open the passenger door, sat drumming the steering wheel, impatient gestures urging Nick to jump in and be nippy about it. The van was flung into racing traffic while Nick was settling in his seat.

After a couple of dangerous attempts, he accepted that the winkling had better wait until they were on the ferry and someone else was driving.

Once aboard, Stig grunted indistinct answers and proved resistant to winkling. He might just as well have been wearing a sweatshirt that said Mind Your Own Business. Irked, Nick sat silently across the table from him, totting up the little he had gleaned. They were taking Victorian furniture to a French antique dealer at Alencon, although the furniture wasn't antique and the dealer wasn't actually in Alencon. The van had been locked when Stig collected it and so he hadn't seen the cargo, although he had called it crap and referred to scuffed and stained armchairs.

Soon Stig perfected his method of fending off questions. While onshore lights remained distinct dots of colour, and the cliffs were a milky swathe across the gloom, he stretched full length on the bench and fell asleep. He didn't stir for a couple of hours, not once while Nick drank a beer, went on deck, pretended to read, made a second visit to the deck, frowned into the gloom where England used to be, shuddered at the sting of rain on his face, and then tossed his mobile into the scrambled water, where it could leave no more trace than the wake written on the surface of the sea.

Karen was casting off London's clamour and heading into her clean, green future. Houses plumped up and spread themselves out on their lawns, classier ones looked like fugitives in a shrubbery. She pressed her toe on the accelerator.

Adele, beside her, had settled into silence edged with reproach. The child had made her views clear: she would never forgive them, look what they had done to her, keeping it secret they were moving house, and she was going to hate the Cotswolds, she just knew she was, but did they care about her, no they did not.

Karen took it with a pinch of salt. Adele was like Nick, a stick-in-the-mud unless given a push. Herself pert and petite, thanks to nature rather than her faddy dieting, she was amused that her daughter was growing to look like him. Adele had his square-shouldered way of advancing on the world and his fudge brown hair, although, when she was ready to switch, Karen could teach her all there was to know about going blonde.

Karen could have married a footballer, as she was inclined to mention after a drink or two. She had gone blonde one week, and the next she met Petey MacAdam, a Millwall defender. Fair and attractive, he had made a profitable transfer and bought a house in Buckinghamshire, but they had split up before the Buckinghamshire bit. Whenever she remembered him she was puzzled how she could have ended up with Nick instead.

Not telling anyone that they were moving was Nick's idea. 'They'll be envious, love, they'll say it won't work out and we'll be back in Romford in no time.'

She had let him have his way, although she was disappointed not to be able to flash the details of the detached house with the couple of acres where they would keep a pony, or describe the smart shops in the town and the good school for Adele.

The secret had turned into a whole series. Carrying on normally had meant making plans with friends who had no inkling she was going to let them down. He had laughed when she complained about her double life, especially the half that didn't feel exciting but out of control.

'Well, it's not out of my control, my sweet. Don't worry, I'm taking care of everything.'

'This new house, it's going to make all the difference to us.'

He had murmured agreement.

Karen had found it, of course. A television property show had put the Cotswolds into her head. By the end of it, a young couple were opting for a honey-coloured house with roof tiles like Ryvita biscuits, and Karen had made up her mind. She picked houses on the Internet, showed Nick. For once he gave in without a fight, perhaps because they had been restless for a while, his relationship with her family had soured, and everyone was on at him about giving up his bread-and-butter work because the man who hired him was bent. As an address, the Cotswolds was a step up from Buckinghamshire, Karen's benchmark.

Karen's excitement bubbled up again as she passed the first sign to their village. 'Look, Adele, we're nearly there.'

Adele grunted, playing with her mobile, committed to showing no interest in the house. How could she trust them about the pony and the dog when they had tricked her out of her friends?

With an unstoppable grin on her face, Karen swept past a jumble of gingerbread houses in the village high street and drew up at the gateway to Flinders. The grin faded. 'Where the hell's the furniture van?'

Forgetting she was 'not speaking', Adele said, 'This is a cool house.'

Karen was tapping into her mobile. Nick's phone was off. She didn't expect him for hours, he had to see someone about a job. 'Never mind, Adele, I expect the van driver's stopped for a break.'

'Mum, I thought the reason we stayed at granny's last night was so they could get our furniture down here early.'

'Yes, it was.'

'And we had to get out of our old house because the Pethies were moving in today.'

'Yes, yes, I know.' She tried Nick again. Still switched off. She had left every detail up to him, everything had gone so smoothly, but now the timings were adrift.

'Can we go in, I want to see inside.'

'But…'

'Oh come on, it's all right for you, you and Dad came and picked it, I didn't even know it existed until three days ago…'

'All right, all right.' She handed them over, a couple of chunky keys, a tag reading Flinders. Adele was off, bounding round the curve of the drive.

From habit, Karen locked the car. She next saw Adele on the front steps, a sweep of stone, carved details to match the drip stones over the mullioned windows. The clumsy child couldn't get the key into the lock. Laughing, Karen ran to help.

She figured it out at once. The front door had a Yale so these heavy keys must be for the back. Just then the door opened. A middle-aged woman in suede trousers stood there.

Karen blurted, 'Oh, you're still here.'

The woman queried her with a frown.

Floundering, Karen tried, 'Our furniture van *isn't* here but *you* are.'

The woman laughed, seeing what must have happened. 'Oh dear, I'm sorry, you've got the wrong house. This is Flinders.'

'Yes, I know it's Flinders. We've bought it and we're moving in today, my furniture…'

The laughing had stopped. 'I'm afraid there's been some ghastly mistake. Flinders hasn't been sold.'

'Ballater Covey showed us round…'

'A shake of the head. They didn't sell it, we took it off the market.'

Then Karen remembered, Nick had gone behind the agent's back, done a private deal with the vendors, got the price way down for a quick cash sale, and she had left it all to him, every little detail. A proprietorial marmalade cat slipped into the house. Karen realised she was gawping, her thoughts too fast, her words too slow. The woman in suede was saying she was sorry, so awfully sorry. And as she was saying it she was backing away, ever so slightly closing the door, afraid the woman on her doorstep was mad.

From the corner of her eye, Karen glimpsed Adele rushing away. She mumbled apology to the bemused lady of Flinders and ran after her daughter.

Adele was in the car, sobbing, jabbing Nick's number into her mobile. Getting nothing. All day they got nothing.

Darkness. Stig driving full tilt down a thin straight French road, the van unremarkable in the skein of vehicles paid out from the ferry. The drum and thrum of the road too noisy for conversation. Radio not working, aerial snapped off. Nick slumped, mesmerised by red tail lights scattered through the distance. The journey's rhythm broken now and then by clattering change of sound as traffic surged through closed-up villages.

Alert now at a turn he didn't expect. He asks. Stig is sharp. 'I'm going this way, all right? I mean, what is this? You putting in a report to Marcus or something?'

'Easy, Stig. I saw us leave the Alencon road, that's all.'

'Short cut, all right?'

'About Marcus... Like I said, I don't know Marcus. It was Nollie who...'

'Yeah, yeah.' Dismissive, disbelieving, all the antis.

And so a day of evasions and deceits added up to this answer: Stig believed someone had said, 'Usual help isn't at hand so nice quiet Nick can go along for the ride and keep an eye on Stig.' Untrue, as far as Nick knew, but hard to blame Stig for thinking it because Nick's role was slight. *Just be there, Nick, if he needs help.*

Nick choked back the smart answers and looked out of the side window. Vague glow of a far off town, gleam of water as they crossed a bridge, but no red lights. They were moving into open country and no one was following. All day long he had been hiding his annoyance, his curiosity, his secrets, and he was weary of it. He didn't doubt Stig had business apart from Marcus and his phoney antiques, all he hoped was Stig would see to it fast and then drop him off near Flers. He was trying to get the map clear in his mind, calculating how to retrieve his package without running into trouble.

Abruptly a sharp left, Stig nearly missing it, throwing the van so hard the back end slid and for a second they teetered above a ditch. Stuff crash-landed on Nick: maps, papers, a bag, a jacket, flying from all around the cab. Swearing, he batted them away, scuffled them aside with his feet. 'For fuck's sake. If you can't drive a sodding motor…'

'Piss off. They didn't do the sign right, did they? Bloody stupid French fuckers nearly had me off the road.'

Nick clamped his jaw, determined not to distract him. Several miles slipped by before he even cleared up. Stig stayed locked over the wheel, chin jutting, urging the vehicle on. Nick shut his eyes but that was no better: he kept hearing the screeching noises of the accident that hadn't quite happened. They raced on, in anger.

Eventually, Nick sensed the speed slackening. Soon there was a petrol station with a cafe. Stig brought the van to rest at the rear of the car-park, swinging it round to face the exit.

They began walking across to the cafe. Near the pumps, Stig faltered. 'Go in, mate, and order some stuff. I'll fill up first.'

'Er… OK.' Nick was convinced Stig was going to drive off. There was a sound reason to fill up straightaway: the pump might switch off for the night. But even so.

He ordered food, sat niggling that Stig ought to have driven straight to the pump and not raised suspicion.

Door swung, Stig hurried in, flushed, saying he was hungry but then picking. Nick, refusing to be told he had ordered the wrong stuff, ignored the picking. At least it meant they would be on their way.

'Another coffee, Nick?'

Nick went to the counter. Away from scrutiny, he read his watch. Getting late. That bothered him, a lot of things were bothering him, especially the danger of being dragged into whatever Stig was up to. All he had ever wanted from this trip was the lift to France. He sighed as he noticed how he had been lowering his aspirations. Don't worry about Flers, Alencon will do. Never mind the delivery, just part from Stig asap. Forget the timetable, sleep in a barn and rejig plans tomorrow. So on.

At the table, Stig was edgy. He had shoved his plate aside and was smoking, rapid little puffs. Nick reached for a discarded chip, utterly casual as he asked, 'This guy in Alencon?'

'Near Alencon.'

'Right, near Alencon. He's expecting us this evening, right?'

Stig shrugged. 'Yeah, well, we had trouble with the motor, didn't we?'

'What I mean is, how late will he wait? We're not going to roll up and find he's gone to bed or anything?'

Stig repeated the shrug, ground out the cigarette beside the chips. He took his time over the coffee.

At last they went outside. To Nick's surprise the van was not to be seen. Then he realised: it was precisely where it had been before the petrol-filling, on the shadowed far side of the car-park. He set off.

Stig, a few yards behind, called, 'Gotta go back in, mate.' Patting his pockets, indicating something lost.

'Hell, at this rate we're never... '

Stig threw the key at him with force. 'Shut it, Nick. Wait in the van.'

Furious, Nick stormed over to it and climbed up. And then there was uproar. Figures were tussling in the fall of light from the cafe, yelling, flinging bodies to the ground. A dog barked. Gunfire. Screams. Nick barged across to the driving seat, started up the engine and fled.

Alencon, Flers, it no longer mattered, he was just desperate to get away. Whatever Stig's scam, he could explain it himself to the gendarmes.

A few miles ahead lay a town. Skirting it, Nick became snared in a network of badly-marked lanes, not certain whether he was escaping or stupidly circling. After too long he admitted he was lost, and searched the map for the name on a signpost. Hopeless, and neither could he work out where he had parted from Stig.

He tossed the map aside. It slid to the floor. Leaning to retrieve it, he spotted something else. Stig's passport, and there was his proper name: Steven Varden. Nick froze. Things had turned several shades darker. Vardens were a worry, you kept clear, you didn't mess with them. If he'd had any idea Stig was one of the Varden family...

He shuddered. 'Thank Christ I did a runner.'

It was then he discovered Stig had failed to fill up. Needle flickered, empty.

Nick detested Stig, but was livid with himself, too. For the sake of a free ride, he had put his future at risk. The set-up was obvious now. He had been hand-picked to take the fall for Stig if things went awry. *Just be there, Nick, if he needs help.* Even if Stig had been killed in the shoot-out, it didn't save him because Nollie and Marcus knew he had gone with Stig. And while they looked for the van, the Vardens would look for Nick. Only Nick could tell them what had happened, and they might not believe him. They were heavy, their business ran on violence. Stig was surely the tiniest cog in their big wheel, but even so.

Once, Nick had tried explaining to Karen the difference between criminals and ordinary people who liked to give themselves an edge, spot a chance, make a few thousand that nobody was going to miss. But she didn't get it. He had always been on the lookout for chances, only gone for excellent odds, and now he had pulled the big one: Internet advertisement, money flowing in, the stash at the farmhouse. It was human nature to be gullible, especially for a good cause, and it was also human nature to take advantage of the gullible. If there was a victimless crime, he thought this was it. The givers had felt noble about giving. Unaware they were conned, no one complained. Happily, it was also undetectable. A dead cert, and all that remained was to collect his hidden treasure. So how could he have been so rash as to hitch a ride with a Varden?

He pictured Stig alive, struggling to extricate himself with his half dozen words of French. From Nick's own point of view, Stig's incompetence was good: no blurting information about his travelling companion. Heartened, he drove on, aiming for the lights of a hill town. At a garage below it, he paid cash to a drowsy youth whose eyes never veered from a television programme.

He ran a finger along the map's printed roads. He knew now where he was and could go straight to the farmhouse. The snag was there were no quick and easy roads. He dared only visit the place at night but it was impossible to get there before daybreak. He swore softly. All his planning had come to this: driving a stolen van loaded with fakes and liable to be caught before collecting his stash. Odds not so good.

Another thought. 'Gendarmes will be looking for the van, not for me. Dump it fast, where it won't give pointers to the farmhouse.'

He studied the map, seeking a spot where he could walk away at first light. Then the hitchhiking, the bus, whatever it took to get to the farmhouse. And after that everything was sure to be different.

Nick chose a riverside track beside a playing field a mile from a large village. The ground was rough, he parked beneath a tree. No hiding place, yet it wouldn't matter if kids spotted it next day. Then he decided to stretch out in the van and sleep for an hour or two. Setting the alarm on his watch, he mocked his optimism. He had slept in vans before, they were hardly comfortable. Round the back, he investigated the lock, expecting to have to be creative to open it without a key. Instead, it opened at a touch. A stuffy smell wafted over him, bringing to mind Stig's remark about stained old armchairs.

He hoicked himself up on to the edge and flicked the thin beam of the torch around the interior. Wooden chair legs, rucked up rug, man's shoe and, as he swung the beam up, he saw the rest of the man, sprawled rigidly in an armchair, head twisted back, gouts of blood… Nick felt his bile rise, felt the world swaying, smashed down behind the van, and lost the torch.

Pitch-black night. No moon, no shine. Panicky, he stumbled around, feeling for it with a foot, guessing where it might have flown as he jerked backwards out of the van. Useless. Shocked and trembling, he sat in the cab, unable to organise his thoughts. That he should have been driving around for hours with… Did Stig know? Was this why Stig…

'Shut up about Stig! *Think*. Can't leave this for kids to find. Serious stuff now. Police don't break sweat for stolen British vans, but when they find one with a dead body by a playing field… '

The questions took over again. Who was the dead man? How had he died? Had he been in the van in England? Did Stig know? Did Marcus know but not Stig? What if they had driven straight to the antique dealer? Could the body have been put there at the petrol station? Or in London, and be the reason Stig was delayed? Grimmer, had the man died while they were driving him around, trapped?

Nick felt sick again. He walked down to the river, a few yards. He was battling not to dwell on those questions, because the only one that mattered was: what was he going to do next?

Fleetingly, he wondered about dropping the body into the bubbling water and letting it become somebody else's problem downstream. Only fleetingly, because without light it was impossible to judge whether that was practical. Whatever he did he must not make matters worse. Leaving a body in a public place was begging for trouble. This was a big empty country, no need to take chances.

Nick jolted the van back down the track, and slipped away into the night-time lanes, seeking out the perfect secret space.

Day break. Softening of blackness, rim of light on mountain top, a bird's faltering call. But no sun. Another day with the sky pressing low, the colours blanked out.

Nick climbed down from the cab, winced to see how close he had parked to the drop. He threw open the rear door, ducking back out of the way until the morning air scoured the van. Then, steeling himself, he confronted the sight.

An older man wearing a charcoal suit, grey-haired and jowly, bullet hole below the left ear, blood and brains on the chair. Yet not enough of them. No neat execution, and if he had been shot in the van there would have been mess all over it. Nick avoided the glaring eye, the sour smell, the hand stuck up in a gesture of hail and farewell. Holding his breath, he lifted the jacket by the lapel.

Pockets empty, so he was no wiser who the man was, which country he came from and where or why he had met his end. He backed out of the van, wiping every surface he had ever touched, used the rug to scuffle away footprints, and drove away. Mountain roads, sparse villages, a haphazard meandering through emptiness, the journey on automatic because he felt safer moving than staying. A few times he worried about the short span of time left to reach the farmhouse before the owners came, with their Dobermans running everywhere so that visitors were certain to be caught. Otherwise he thought about the van.

Once, he decided to stay overnight in a motel, but was frightened off by a warning in its car-park about vehicles being broken into. Another time he chose a screened spot in a secluded camp site, only to have a family in a camper van pull in. Their dog sniffed him out instantly, persuading him that the smell was escaping from the van.

Isolated, with little sleep and less food, he began to believe the odds were hopelessly against him. He felt like an actor in a film where twists of fortune send lives careering off in unexpected directions. If he could reel it back to the evening Nollie phoned to ask him to help, he would say no. Or when the white van slewed into the cafe car-park he wouldn't rush out to climb in beside Stig. Maybe he would disappear once they berthed at the French port, rather than set out on the journey to Alencon. Even if he left it as late as the ambush, he wouldn't steal the van.

The absurdity struck him: he had got the free and roving life he had schemed for. Who was it who said be careful what you wish for lest your wishes come true? Racked by uncontrollable laughter, he sat on an empty hillside, watching evening fall. The swift closing down of a day without sun worth the name; the wind changing to run down-hill bringing different scents; the stirrings as the shift changed – day creatures to bed, the other lot on patrol.

Calm again, he faced things coolly. He admitted he no longer believed in the police raid. Nothing he remembered seeing in the patchy light suggested it. People had been ambushed but the rest was conjecture, and he couldn't guess which side Stig was on. Then the body. Either Stig had been disposing of it, or it had been put there as a warning to Stig and whoever he worked for. Planting a body is making a statement, it's usual to hide them. Nick resolved to hide it next day. Bad enough imagining the police in pursuit of the van, but he was under a more dangerous threat. The passenger's friends might want the van back, and so might the passenger's enemies.

The following morning Nick filled the petrol tank, filled a can besides, and took the van up through hairpin bends to a rough lay-by. In a while, he realised the site wasn't good enough. Unless he managed to send the van straight down, it might swerve into a large shrub which would slow its fall and prevent it burying itself in the vegetation lower down. Nick drove further up, picked another point, but that was close to a tourist spot so he drove on again. Scenery changed, trees thinned, and he wasn't happy because he wanted cover. He tried to turn the van round and wind down to the shrubby areas below, but the steepness of the track and the narrowness made it desperately difficult. So on up he went. Where the track was reduced to a jagged edge above a rocky gorge, Nick pulled on the hand brake. This was it.

He wiped every surface in the cab, wrenched off number plates and anything that identified the vehicle. Then he sloshed petrol inside the rear, fixed a taper, and inched the van as close to the edge as he dared. At dusk, he lit the taper and gave the van a shove. It juddered but resisted. He shoved again. It rocked. He dashed to tamp out the taper, then ran to check the nearside wheel. Snagged on a stone. He swore. He had failed to notice the front wheels were angled towards it. The other one was already airborne. Nick grimaced, thinking how having no options saved struggling with decisions. He fixed the jack near the trapped wheel, raised it slightly, lit the taper, raised the jack again and leapt out of harm's way as the van's weight sent it plunging and slithering in a grating rush of scree.

Winded, Nick lay listening to its noisy exit as it banged against rocks, flattened shrubs, the racket ricocheting around the mountains. And then, just as he feared it was finishing, the flare and boom of the explosion. Nick watched the fiery trace for a few minutes. Then there was only the heavy silence of the mountain and darkness.

Nick tore up and burned the documents, he buried the number plates.

It was a German lorry and the driver spoke English with an American accent. Non-stop.

'Where did you say your car broke down?'

'Eh?' Nick had said nothing of the sort, just snagged a lift by a junction.

'Your clothes give it away, the petrol stains... '

Nick laughed, not feeling like it. True, he looked a wreck and he stank. 'It wasn't mine, though. I was helping someone.'

Although he was being edged into telling more, he put a stop to it, afraid of being caught out. He did what Stig had done to him, grew vague or said nothing.

Thwarted, the driver switched on music for company instead.

Bluegrass and loud. On the straight bits between the mountain bends, he beat out the rhythm on the steering wheel. Nick kept his eyes shut, demanding the Almighty tell him what was happening to his luck that he had got another crazy driver.

A whoop and a yell beside him. 'Wheee! Look at that? Damn near set fire to the whole valley.'

Nick gulped. Apparently, his blundering walk through the night had been a waste of effort. From this angle he could see the raw scar that ended in a streak of blackened scrub.

He said, 'A bad crash. No one could walk away from that.'

'Naw, that's an insurance job. Shove the thing over, collect the cash. But looks like this one went wrong.'

'Wrong?' He had spoken too quickly, too nervously perhaps.

'Well, how's it gonna stay hidden with that fire trail pointing it out?

Nick shot back. 'Maybe it was better to burn it.'

Sideways look. 'Yeah?'

'I mean, there'll be nothing *to* find. Right?'

'Sure. Bit of metal, no evidence.'

'Evidence?'

The driver dragged through a bend before replying. 'Whatever crime they're covering up. You know, fingerprints, body in the boot, whatever.'

Nick said nothing. The driver looked at him.

They passed a sign for a town in three kilometres. Nick said he would get out there, but the driver argued he would be better off staying until they reached a bigger place. So Nick grabbed his chance when they were stuck in a tailback at a roundabout. As he walked away, he sensed the man giving a final appraising look, at the grime and the guilt, the stained trousers and the charred cuff.

The town was packed because it was market day. Nick bought a change of clothes. He caught a train north, wondering how many people the lorry driver had talked to about him by now. It was a certainty he *would* talk, because that was what the man did, without respite. Nick had heard him on global warming, the wickedness of politicians, the countries he drove through, the chances of winning a

lottery, and life in general. On life in general he had cited Damon
Runyan's 'All life is 6-5 against.'

'Some days,' said the driver, 'I think he's being too hopeful.'

Nick had thought so too.

He recognised the outline of the lofty trees protecting the farmhouse.
He had last been there on a summer day, shortly after withdrawing
the money in euros. He tried to forget his panic when he had suddenly
needed to return to London. Misguided, the police were querying a
legit job, but he could hardly afford to act guilty by running off.
Neither could he take home a sack of unexplainable foreign cash.
Luckily, he had remembered the farmhouse, the one Karen's friends
had rented because the owners only used it during school holidays.
He and Karen had stayed with them on their way back from Spain, a
stopover spoiled by their dog taking against Nick, as dogs often did.

Approaching the farmhouse secretly across a field, heart skipping
a beat at each sound, the cry of a rook was the bark of a dog, a plane
became a car in the lane. Tension giving him a headache. Relax, he
told himself, this is easy. Anyone comes, ask for somebody who can't
be here. Not going to be seized or reported, going to be all right. But
even so.

Crouching by the barn, checking for movement. Bravely creeping
up to the house, flashing a torch through the kitchen window. That
unused look places get. Relieved, he teased open the padlock on the
barn door. And then calamity. The barn was full of bales and his
hiding place was beneath the floor. He dashed outside, looking for a
way in under the building, but there was nothing. Then his torch
bothered a wandering terrier. Cursing he backed off, afraid of being
caught, afraid of having to wait weeks until the barn was cleared. His
head was pounding. Don't worry, he was thinking, take a closer look
in daylight, maybe shift some of the stuff . A car came up the lane.
Nick hid behind a hedge and watched lights come on in the farmhouse, heard the Dobermans rampaging. Wearily he walked away,
leaving it for another day, another week, whatever.

Mortified, Karen had pieced it together, the tricks and the treachery.

He had never meant to go to the Cotswolds, he had just meant to go. He had taken the money he'd received from selling the house and hadn't bought another one. She had left every little detail to him, her only role had been to help keep it secret. He had left her, and without a roof over her head. She was staggered.

Adele, for once appreciating the seriousness of an adult situation, had wisely shut up. Even when Karen, out of the blue, burst out with, 'But I could have married a footballer!' Adele ignored her.

Karen rented an unpleasant cottage in the Cotswolds. Adele said, 'This is a cold house.' Karen sent her family picture postcards bearing misleading messages. She wondered whether to hire a detective to find Nick and wrest her share of their money from him. It didn't take two to buy a house in the Cotswolds, it only took money.

Karen phoned Nollie at the garage. She had avoided getting involved in Nick's business, which meant she couldn't trace people she knew only by first names, but it was easy as pie to get the number of a garage. She was cagey and noted that so was Nollie. She left a number. An hour later she had a Marcus on the line, a growling man she thought sounded as though he could eat Nick for breakfast. He was more fussed about his missing van than about her missing husband.

Stupidly she asked, 'Have you reported it?'

The growl turned to a squeak of disbelief, which she sensed spoke eloquently about the nature of Nick's latest bit of business. She had hated him sailing close to the edge, not sharing his belief that he knew where the edge actually was. By the time the call ended, she was certain she didn't need a detective because determined people were on the trail. It was going to make all the difference.

She sat back to play the long game. If they found him alive she would get her money. If they found him dead she would get his share too. And if they didn't find him at all she she would have him declared missing presumed dead. Karen was hungry for revenge but the money would do.

Weeks went by. She had her ups and downs, went on a new diet and gave it up in a binge. Just when she had put on six pounds and her morale was lowest, the story about Petey McAdam broke. The footballer was being done for corruption, fiddles in his heyday when he went to live in Buckinghamshire. In a way, Karen minded more about this than all the rest.

# Asylum
## John Harvey

*John Harvey remains best known for his series of novels about Nottingham cop Charlie Resnick, but his short stories (and the occasional anthologies that he has edited) are also well worth seeking out. 'Asylum' features Harvey's latest leading character, Jack Kiley, and is notable for its topical subject matter. But the power and compassion of the story is likely to linger in the reader's memory long after sensationalist tabloid headlines about migrant workers and people trafficking have been forgotten.*

The van had picked them up a little after six, the driver cursing the engine which had stubbornly refused to start; fourteen of them cramped into the back of an ailing Ford as it rattled and lurched along narrow roads, zip-up jackets, boots, jeans, the interior thick with cigarette smoke. Outside, light leaked across the Fens. Jolted against one another, the men sat, mostly silent, head down, a few staring out absently across the fields. Field after field the same. When anyone did speak it was in heavily-accented English, Romanian, Serbo-Croatian, Albanian. There were lights in the isolated farms, the small villages they passed through, children turning in their beds and waking slowly to the half-remembered lines they would sing at Harvest Festival. Thanks for plenty. Hymns of praise. The air was cold.

Some ten miles short of Ely, the van turned off along a rough track and bumped to a halt behind a mud-spattered tractor and several other vans. On trestle tables beneath a makeshift canopy, men and women were already working, sorting and wrapping cauliflowers in cellophane. Towards the far side of the field, indistinct in the havering mist, others moved slowly in the wake of an ancient harvester, straightening and bending, straightening and bending, loading cabbages into the low trailer that rattled behind.

A man in a dark fleece, gloves on his fists, stepped towards the van.

'What sort of fuckin' time d'you call this?'

The driver shrugged and grinned.

'Laugh the other side of your fuckin' face, one o' these fine days.'

The driver laughed nervously and, taking the makings from his pocket, started to roll a cigarette. Most of the men had climbed down from the van and were standing in a rough circle, facing inward, hands jammed down into their pockets as they stamped their feet. The others, two or three, sat close against the open door, staring out.

'You,' the foreman said, waving his fist. 'You. Yes, you. What d'you think this is? Fuckin' holiday? Get the fuck out of there and get to fuckin' work.'

Across the slow spread of fields to the west, the blunt outline of Ely Cathedral pushed up from the plane of earth and bulked against the sky.

A hundred or so miles away, in north London, the purlieu of Highbury Fields, Jack Kiley woke in a bed that was not his own. From the radio at the other side of the room came the sounds of the *Today* programme, John Humphrys at full bite, castigating some hapless politician for something he or she had done or failed to do. Kiley pushed back the quilt and rolled towards the edge of the bed, feet quick to the floor. In the bathroom he relieved himself and washed his hands, splashed cold water in his face. At least now Kate was allowing him to leave a toothbrush there, a razor too, and he used both before descending.

Kate sat at the breakfast table, head over her laptop, fingers precise and quick across the keys. Kiley knew better than to interrupt. There was coffee in the cafetière and he poured some into Kate's almost empty mug before helping himself. His selflessness was acknowledged by a grunt and a dismissive wave of the hand.

A mound of the day's papers, including the *Independent*, for whom Kate wrote a weekly column, was on a chair near the door, and Kiley carried them across to the padded seat in the window bay. Through the glass he could see the usual dog walkers in the park, joggers skirting the edge, more than one of them pushing those three-wheeler buggies that cost the price of a small second-hand car.

Automatically, he looked at the sports pages first to check the results and saw, with no satisfaction, that one of the teams he used to play for had now gone five matches without scoring a goal. Below the fold on the front page, the second lead was about the wife of a Home Office minister being attacked and robbed not so very far from where he was now.

*In the early hours of yesterday morning, Helen Forester, wife of ...*

What in God's name was she doing, Kiley thought, wandering around the nether end of Stoke Newington at two in the morning? He checked the other papers. Only the disintegrating marriage of a B-celebrity soap star prevented the story from making a full sweep of the tabloids, *Minister's Wife Mugged* and similar dominating the rest in one inch type. A library photograph of Helen Forester accompanying her husband to the last party conference was the most popular, her narrow, rather angular face strained beneath a round, flat-brimmed hat of the kind worn by Spanish bullfighters, her husband mostly cropped out.

*Mrs Forester was found in a dazed state by passers-by and taken to Homerton hospital, where she was treated for minor injuries and shock.*

'I know her,' Kate said, looking up from her work. 'Interviewed her for a piece on politicians' wives. After all that fuss about Betsy what's-her-name. I liked her. Intelligent. Mind of her own.'

'Must have been switched off when this happened.'

'Maybe.'

'You think there's more to it than meets the eye?'

'Isn't there always?'

'You're the journalist, you tell me.'

Kate shot him a sour glance and went back to the piece she was writing – *No More Faking It: the rehabilitation of Meg Ryan in 'In the Cut'*.

'At least it makes a change,' Kiley said, 'from MPs caught out cottaging on Clapham Common.'

But Kate had already switched him off.

By midday the Minister concerned had issued a brief statement. *My wife and I are grateful for all of the flowers and messages of support...* The Shadow Home Secretary materialised long enough to fire the usual tired salvos about the unsafe streets of our cities and the need for more police officers on the beat. Nothing yet about what the unfortunate Mrs Forester had been doing out alone when she might more properly have been tucked up alongside her husband in the safety of their Islington flat or at their constituency home. That, Kiley was sure, would come.

Café tables were spread along the broad pavement north of Belsize Park Underground station, and Kiley was sitting in the early autumn sunshine nursing a cappuccino and wondering what to do with the rest of the day.

Almost directly opposite, above the bookshop, his small two-room office held little attraction: the message light on the answer-phone was, as far as he knew, not flickering, no urgent faxes lay waiting, any bills he was concerned with paying had been dealt with and his appointment book, had he possessed one, would have been blank. He could walk up the hill on to Hampstead Heath and enjoy the splendours of the turning leaves or stroll across to the Screen on the Hill and sit through the matinée of something exotic and life-affirming.

Then again, he could order another cappuccino, while he considered the possibility of lunch. Irena, the young Romanian waitress who moonlighted two mornings a week as his bookkeeper and secretary, was not on duty, and he caught the eye of a waiter, who by his accent was Spanish and most probably from Latin America. At one of the nearby tables, a May-November couple were holding hands and staring into one another's eyes; at another, a man in a *Fight Global Capitalism* T-shirt was listening contentedly to his I-Pod, and just within his line of vision, a young woman of twenty-two or -three, wearing dark glasses and a seriously abbreviated cerise top, was poring over *The Complete Guide to Yoga*. In small convoys, au pairs propelled their charges along the pavement opposite. The sun continued to shine. What was a seemingly intelligent, middle-aged middle class woman, doing, apparently alone, at the wrong end of Stoke Newington High Street at that hour of the morning? Like a hangnail, it nagged at him and wouldn't let him rest.

*

Dusk prevailed. Lights showed pale under the canopy as the last supermarket loads were packed and readied. The workers, most of them, stood huddled around the vans, the faint glow of their cigarettes pink and red. Mud on their boots and the backs of their legs, along their arms and caked beneath their fingernails. The low line of trees at the far field edge was dark and, beyond it, the cathedral was black against the delicate pink of the sky.

The foreman had counted his men once and now was counting them again.

One short.

He'd had a shouting match with one of them earlier, some barrack-room lawyer from Dubrovnik or some other Godforsaken place, there was always one of them, mouthing off about rest periods and meal breaks.

'You,' he said, poking the nearest with a gloved finger. 'That mate of yours, where is he?'

The man shook his head and looked away. The others stared hard at the ground.

'Where the fuck is he, that fucking Croat cunt?'

Nobody answered, nobody knew.

'OK,' the foreman said finally, the driver with his engine already idling. 'Get 'em out of here. And tomorrow, be on fuckin' time, right?'

It was later that evening, after a warming dinner of lamb shanks with aubergine and cinnamon and the best part of a bottle of Côtes de Ventoux, the moon plump in the sky, that Audrey Herbert left her husband to load the dishwasher, donned her wellingtons and waterproof jacket and took the labrador for its final walk. Halfway along the track that ran beside the second field, the dog started barking loudly at something in the drainage ditch and Audrey thought at first he had unearthed a rat. It was only when she shone the torch and saw the body, half-submerged, she realised it was something more.

Kate stood Kiley up that evening to have dinner with Jason Cameron. Cameron, until a rather public falling out and resignation, had been press officer to the Prime Minister and still had close connections with the inner sanctum of government.

'Seems the PM went ape shit,' Cameron confided. They were in an Indian restaurant in Kentish Town, a table well away from the door. 'Tore a strip off the Home Secretary right outside the cabinet room. Told him if he couldn't keep his underlings and their bloody wives in order, he'd replace him with someone who could.'

'Bit of an overreaction?'

Cameron shrugged. 'You know how he is, scared about weevils coming out of the woodwork. Or wherever it is they come from.'

Kate thought it was flour.

'His ratings, this past six months, last thing he needs now is a juicy bit of scandal.'

'Is that what this is?'

'I shouldn't think so.' Cameron smiled winsomely. 'How's the tarka dhall, by the way?'

'A little too runny, actually.'

'Shame.'

'So. When's it going to hit the fan?'

Cameron looked at her appraisingly. 'First editions tomorrow, most likely.'

'Are you going to make me wait till then?'

'You could always phone your editor.'

'I'm having dinner with you.'

Cameron sighed. 'It seems Helen Forester has not been averse, shall we say, to seeking a little solace on the side. When her husband's work has made him less than attentive.'

'She screws around.'

'Not compulsively.'

'Anyone notable?'

Cameron named a junior MP and a writer whose dissections of political life under the Tories had come close to earning him a CBE. 'That's over a period of ten or twelve years, of course. Restrained by some standards.'

'And Forester knows?'

Cameron nodded. 'There was some talk of divorce, I believe, but all the usual factors came into play. Children. Careers. Forgive and forget.'

'So the tabs are going to dish the dirt, encourage their readers to join the dotted lines. What else was she doing in the wee small hours if she wasn't on her way home from some love nest or other?'

'Something like that.'

'Any names being bandied about?'

'Ah ... ' Cameron leaned back in his chair. 'I was rather hoping you might help me there.'

'Me?'

'You interviewed her recently, got on famously by all accounts.'

'And you think she might have been a little indiscreet?'

'Two women chatting together, relaxed. It's not impossible she'd have mentioned a name or two, purely in passing. Besides, it's what you're good at. Getting people to say things they'd rather keep to themselves.'

Kate smiled and let a piece of well-spiced lady's finger slide down her throat. 'It's you, actually, Jason. Fancies the balls of you, she really does. Maybe I'll give my editor a call as you suggest.'

There were times and recently a goodly number of them, when Kate despaired of her profession. The following morning, when the press spewed up a mess of private folly and unsubstantiated rumour, was one of them. In the cause of public interest, the tabloids took their usual lead, while the broadsheets, keen to maintain their superiority, merely reported their assertions in words of more than two syllables.

After a decent interval, Kate phoned the number she had for Helen Forester but there was no answer. By the time she tried again later, mid-morning, the line had been disengaged. Jason Cameron's mobile was permanently switched off. Kiley, she remembered, had promised to do a little background checking on the client of a barrister friend. She wondered if a visit to the Olafur Eliasson sun installation at Tate Modern might lift her into a better frame of mind.

It was late afternoon before Kiley reported to the offices of Hamblin, Laker and Clarke, a summary of his findings inside a DL manilla envelope, along with a bill for his services. Margaret Hamblin, quietly resplendent in something from Donna Karan, came out into the reception area to thank him.

'I would suggest a glass of wine, Jack. There's a quite nice white from Alsace I'm giving a try. Only there's someone here who wants to see you. Special Branch. You can use my office.'

Someone was plural. One brusque and unsmiling, slight hints of a Scottish accent still lingering, the other, bespectacled, mostly silent and inscrutable.

'Masters,' the first man said, showing identification. 'Detective Superintendent.' He didn't introduce his companion.

'Jack Kiley.'

'You're a private investigator.'

'That's right.'

'And you can make a living doing that?'

'Some days, yes.'

In the parlance of Kiley's recent profession, Masters was a skilful midfielder, not especially tall, wiry, difficult to shake off the ball. He nodded and reached into his pocket. The by-play was over. Inside a small plastic envelope was one of Kiley's business cards, dog-eared and far from pristine.

'Yours?'

'Cheaper by the thousand.'

'There's a phone number, just above your name.' He held it up for Kiley to see. It was Margaret Hamblin's number. 'Is that your writing?'

'Seems to be.'

A Polaroid photograph next, head and shoulders, a deep gash to one side of the temple, lifeless eyes.

'Anyone you know?'

'No.'

'He was found dead in a field last night. Village outside Ely.'

Kiley shook his head.

'Here,' Masters said, handing Kiley the envelope containing the card. 'Turn it round.'

On the back, smudged but still readable was the name *Anna*. Just that.

'Ring any bells?'

It rang a few. Anna was a friend of Irena's from Costanza on the Black Sea coast of Romania. Smuggled into the country, she had worked as an exotic dancer, paying off the exorbitant fee for transportation. She had got into a little trouble and Kiley had helped her out. That had been a year ago. Somewhere in that time she had sent Irena a card from Bucharest.

'You rode to the rescue,' Masters said. 'Knight in shining armour.'

'Dark armour,' the second man corrected, as if to prove he'd been listening. "A knight in dark armour rescuing a lady".'

'Harry Potter?' asked Kiley guilelessly.

'Philip Marlowe. *The Big Sleep.*'

'You know where she is now, this Anna?' Masters asked.

'Romania?'

'I don't think so. And Alen Markovic... '

'Who's that?'

'The man in the photo.'

'The dead man.'

'Exactly. You've no idea how or why he might end up in a drainage ditch with your card on his person? Complete with the name of an illegal immigrant you befriended and the telephone number of a barrister with a reputation for handling appeals against deportation. And let's discount, shall we, pure chance and coincidence.'

'If I had to guess,' Kiley said. 'I'd say he got it from Anna.'

'You gave it to her, she gave it to him.'

'Something like that.'

'In case of trouble, someone to contact, someone to ring.'

'It's plausible.'

'He didn't call you?'

'No.'

Kiley wondered if they were merely following up stray leads; he wondered if the one blow with a thick-edged implement to Alen Markovic's head had been enough to kill him. On balance, he thought both less than likely.

'We could always try asking this Anna,' Masters said softly, as if the suggestion had just that second occurred to him.

'If we could find her,' Kiley said.

'If she isn't still tied to a tree,' said the second man. He really did know his Chandler backwards.

A light rain was beginning to fall. Most of the outside tables had been cleared. Kiley intercepted Irena on her way up from the tube. Masters stood a little way off, coat collar up. Through the pale strobe of headlights climbing the hill, Kiley could see Masters' colleague in the bookstore opposite, innocently browsing through this and that.

'What is it?' Irena said. 'What's happened?'

Kiley moved her close against one of the plane trees that lined the street. Her features were small and precise and the rain that clung to her short, spiky hair made it shine.

'Anna,' Kiley said. 'Is she back in England?'

'No, of course not.'

Kiley waited, fingers not quite touching the sleeve of her coat. Her eyes avoiding his. 'I shall be late. For work.' Absurdly, he wanted to run his hand across the cap of dark, wet hair.

'Why? Why do you want to know?'

'It's complicated.'

'Is she in trouble?'

'I don't think so.'

'She made me promise not to tell you. She thought, after everything you did, she thought you would be angry. Upset.' There were tears on her face or maybe it was only the rain, which had started to fall more heavily. 'She is working at a club. I think near Leicester Square. I don' t know the name.'

'You know where she's living?'

Irena took a set of keys from her pocket and put them in his hand.

'She is living with me.'

Kiley watched her walk away, head down, and then waited for Masters to join him. The dark blue Vauxhall was parked in a side road opposite.

Masters' bibliophile friend was standing by the car, a plastic bag containing several paperbacks clutched against his coat. 'You're lucky,' he said to Kiley. 'More than decent bookshop, that close to

where you work.' The glow from the overhead light turned his skin an
unhealthy shade of orange.

'You've got a name?' Kiley asked.

'Several.' He took off his glasses, shook them free from rain,
blinked, and put them back on again.

'How about one that matches some ID?' Kiley said.

'Jenkins?'

'And you're Special Branch too?'

'Not exactly.'

'Let's get in,' Masters said. 'We're wasting time.'

At the lights by Chalk Farm station, Masters said, 'All we want
from your friend is a little information, clarification. We've no interest in her immigration status at this stage.'

Kiley trusted him like he trusted the weather.

Irena lived in two rooms off Inverness Street; actually a single
room let into the roof and divided by a rickety partition. A small
Velux window gave views towards the market and the canal. Kiley
had been there once before, a party for Irena's friends, enough of the
Romanian diaspora to cover every available inch of floor and spread
back down the stairs.

He had hardly let himself in when Anna came bounding after him,
scarf tied round her raven hair, cursing. She was wearing a bustier
beneath a flimsy cotton top, skin tight emerald green trousers and
what, after several visits to Cinderella at an early age, would, to Kiley,
forever be Dandini boots, folded back high above the knee

'Oh, my God!' she exclaimed, seeing him. 'Oh, my God, what are
you doing here?'

'It's all right,' Kiley said. 'Irena gave me a key.'

'I am just here,' Anna said breathlessly, 'for visit. Holiday.'

'Irena said you were working.'

Anna dumped her things on the floor and threw herself into a
chair. 'Work, holiday, what does it matter?'

The headline on the evening paper read *MINISTER'S WIFE'S
MIDNIGHT ASSIGNATION*. What was an hour or so up against
some nice alliteration?

'Anna, there are some people who want to see you.'

'I have visa,' she said. Probably a lie.

'It's not about that.' He paused, the rain persistent on the window. 'You know someone named Alen Markovic?'

Anna jerked forward. 'What's happened to him?'

'You do know him then?'

'Something has happened.'

'Yes.'

'They have killed him.'

'Who?'

She shook her head. Her hair bounced against the tops of her breasts. He thought she might be about to scream or cry, but instead she brought her forearm to her mouth and bit down hard.

'Don't,' he said.

'These people,' Anna said, 'they are police?'

'Yes.'

'Of course they are police.' She stood up and studied the bite mark on her arm. 'You trust them?'

'I don't know.'

'OK, for Alen's sake I will talk to them. But you must be there with me.'

Kiley nodded. 'The café across the street.'

'Portuguese or Italian?'

'Portuguese.'

'You go. Five minutes, I come.'

'Don't duck out on me.'

'Duck out?'

'Never mind.'

Jenkins sat reading a short history of Europeans and the Rest of the World from Antiquity to the Present. Masters held a small espresso cup in his hand and stared at a lithograph of Lisbon on the wall. Kiley ordered coffee for himself and, believing one of those intense little Portuguese custard tarts was never quite enough, bought two; he didn't offer to share them round.

'When you were helping your friend out of her little difficulty,' Masters said, 'you ran across Sali Mejdani. Aldo Fusco, he sometimes likes to call himself.'

'We had a conversation.'

Jenkins chuckled softly, possibly at something he'd just read.

'He brought her into the country, your Anna?'

'Not directly.'

'Of course. From Romania to Albania and then to Italy, Italy to France, Belgium or Holland. Into Britain from somewhere like Zeebrugge. Fifteen or twenty people a day, seven days a week, three hundred plus days of the year. Approximately £5,000 sterling per head. Even after expenses – drivers, escorts, safe houses, backhanders...'

'Plenty of those,' Jenkins said, without looking up.

'...it all adds up to a tidy sum. And the punters, what they don't pay in advance, they pay with interest. For women and boys it's the sex trade, for the rest it's hard labour.'

'Mejdani,' Kiley said, 'why can't you arrest him, close him down?'

'Ah,' said Jenkins.

'For the last couple of years,' Masters said, 'we've been building a case against him. Ourselves, Immigration, Customs and Excise, the National Crime Squad.' He set down his cup at last. 'You know when you were a kid, building sandcastles on the beach, Broadstairs or somewhere, you and your dad. You're putting the finishing touches to this giant, intricate thing, all turrets and towers and windows and doors, and just as you turn over the bucket and tap the last piece into place, one of the bits lower down slides away, and then another, and before you know it you're having to start all over again.'

'Accident?' Kiley said. 'Over ambition?'

Masters sat back. 'I prefer to think the fault lies in the design.'

'Not the workmanship?'

'Get what you pay for, some might say.'

Jenkins laid aside his book. 'Mejdani certainly would.'

'He's bribing people,' Kiley said, 'to look the other way.'

'I didn't say that.'

Kiley looked across at Masters. Masters shrugged.

'Tis but the way of the world, my masters,' Jenkins said.

'Not Chandler again?'

'A little earlier.'

They all looked round as Anna stepped through the door. She had changed into black jeans and a black roll neck sweater, an unbuttoned beige topcoat round her shoulders. Some but not all of the make-up had been wiped from her face. She asked at the counter for a Coke with lemon and ice.

Kiley made the introductions while she lit a cigarette.

'Alen,' she said, 'what happened to him?'

Masters showed her the photograph.

For a long moment, she closed her eyes.

'You're not really surprised,' Masters said.

'I don't understand.'

'You thought he might get into difficulties,' Kiley said. 'You gave him my card.'

'Yes, I thought... Alen, he was someone important in my country, high up in trade union...'

'We used to have those,' Jenkins said, as much to himself as anyone.

'...there was disagreement, he had to leave. Rights of workers, something. And here, I don't know, I think it was the same. Already, he told me, the people he work for, they warn him, shut your mouth. Keep your mouth shut. I think he had made threat to go to authorities. The police.'

'You think that's why he was killed.'

'Of course.'

Masters glanced at Jenkins, who gave a barely discernible nod. 'We have a number of names,' he said, 'names and places. We'd like to run them past you and for you to tell us any that you recognise.'

Anna held smoke down in her lungs. What was she, Kiley wondered? All of twenty? Twenty-one? She'd paid to risk her life travelling to England not once, but twice. Paid dearly. And why? Because the strip clubs and massage parlours of London and Wolverhampton were better than the auto routes in and out of Bucharest? As an official asylum seeker, she could claim thirty quid a week, ten in cash, the rest in vouchers. But she was not official. She did what she could.

She said, 'OK. If I can.'

'Wait,' Kiley said. 'If she helps you, you have to help her. Make it possible for her to stay, officially.'

'I don't know if we can do that,' Masters said.

'Of course we fucking can,' Jenkins said.

Anna lit a fresh cigarette from the butt of the first and asked for another Coke.

Kiley caught the overground to Highbury and Islington. In an Upper Street window a face he recognised stared out from a dozen TVs; the same face was in close up on the small Sony Kate kept at the foot of the bed.

'Kramer seems to be getting a lot of exposure,' Kiley said.

'The wrong kind.'

Dogmatic, didactic, distinguished by a full beard and sweep of jet black hair, Michael Kramer was an investigative journalist with strong anti-capitalist, anti-American left wing leanings and a surprisingly high profile. Kiley had always found him too self-righteous by half, even if, much of the time, what he said made some kind of sense.

Kate turned up the volume as the *Newsnight* cameras switched to Jeremy Paxman behind an impressive looking desk. '...if it really is such a small and insignificant point, Mr Kramer, then why not answer my question and move on?'

She flicked the sound back down.

'What was the question?' Kiley asked.

'Was he entertaining Helen Forester in his flat on the night she was attacked?'

'And was he?'

'He won't say.'

'Which means he was.'

'Probably.'

Sitting, propped up against pillows, Kate was wearing the faded Silver Moon T-shirt she sometimes used as night wear and nothing else. Kiley rested his hand above her knee.

'They were at Cambridge together,' Kate said. 'Maybe they had a thing back then and maybe they didn't.'

'Twenty five years ago,' Kiley said. 'More.'

Kate turned in a little against his hand. 'Kramer's been making this programme for Channel 4. Illegal workers, gangmasters, people trafficking. Pretty explosive by all accounts.'

'Not the best of times for the wife of a Home Office minister to be sharing his bed.'

'Needs must,' Kate said. 'From time to time.'

Helen Forester denied and denied and finally admitted that she had, indeed, had dinner with Michael Kramer on the night in question, had enjoyed possibly a glass of wine too many, and gone for a stroll to clear her head before returning home.

Kramer's programme was moved to a prime time slot, where it attracted close on seven million viewers, not bad for a polemical documentary on a minority channel. Standing amidst the potato fields of East Anglia, Kramer pontificated about the farming industry's increasing dependence on illegal foreign labour, comparing it to the slave trade of earlier centuries, with gangmasters as the new overseers and Eastern Europeans the new Negroes; from the lobby of a hotel in Bayswater he talked about the dependence of the hotel and catering trades on migrants from Somalia and south-east Asia; and at the port of Dover he made allegations of corruption and bribery running through customs and immigration and penetrating right up the highest levels of the police.

'That's the thing about Kramer,' Masters said, watching a video of the programme in Jenkins' office high above the Thames. 'He always has to go that little bit too far.'

Two days earlier, with the assistance of officers from the Cambridgeshire force, they had arrested two of Alen Markovic's fellow field workers for his murder. The foreman, they claimed, had given them no choice: get rid of him or get sent back. They had clubbed him to death with a spade and a hoe.

In one of his last actions as a minister before being shuffled on to the back benches, Hugo Forester announced a further toughening of the laws governing entry into the country and the employment of those who have gained access without proper documentation. 'The present system,' he told the House, 'in its efforts to provide refuge and succour to those in genuine need, is unfortunately still too open to exploitation by unscrupulous individuals and criminal gangs. But the House should be assured that the introduction of identity cards to be announced in the Queen's speech will render it virtually impossible for the employment of illegal workers to continue.'

Co-ordinated raids by the police on safe houses and farms in Kings Lynn and Wisbech resulted in twenty-seven arrests. Two middle-ranking officers in the Immigration Service tendered their resignations and a detective chief inspector stationed at Folkestone retired from duty on medical grounds. A warrant was issued for Sali Mejdani's arrest on twenty seven separate charges of smuggling illegal immigrants into Britain. Mejdani, travelling under the name of Aldo Fusco, had flown from Heathrow to Amsterdam on the previous morning, and from there to Tirana where he seemed, temporarily, to have disappeared.

Anna was duly given a student visa and enrolled in a course in leisure and travel at the University of North London.

Hugo and Helen Forester announced a trial separation.

Kiley, feeling pleased with himself and for very little reason, volunteered to treat Kate to one hundred and thirty-eight minutes of *Mystic River* with supper afterwards at Café Pasta. Kate thought she could skip the movie.

When she arrived, Kiley was already seated at a side table, Irena bending slightly towards him, the pair in conversation.

'Ordered the wine yet, Jack?' Kate said, slipping off her coat and handing it to Irena. Irena blushed and backed away. 'Oh, and bring us a bottle of the Montepulciano d'Abruzzo, will you? Thanks very much.'

'She was telling me about Anna,' Kiley said.

'How was the film?' Kate asked.

'Good. Pretty good.'

Irena brought the wine and asked Kate if she would like to taste it, which she did.

'She's lovely, isn't she?' Kate said as Irena walked away.

'Who?'

'Irena.'

'Is she?'

# A Shameful Eating

## Reginald Hill

*Like Michael Gilbert, Reginald Hill has received the highest award that can be made to a British crime writer, the CWA Cartier Diamond Dagger, to mark an outstanding career of crime writing. Whether or not writing about Dalziel and Pascoe, Hill always guarantees entertainment and his non-series work is as impressive as the books about Mid-Yorkshire's finest. This macabre story, first published in an anthology celebrating the Diamond Jubilee of the late lamented Collins Crime Club, is relatively little known but a splendid example of historical crime fiction.*

A shameful eating is better than a shameful leaving, my dear old gramma used to say as she urged me into a second circuit of her groaning table. And I never saw any need to disagree with her, not until the start of my third week in that wallowing lifeboat.

The *Needle's Eye* had gone down fourteen days earlier, split apart by a squall so sudden that only the three of us on deck at the time had any hope of surviving. The youngest was Perkin Curtis, a fresh-faced lad on his very first voyage, with a fine tenor voice whose rendition of *A poore soule sate sighing by a sicamore tree* brought tears to the rheumy eyes of those same grizzled tars who lusted after his pink and white flesh. Three of them would have had him across the long cannon on the poop deck during the dog watch one night if I hadn't come up for a breath of air from the afterhold which I was using as a sickroom during an outbreak of Yellow Jack. I swear the boy was so innocent that he thought it no more than a bit of boisterous fun. I told him to pull his britches up, ordered two of the men below with a promise that they'd be up for captain's punishment in the morning, and kept their ringleader beside me. This was Josh Gall, the bosun's mate, a small plump man whose surface of placid amiability had scarce been touched by half a century of evil habits and riotous behaviour. But he was a fine seaman, none better for anticipating and dealing with a nautical emergency.

I should have remembered this as I savaged him with my tongue, promising him the extremities of the law for his assault on young Curtis. But I took no notice of a sudden change in his expression from abject contrition to active alarm, save to congratulate myself on having pierced his carapace with my threats.

'Sir,' he tried to interrupt, 'will you listen—'

'Too late for excuses now, Gall,' I shouted him down. 'This time it's the lash for you!'

Alas, it wasn't his excuses he wanted me to listen to, but that change in the wind's note which gave him warning of the fury that was almost upon us.

'For God's sake, bring her round!' he yelled suddenly, trying to spring by me towards the wheelhouse. Still deafened by my own rage, I caught his arm and held him fast.

Then in a trice the wind shifted from west to south, from light airs to a near-tornado, which hit us like a man-o'-war's broadside. The *Needle's Eye* went over till her masts lay parallel with the sea, then a wave like a giant's fist struck her amidships, and the poor old tub folded in two and turned submarine.

Somehow a lifeboat was ripped free, and somehow Josh Gall with his instinct for being in the right place at the right time came up alongside it and scrambled in. I surfaced half a furlong away and saw him quite clearly, for despite the fury of the wind there was not a cloud to be seen in the huge starry sky. I shouted, then went under again, so deep that I saw as in a dream the bow section of the ship with its figurehead of a full-breasted mermaid drifting downward to its eternal rest. Perhaps I did dream that I could see desperate hands clawing at the foc's'le ports, but the image gave me strength to kick upwards one last time, and when I broke the surface I saw the lifeboat bobbing past within a couple of feet. Gall lay sprawling over the gunwale. His eyes met mine. I called for help but he regarded me indifferently and made no move, and the boat would next moment have been beyond my reach had there not been a line trailing behind. This I seized and with my last strength hauled myself along it till I could grasp the stern and drag myself aboard.

I had no strength or breath to express my contempt for Gall, but lay there, giving God what proved premature thanks for my deliverance. Then I became aware Gall was standing upright in that rocking cockleshell with a sailor's ease, pointing and shouting.

'Over there,' he cried. 'Do you not see?'

I forced my head up and looked. About fifty yards away in the surging sea I glimpsed a wooden cask with a man clinging to it by one arm.

'Quick!' urged Gall. 'I can't manage on my lone!'

He was trying to paddle towards his shipmate, using a length of wood ripped from the shattered thwarts. I pulled free another piece and taking my place on the opposite side of the boat, joined my efforts to his. I confess I felt a little shame at my recent condemnation of Gall for his apparent failure to offer assistance to me. And my shame grew when I saw that it was no special crony of the man's we were trying to rescue, but young Perkin Curtis.

We would probably not have reached him had the storm not abated as suddenly as it came and the ocean rapidly deflated from Pennine peaks to Lincolnshire levels. But as we drew alongside Curtis, my new respect for Gall died like the wind.

He reached out, seized the boy's arm, prised it loose from the cask – then thrust the unhappy youth down into the sea!

For a second I believed he had merely lost his grip. Then I realised that what Gall was concerned to rescue was not the boy, but the cask he was clinging to!

'For God's sake, man!' I cried. 'Will you let a fellow human perish?'

'Without water, we all perish,' he snarled. 'Give us a hand to get this aboard.'

There was no point in cutting off my nose to spite my face, so I helped him drag the cask over the gunwale. Then as I stared sadly into the ocean which I thought had closed over the unfortunate youth for ever, to my joy and relief I saw Curtis's head break the surface only an arm's length away. He was clearly *in extremis,* perhaps even past relief, but I reached out my hand and grasped his shock of corn-blond hair.

'Help me!' I screamed at Gall, who regarded me with a sneering indifference for a moment. Then perhaps his cunning mind took into consideration that if we survived, my evidence to an Enquiry might yet do him some harm, and he leaned out to take Curtis by the collar and between us we pulled him aboard. He collapsed in a heap in the bow, looking for all the world like a dead man, but I have had plenty of experience of dealing with men snatched from the deep and knew what to do. Rolling him on his back, I knelt beside him and pressed hard against his stomach. A great gush of water issued from his mouth but he did not start to breathe, so I used a technique I had learnt from the savages of the Carolinas and, putting my mouth to his, filled his lungs with air from my own, then expelled it by pressure to his chest. This I repeated three or four times till of a sudden he retched, bringing up more water, and I turned him on his side, seeing that he could now breathe on his own.

I looked up to catch Gall's twisted smile.

'It's a strange world, Mr Teasdale,' he said. 'Less than thirty minutes ago you were threatening to have the skin off my back for little more than what you've just been doing.'

'You're a foul creature, Gall,' I said contemptuously. 'You sit there sneering when you should be giving gratitude to God for sparing this boy's life.'

'Oh, I'm grateful enough, Mr Teasdale, sir,' he said. 'God moves in mysterious ways, and the lad is certainly well fleshed.'

I thought his mind was simply dwelling on its usual vile carnal obsession, but perhaps already his undoubted seaman's nous was anticipating the trials ahead and providing his own unthinkable answer to them.

Now he turned his attention from me to the cask. The way it had floated told that it could be no more than half full but if that half were water, then it was indeed a priceless discovery. Gall gently twisted the spigot till a thick liquid started to ooze out. He let it touch his fingers, sniffed, tasted, and laughed his grating laugh.

'God's good to patriots, it seems,' he said. 'We can drink the King's health afore we light our pipes tonight. This here's our late lamented skipper's best rum!'

I reached over and tasted. He was right. It was one of several casks which Captain Danby had insisted on taking on board in Jamaica despite my advice that we would do better to cram our limited storage space with fresh fruit and vegetables.

'At least we can wet our whistle and die merry,' said Gall.

'Die you will if you take too much of this, Gall,' I said sternly. 'Alcohol dries up the blood and redoubles a man's thirst. But yet it is a good restorative and may help this poor boy.'

So saying, I caught half a gill in the palm of my hand and gently poured it into Curtis's mouth. It set him coughing and spluttering once more, but when the fit was passed, he had some colour in his cheeks and was able to struggle upright. He looked all around him. The sea was smooth as his own unrazored cheeks and the moon lacquered it with light so that he could see for miles in all directions. Save for a few spars from the wrecked ship, we were the only thing to trouble that polished surface. I think it was only now that his desperate plight struck him, for the tinge of colour the rum had restored drained from his cheeks once more and he cried, 'Mr Teasdale, where are the others? Where is the *Needle's Eye?*'

'Sunk, lad,' I said. 'And all your shipmates with it, God rest their souls. But do not despair. The Almighty has seen fit in His infinite mercy to spare us the full measure of His wrath, and I cannot believe that He has preserved us from the deep but to watch us perish in plain air.'

My words of comfort had but little effect, I fear. Young Curtis collapsed to the bottom of the boat once more, sobbing and howling, and his eyes gushed forth as much water as his belly had after his submersion.

Gall meanwhile had settled himself comfortably against the tiller on the one unshattered thwart in the stern. I glared at him angrily. As the one surviving officer of the *Needle's Eye,* it was time to assert my authority.

'Gall,' I said coldly, 'will you be good enough to move? It is the captain's place, I believe, to be at the helm.'

For a second I thought he would defy me, then he grinned and said, 'Aye, aye, *Cap'n* Teasdale, sir,' and shifted down the boat.

I took his place on the stern thwart and grasped the tiller. It moved in my hand like a twig on a sapling, I peered over the stern and saw that the rod linking tiller and rudder had shattered.

'Shouldn't worry about that, Cap'n,' said Gall. 'No great loss not being able to steer when we've only the currents to carry us.'

He was right. There were no oars, no mast, no sail.

'We can paddle, with the broken thwarts,' I said with a show of authority. 'Come, best make a start before the sun comes up and the heat saps our strength.'

Gall grinned again, picked up the length of broken wood and said, 'Aye, aye, Cap'n Teasdale. What's your course, Cap'n?'

I saw his game. He knew well that, as ship's doctor, my expertise lay in charting the course of men's ailments, not the ways of the sea. But with the stars showing in their full refulgence, I at least had no problem in finding directions out.

'West,' I said, pointing. 'We will head west.'

'Back to the Americas?' he said. 'Well, 'tis certainly a large target, sir, and one that would be hard to miss. Trouble is in these waters, west's the direction the prevailing winds came from and also the great currents, and while I dare say two men paddling hard might hold their own for a while, yet I do not see how they could hope to make any progress.'

'You would have us go east, then?' I asked, swallowing my pride.

'East? Now certainly that would mean we had wind and water in our favour, but betwixt us and Africa there is nothing but the Azores, and they are such a tiny target I doubt that we could hit it even if our strength held out that long.'

'So what do you suggest, Mr Gall?' I demanded. 'Bob around here, doing nothing?'

'What point in doing anything else?' he asked. 'We are as like to meet with a ship here as anywhere else. We are close to the main lanes to and from the Indies. Here let us rest, and the Lord have mercy on our souls.'

And so our ordeal began. We pooled our resources. They were poor enough in all faith. All I could supply was a tinderbox which lived up to its claim to be waterproof, a clay pipe broken in three pieces, a pouch of sodden tobacco and, most useless of all, a few silver guineas in a wash-leather purse I kept hung round my neck. Gall had even less to offer: a piece of twine about four feet in length and a broad-bladed knife such as butchers use for the dressing of meat. Young Curtis's pockets provided the best trove. Clearly he had a boy's endless appetite and out came two apples, a block of treacle toffee, a wedge of cheese, and a hunk of bread turned by its immersion in the sea into a grey and glutinous putty which nevertheless I spread out to dry, foreseeing that a time would soon come when we would be ready to eat anything.

These, with the cask of rum, were our provisions. I took charge of the rum, doling it out in the smallest of measures, fearful of the effect it could have on our weakened frames and also eager to save some in case we had to signal a distant ship. I discovered that the strong fumes given off by the heavy treacly liquor were readily ignitable by the flint from my tinderbox, and though fire is a dangerous companion on a small boat, yet it would be worth the risk if it meant a chance of rescue.

Water we had none, but God soon sent the mixed blessing of rain, which slaked our thirst while drenching our skins again, for we had no means of shelter either from clouds or the sun.

Despite my utmost parsimony, our small store of rations did not last beyond a week. Some of the cheese we sacrificed on a hook made from a shoe buckle tied to the end of Gall's piece of twine, in an effort to catch fish, but without luck. Gall slashed wildly with his knife at the occasional seabird which curiosity brought near our craft and though he once disturbed a feather, he got no closer.

We passed the second week chewing salty tobacco, sipping minute quantities of rum, and moistening our lips with rainwater. I think that I possibly suffered the most. The other two were well fleshed but I was ever lean and bony, and while they fed on their own fat, I became skeletal. But it was young Curtis who suffered the worst in his morale. Despite all my efforts at comfort, he would weep for hours on end, raving of his mother and his sisters, till finally he had no strength to weep or talk, and would not even have roused himself for his ration of water and rum had I not forced it through his flaked and bloodless lips.

'It's a waste,' said Gall one day as he watched me.

'A waste,' I said. 'Why? Do you think if you took his share it would prolong your miserable life by more than a miserable minute?'

'No, I meant it's a waste that we starve when there is victuals aplenty before us,' said Gall.

It took me a long moment to get his meaning and when I did, I looked at him aghast.

'What new depth of foulness is this?' I cried in disbelief.

'Don't preach at me, you poxy quack,' he snarled. 'The lad's good as dead. Why strive to keep him alive just so that we can all die together? Let's make an end of him now and save ourselves. You're a surgeon, you should know best where the most nutrition lies in human meat!'

He had his knife in his hand and on his face was a look of madness which warned me I must be careful how I interfered.

I said, 'Let me have the knife, Gall. Come, you said I was the surgeon and thus best fitted to do the carving. The knife, if you please.'

He looked at me doubtingly, then slowly he handed over that dreadful weapon. I drove it into the thwart beside me.

'What? Do you betray me then? Will you not do it?' he cried.

'I am a doctor, Gall,' I answered. 'I have taken vows to preserve life, not to destroy it.'

'That's all I'm suggesting we do,' he answered with the cunning logic of insanity. 'Save two lives at the expense of one. Like you said to Curtis at the start, God won't have saved us from drowning at the bottom of the ocean just so's we can starve on top of it!'

'No,' I cried. 'Thou shalt not kill! God is just testing us. He will provide. He will show us another way.'

'Then He'd better show it quick, Cap'n Teasdale,' mocked that vile and villainous creature. 'Else, if He waits another few hours, He'll be able to tell us what we ought to have done face to face!'

I think my faith in a loving God died at that moment. I turned the spigot on the rum cask and filled the wooden cup which Gall had roughly fashioned from a piece of the useless tiller. When I handed it to him he looked at me speculatively, then downed the lot. I refilled the cup and poured the liquor down the unresisting Curtis's throat. Then I passed another brimming measure to Gall.

'Mr Teasdale, sir,' he said. 'I see you're a true gent after all. If a man must die, then let him die merry. Here's health.'

He downed the rum in a single draught. In his weakened state his old capacity for hard drinking was of no avail and I could already see the fiery liquor taking effect, while after a single draught the boy was almost unconscious. I filled the cup again.

We were picked up ten days later by a Portuguese brigantine hauling copra from the Leeward Islands. She had sprung a seam and was making heavy weather to the Azores, and our new conditions were but little improvement on those we endured in that open boat. Yet the Promethean spark at the heart's core is most obstinate against extinction, and my two companions were carried ashore at Ponta Delgada on San Miguel with breath enough still to mist an eyeglass. We were taken to the town's infirmary, run by Father Boniface, a Catholic priest more skilled at steering his patients to the next world than keeping them in this. He expressed great amazement at our survival, especially as we were all three Protestant, but his admiration for me as a fellow doctor was unstinted.

'Gangrene, you say?'

'Aye, gangrene,' I replied indifferently.

'And with a carving knife?'

'Aye, a carving knife.'

'And how did you cauterise the arteries?' he asked eagerly.

'With the lees from a keg of rum which I then fired with my tinderbox,' I said wearily. 'Enough of these questions. They are in your care now, Father. My responsibility for them is done.'

'*Non nobis, Domine,*' he proclaimed. 'Not unto us, my friend. They are in God's care and always have been, for truly His hand must have guided thine.'

'Your care, God's care, take the credit who will,' I cried wildly. 'Only they are out of my care. And if they now die, as seems most likely, it cannot lie at my door!'

He put my outburst down to a hysterical fever and mixed me a filthy potion which I poured down the jakes after he had gone. It did not seem possible that my companions who had no such strength to resist could long survive such divine ministrations.

I slept well that night and felt stronger in the morn, and when I learnt that the brig which had brought us here was now repaired and ready to resume its voyage to Lisbon, I announced that I purposed to sail with her. Some money from the purse I wore about my neck I gave to the good Father.

Perhaps it was the clink of the coins which penetrated Gall's ears, for he opened his eyes and spoke the first words he had uttered since our arrival.

'What? Are you leaving, Mr Teasdale? Nay, you are right not to delay on our account. God speed. And rest assured young Curtis and I will never forget what you have done for us.'

His voice was low but every word fell on my ears like a bell-note. Then he closed his eyes once more.

I made for the door, pausing only to shake hands with Boniface.

'You have two friends forever here, I think,' he said, smiling. 'Let us pray they survive.

'I know you will do your best for them, Father,' I said. 'Be not sparing of your prayers. Nor your potions either.'

And with that I hastened down to the harbour where the brigantine was already hoisting her sails to catch the freshening western breeze.

I gave up the sea after that and went back north to my native Derbyshire, where I set up practice in the wild country of the Peak. Here distances were long, weather was wild, and payment was as like to be in eggs and vegetables as coin of the realm. Yet it was a comfort to me even as I laboured through the wildest storm to taste no tang of salt in the rain, and to know that the nearest sea was three days' hard riding to east or west. My patients apart, I saw little company for I proved far too abstemious for our hard-drinking, hard-eating, hard-hunting squire, and far too contentious for our prating parson. Once a week I would ride the seven miles to the Black Tor Inn which stood high on an edge overlooking the road from Buxton to Sheffield and learn what news the mail coach had brought in. Occasionally there might be some respectable company to talk to, but usually I made do with John Farley, the landlord, swapping local gossip over a pint of his sour ale. Then, after a plain repast of bread and cheese, with perhaps a bowl of vegetable broth if the weather were chill, I would take my leave. At my first coming to those parts, the landlord had tried to press me to a joint of meat or a bowlful of beef stew, convinced as such men are that flesh is necessary to human health. But my continual refusal, and I dare say my continual survival, persuaded him in the end that a man might live on cheese and vegetables alone, though he begged me not to recommend such a diet to my patients and his customers.

'There's little profit to be made in such plain fare,' he confided. 'For when a man can see exactly what he is eating, he can add up the cost of the parts and complain bitterly if he thinks a poor innkeeper is seeking too much profit. But once let there be meat in it and gravy and spices and herbs, though it be but in truth three parts vegetable water, then is he more willing to pay what I ask without quarrel!'

He spoke thus familiarly with me only after long acquaintance, and also because he was convinced by my frugal method of life that I lived up to the old reputation of my profession and loved gold as much as he did.

I smiled and thereafter joined him in long plaints about the rising cost of things and the parsimony of our shared customers, and on such plain fare for the stomach and for the mind, I existed quite happily for near on ten years.

*Happily*, I say. Well, it is a question of degree; and though I ofttimes felt that I would be as well out of this world as in it, yet it is a brave surgeon who can practise on himself, and an unbroken pattern of life can come to be pleasant though no single part of it has much power to please.

So my life passed till this bleak November day. It was a wild dark morning with the promise of winter's first snow in the blast and I almost abandoned my customary ride to the Black Tor. Yet, perhaps because I knew such a break in the pattern of my existence would make me feel unsettled, I saddled my patient old mare and set out. The stage had been and gone when I reached the inn. Some passengers had alighted, I was told, but they were resting after their long bone-shaking ride and had left orders not to be disturbed till their dinner was ready, so I went and sat alone in the upstairs parlour till John Farley came to join me.

'It's blowing up a real hurricane out there,' he pronounced. 'Feel how it makes the old timbers shake. You'd almost think we were out at sea.'

I smiled thinly, thinking how little he knew of what it really felt like to be in a storm in the Atlantic's bubbling cauldron. But he was right about the rising wind for I could hear it singing in the chimney and round the shutters, and from time to time it did indeed seem as if the boards beneath my feet vibrated like a ship's deck.

'It will be good for trade, John,' I joked. 'Those who are here will not be able to leave for home.'

'Nay,' he said gloomily. 'You mean those who are at home will not set out to come here.'

So we talked of nothing in particular, and smoked a pipe, and supped our ale, till there came a knock at the door, or rather a thud low down, as if someone had kicked it.

'Who's there?' called Farley.

'Doctor's dinner,' came back a voice I recognised as belonging to Willie Bell, a slow-witted youth who worked in the kitchen.

'Well, fetch it in, you great lubbock!'

'Can't open the door, maister,' replied Willie.

With an exasperated groan, Farley rose and pulled the door open.

It was immediately apparent why Willie could not turn the handle himself.

Instead of the usual small tray with a loaf and a wedge of cheese, he was carrying a huge pewter salver with a great domed lid.

He staggered forward and deposited it on the table in front of me, then waved his hands in the air, saying, ''Tis hot.'

'Hot? What's hot?' cried Farley. 'What's this you've brought, you idiot?'

And so saying, he snatched the lid off the salver.

A great cloud of aromatic steam arose, obscuring what lay there for a moment. Then as the morning mist is sucked up the fellside by the reddening sun, it cleared to reveal two mountainous joints of roast meat, one a leg of pork, the other a shoulder of mutton.

My first thought was that this must be some monstrous joke of mine host's, and I leapt to my feet, ready to vent my indignation upon him. Then I looked into his face and saw that his amazement was as real as mine.

'Numbskull!' he yelled, raising his fist threateningly above the potboy's head. 'What stupidity is this? Have you not been working here long enough to know what manner of vittles his honour prefers?'

Willie cringed away, crying, 'Aye, maister, but the missus told me as he wanted this here today.'

'The missus?' Farley looked at me with wild surmise. 'Doctor, I'm sorry. Clearly this fool has got more muddled than he usually is, if that's possible. We'll have this sorted in a trice. Dora!'

His bellow shook the room almost as much as the storm without, which was increasing in intensity with each passing minute.

A few moments later Mrs Farley – a stout good-natured woman whose natural generosity when it came to loading plates brought her into frequent conflict with her husband – appeared in the doorway.

'This idiot says you gave him this as the Doctor's dinner,' said Farley, pointing at the steaming salver.

'That's right,' said his wife. 'Is something wrong wi' it?'

'Wrong? A leg of pork and a shoulder of mutton, and you ask if something's wrong?' cried Farley. 'When did you know Dr Teasdale let a morsel of meat pass his lips? What are you thinking of, woman?'

'I'll thank you not to *woman* me,' said his wife with spirit. 'It was the Doctor's friends as told me to send it up.'

A blast like a giant's hand struck the building so that it seemed that at the very least it must tear the chimneys off, and for about half a minute speech was impossible. Then the wind subsided to a steady roar, and I moistened my lips with beer and asked faintly, 'What friends, Mrs Farley?'

'The two gentlemen who got off the coach,' she replied. 'They

ordered a roast leg and a roast shoulder as soon as they arrived and
naturally I thought it was for them, though a lot it seemed for just the
two of them. But when they came down just now they said, no, it
weren't for them, it was for their friend, Dr Teasdale, and would I
send it straight up? I hope I didn't do wrong.'

Farley was looking at me. What he saw in my face must have
assured him that these men were no friends of mine, for he said,
'Right, wife. Let's you and I have a talk to these two gentlemen who
make themselves so pleasant with decent folk.'

'Oh, it's too late for that,' said his wife. 'They've gone.'

'Gone?' said Farley, looking aghast at the loaded salver. 'Did they
pay their reckoning?'

'Oh aye. They paid in full. For their room, the food, and the other
things they bought. I asked 'em if they didn't want a word with the
Doctor, and they said no, they'd likely see him at home later.'

'Well, this beats cockfighting,' said Farley with undisguisable relief
at learning that this jape was not going to cost him money. 'What do
you make of it, Doctor?'

'Mrs Farley,' I said with difficulty. 'What did they look like, these
two men?'

'Oh, if it's a description you want for the constable, I'd know 'em
again anywhere,' she cried. 'They were the oddest pair. Him, the older
one who did the talking, he had one of them peg-legs and walked with
a crutch. And the other, the younger one, who never opened his
mouth, poor lad, he had his sleeve pinned across his chest like he had
no arm to go in it.'

I could speak no further but Farley's curiosity was bubbling over.

'You said they bought some other things, wife. What manner of
things did they buy to carry out into this terrible storm with them?'

'The oddest set of things you can imagine,' she replied, shaking her
head in puzzlement. 'But they did not carry them off with them. No,
they said they was sure the Doctor, understanding their disabilities,
would oblige them by fetching them along hisself. And they left them
on the kitchen table.'

'Left *what*, for God's sake, woman?' cried Farley in desperation.

But I did not stay for her answer.

Rudely thrusting her aside, I clattered down the narrow stairway to the kitchen, and flung open the door.

There on the great oak table, in a miasma of smoke and steam and the reek of roasting meat, stood a cask of rum; a tinderbox; a carving knife.

# Vanishing of Velma

## Edward D Hoch

*A story about a girl who vanishes from the top of a ferris wheel seemed to me to be a natural for* Crime on the Move. *'The Vanishing of Velma' is a classic tale featuring one of Edward D Hoch's most popular characters, Captain Leopold. Ed Hoch has been a loyal supporter of the CWA anthology and, when we met at an international crime writers' reception in Nevada last autumn, he immediately agreed to my request to reprint the story. As he has done on so many other occasions, he provides an enjoyable spin on the idea of the 'impossible' crime – an appealing subgenre which has been given a new lease of life by the popularity of the BBC television series* Jonathan Creek.

Remember Stella Gaze?' Sergeant Fletcher asked, coming into Captain Leopold's office with the morning coffee.

'Stella Gaze? How could I forget her?' It had been one of Leopold's oddest cases, some three years back, involving a middle-aged woman who'd committed suicide after having been accused of practising witchcraft. He thought of Stella Gaze often, wondering what he could have done to handle things differently. 'What about her?' he asked Fletcher.

The sergeant slipped into his favourite chair opposite Leopold's desk and carefully worked the plastic top off his cup of coffee. 'Well, you remember that her house was directly adjacent to Sportland Amusement Park – in fact, when they couldn't buy her land they built the ferris wheel right next to the house, with only a wire fence separating them.'

'I remember,' Leopold said. Stella Gaze – no witch, certainly – but only a neurotic woman whom no one understood. She'd tried suicide before, and in the end had been successful.

'Well, listen to this! Last night about ten o'clock, a girl vanished from the top of that same ferris wheel! What do you think the newspapers will do with that when they get it?'

'Vanished?' Leopold scratched his head. 'How could she vanish from the top of a ferris wheel?'

'She couldn't, but she did. It wasn't reported to the police till later – too late for the morning editions, but the papers will be on to it any minute.'

As if in answer to Fletcher's prediction, the telephone buzzed, but it was not a curious newsman. It was Leopold's direct superior, the chief of detectives. 'Captain, I hate to ask you this, because it doesn't involve a homicide not yet, anyway. But you worked on the Stella Gaze case out at Sportland – three years back, didn't you?'

'That's right,' Leopold answered with a sigh, already sure of what was coming.

'We've got a disappearance out there. A girl missing from the ferris wheel. I know you're not working on anything right now, and I thought you might help us out by handling the case with Sergeant Fletcher. The papers are already trying to tie it in somewhat with the Gaze thing, and you'll know what to tell them.'

'I always know what to tell them,' Leopold said. 'What's the girl's name? '

'Velma Kelty. She was there with a boyfriend, and he's pretty shook about it.'

'I'll talk to him,' Leopold said. 'Any special reason for your interest?' He'd known the chief of detectives long enough to ask.

'Not really. The boy is Tom Williams, the councilman's son.'

'And?'

A long sigh over the phone. 'It might turn out to be sort of messy, Captain, if anything's happened to her. She's only fifteen years old.'

So Leopold drove out to visit Tom Williams at his home. He'd never met the boy, and knew his father only slightly, in the vague manner that detectives knew councilmen. The house was large and expensive, with a gently curving driveway and a swimming pool barely visible in the back area.

'You must be the police,' the boy said, answering the door himself. 'Come in.'

'Captain Leopold. You're Tom Williams?'

'That's right, sir,' He was about twenty, with sandy hair cropped short and a lanky look that was typical of college boys these days. 'Have they found her yet?'

'No, I guess not. Suppose you tell me about it.' Leopold had followed him on to a rear terrace that overlooked the pool. It was empty now, with only a rubber animal of some sort floating near the far corner.

'She went up in the ferris wheel and she didn't come down,' the young man said simply. 'That's all there is to it.'

'Not quite all,' Leopold corrected. 'Why don't you start at the beginning. How old are you, Tom?'

The young man hesitated, running a nervous hand through his sandy close-cropped hair. 'I'll be twenty-one in two weeks. What's that got to do with anything?'

'I understand Velma Kelty is only fifteen. I was just wondering how you two happened to get together, that's all.'

'I met her through my kid sister,' he mumbled. 'The thing wasn't really a date. I just took her to Sportland, that's all.'

'How many times had you been out with her this summer?'

He shrugged. 'Two or three. I took her to a movie, a ball game. Anything wrong with that?'

'Nothing,' Leopold said. 'Now suppose you tell it like it was, in detail this time.'

He sighed and settled a bit deeper into the canvas deck chair. 'I took her out for a pizza earlier, and she suggested we play some miniature golf. Sportland was the closest place, so we went there. I parked my car in the lot by the golf course and driving range, but when we'd finished she suggested going on some of the rides. We went on a couple, but the rides right after the pizza upset my stomach a bit. When she suggested the ferris wheel I told her I'd watch.'

'And you did watch?'

'Sure. I paid for her ticket and watched her get into one of those little wire cages they have. It was dark by that time, around ten o'clock. You know how they light the wheel at night?'

'I haven't seen it in a few years,' Leopold admitted.

'Well, they have coloured neon running out on the spokes of the wheel. It looks great from a distance, but close up it's a little over-whelming. Anyway, I didn't remember exactly which of the coloured cages she was in, and by the time it had reached the top of the wheel, I'd lost it in the lights.'

'Was she alone in her cage?'

'Yeah. The guy tried to get me in at the last minute, but my stomach wasn't up to it. The wheel was almost empty by that time.'

'What happened then?'

'Well, I waited for her to come down, and she didn't.'

'Didn't?'

'That's right. I watched each cage being unloaded. She wasn't in any of them. After a while I got sorta frantic and had the operator empty them all out. But she wasn't in any of them.'

'Who did get out while you were standing there?'

'Let's see... the ones I remember were a father and two little kids, a fellow and girl who'd been necking – they were right ahead of us in line – and a couple of college girls who seemed to be alone. I suppose there were others, but I don't remember them.'

'Could she have gotten off on the other side of the wheel?'

'No. I was watching each car when it was unloaded. I was inter-ested in the way the guy was doing it giving the good-looking girls a quick feel as he helped them to the ground.'

'Why did you wait a couple of hours before calling the police?'

'I didn't believe my eyes, that's why! She couldn't have just vanished like that, not while I was watching. The guy operating it told me I was nuts.'

'Didn't he remember her?'

'No.'

'Even though he wanted you to join her?'

'He said he was busy. He couldn't remember everybody.'

Leopold glanced at the official report of the patrolman who'd been summoned. 'That would be Rudy Magee?'

'I guess that's his name. Anyway, he dismissed the whole thing, and I guess for a minute I just thought I was cracking up. I walked around for a half hour, just looking for her, and then went back to the car and waited. When she didn't come, I walked over to the ferris wheel again and told the guy Magee I was going to call the police.'

'I see,' Leopold said, but he didn't really see very much.

'So I called them. That's it.

Leopold lit a cigarette. 'Was she pregnant, Tom?'

'*What?*'

'You understand it's my job to ask all the questions, and that's one of them. You wouldn't be the first boy who wanted a fifteen-year-old pregnant girlfriend to disappear.'

'I never touched her. I told you she was a friend of my sister's.'

'All right.' He stood up. 'Is your sister around now?' he persisted.

'She's out.'

'For how long?'

He shrugged. 'Who knows? She's sorta loose.'

'I'll be back,' Leopold told him. 'What's your sister's name?'

'Cindy. They call her Cin.'

'Who does?'

'Her crowd.'

'Is she fifteen, too?'

'Sixteen.'

Leopold nodded. As he walked around the side of the house, he looked a bit longingly at the swimming pool. The day was warming up, and a dip in the clear blue water would have felt good.

He got back in the car and drove out to Sportland.

Sportland was still big, but it had perhaps retreated a little into itself since Leopold's last visit. The lower portion, once given over to kiddies' rides, had been sold off to a drive-in movie, and the rides in the upper part now seemed closer together. The ferris wheel was still in the same place, of course, but Stella Gaze's house had been torn down for parking.

'You Rudy Magee?' Leopold asked a kid at the ferris wheel.

'He's on his break. Over there at the hot dog stand.'

Magee was a type – the sport-shirted racetrack tout, the smalltime gambler, the part-time pimp.

Leopold had known them through all of his professional life. 'I want to talk about last night,' he told the thin, pale man, showing his identification.

'You mean that kid – the one who lost his girl?'

'That's right.'

'Hell, I don't know a thing about it. I think he dreamed the whole bit.'

Leopold grunted. 'You worked here long? I don't remember you.'

'Just since the place opened for the season in May. Why? I gotta be an old-time employee to know people don't disappear from ferris wheels?'

Leopold was about to answer, but a third man had joined them – a stocky, thirsty-looking fellow who looked vaguely familiar. 'Well, Captain Leopold, isn't it? You working on this Velma Kelty case?'

Leopold looked him up and down. 'I don't believe I caught the name.'

'Fane. Walter Fane from the *Globe*. You've seen me around headquarters.' He pulled an afternoon paper from under his arm. 'See? We've got it on page one.'

They had indeed. *Girl Vanishes at Amusement Park; Councilman's Son Quizzed.*

'Is that the way it is, Captain? Or have you found the body?'

'What body?' Leopold asked.

'You're a homicide captain, right? If you're on the case, there's a body.'

'Not this time. I'm just helping out.'

'Give me a break, Captain. I can still phone in a new lead for the late sports edition.'

Leopold gazed over at the ferris wheel, and at the new parking lot beyond. 'Are you superstitious, Fane?'

'Huh?'

'Three years ago, a woman named Stella Gaze was accused of witchcraft.'

'Yeah.' His eyes brightened a bit. 'She lived out here somewhere.'

'Right next to the ferris wheel. The house was torn down after she killed herself. But if a girl really did vanish from that ferris wheel, who's to say Stella Gaze's spirit isn't still around?'

'You believe that bunk, Captain?'

' You wanted a new lead. I'm giving you one.'

The reporter thought about it for a moment and then nodded. 'Thanks,' he said, heading off toward a telephone.

'We can go back to your wheel,' Leopold told Rudy Magee. 'I want you to tell me how it happened.'

'Nothing happened. Nothing at all,' Rudy insisted vehemently.

'Well then, tell me what *didn't* happen.'

They reached the wheel and Rudy took over from the kid, standing on a raised platform where the cars came to a stop, helping people in and out over the foot-high metal sill. 'Watch your step,' he told two teenage girls as he accepted their tickets and shut the wire cage on them. Though Leopold could see only their knees and upper bodies from the ground, he knew Magee was getting a good view from his position.

Rudy let a few cars go by with empty seats before he stopped the wheel again to load the next passengers. 'When there aren't many customers, I balance the load,' he explained to Leopold.

A young hippie type with sideburns and beads came by. 'Is Hazel here?' he asked Magee.

'Not now,' the pale man answered. 'Maybe later,'

Leopold watched the wheel turning against the sky, noting a tree too far away, a lamppost just out of reach. He tried to imagine a fifteen-year-old girl swinging like a monkey against the night sky, trying to reach one of them, and then decided it was impossible. If Velma had gone up – and that was the big if – then she'd surely come down as well.

'Satisfied?' Rudy asked curtly. 'Not quite. I understand you've got an easy hand with the girls when you're helping them in and out. You must have seen Velma.'

'I told you, and I'm telling you. It was busy. I didn't notice anybody.'

But his eyes shifted as he spoke. He was a poor liar. 'All right,' Leopold said. 'Let's try it another way. Lying to me is one thing, lying before a grand jury is something else. The girl is missing and we want to find her. If she turns up dead and you've been lying, that's big trouble for you.' He took a chance and added, 'They know about your record here, Rudy?'

'What record? A couple of gambling arrests?'

Leopold shrugged. 'Why make more trouble for yourself?'

The thin man seemed to sag a little. 'All right. I was just trying to stay outa trouble. Understand?'

'Everybody wants to stay outa trouble, Rudy. Now suppose you tell me about it.'

'Well, the guy shows up just before ten o'clock with his broad. She's got long black hair and looks about eighteen. They argue for a couple of minutes, because she wants him to go up with her and he doesn't want to. Finally he buys her a ticket and she goes up alone. All alone nobody sharing the seat with her – just the girl alone.'

'And?'

'And she never comes down. Just like he said. Damnedest thing I ever seen.'

'You're sure?'

'I'm sure. I was sorta watching for her. You know'

'I know, Rudy. What did you think happened?'

'Hell, I was scared. I thought she opened the cage and jumped. I figured we'd find her body over in the parking lot somewhere.'

'But you didn't.

'No. Besides, somebody would have seen her, you know. But I just couldn't figure anything else. Say, do you believe that stuff about the witch and all? Do you think she put a curse on this place before she died?'

Leopold shrugged. 'It'll make a good story for a few days, keep them off the kid's back. Maybe by that time we'll find out what really happened to Velma Kelty.'

The missing girl had lived with an aunt and uncle in the East Bay region of town, ever since her parents had died in the crash of a private plane some eight years earlier. Captain Leopold drove over to the house, knowing that he was only retracing the steps covered earlier by the missing persons people.

The uncle was a lawyer named Frank Prosper. He was a bulging, balding man whom Leopold had seen occasionally around City Hall. 'You mean you've only come to ask more questions?' he challenged, 'and not to give us any word of her?'

'There is no word,' Leopold said. 'I wanted to ask you a few things about her. And about Tom Williams. He seems a little mature to have been dating her.'

'We've always had trouble with that girl,' Prosper said, biting off the tip of a cigar. 'My wife's brother was a wild sort and she takes right after him.'

'What do you think about Williams? Do you think he might have harmed her?'

'I don't know. He's not a bad kid. Only thing wrong with him is that he thinks his father's God's gift to politics. Old man Williams is the last of the old cigar chompers.'

Leopold thought this last was a somewhat odd comment from a man who himself was smoking a cigar at the moment.'

'You mean he's crooked?'

'Nothing of the sort! He's just a man who believes in political power at the ward level, the way it was practised a couple of generations ago. The country has passed men like Williams by, but he doesn't seem to realise it.'

'I'd like to know more about your niece. Do you have a picture of her? A snapshot would be fine.'

'I gave one to the missing persons people. Here's another.' He held out a framed photograph of a shyly smiling girl in a short red dress. She wore her black hair long, half covering a pretty, if unexceptional, face. She seemed several years older than fifteen. Leopold would have taken her for a college girl.

'She doesn't look like the wild sort. What was the trouble?'

'She hung around with a fast crowd. Hippies. That type.'

'Tom Williams, a hippie?' Somehow the scene didn't ring true to Leopold.

'Not Williams. His sister. Talk to his sister.'

Leopold nodded. 'I was thinking of doing just that.'

She was in the pool when he returned to the Williams house, splashing around in a brief two-piece suit that stopped just short of being a true bikini. When Leopold called to her from the water's edge, she left the rubber animal to float by itself and kicked out with energy toward where he stood.

'You're Cindy Williams?' Leopold asked, stretching out a hand to help her from the water.

'Just call me Cin,' she replied.

He shook the dampness from his cuffs and took a good look at her. Yes, he supposed even in the bathing suit she could have been called a hippie – especially by a paunchy lawyer like Frank Prosper. Her hair was long and stringy, not unlike the missing girl's, except that it was blonde. She had the same sort of pretty but unremarkable face. He'd seen her type many times before, downtown, wearing tight jeans and laughing a bit too loudly on a street corner. He wondered what her father, the councilman, thought about it all.

'Velma Kelty,' Leopold said. 'She was your friend.'

Cin Williams nodded. 'A year younger than me, but we're in the same class at school.'

'I'm investigating her disappearance. Any idea what might have happened to her?'

Cin shrugged her loose, bony shoulders. 'Maybe it was the witch.' She gestured toward the final edition of the newspaper, where the headline now read: *Girl Vanishes at Amusement Park, Witchcraft Hinted*. Walter Fane had phoned in his story on time, and Leopold supposed it was a slight improvement over the earlier headline.

'Were there any other boys beside your brother?' he asked the girl in the bathing suit. 'Someone else she might have dated?'

'Gee, I don't know.' She was starting to dry off her long suntanned legs with a towel.

'I hear she hung around some with hippies.'

'I don't know.'

'We'll find out,' Leopold said.

A voice called from the terrace at the back of the house. 'Cindy, who's that you're talking to?'

'A detective, Daddy. About Velma.'

Councilman Williams, whose first name was also Tom, came down the flagstone walk. His son looked a great deal like him, as did the daughter to a lesser extent. There was not a cigar in sight, and despite what Prosper had said, Leopold doubted that he smoked them. 'You're Leopold? The chief said he'd put his best man on this thing.'

'Captain Leopold, yes.'

'Any clues yet, Captain?'

'No clues. It's not the sort of case where you look for clues.'

'But the girl disappeared from the ferris wheel.'

'Perhaps.'

'If there's any way I can help out, down at City Hall… '

'Do you know the girl's uncle? Frank Prosper?'

'Yes. He's a lawyer, active in politics. I know him.'

The tone was one of prompt dismissal. Perhaps they only belonged to different parties. Leopold looked back to where Cin had finished drying herself. 'I was asking your daughter about hippies. I understand Velma travelled with a pretty wild crowd.'

'What gave you that idea?' Williams asked. 'She was with my daughter a great deal. And with my son recently, of course.'

Young Tom Williams came out then, to join them and stand beside his father. He seemed very young, still a boy. 'Is there any news about Velma?'

'No news.'

'She'll turn up,' the father decided. 'It's probably just some gag.'

Leopold didn't have an answer for that. Standing there with the three of them beside the pool, he didn't have an answer for anything.

Fletcher came in with coffee the next morning. 'Anything on the girl, Captain?' he asked, settling into his usual chair.

'Nothing.'

'You going to turn it back to missing persons?'

Leopold sighed. 'The chief wants me to stay on it another day. He promised Councilman Williams we'd do our best.'

'What do you think happened to her?'

Leopold leaned back in his chair. 'What do I think happened? I think somebody's trying to pull a neat trick. I think the ferris wheel was chosen because of Stella Gaze and all that talk of witchcraft. But I don't know who's behind it, or what they're trying to accomplish.'

'Young Williams?'

'Yes. He has to be in on it. You see, whatever the plan was, it called for witnesses at the wheel to verify the boy's story. Unfortunately for him, Rudy Magee wasn't about to verify anything. That threw him into such confusion that he walked around for an hour or two before even calling the police. That tells us something very interesting, if just a little bit sinister.'

'Sinister?'

'Look at it this way. Young Williams and the girl are going to fake a disappearance for some reason – publicity, a joke, anything. She goes up in the ferris wheel, after a big scene with him to draw attention – and then does her vanishing act. Big witchcraft thing, Stella Gaze and all that. Except that it doesn't work because Magee gets scared and denies everything. So what happens? Williams goes away for a while, *but then he comes back and calls the police.* Why? There were two other courses open to him. He could have forgotten the whole thing, or the two of them could have tried it again some other night. Why did he call the police with the weak story he had?'

'You said it was something sinister.'

'It is.' Leopold swivelled in his chair to stare out the window. The headquarters' parking lot was damp and misty, its asphalt surface dark with water from a morning shower. The view wasn't much.

'Sinister how? Like witchcraft?'

'Like murder,' Leopold said. There were other crimes that day, the usual assortment of a city's troubles, and it was not until late in the day that Leopold's mind went back to the vanishing of the fifteen-year-old girl. It was yanked back suddenly by a telephone call.

'Captain Leopold?' A girl's voice, soft.

'Yes.'

'This is Velma Kelty.'

'Who? You'll have to speak louder.' Already he was signalling Fletcher to trace it.

'Velma Kelty. The girl on the ferris wheel.'

'Oh yes. I'm glad to hear from you, Velma. Are you all right?'

'I'm all right.'

'Where are you, Velma?'

'At Sportland. I'd like to meet you here, later, after dark.'

'Couldn't I come out now?'

'No. Not yet. After dark.'

'All right, Velma. Where should I meet you?'

'Ten o'clock. By the ferris wheel.'

'Yes. Of course. I'll be there, Velma.'

He hung up and called to Fletcher, but there'd been no time to trace it. There was nothing to do but wait till ten o'clock.

The rain came again about eight, but it lasted only a few minutes. It left behind a summer dampness, though, and a light mist that clung to the road as Leopold drove. Approaching the Sound, he might have been driving toward the end of the earth, were it not for the bright neon of Sportland that told him some sort of civilisation still existed out there at the water's edge.

It was five minutes to ten when he reached the ferris wheel. Rudy Magee was on duty again. 'You must work all the time,' Leopold observed. 'You're always here.'

'Every other night, alternating with the afternoons,' Magee said. 'What's up?'

'I thought I might ask you. Seen anybody familiar tonight? '

'Yeah. Now that you mention it, that reporter Fane was nosing round.'

'Oh?' Leopold lit a cigarette. 'Anybody else?'

'Like who?'

Leopold glanced at his watch. It was just ten o'clock. 'Like Velma Kelty, the missing girl.'

'Never laid eyes on her. I'd know her from the picture the papers published.'

'She's not on the wheel now?'

'I told you I'd know her. There's nobody but a middle-aged couple and a few strays.'

He slowed the wheel to a stop and released a young man from his cage. Then he slowed it a few cages on and opened it for a young lady. Leopold saw the hair first, and knew. Rudy Magee saw her too, and let out a muffled gasp.

Velma Kelty had come back.

Leopold beckoned to her and they walked away from the shaken Magee.

'I suppose you're going to tell me you were riding around on that ferris wheel for the last forty-eight hours,' Leopold said.

'Sure. Why not?'

He peered at her in the uncertain light. 'All right, young lady. You nearly scared that ferris wheel operator to death. I'm taking you home to your uncle.'

'I can find my way,' she told him. 'I just wanted to see you, to show you I wasn't really missing.'

'Sure.' They were in better light now, crossing to the parking lot. He glanced sideways at her and reached out to touch her long black hair. Then he twisted and gave a sudden tug. It came away in his hand.

'You creep!' Cindy Williams shouted at him, clutching for the wig.

'Now, now. You're playing the big girls' game, Cindy. You have to expect these little setbacks.'

'How'd you know it was me?'

'I guess because it looked like you. That's a pretty old trick, to start out a blonde and then change to a brunette. You fooled Rudy Magee, anyway. Of course you had the wig hidden in your purse when you got on the wheel a while ago.'

'I just wanted to show you it could be done,' she said. 'Velma could have worked it just the opposite – gotten on the ferris wheel as a brunette and gotten off as a blonde.'

'But you didn't show me anything of the sort, because it didn't work, did it? I recognised you as I got you in the good light, and Tom would have recognised Velma a lot sooner than that, wig or no wig, because he was watching for her.' He sighed with exasperation. 'All right, get in the car. I'm still taking you home.'

She slid into the front seat, pouting for several minutes as he turned the car out of the Sportland parking lot. Presently the garish neon of the amusement park subsided into the background as they drove toward town.

'You think I'm involved, don't you?' she asked.

'I didn't, until tonight. That was a pretty foolish trick.'

'Why was it?

'I might have told Prosper she was alive, gotten his hopes up.'

'You think she's dead?'

Leopold kept his eyes on the road. 'I think Tom was playing a stunt of some sort and it didn't come off. He waited two hours before calling the police. Why? Because he was trying to decide what he should do. But then he called them after all, even though Magee didn't back up his story. Why again? Because he couldn't come back and try his stunt the next night. Because Velma Kelty really had vanished, only not in the way he made it appear.'

'How, then?'

'I wish I knew.' He pushed in the cigarette lighter that rarely worked and reached for his crumpled pack. In the light from passing cars her face was tense and drawn. Once again, she looked older than her age.

'You must have some idea.'

'Sure I do, lots of them. Want to hear one? Velma Kelty died some-how at your house, maybe in the swimming pool, and your father the councilman is implicated. To protect him, you and Tom cook up this disappearance, with you using that black wig. How does that sound to you?'

'Fantastic!'

'Maybe.'

They drove then rest of the way in near silence, until they were almost to her house. 'By the way,' he asked, 'how'd you get out to Sportland tonight?'

'Tom drove me,' she mumbled. 'He dropped me off.'

He pulled up in front of her house. 'Want me to come in with you, have a few words with your father?'

'N-no.'

'All right. This time.'

He watched till she reached the door and then drove on. He was thinking that if his own marriage had worked out he might have had a daughter just about her age – fifteen or sixteen – but that was a heck of a thing for a cop to have on his mind. Velma Kelty might have been his daughter too, and now she was gone.

He went home to his apartment and turned on the air-conditioner He fell asleep to its humming, and when the telephone awakened him he wondered for an instant what the sound was.

'Leopold here,' he managed to mumble into the instrument.

'It's Fletcher, Captain. Sorry to disturb you, but I thought you'd want to know. We found her.'

'Who?' he asked through bleary cobwebs.

'The missing girl. Velma Kelty.'

'Is she all right?'

'She's dead, Captain. They just fished her body out of the Sound near Sportland.'

He cursed silently and turned on the bedside lamp. Why did they always have to end like this?

'Any chance of suicide?'

Fletcher cleared his throat. 'Pretty doubtful, Captain. Somebody weighted down the body with fifty pounds of scrap iron.'

Leopold went back to the house with the swimming pool, rousing Tom Williams from his bed just as dawn was breaking over the city. 'You'll wake my father,' young Williams said. 'What do you want?'

'The truth. No more stories about ferris wheels, just the truth.'

'I don't know what you're talking about.'

'They just fished Velma's body from the Sound. Now do you know what I'm talking about?'

'Oh no!' He seemed truly staggered by the news, as if he refused to comprehend the truth of it.

'That trick with your sister was a bit of foolishness. Is that the way you worked it the other night, with a wig?'

'I swear, Captain, Velma Kelty got on that ferris wheel. She got on and she never got off. I can't imagine what happened to her, or how she ended up in the Sound. What killed her?'

'They're doing the autopsy now. Her body was weighted to keep it at the bottom, but not heavily enough, apparently. It wasn't any accident.'

'I... I can't imagine what happened to her.'

'You'd better start imagining, because you're in big trouble. You and your sister both. Someone killed the girl and threw her body in the Sound. Maybe she was raped first.'

'You don't know that!'

'I don't know much of anything at this point, but I can speculate. Did you do it, Tom? Or maybe your father? Or maybe some of the hippie crowd she hung around with? Anyway, the body had to be disposed of, and Velma's disappearance had to take place somewhere else. The ferris wheel seemed logical to you, because of the witch stories, so Cindy put on her wig and you pulled it off. Except that the wheel operator was ready to deny everything. That threw you for a loss, and you spent a couple of hours wondering what to do next.'

'No!'

'Then why did you wait all that time before reporting her disappearance? Why, Tom?'

'I... I...'

Leopold turned away. 'You'd better think up a good story. You'll need it in court.'

Fletcher looked up from his desk as Leopold entered the squad room and crossed to his private office. 'Did you bring the Williams kid in, Captain?'

'Not yet, soon.' His lips were drawn into a tight line.

'Crazy story for him to make up, about that damned ferris wheel.'

'Yeah.' Leopold shuffled the papers on his desk, seeing nothing. 'How's the autopsy report?'

'Nothing yet.'

'I'm going down there,' he decided suddenly.

The medical examiner was a tall, red-faced man whom Leopold had known for years. He had just finished the autopsy and was sitting at his desk writing the report. 'How are you, Captain?' he mumbled.

'Finish with the Kelty girl?'

'Just about. I have to submit the report. Her things are over there.'

Leopold glanced at the clothes, still soggy with water. Dark blue slacks and sweater, sneakers, bra and panties. A heavy piece of cast iron, entwined with damp cord, rested nearby. He looked back at the doctor. 'Was she raped, Gus?'

'No. I wish it were that easy. Something like that I could understand.' His face was suddenly old.

'What was it, Gus?'

'Fifteen. Only fifteen years old...'

'Gus...'

The doctor stood up and handed over his report. 'There it is, Captain. She died of a massive overdose of heroin, mainlined into a vein near her elbow...'

It was late afternoon when Leopold returned to Sportland. He could see the ferris wheel from a long way off, outlined against the blue of a cloudless sky. For the first time he wondered if Stella Gaze really had been a witch, if she really had put a curse on the place. Maybe that was some sort of an explanation.

'You're back!' Rudy Magee said, strolling over to meet him. 'I hear they found the girl.'

'They found her.'

'Not far from here, huh!'

'Close, Rudy. Very close.'

'The kid was lying, then?'

'Let's go for a ride, Rudy, on your ferris wheel. I'll tell you all about it.'

'Huh? All right, if you really want to. I don't usually go on the thing myself.' The kid took over the controls, and he preceded Leopold into one of the wire cages. As the wheel turned and they started their climb, he added, 'Great view from up here, huh?'

'I imagine with all this neon lit up at night it's quite a ride.'

Rudy chuckled. 'Yeah, the kids like it.'

'I know how Velma disappeared,' Leopold said suddenly.

'You do? Boy, I'd like to know myself. It was a weird thing. The kid played some trick on me, huh?'

'No trick, Rudy. You were the one with the tricks.'

The pale man stiffened in the seat beside him. 'What do you mean?' The caged seat swayed gently as it reached the peak of its ascent and started slowly down.

'I mean that you've been selling drugs to these kids – hippies, college kids, fifteen-year-old girls. I suppose it was a big kick to go up on this wheel at night with all the coloured neon and stuff while you were high on LSD.'

'You'd have a tough time proving that,' Rudy said.

'Maybe not. Maybe Tom Williams has decided it's time to talk. That was the key question, after all – why he waited so long to report Velma's disappearance to the police. The reason, of course, was that he was high on drugs at the time, probably on an LSD trip. He had to wait till it wore off a little. Maybe you even had him convinced that

Velma never did get on your ferris wheel.'

'I told you she got on,' Magee mumbled. 'But she never got off.'

'She never got off alive.' Leopold watched the scene shifting. beneath them as they reached bottom and started up once more. 'LSD had become too tame for Velma and her hippie friends. So you maybe sold her some marijuana. Anyway, before long you had her on heroin.'

'No.'

'I say yes.'

He rubbed his palms together. 'Maybe I sold the kids a little LSD, but never anything stronger. Never horse.'

'Some people call it *horse,* Rudy. Others call it *Hazel* I heard the kid ask you for Hazel the other day, but it didn't register with me then. Velma Kelty bought the heroin from you, and mainlined it into her vein as she was going up in the ferris wheel. It's a pretty safe place, when you consider it. Only she was fairly new at it, or the stuff was a bad batch, or she just took too much. She crumpled off the seat, into this space at our feet – and she rode around on your ferris wheel for the rest of the night, until the park closed and you could weight the body and toss it in the Sound.'

'You're as nutty as he was. Somebody would have seen her there.'

'No, not from ground level. This metal sill is a foot high, and I noticed that from the ground you couldn't see below girls' knees. A small fifteen-year-old girl could easily crumple into that space, seen by you on that platform every time the wheel turned, but invisible from the ground. The seat just looked empty and of course you were care-ful to skip it when loading passengers.'

'The people in the seat above would have seen her there,' Magee argued.

'So you kept that seat empty too. Williams said you weren't busy that night. There were only a few others on the wheel. Besides, Velma was wearing dark blue slacks and sweater, and she had black hair. In the dark no one would have seen her there, especially with all this neon blinding them.'

'So you're going to arrest me for disposing of a body?'

'For more than that, Rudy. The narcotics charge alone will keep you behind bars a good long time. But you know the effects of an overdose as well as I do. Velma Kelty was still alive after she collapsed – physically incapacitated, stuporous, with slow respiration, but still alive. She could probably have been saved with quick treatment, but you were too afraid for your own skin. So you let her slowly die here, crumpled into this little space, until the park closed and you could get rid of the body.'

'The policeman came, he looked.'

'Sure. He came and looked two hours later. Naturally he didn't check each individual seat, because no one would believe she could still be there unseen. Perhaps by that time you had stopped the wheel anyway, with her body near the top. Or maybe you'd even managed to remove it, if business was bad enough to give you a few minutes' break.'

Rudy Magee's hand came out of his pocket. It was holding a hypo-dermic syringe. 'You're a smart cop, but not smart enough. I'm not going back inside on any murder rap, or even manslaughter.'

Leopold sighed. The wire cage was nearing the ground again. 'Do you see that man watching us from the ground? His name is Sergeant Fletcher, and he's awfully good with a gun. I wouldn't try to jab me with that, or yourself either.'

As he spoke, Leopold's hand closed around the syringe, taking it from Rudy's uncertain fingers. 'How did you know it all?' he asked, quietly, staring into Leopold's eyes.

'I didn't, until I saw the autopsy report. Velma died of an overdose of heroin, and she was last seen alive getting on to your ferris wheel. I put those two facts together and tried to determine if she could have died on your wheel, and just kept going around, without being seen. I decided she could have, and that she did.'

The wheel stopped finally, and they got off. There was a bit of a breeze blowing in off the Sound, and it reminded Leopold somehow of Velma Kelty – the living girl, not the body in the morgue. He wished that he had known her. Maybe, just maybe, he could have saved her from Rudy Magee – and from herself.

# Death Ship
## Bill Kirton

*Five years back, Bill Kirton contributed an excellent story 'Missing', to the CWA's Missing Persons anthology. He has kept a relatively low profile since then, which is a pity, for he has the gifts of a real story-teller. 'Death Ship' is a lively story with a well-evoked setting on board. Its appearance in this book offers an introduction to the work of an author with whom many readers will be unfamiliar. I hope that the publication of 'Death Ship' will encourage Bill Kirton to make more time for crime writing in the future*

We were less than a day out of Kristiansand when the first body was found. The seas were piling into the Skagerrak Strait under a force eight. It had been blowing for four days. We'd set just two jibs and the fore topmast staysail, the courses, lower topsails and lower staysails on all three masts and the spanker to steady her. As she beat out into the North Sea, the carpenter's workshop was the last place anyone wanted to be. There, up in the bows, you felt the sea's full violence. Jack Stretton had no choice. As part of his watch, he had to start his fire inspection rounds under the foredeck. In the gloom, he heard the carpenter's door banging back and forth. He pushed it open. Davie Strachan's body lay against the workbench. His head had been held face down in the vice and then beaten until it resembled a crude bowl filled with silvery red substances in which floated fragments of bone.

A few minutes later, I was looking at it with the captain, Big John Michie. We were wondering how to report it to Mr Anderson.

'If the police hear about it, we'll be held alongside for days, maybe weeks,' said Big John.

'Aye,' I said. 'I can just hear what he'll say to that.'

Big John nodded.

'We canna keep quiet about it, though. Not with the crew telling the tale in all the bars.'

'Is it something you want to hide, then?' I asked.

He shook his head. I looked again at Davie's open skull.

'No easy matter to pretend it's an accident,' I said. 'That vice is deep in his cheeks. There was a lot of pain.'

'Aye. But I canna just leave him there. With this wind we'll soon be needing work done down here.'

As if she agreed with him, the ship dived steeply into a trough and we had to hold the rails tightly to keep our footing. Only the vice kept Davie from sliding under the bench.

'And where can I put him?' Big John went on. 'God knows how long it'll take us to get home with the wind on our nose like this. He'll smell worse than a hold full of herring.'

It was interesting that he seemed to have less curiosity about the killing than about how it would interfere with sailing the ship.

'You're the master. It's your decision,' I said.

'Aye, thanks.'

He wasted little time reflecting. He was right: he couldn't store a decomposing body in a fully laden ship where there was hardly space enough for the crew. And, with superstition a part of every seaman's thinking, other troubles would inevitably grow from the corpse. When we went back on deck, he ordered the sailmaker to break out some canvas and sew the body up in it. We'd then cover it with pitch and drop it over the side. The death would have to be reported but, with no body to look at and no-one caring much about what happened to Davie anyway, Big John hoped that Mr Anderson's trade would not suffer unduly.

Mr Anderson was our employer. One of the most successful of Aberdeen's many rich merchants, he'd built a fleet of vessels which carried people to the Americas and brought back timber. To my delight, he was resisting the call of the new steamships, reasoning that they were not always faster than sail and that boilers, engines and coal took up space that could be better used for cargo. He still preferred the traditional ways and his growing fortune seemed to confirm that he was right to do so. The ship we were sailing, the *Christian Rose*, would soon be expanding his influence even further, taking labourers and mechanics to Jamaica and, if the captain was willing, shepherds and agricultural labourers to New South Wales, at the bottom of the world.

Usually, as his shipwright, it was I who was charged with building any additions to his fleet, but news had come to him that the Norwegian merchant who had commissioned the *Christian Rose* had been killed in a dockside accident and that the builders were anxious to find a new buyer. With his customary skill, he'd not only negotiated a good price but also found a cargo of pulp and timber to bring back to Scotland. I'd inspected the final fitting out and was now part of the crew which was taking her back to Aberdeen.

We'd sailed across to Norway in another of his ships, not as passengers but as extra hands. It had been a crowded trip but, with a strong south-westerly on our quarter and a double crew to haul canvas, we'd flown across in little more than three days. This return voyage, though, was a different story. It gave us little time to brood on Davie's death because, with a strong westerly blowing, the sailing was hard. We had to lay well off our preferred course and, when the time came to tack or wear ship, all hands were needed to clew up the sails, brace round the yards and get her on her new heading.

It was the continual bucking and crashing of the ship that explained the condition of the second body. Less than twenty-four hours after Davie had been sewn into his bag, the new discovery fell, once again, to Jack Stretton. He'd gone forward to the point of the bows to relieve Rab Robertson as lookout and was surprised to see no-one there. It was a cold, lonely, uncomfortable watch, but everyone knew how important it was and no-one, not even Rab, would be foolish enough to leave before his relief arrived. Jack had been in position for several minutes, scanning the grey sea with its boiling white crests, when he noticed that one of the forward belaying pins had no rope around it. It should have held the outer jib downhaul and, when he followed the line of the bowsprit out to where the rope was attached to the sail, he saw that it was hanging down into the water, held taut by some sort of load. He raised the alarm, the rest of his watch were called forward and, after some heavy hauling, they brought the load inboard and laid it on the foredeck.

It was the remains of Rab. The end of the rope had been knotted around his throat and the angle of his head showed that his neck had been broken. As the ship had ploughed through the big seas, he had constantly been smashed against the hull down at the waterline. His limbs all lay at unnatural angles and the ship's bow had flayed and chopped the flesh from various parts of his body.

When Big John and I arrived, the men were standing or squatting around Rab. No-one was speaking. Jack Stretton's eyes kept flicking from the sea ahead to the bundle of rags and blood beside him. I looked round at them all. These were the men who, on the way over, had been singing and hauling away, laughing and cursing as we rushed across the water. Now, in their faces, there was just fear.

Big John put the sailmaker to work again and asked me to come back to his cabin with him. As soon as the door closed behind us, he swore and threw his heavy jacket across the chart table.

'What is it, Joe? A curse?'

I just shook my head.

'It's worse than Baffin Island,' he said.

I knew that Big John had spent many years on whaling ships in the North Atlantic but I had no idea what he meant. My expression must have shown my puzzlement. He sat down and leaned forward.

'Dropped like flies there. We'd get stuck in the ice, victuals got low and you'd have them with their gums peeling back off their teeth from scurvy or their fingers snapping off with the frost. You'd see them going mad, dropping over the side and wandering away over the ice. Sometimes, there'd be hardly enough crew to sail her back when the thaw came. But at least you knew why. It was the ice, the cold. Here, there's no reason.'

'There has to be. Two in two days. And no question but that they were murdered. And that they suffered. No-one murders by accident. Or just for pleasure.'

'Why those two then? And who's next?'

I couldn't answer him. He started filling his pipe.

'Jack Stretton found them both. A coincidence?' he said, half to himself.

'Can you see Jack doing such things?' I asked.

He shook his head.

'They're all capable of it onshore, when they've had a few drams, but Jack would never be the first. And anyway, Davie and Rab, they're not regular crew. Remember where we got them. Maybe that's it. Maybe it's unsettled business from back there.'

I waited. I knew what he meant. The opportunity of the *Christian Rose* had taken Mr Anderson by surprise. When his offer had been accepted, he still had not had time to gather a full crew. He always liked to talk to all of the men separately, to test whether they understood his special ways of doing business and make sure that they would ask no questions about what they saw. He'd come to see me in my boatyard on the afternoon before we'd sailed for Norway.

'I'm still wanting some half a dozen men,' he said. 'And there is no time to find them.'

'Then we'll have to be short-handed. Given a fair wind, it will not add too many days to the voyage.'

'One day is too many. All I need is six men. For two weeks, perhaps less.'

'But we need people who understand the Anderson style.'

'No,' he said. 'They can be from anywhere. They need understand nothing. Their sole instruction is to sail with Captain Michie and do as he tells them. In a matter of days, they'll be back in Aberdeen with money in their pouches and the freedom to do as they please. In the meantime, I shall look for proper crewmen to take their places when she sets sail for Jamaica.'

'So you don't care whether they have experience at sea?'

'God, man, anyone can haul on a rope.'

'Then we should perhaps look in Sinclair's Close or Pensioners Court.'

His look told me that it was an idea that had already occurred to him. The alleyways I'd mentioned were the breeding ground for pickpockets, prostitutes and others who grow like scabs on our society. Every evening, the cobbles are awash with drunken men and women, singing, sleeping, cursing and behaving like beasts. For anyone brave enough to risk the contamination of their proximity, it would be a simple matter to find six or more men drunk enough to be persuaded to take a short sea trip, at the end of which they would receive more money than they could beg or steal in the equivalent time onshore.

'Six men, then,' said Mr Anderson. 'I leave it to your best endeavours. I shall talk to Captain Michie. I suggest you accompany him there this evening.'

I inclined my head by way of answer. I would have preferred to spend the evening with my Emma, but I was used to carrying out unplanned commissions on his behalf, many of them completely unconnected with the construction of ships, and, once you were part of his trusted circle, he paid well.

I have been to Pensioners Court only infrequently and, each time, the degradation of the place has made me shudder. Drunks lie still and silent in their own and others' urine. Groups rage and argue over a woman, a half empty bottle of whisky, or nothing. Few of Aberdeen's forty-seven night watchmen ever venture there. For the most part they are older men and the eleven shillings a week they're paid is not enough to persuade them to risk the fists, boots and knives which await them there. Every black doorway holds menace. Figures wait in their shadows, still and watching, and many innocents, children and adults alike, have been dragged into these corners to be filled with their own darkness by the knife which slides quickly across their throat. In Pensioners Court, life is brief and cheap.

I was glad of the company of Big John. He'd fought in bars from Newfoundland to the East Indies and China and feared no-one. He also seemed to know who he was looking for.

'Noah McPhee, we'll start with him,' he said. 'Find him and you'll find all the scum you want.'

It was a name I knew well.

'Is it not dangerous to have such a man on board?' I asked.

Big John laughed. There was no joy in it.

'He's no man. He's raped and killed and robbed, but he chooses women and old men, or people too far into their drink to know who they are. He's a coward. Take him away from his whisky and set him on a slippery deck. That'll pull his teeth.'

I wanted to share his confidence, but I could not dismiss with such ease the history of McPhee and his gang. With Cammie Drewburgh, Rab Robertson and Davie Strachan, he seemed to have set out to move beyond mere crime into evil itself. Even as youngsters, they'd built themselves reputations as the blackest rogues, running into Mother Watson's alehouse with live rats and throwing them on the fire, cutting the tendons of horses waiting patiently in the shafts of their carts. Once, they hacked off a dog's leg and set the animal to run free in the street, trailing its blood amongst terrified mothers and children. And then, as they grew into men, their attention turned to women, whom they treated just as they had the animals, perpetrating crimes on girls as young as eight, systematically raping them, selling their pale bodies to visitors in Pensioners Court.

They spent many months in the Bridewell Prison in Rose Street and seemed only to use their time there to refine their villainy. Everyone was afraid of them. Their crimes were rarely reported and the police officers themselves preferred to stay away from them.

'They should have been hanged long ago. Or sent to Australia,' said Big John, his voice low, barely audible.

I just nodded.

'What they did to those lassies,' he went on. 'Slashing their horse's neck, dragging them out of the carriage.'

I knew the incident he was speaking of. Everyone in Aberdeen did.

'The old one,' he said. 'Stripping her, beating her, taking everything and sending her crying through the streets like that. In just a shift.'

'She was the lucky one,' I said.

'Aye. I've thought many times how the young one must have felt, lying on the cobbles, in the dung, the vomit, with the four of them taking their turns with her.' He shook his head. 'A lassie, Joe. What enters into men to make them do it?'

I could only shake my head.

'And then throwing her behind a fish store, like a bundle of rags. It would've been better if she'd died.'

'I don't think so,' I said. 'She survived. She beat them in the end.'

'Aye, but she canna say so. Canna speak, canna walk, canna even wave her arm. It's the devil's work they do.'

It was hard to disagree with him. There had been no punishment. The drunken crowd in Sinclair's Close had been entertained by it all but no-one was ready to speak to the police about it and the two women felt such shame that they simply retreated behind their doors to fight the memories in silence.

And these were the men who were sharing our ship. We'd found them in the London Tavern on Waterloo Quay, drinking with Windy Geech and Tam Donald. I was surprised to see Tam with them. His daughter had been one of their early victims. Perhaps time does let you forget. But Big John was in a hurry. He told them that he had two 'spare' bales of Mr Anderson's silk in his hold and that whoever helped him to bring them ashore would share the money they fetched. The six of them stumbled to the ship and down into the hold. Once they were below, Big John simply fastened the hatch over them and there they stayed until we were well out of Aberdeen the following day.

And now two of them were dead. Big John's remark about 'unsettled business' made sense.

He finished filling his pipe, lit it, and the blue smoke hung in the air of the cabin.

'Death follows them wherever they go,' he said.

'Aye, and we've brought it on board.'

'Better to have it out here than stalking the good folk of Aberdeen. We've no family at home to worry about, and I'm glad of that every time I sail.'

I said nothing. Neither Big John nor any of the others knew that Emma Fielding, the woman I was to marry, was already living in my house in York Place. It was an arrangement that would scandalise the 'good folk' Big John was speaking about, so we kept it our secret, shared only by Lizzie, our maid. And, as for Big John's own marital status, everyone knew his appetites. Each time he sailed, he left not one but a dozen women behind him.

'Does that not chill you,' I asked, 'that we have a monster on board?'

He thought for a moment.

'Aye, but it's an ill wind...'

He sucked long and hard at his pipe, coughed, and then continued.

'I'm thinking there'll be a fuss when we get alongside, but that Mr Anderson will maybe not be too upset by it.'

'I don't understand.'

'By the look of it,' said Big John, setting his pipe in a bowl on the chart table, 'we're going to be another week or more at sea.'

I nodded. The wind was still steadily against us.

'He's paying the six rogues we found in that tavern a shilling a day. With two of them dead, he's already saved himself a guinea or two.'

I laughed.

'Have you not thought, then, how much more he could save if the victims were yourself or me?' I said.

He looked at me, his eyes dark, unsmiling.

'Look,' I said, 'I know our master is a powerful man, but he's in Aberdeen. Not even he can kill men on a vessel some five hundred miles distant.'

'But someone could do it for him.'

'Who?'

He raised his shoulders and spread his hands.

'Mr Anderson has enemies, too,' I said. 'Perhaps they have a hand in it. Perhaps these deaths are not meant to help, but to embarrass and inconvenience him.'

Big John nodded.

'In that case, we're all in danger. We're going to have to stop him doing it again. I'll make sure the crew always work in pairs.'

'Which means that someone will be with the killer,' I said.

Big John gave one of his great laughs.

'Grand. So when the next body's found, we'll put the man he worked with in irons and sail home happy.'

I was surprised at how quickly he could find amusement in it all.

'And who will you and I be paired with?' I asked.

His response was immediate.

'Each other.'

I was glad of his choice and saw the sense in it. Our responsibilities for the trip overlapped in many areas and we were both answerable directly to Mr Anderson.

'It's the way our master would want it,' he added.

He put on his jacket and we went back on deck. We left just the helmsman and the lookout at their posts and Big John called everyone else together in the forward hold where they'd slung their hammocks. Their small sea-bags were jammed into corners and gaps in the timber and they crowded together in the low, narrow gloom. There were two mates and twenty-two men and boys there, including three of the four remaining of the six Big John and I had found in the London Tavern. Cammie Drewburgh was on lookout duty. As I listened to Big John, I thanked God that my trade was building ships rather than sailing them. The constant noise and movement, the filthy, cramped conditions on board, the stinking, insistent presence of others, all gnawed at me, and only the need to work together to survive kept the frustrations and angers beneath the surface. And now, this extra, nameless fear brought new tensions to our exchanges. For myself, I wanted only to be done with it all, and back with Emma.

'He seems to prefer your friends,' Big John was saying to Noah McPhee. 'So maybe the four of you should work together.'

'We shouldna be here,' said Noah. 'Shouldna be working for Anderson.'

'Well, you are, so look out for yourselves.'

'I'm no wanting to be paired up with anyone,' said Tam Donald.

'I'm no asking you to do it, I'm telling you that's how it'll be,' said Big John.

Tam stared at him but kept his lips shut tight.

'Should we double up on helm and lookout too?' asked Daniel McStay, the boatswain.

'Not the helm. I can see him from the charthouse. Anyway, nobody would be foolish enough to leave the ship drifting. But we'll keep two up forward.'

He looked round at the men. Their bodies swayed with the ship's pitching and rolling and there was a strange silence in the hold, a stillness at the heart of the rushing wind and sea. All their eyes were on him.

'Right, Daniel,' he said. 'Get the new watches made up and organise the pairings.'

He motioned for me to follow him as he climbed up to the deck.

'Do you trust me?' he asked as we turned to keep the wind at our backs.

'Of course.'

'Good. I like your company well enough, but the thought of spending every minute with you pains me. I'm going to settle the course then have a silent pipe in my cabin.'

'Then I shall go back down and see what the crew are saying.'

He swayed his way back along the deck, moving easily to counter the ship's movement. His strength with the men and with the unusual situation in which we found ourselves was admirable. I can only think that he had seen more things at sea than I could imagine and that the killings were almost a diversion in the daily task of thrashing across the wind towards Scotland.

By the time I got back down to the hold, some of the crew had already left. Others were climbing into hammocks and the boatswain was still arguing with Noah.

'We shouldna have to do any of it,' Noah was shouting. 'We're no sailors. You ken what you're doin', you can look out for yourselves, we never know what's comin' at us.'

The boatswain bunched his fist in front of Noah's face.

'This is what'll be comin' at you if you dinna do as you're told.'

He was a big man. Too big for Noah.

'Ach, leave him, Noah,' said Tam Donald. 'Come away. We're on lookout in a while. Just think of the money.'

Noah spat on the deck, pushed the boatswain's fist aside, shoved Tam out of the way and started back up the steps.

'He'll be all right,' said Tam. 'I'll keep him quiet.'

'If you dinna, he'll be next. And it'll be me who does it,' said the boatswain.

Tam grinned.

'I'm surprised to see you with them,' I said, as he turned to follow Noah.

'Why?'

I didn't want to mention his daughter but I think my face must have shown my embarrassment.

'Life goes on,' he said. 'Anyway, I'm no with them. It was just chance that I was there that night you kidnapped us.'

'You seemed happy enough.'

'Does drink no make you happy?'

'Not if I'm with a man who's... '

I stopped. I couldn't say it.

He shook his head and looked hard at me.

'Nobody kens what goes on in folks' heads,' he said.

I thought of following him as he climbed up to the deck, but I was weary. I hauled myself up into my hammock and watched the bulkheads moving up and down as I hung steady between them.

I don't know how long I slept but I was woken by shouts and a rough hand shaking me. It was the boatswain.

'On deck,' he said. 'We've lost another one.'

Others were stumbling from their hammocks and it was a while before I could pull on my boots and go up to join the crew around the foot of the mainmast. The word was that Tam had gone forward looking for Noah. It was their lookout watch but there was no-one there. In the end, Noah joined him and it was only when they started talking that they realised that Cammie hadn't been there to be relieved. It was Tam who raised the alarm and all hands had been called to search the ship from stem to stern. Noah was still at his lookout post in the bows, one of the mates was at the wheel, and Big John had some questions for Tam. The rest of us spread through the holds and spaces, crawling into the bilges, opening every compartment.

We searched for a good hour but there was no trace of Cammie. No-one doubted that he was now at the bottom of the black North Sea. Big John got us together again. We stood there, listening to his new orders and knowing that, for all the wind's whistling and the sea's crashing against the hull, the real dangers lay somewhere in the crew. Some of them had been shipmates for many years, but their eyes were flicking around, each man unwilling to trust any other.

'So forget about being in pairs, we all work together from now on,' Big John was saying. 'Wherever you are, make sure there are always at least three other men with you. We'll take a chance and set more sail. I want to get us back while I've still got a crew.'

He nodded to the boatswain, who immediately started shouting his orders.

'All hands. Clew up the mainsail. Stand by the braces.'

'What about Noah?' said Tam. 'He's still on lookout.'

'Stay with him,' said Big John. He jerked his thumb at me. 'You, too, Joe. And keep your eyes aloft, too.'

I nodded and climbed up on to the foredeck with Tam. The ship was heeled over on the larboard tack and we bent into the wind to crab our way up the slope to the bows. Suddenly, Tam stopped.

'Where is he?' he shouted.

We both scanned the deck ahead of us. Tam was right. We saw only the silhouettes of the bell, the rails and a single vent. The wind and movement had uncoiled several of the ropes from their belaying pins and they shifted back and forth on the deck. It was only when we came right up beside them that we saw that the bundle was made up of more than ropes.

Noah McPhee lay among them, his left leg tangled with them, his arms flung out and his neck a long cut from ear to ear, so deep that his head lay back at a preposterous angle. His blood had poured every-where but there was still some left in him and it oozed out on to the deck and slid beneath his shoulders. I grabbed him and pulled him clear of the ropes, pushing his head forward to try to close the gaping flesh at his throat. The chill of the wind seemed to bite more deeply into me. I stood up and looked ahead at the grey tumbling seas. I grabbed Tam's shoulder and pointed back at the rest of the crew. Together we made our way towards them and, from the top of the foredeck steps, I shouted to Big John.

It took a while to get his attention but, at last, he came forward and stood looking at the body, his head shaking slowly before he raised it to look across the waves running towards us. He turned once to where the crew was beginning to climb the rigging to set more sail on the topgallants and royals. As he watched them, he suddenly shrugged and turned back.

'Grab his shoulders,' he said to Tam and me.

We moved to Noah's head while Big John bent to take his feet.

'Right,' he said, when we'd lifted him clear of the deck. 'This one's going straight over the side. I've wasted enough time with villains this trip.'

Tam and I looked at one another, but Big John was already pulling Noah towards the starboard rail. We had no choice but to follow and, as soon as we were near enough, Big John heaved the legs over and, as Noah's chest lifted, we stumbled forward and let go of his shoulders. We had no time to see the splash and heard nothing over the shrill wind.

'You say nothing of this,' said Big John. 'I'll tell them in good time. But now, I want to get on as much sail as she'll carry to get us out of here and back on shore. Understand?'

We both nodded.

'Right. Are you willing to stay together as lookouts? Just the two of you?'

Tam and I looked at each other and said nothing.

'It's either that or one of you stays here and takes his chance with whoever comes along.'

'Aye,' said Tam. 'We'll stay.'

I nodded my agreement.

'I'll send a boy up with a bucket and scrubber,' said Big John. He pointed at the dark stains on the deck. 'You can start getting rid of this.'

We said nothing when he left us and, for a while, we took turns in looking at the sea ahead and scrubbing the blood from the deck. Then, as we stood with our arms bracing us against the forward rail, I saw Tam's head nodding. His lips moved but I couldn't hear what he said.

'What?' I shouted.

He looked at me, as if surprised to see me there.

'I was just saying a wee prayer for my lassie. She can rest now,' he said.

I just nodded.

'Every time I saw them,' he went on, 'I couldna get her out of my head. Thirteen year old, she was.'

There was nothing I could say. Tam's daughter had been raped and strangled. They'd found her in a fish barrel.

'Now they're away,' he said. 'Down with the devil they've been serving all these years.'

'It must make you happy,' I said.

He shook his head.

'If I could still hear her singin', that'd make me happy. But at least they've paid. That doesna happen all that often.'

'There are many who think like you,' I said. 'Many who'll be grateful they're gone.'

The words made him turn to look straight into my eyes. He was quiet for a long moment.

'We've all got our secrets,' he said at last. 'Who's going to care who killed them? The world's better off without them.'

I nodded and we fell back into our silence again.

It wasn't until we were relieved by the next two lookouts that he spoke again.

'Dinna be feared, Joe,' he said. 'I don't think there'll be any more. Do you?' And he skipped down the steps without waiting for me to answer.

As I said, my experience of being on board ships was confined to testing the planking while they were still on the stocks, so I had no way of measuring just how different the voyage was from the usual. Tam's confidence was certainly not shared by the rest of the crew. The silences and the strange groupings and the number of lamps that were kept alight through the dark hours all spoke of the fear that still haunted everyone. They worked hard to keep the ship pushing through the water, all desperate to be on land and away from the hands that had killed four of their fellows.

In the afternoon of the day after Cammie and Noah had been killed, the wind backed through a hundred degrees and we were suddenly dancing along under full canvas with a force six coming over the larboard quarter, the figurehead's outstretched arm pointing directly at Aberdeen. We moved around in groups, watchful, trusting no-one. I spent most of my time with Big John and the boatswain, and we were rarely out of sight of several others. When we eventually saw the low profile of the Scottish coast up ahead, Big John laughed, slapped me on the shoulder and said, 'Well, Joe. We kept him quiet after all.'

I couldn't help smiling with him.

'What of the dead men?' I said. 'You'll have to tell the police.'

'Just consider, though,' he said, his arm still at my shoulder, 'Noah McPhee, Cammie Drewburgh, Rab Robertson, Davie Strachan. There winna be much grieving for the likes of that. They may even give me a reward.'

'And what about Mr Anderson?' I said.

'You can do the sums,' he said. 'Four men times the number of days since we left Aberdeen. That's how many shillings he's saved. I canna see him shedding too many tears.'

He was right, of course. When we made harbour, Mr Anderson came on board and quickly dismissed the 'worthless scum', as he called them, concentrating instead on asking Big John and myself about how the ship handled and how she'd fare on the crossing to Jamaica. He charged me with the task of keeping him informed of how the police investigations progressed and invited us both to take a drink with him. Big John had no woman to go back to and so was glad to accept. I gave my excuses, anxious as I was to be back with Emma and tell her of the strangeness and horrors of the voyage.

As I walked down York Street, the sounds of horses, handcarts and the calls of the people working on the quays were soothing. They reminded me that I was back where I belonged, and safe in my own element again. I opened the door and went through to the bedroom. Emma was lying in her usual place, her eyes fixed on the door. As she saw me enter, the happiest smile came across her face. I smiled back, went across and kissed her. With great difficulty, she pulled her left arm from under the covers and lifted it to touch my cheek. Her right arm lay, still and useless as always, hidden in the sheets.

At first, we said nothing, I because my throat was full of tears, she because one night, in Sinclair's Close, her voice had been ripped from her.

Then, 'They're gone, my darling,' I said. 'All of them.'

# Of a Bicycle Made For Two

## Keith Miles

*Keith Miles' achievements are diverse in the extreme, but he is perhaps best known as a successful author of historical novels under the name of Edward Marston. Much of his writing is in a light vein and 'On a Bicycle Made for Two' is no exception. As with his contribution to last year's CWA anthology,* Green For Danger, *Keith has made good use of the tensions in a small village community in another agreeable story.*

It was at the Annual Summer Fete that they first heard about the event. Peter Figgis, dressed in white flannels, an ancient striped blazer and a straw hat, was surprised by their ignorance. He was enjoying a drink with the newcomers outside the beer tent when the subject came up.

'Nobody's told you about the Bossingham Dash?' he asked.

'No,' replied Malcolm Whipple with a shrug. 'We only moved into the village three months ago. What is it – a 100 metres sprint?'

'It's much more interesting than that, Malcolm. It's less of a dash than a middle-distance race, with one or two unusual features.'

'Such as?' wondered Daisy.

'Such as the fact that only married couples can take part.'

'Why?'

'Because it's in the rules laid down by the man who founded the Bossingham Dash. It's the fiftieth anniversary this year. With a name like yours, Daisy, you simply have to take part.'

'Do I?' she said.

'Yes,' insisted Figgis. 'It's a tandem race, you see.'

Raising his beer glass to her, he broke into a song in a rich baritone voice:

*For you'll look sweet, upon the seat*
*Of a bicycle made for two.*

There was a spontaneous round of applause from the crowd outside the tent. Figgis lifted his straw hat in acknowledgement.

Daisy exchanged a fond smile with Malcolm. Bossingham was a tiny village some six miles away from Canterbury and the couple had moved there after living in the heart of Manchester. They had still not adjusted properly to the more leisurely pace of rural life or to its quainter eccentricities. Malcolm Whipple was a tall, slim, bearded man in his early thirties with handsome features. His faint northern accent marked him out as a stranger to Kent. Daisy hailed from London but three years at Manchester University, and another five in the city itself, had not robbed her altogether of her Cockney twang. She was a bright, attractive young woman in her late twenties with auburn hair and a toothy grin.

Peter Figgis was chairman of the committee that had organised the fete and, as such, took on the role of greeting any new faces. Now retired from his job as a bank manager in Ashford, he had thrown himself with vigour into village activities and, in spite of his age, still played regularly in the Bossingham Cricket XI. He was a plump man of medium height with a rubicund face and a permanent smile. Figgis had warmed to the Whipples as soon as he had introduced himself to them.

'No children, I see,' he observed.

'Not yet,' said Malcolm.

'And you're both fit and healthy.'

'We play tennis twice a week, and Daisy goes to dance classes.'

'Better and better.'

'Malcolm is the real fanatic,' explained Daisy. 'He runs almost every day. He took part in the London Marathon last year and he's been in the Great North Run twice.'

'This is wonderful,' said Figgis, downing the remains of his drink. 'You simply *must* compete in the Bossingham Dash. We could finally have found someone who can actually beat them.'

'Beat them?' echoed Daisy.

'The Stallards – Roy and Sarah of that name.'

'Do they go in for this tandem race as well?'

'They've taken it over, Daisy,' said Figgis, rolling his eyes. 'They've won it four times in a row. According to the rules, a fifth consecutive win means that they can keep the trophy in perpetuity. That would be an absolute disaster.'

'Would it?'

'Yes. Technically, it would mean the end of the Bossingham Dash.'

'Couldn't a new trophy be bought?'

'Not if we abide by the rules, and they're sacrosanct.'

'Can't they be changed?'

'Only by the man who drafted them and that poses a problem. Arthur Luckhurst died twenty years ago. Much as he loved the event, I doubt if even Arthur is able to tinker with the rules posthumously.'

'We're not really cyclists, Mr Figgis,' said Malcolm, defensively. 'In fact, we've never been on a tandem in our lives. Besides, we don't own one so there's no chance of our getting involved.'

'Most of the competitors don't own tandems,' Figgis told them. 'They simply hire them for the race. There's a bicycle shop in Canterbury that has half-a-dozen of them to rent out each year. Of course,' he added, darkly, 'nobody is allowed to hire the finest machine in the shop.'

'Why not?' asked Daisy.

'That's reserved for the people who actually run Mercury Cycles.'

'And who are they, Mr Figgis?'

'Who else? Roy and Sarah Stallard!'

Sarah Stallard cleaned the cup every day. It occupied pride of place on their mantelpiece between large framed photographs of them winning the trophy in previous years. Made of silver, it was almost two feet tall, its lid surmounted by a couple on a miniature tandem. Inscribed on a silver plaque attached to the base were the names of those who had won the Bossingham Dash over the past forty-nine years. Roy and Sarah Stallard were intensely proud of their own record in the event.

Sarah was still putting a shine on the cup when her husband got back to their cottage that evening. She gave him a welcoming smile.

'Busy day, darling?' she asked.

'Lots of people in the shop,' he said, 'but only one genuine sale.'

'Never mind. It's been a wonderful summer for us. We've sold more mountain bikes than ever before, and the skateboards have been snapped up in dozens.' She stepped back to admire the trophy. 'It was a good idea of yours to branch out into skateboards, Roy.'

'If we're going to stay in business, we have to diversify.'

'We should have a real boost next month,' she said, complacently. 'When we win the Bossingham Dash for a record fifth time, we're sure to get lots of publicity. After we had our picture in the papers last year, we sold two tandems. We may do even better this time.'

'Assuming that we win, Sarah.'

'There's no doubt about that, is there?'

'I hope not,' he said, 'but I've been hearing whispers. We've got the usual bunch this year and we can beat them hollow. What worries me is these newcomers.'

'Newcomers?'

'Malcolm and Daisy Whipple. That couple who moved into Meadow View. You must have spotted them.'

'That handsome man with a beard?' she said with a flicker of lust. 'Oh, yes. I spotted him when I walked past their house with the dog. If I were ten years younger, I'd fancy him like mad. Actually,' she added with a shrill laugh, 'I'd fancy him if I were ten years older as well.'

'Behave yourself, Sarah!' he chided.

'He's drop-dead gorgeous. You should see him in a pair of shorts.'

'I will – when he races against us in the Bossingham Dash.'

Sarah was jolted. Now in her late-forties, she had long, narrow face that featured an aquiline nose, a large mouth and a pair of piggy eyes that began to dart with apprehension. Her cadaverous body suggested years at the mercy of various Spartan slimming regimes. Roy Stallard, by contrast, was a big, solid man with rapidly thinning hair and a weather-beaten face. Ten years older than his wife, he shared the same manic pride in their cycling achievements. News that they might at last have serious rivals in the tandem race had disturbed him.

'Are they any good?' demanded Sarah, hands on her hips.

'Who knows? I've never seen them in the saddle.'

'We can't let anyone beat us, Roy.'

'I know,' he said, gritting his teeth. 'Lose this year and we'd have to win for the next five in order to keep the trophy for good. My dodgy knee is not going to last that long, Sarah.'

'Neither is my bad back,' she moaned. 'What are we going to do?'

'Keep calm, for a start.'

Sarah stamped her foot. 'How can I keep calm when someone is threatening to take the cup away from us? I've set my heart on winning it for good. I won't have some Johnny-Come-Lately and his wife, swanning into the village and stealing the thing from under our noses.'

'That may not happen, Sarah,' he said, trying to soothe her. 'All I know is that Peter Figgis has persuaded them to take part.' Raising a hand to silence her protest, he went on quickly. 'Yes, I know that Figgis will do anything to spike our guns but that doesn't mean he's found a couple who are good enough to beat us. We still hold the course record, remember. Nobody else has got within two minutes of that.'

'*He* might,' she said, bitterly. 'Malcolm Whipple. He looks really fit, Roy, and he's much younger than us.'

'Let's check him out. After all, it takes two to ride a tandem. He may be a wizard on wheels but this wife of his – Daisy – may turn out to be a hopeless. We may find that the Whipples are no threat at all.'

'But what if they are, Roy?'

'In that case,' he said, grimly, his eye falling on the trophy that was now gleaming on their mantelpiece, 'measures will have to be taken. Drastic measures, if need be. That cup is our personal property.'

Since the village had no shop, residents of Bossingham who wanted a morning paper had to go to the neighbouring village of Stelling Minnis, a mile and a half away. The shop there was a veritable Aladdin's Cave, selling, in addition to newspapers and magazines, alcohol, hardware, lottery tickets, haberdashery, cigarettes and tobacco, basic medical supplies, fresh fish, game in season, an astonishing range of groceries, fruit and vegetables, and, during winter months, a selection of green Wellington boots. Videos could also be hired and those who penetrated to the inner recesses of the establishment found the smallest post office in the county at their service.

Daisy thought the place was enchanting. She loved its amiable clutter and its strange blend of aromas. She also found that it was ideal place to meet people. When she collected her newspaper that Saturday morning, she bumped into Peter Figgis, who was coming in to pick up his copy of the *Daily Mail*. He was pleased to see her.

'Have you gone into training yet?' he asked.

'No, Mr Figgis,' she confessed. 'To be honest, we've been having second thoughts about the whole thing.'

'Nonsense! You must take part.'

'Malcolm and I are not sure that we really qualify. Let's face it, we've only been here five minutes. We feel rather like interlopers.'

'I don't care if you've been here five minutes or five years,' said Figgis, jovially. 'The rules are quite clear. Everyone living within the boundaries of Bossingham is entitled to compete in the Dash. That's why Jack and Enid Haynes sold their bungalow in Stelling Minnis and moved a mere mile and a half down the road. They were desperate to take part.'

'Did they win?'

'Unfortunately, no,' he admitted with a sigh. 'They hit a pothole and took a bit of a tumble. Jack still walks with a limp but you can hardly notice the scars on Enid's face since she had cosmetic surgery. Mind you,' he went on, 'they were leading the race at the time.'

'I had no idea that it was so dangerous.'

'It's very dangerous,' said a woman's voice behind her. 'It's only fair that you should know that before you even consider taking part.'

Daisy turned round to find herself looking into the unforgiving face of Sarah Stallard, all narrowed eyelids and cold smile. Figgis introduced the two of them and beamed like the manager of a champion boxer.

'Daisy is here to take your crown away, Sarah,' he warned. 'She and her husband have set their sights on the Bossingham Dash.'

'That's not true at all,' said Daisy, timidly. 'We're raw beginners.'

'You've got three weeks to get yourselves in trim.'

'Roy and I have been in training for months,' boasted Sarah. 'And, of course, we've been cycling together for years now. More to the point, we know the course. It's very tricky.'

'Is it?' asked Daisy.

'Several competitors have got lost in the past.'

'Not if they've been over the route enough times,' argued Figgis. 'Don't listen to her, Daisy. If you'll pardon a dreadful pun, there are wheels within wheels here. Sarah is trying to frighten you off.'

'On the contrary, Peter. We want a proper race this year – all the more the merrier. Besides,' she went on, glancing at Daisy's newspaper, 'the Bossingham Dash has never been won by *Guardian* readers before. Roy and I are *Daily Telegraph* people, like most winners of the trophy.'

'It doesn't matter if Daisy and her husband read the *Guardian* or the *Greyhound Fancier's Gazette*,' said Figgis, confidently. 'My guess is that they'll be the team to beat.'

'Only if we take part,' noted Daisy, 'and that's highly unlikely.'

'Why?' challenged Sarah. 'Are you afraid to be humiliated?'

'Of course not, Mrs Stallard.'

'Then you're probably scared of all those potholes on the course.'

Figgis clicked his tongue. 'Stop trying to put her off, Sarah.'

'I want to encourage her, Peter. It may be that she actually likes being chased by dogs.' Sarah grinned as she saw the look of horror on Daisy's face. 'Yes, that's one of the many hazards of the Bossingham Dash. The two Alsatians at Cragg's Farm are the worst, though the Yorkshire terrier at the White Hart can give you a nasty bite. Martin Baber still has the marks on his leg to prove it.' She patted Daisy on the back. 'It's not so much a cycle race as an obstacle course,' she said. 'I think the two of you are very brave even to think of joining in.'

Roy Stallard was cleaning his car that afternoon when he saw the lone figure running towards him. Realising who it was, he broke off and leaned on his gate so that he could speak to the man. Malcolm Whipple was moving with speed along the lane, his stride long, low and economical, his breathing easy. In his shorts, vest and running shoes, he looked like an Olympic athlete. Roy raised a palm to stop him.

'Hello, there,' he said, cheerily. 'Welcome to the village!'

'Thanks.'

'I'm Roy Stallard.'

'Pleased to meet you,' said Malcolm, shaking the proffered hand. 'Malcolm Whipple. You run a bike shop in Canterbury, I hear.'

'My fame goes before me. What's your line, Malcolm?'

'The book trade. I manage Ottaker's in Folkestone.'

'Does your wife work?'

'Oh, yes,' replied Malcolm. 'Daisy is no stay-at-home. She teaches English at a school in Ashford. The beauty of it is that we get to use their tennis courts free. That's our mutual passion – tennis.'

'What about running?'

'I'm easing off a little. I only do five miles a day now.'

'Five miles!' gulped Roy. 'I'm not sure that I could *walk* that far. But, then, I've always been a cycling man myself,' he said, airily. 'Been all over the country on two wheels – and across to France. Sarah and I more or less live on that tandem.'

'So I understand. You're the stars of the Bossingham Dash.'

'In a manner of speaking,' said the other, feigning modesty. 'Is it true that you and your wife may be among the starters this year?'

'It's only an outside possibility.'

'Oh?'

'The truth is that we're complete novices, Mr Stallard. We can both ride bicycles, of course, but we've never been near a tandem. And we've certainly never raced one.'

'They're not as easy to ride as they look. Tony found that out.'

'Tony?'

'Tony Preston,' said Roy, pointing to the pub nearby. 'Landlord of the Hop Pocket. He and his missus tried to overtake us on a bend in last year's Dash and Tony lost control of the steering. Pair of them went arse-over-tip. That's how Tony got that broken nose. At least,' he added with a chuckle, 'he *says* it was. I reckon that his wife punched him on the hooter for colliding with that tree. Marion Preston has a vicious streak.'

'Will they be competing this time?'

'No way! Tony swears he'll never even look at a tandem again.'

'Just as well, by the sound of it.'

'In any case,' Roy went on, 'we wouldn't be able to hire out one of our machines to him this year. That goes for you as well, I'm afraid.'

'Does it?'

'All our tandems are booked.'

'Oh, I see,' said Malcolm with a hint of disappointment.

'So you wouldn't be able to enter the Dash, even if you wanted to.' Roy bared his teeth in a triumphant grin. 'Tell you what,' he suggested. 'Instead of chafing your balls against the saddle of a tandem, why don't you *run* against us in the race?'

After he had showered, Malcolm came downstairs to find that Daisy had a cup of tea waiting for him in the kitchen. Sipping it gratefully, he told her about his encounter with Roy Stallard. Daisy seized on the excuse to drop out of the Bossingham Dash.

'That's it, Malcolm,' she decided. 'If we have no machine to ride, we'll simply have to forget it.'

'I'm not so sure.'

'But you just said that all the tandems were booked.'

'That's what he told me,' agreed Malcolm, 'but I don't know that I believed him. I think he was deliberately trying to stop us from entering, Daisy. First of all, his wife puts the wind up you with stories about crashes and dangerous dogs. And now, he has a go at me.' He took another sip of tea. 'They're worried. They think we can beat them.'

'How? They've been training for months.'

'Only because they *need* to train,' he said. 'Roy Stallard looks unfit and overweight to me. OK, they've won the trophy four times in a row but that's because they've never been pushed. According to Mr Figgis, most people only take part in the race for fun. It's all a laugh to them. They don't even try to win. So the Stallards romp home time and again.'

'I didn't take to the wife at all,' said Daisy. 'She reminded me of a kid I teach in the Third Form – sly and deceitful. You know, the kind who'll stop at nothing to drop others in the shit.'

'Then she and her husband are well-matched. Roy Stallard was one of those clever buggers who always has to have the whip hand over you. Didn't like him one bit.'

'Mr Figgis reckons that nobody in the village likes either of them.'
She remembered something and giggled. 'Apparently, Sarah Stallard's
nickname is Lady Macbeth. She's the one who eggs her husband on.'

'I doubt if he needs all that much egging, Daisy.' He sat back in his
chair and pondered. 'Do you know?' he said at length. 'I wonder if we
shouldn't throw our hat into the ring, after all.'

'We can't, Malcolm – and you know why.'

'Do you want those monsters to crow over everyone in the
village?'

'No,' said Daisy, mindful of her conversation at the shop that
morning. 'I'd really love to wipe that supercilious expression off
Sarah Stallard's face. I hate it when people look down their noses at
me.'

'Then why don't we take them on?'

'We don't have a tandem, Malcolm.'

'We find one. They don't have a monopoly.'

'But they're experts.'

'If we practice hard enough, we can become experts as well. The
Stallards have a psychological advantage. They convince everyone
else in the race that they can't possibly win. That's why Lady Macbeth
and hubby have snatched the trophy four times. If they're such ace
cyclists,' he reasoned, 'why are they troubled by a couple of tender-
foots like us?'

'Maybe they're not as good as they pretend.'

'There's only one way to find out, Daisy.'

She shook her head. 'No, it would be wrong for us to enter.'

'Not any more,' he said, eyes glinting with determination. 'After
the way they treated us, they deserve to be taken down a peg or two.
We're not only going in that race – we'll damn well win it!'

'I don't believe it!' exclaimed Sarah Stallard, hurling the secateurs to
the ground with anger. 'Where on earth did they get their tandem?'

'Peter Figgis borrowed it from a friend in Chartham.'

'I might have known that *he'd* be behind this.'

'He's shown the Whipples around the course,' said her husband.
'Figgis is coaching them and that disturbs me, Sarah. Don't forget that

he and his wife actually won the race thirty years ago. He knows what it takes to lift that trophy.'

'Our trophy!' she cried. 'It belongs to us, Roy.'

'Only if we're first past the post again this year.'

Sarah was pulsing with fury. She had been pottering in the garden when Roy broke the news to her. Reclaiming the secateurs, she held them up and snapped them shut.

'I know what I'd like to do with these,' she said, menacingly. 'I'd like to send Peter Figgis's interfering voice two octaves higher.'

'He's not the problem, Sarah. It's them. The Whipples.'

'So young, so fit, so bloody earnest.'

'Nevertheless, we might still beat them fair and square.'

'We can't take that chance, Roy. There's far too much at stake.'

'Yes,' he conceded. 'Talking of stakes, I've got some more bad news for you. Tony Preston has chalked up the odds on the board at the pub. He's made Malcolm and Daisy Whipple the favourites.'

'That's an insult!' she exploded.

'So I told him.'

'How can he put them above us? For heaven's sake, we've won the race four times – they've never been on a tandem before.'

'Peter Figgis is to blame. He convinced Tony that he's found a team that can knock us off our perch. Annoying thing is that lots of people in the village believe him. All the early money has been bet on the Whipples so far.'

'We're not going to put up with that, Roy!'

'I know. Steps will have to be taken.'

'The sooner the better. I want those two out of the race.'

'Leave it to me, Sarah.'

'Remember one thing,' she said, pointing the secateurs at him.

'What's that?'

'Be ruthless. All's fair in love, war and the Bossingham Dash.'

Once they got the hang of it, Malcolm and Daisy began to enjoy riding on the tandem. Starting off was the only thing they found difficult at first. As soon as they had mastered that, their confidence steadily grew. They were amazed at how much speed the two of them could generate on a long, straight stretch of road. There was another bonus. It somehow drew them even closer together. The perfect coordination they achieved in the saddle was reflected in their domestic life.

Notwithstanding the efforts of Peter Figgis to talk up their chances, they knew that it would not be easy to win. Had they been racing on a main road, they would have backed themselves against the Stallards, but the course over which they had to ride was strewn with hazards. Going up and down hills, it twisted and turned along a series of narrow lanes that, in some places, became little more than rutted tracks. They soon made the acquaintance of the dogs. Fear put a surge of power into their legs as they sought to outrun the gnashing teeth.

But it was the other setbacks that really irked them. As they came round a bend during one training session, they saw that broken glass had been scattered across the ground. Both tyres were soon flat. They had to trudge all the way home, pushing the heavy machine. As they passed the Stallard cottage, they saw the curtain twitch.

'I fancy it was *their* doing,' said Daisy, ruefully.

'I'm sure it was,' agreed Malcolm, 'but we must pretend that the thought never crossed our minds. Rise above them, Daisy.'

'But they're cheats.'

'Cheats never prosper.'

'Then how did they win the race four times in a row?'

'We'll ask them as we overtake them this year.'

Daisy was lifted by his buoyant optimism. Having mended the punctures, they were soon back on the tandem, but this time they rode more slowly so that they see any obstacles in their path. There were none. On the following evening, however, they learned just how perilous their training run could be. Not only was a large stone thrown at them by an unseen hand, they also had to negotiate their way past more broken glass and avoid being knocked to the ground by a trailer that suddenly rolled down a hill after them.

When they got back to the safety of their home, Daisy was shaking.

'That was scary, Malcolm,' she said.

'We survived.'

'They tried to kill us.'

'No, Daisy,' he said, giving her a consoling hug. 'They're tried to frighten us, that's all. Mr Figgis warned us that they'd have a few tricks up their sleeve.'

'Those were more than tricks. If that trailer had hit us, we'd both have ended up in hospital. I think we should tell the police.'

'What evidence do we have?'

'The evidence of our own eyes, Malcolm.'

'It's not enough,' he pointed out. 'Besides, we mustn't let them get to us. Call in the police and the Bossingham Dash might be in jeopardy. No, the only way to get even with the Stallards is to rub their noses in it. We take all they can throw at us then come back to win the race.'

She was dubious. 'Will we still be alive to take part?'

'Of course.' He kissed her softly on the forehead. 'Hey, I've got a great idea. Next time we go out on the tandem, you ride at the front.'

'Me? Why?'

'Because your bum is much nicer to look at than mine.'

Roy and Sarah Stallard were reaching the point of desperation. Every time they tried to sabotage their main rivals, they failed. They even made a nocturnal attempt to steal the Whipples's tandem from their garage, but, when they broke in, they discovered that the machine had been moved into the house itself. The day of the race got nearer. Panic set in.

'We've got to stop pussyfooting around like this,' declared Sarah. 'I'll finish them off this time.'

'How often have I heard you say that?'

'I'm taking no chances, Sarah,' said her husband, reaching into the cupboard for his air rifle. 'I've found the perfect place for an ambush. It's halfway down that steep hill. If I wing Malcolm with a pellet, he'll lose control of the tandem and the pair of them will come off when they're travelling at maximum speed. The least we can hope for is a broken leg.'

'What if you miss?'

'From a distance of five yards? No chance. In any case,' he went on, pulling his air pistol from the cupboard. 'I can take a second shot with this to make sure.'

'No, you can't, Roy.'

'Why not?'

'Because *I'll* do that,' insisted Sarah, snatching the pistol from his grasp. 'Malcolm Whipple won't know what hit him.' She checked her watch. 'Come on. We'd better go. They always do a practice run at seven. Since it's their last ever ride on a tandem, we don't want to miss it.'

Before they set out that evening, Malcolm Whipple took the precaution of driving around the five-mile course in his car to make sure there were no obstacles or booby traps left there by the Stallards. When he got back, he assured Daisy that they would have a clear run for once. She was both comforted and emboldened.

'Do you think that I *could* ride in front for a change?' she asked.

'Please do. I'd much rather take a back seat.'

'How good are the brakes?'

'Very good,' he told her. 'You'll be fine, Daisy.'

'I'd just like to try it once.'

He grinned. 'Remember the last time you said that?'

She punched him playfully then led the way to the hall, where the tandem was waiting in readiness. They were soon on the road. Daisy was tentative at first but she gradually got better and elected to increase speed. By the time the steep hill came into view, they were moving at a fast pace. Even when they stopped pedalling, they were still haring along.

'Watch out for the bend on the hill,' he warned.

'I can manage.'

'It's sharper than it looks, Daisy.'

'Who's in charge of this machine – me or you?'

To prove how confident she felt, she started to pedal again until she met the gradient. Having only seen it from the rear seat before, Daisy had not realised how difficult it was to negotiate the bend at speed. She tried to put the brakes on but the tandem had built up momentum by now and it hurtled downward. Daisy lost her nerve.

Unable to steer around the bend, she instead took them through an open five-barred gate and down a grassy bank, shrieking with fear as they bumped along. Her screech produced an unexpected result. Seeing that the machine was headed straight for them, Sarah and Roy Stallard emerged from the bushes in which they had been concealed and began to run madly down the field. Daisy did her best to avoid them but steering was impossible in the circumstances.

Sarah's bad back was made considerably worse as the tandem ploughed into her and sent her somersaulting crazily in the grass. Roy's dodgy knee gave way completely as he put his foot in a rabbit hole. The two of them lay moaning on the ground while Malcolm and Daisy picked themselves up. Miraculously, the riders had escaped injury but they had no sympathy for the wounded Stallards. They had clearly been waiting in ambush. Lying on the grass beside Roy was the telltale air rifle. Clutched in Sarah's hand was the pistol she had intended to fire.

Malcolm looked with amusement from one to the other.

'Well,' he said. 'It looks as if you've shot yourselves in the foot.'

Winning the Bossingham Dash was a mere formality. With the Stallards out of the race – and facing stern police questioning – Malcolm and Daisy had nobody who got within a hundred yards of them. As they rode past the finishing line at the Hop Pocket, it was a delighted Peter Figgis who led the cheers. His proteges had won the race, earned him a handsome profit on his bet and whisked the trophy off the mantelpiece in the Stallard Cottage. It was a fitting end to the Fiftieth Anniversary Dash. There was, however, a surprise in store for him and for the crowd that had gathered outside the pub.

Malcolm Whipple held up both hands to still the loud applause.

'Thank you, everyone,' he said. 'It would be wonderful to take the cup home with us, but there's been a slight hitch. Or, to be more exact, there *hasn't* been a hitch at all.'

'We don't really qualify for the race,' admitted Daisy, shyly. 'That's why I was so hesitant to take part. We're not married, you see.'

'Why didn't you say so?' asked Figgis.

'It's not something we wanted to broadcast, Mr Figgis. We tried to

get out of the Dash but Roy and Sarah more or less goaded us into it.
So, although we won today, the cup will have to go to the tandem that
came second. We were just pacemakers.'

'However,' announced Malcolm, gallantly, 'we may not have won
the Bossingham Dash this time, but I'm determined that we will next
year. With luck, we'll qualify by then.'

Dropping to one knee, he held out both hands and sang aloud:
*Daisy, Daisy, give me your answer do,*
*I'm half crazy, all for the love of you*
Everyone there joined happily in the collective proposal.
*It won't be a stylish marriage,*
*I can't afford a carriage*
*But you'll look sweet, upon the seat*
*Of a bicycle made for two.*
Daisy laughed. 'I suppose that I'd better say yes, then.'

# Landfall

## Stephen Murray

*Stephen Murray first came to prominence over a decade ago, with a series of books featuring a police investigator, Alec Stainton. In recent years, like one or two other contributors to this anthology, he has published little in the crime field. So I was delighted to receive 'Landfall' and had no hesitation in selecting it for inclusion in* Crime on the Move. *It is an excellent story and a reminder of Murray's talent, which readers have been missing for too long*

'Cup of tea, sir?'

'Thank you.'

'I've made a sandwich, sir. Potted meat.'

'Lovely grub.'

She flashed him a neat smile and took her tray through into the other room. It was easy to make fun of Fl Lt Dobbs, with his cardigan and his old pipe and his thinning hair, but she had come to feel very comfortable about their long hours on watch together. Fl Lt Dobbs had a wife and two daughters to whom he wrote affectionate letters illustrated with little drawings in the margin, and wasn't at all over-awed in the company of women. He didn't feel compelled to gallantry or innuendo and he kept his hands to himself. He had been a pilot himself in the first war, but he never spoke of it, for which she rather admired him.

The other girls grumbled about the long night shifts, but Joan found them agreeable enough. From time to time she would make a pot of tea or some sandwiches, and around half-past two Fl Lt Dobbs would disappear to the lavatory at the end of the corridor for half an hour, to emerge with the squares of his *Times* crossword filled in. Otherwise, there was nothing to upset the steady hours of duty.

Her job was to scan the cathode ray tube while outside on the bleak headland, buffeted by the winds, a rotating aerial sent its unseen beams far out over the ocean, piercing darkness and cloud, searching for distant aircraft. Inside the low brick building, the display was swept by the index line every eight seconds, and anything the aerial picked up appeared as a green dot. From the grid superimposed on the display, she could work out the approximate distance and bearing of the contact. A powerful radio enabled her to speak to the crews in an emergency, and her job was to guide a lost or damaged aircraft back into visual contact with the land. That at least was the theory. In practice, the equipment was too new, too hastily devised, the atmospheric conditions too often unfavourable. Getting the best out of the rudimentary sets required patience, skill and dedication. It was exhausting work constantly scanning the instrument, forever alert, always keyed up for action which mostly never came.

She sipped her tea. It was hot and strong and heavily sugared. Her mother would have sniffed and called it workmen's tea.

She thought of her cloistered upbringing – the comfortable professional household, the daily bus ride to the girls' grammar school, lacrosse and hockey and pashes for the gym teacher, piano lessons and evenings of homework and Horlicks at bedtime. A year ago, she had been a well-brought up girl, rather on the shy side, no beauty to be sure, but personable enough. A girl sought out at tennis club dances and under the mistletoe but whose heart had never been touched.

But that was then. This was now: sitting in uniform operating highly scientific top-secret equipment with people's lives depending on her.

That was Before Patrick; and this was after.

The sea, five hundred feet below, was differentiated from the night sky only by a dull iridescence, and all that kept them from death was Patrick's continuing ability to distinguish between the two.

Eight convoys were traversing the ocean, on their way to or from America, India, the Cape or the Mediterranean, laden with troops and grain, petrol and tanks. Hundreds of fishing boats were at sea. Eleven U-boats had been reported as having left their bases. But since leaving the Scillies astern four hours ago, Patrick had strained his eyes across that oily waste and seen nothing except the greasy, heaving waves.

He blinked his eyes and adjusted the cockpit heating. His navigator's head turned resentfully and his voice came robotically over the intercom.

'Must you have it so bloody cold?'

'If you want to stay alive, yes.'

It was an old dispute; one of those silly niggles which soured things between people whose lives depended upon their co-operation. It *was* cold in the cockpit. But if it was any warmer, Patrick's head would droop, his eyelids close just for a moment – and the sea would swallow them without a murmur. So for the moment, cold it would stay.

His navigator scanned the instrument panel and then stared out of the cockpit windows.

'See the way that sea's moving? There's a storm ahead.'

'Jonah.'

'And look what he went through.'

'Tell me when you spot a whale.'

The navigator reached for the Thermos flask in its webbing straps. 'Fancy a brew?'

'Sounds good.'

Peace was restored. Patrick brought the machine up another five hundred feet, set the trim, yawned and took his hands and feet off the controls. The tea was hot and strong and loaded with sugar. Two more hours and they'd be on the ground. Debriefing, breakfast and then he'd be tucked up in bed. And when he woke...

Joan.

He had noticed Joan some weeks before, walking a little apart from a gaggle of other WAAFs, quiet and self-contained. He began to look out for her dark hair and composed, enigmatic face around the station. But he never quite knew what prompted him to call out to her, as she cycled past him one sunny afternoon.

He asked her where she was going and she told him, her manner saying plainly that it was none of his business. And he said: Did you know you look rather wonderful when you're angry?

And she had met his eyes for the first time and he had seen that hers were light brown flecked with gold, and the arch of her lips heart-breakingly innocent. And he had said: if you are going out tomorrow, perhaps we could meet somewhere. This weather's too lovely to be stuck on the station all the time.

And she had said: yes, of course. And cycled on. And he had walked across to the parachute shed ten feet high, the sky technicolor blue and the birds singing at twice their normal volume.

Later she told him that she hadn't been cross at all, only nervous, and he was amazed and flattered at the idea that she could be afraid of him. And she laughed and said it *was* rather frightening – *then*. But that was before she knew him. And he said, Promise you'll never be frightened of me again. And it was all so different from the coy young women at church socials and the predatory sisters of his school friends. And in the mess he lay on his bed realising that this was what it was like to be in love.

Joan smiled as she sipped her tea, remembering how it had all started.

Patrick had called out to her as she cycled from her hut towards the guardroom. She had tried to salute and brake at the same time and ended up riding into the kerb. Her heart was palpitating with anxiety. She was sure she must have done something wrong to be shouted at by an officer she didn't know.

He had asked her where she was going, and still thinking herself in trouble she had said: just out – just for a ride – it was her afternoon off; was there some difficulty? – talking too much in her nervousness, unable to meet his eye. And he had said: You look wonderful when you're angry. And she had looked at him for the first time and seen that he was grinning at her. And he had said: if you are going out tomorrow, perhaps we could meet somewhere.

And she had said: yes, of course. And cycled on. And only after-wards realised, wondering, that he had stopped her because he wanted to know her better.

Later, of course, she told him that she hadn't been cross at all, only nervous, and he laughed and made her promise never to be frightened of him. And it was all so different from the bashful young men at the tennis club and the whiskery, whisky-smelling uncles under the mistletoe. And in the hut, when the girls swapped experiences, crude as only girls can be, she lay on her bed hugging her own private miracle to her: the miracle of love given, and returned.

Her life fell into a new, wonderful pattern. When she'd been on duty, the truck returned her to the base at breakfast time. She'd snatch a few hours' sleep. By two-thirty she'd have wolfed a late lunch in the mess and be cycling past the guardhouse. They'd meet where the lanes crossed high on the rolling down, where larks trilled all around and the view stretched past combe-folded village and shy church spire to the silver sea. Together, they'd sit by their bicycles and talk, before pedalling off side by side down narrow lanes where the hedges pressed tightly on each side, past farms squeezed in green clefts, where dogs raised lethargic heads in the shimmering heat; past derelict cottages and new-sprouted radio masts; spinning down to secret coves and toy-town harbours.

Love electrified every part of her life. She'd never done her job so well; never seen the colours so bright; never loved her fellow men and women so much.

They'd kiss in gateways framed with cow-parsley and herb robert, and she'd marvel at the hardness of Patrick's body beneath the severe lines of his uniform, and the laughter in his mesmerising blue eyes; and shiver at the touch of his hands inside her clothes, where no man had ever touched her before.

And he would exclaim at the softness of her skin, the depth of her brown eyes and the silky thickness of her hair when she released it from its pins and bands, telling her over and over how wonderful she was. And the knowledge that she, who had never thought of herself as attractive, could make a man feel like that was unbearably heady.

Patrick glanced at the clock on the instrument panel. Ten to two. He'd land back at base at four. The truck took him over to Intelligence for debriefing. He'd snatch bacon and egg in the mess followed by a few hours' sleep. By two he'd be bolting a late lunch, and half an hour later he'd be cycling past the guardhouse. They'd meet where the lanes crossed high on the rolling down, the wide unfenced byways where the sheep roamed free.

He was flying better, sleeping better, eating better, getting on with the other chaps in the mess better. He'd never seen the colours so bright; never loved the countryside so much. So this was what it was like, being in love. No wonder they wrote so many songs about it.

He wondered where Joan was at this moment. She might be on duty, in the brick hut on the headland, ready to reach out to him in his moment of need. She might be reading or listening to the wireless or playing snap, or back in her billet, mending a blouse with patient stitches.

He never told Joan how the simple knowledge of her presence, hundreds of miles away across the ocean buoyed him up; how her love enabled him to endure the tremendous effort of concentration needed for flying so close to the greedy heaving seas for hours at a time, incessantly scanning the dark water for the darker shadow which might be a ship; constantly on edge for the moment which might never come, when the tedium exploded into a few short minutes of action which might mean his death.

Sometimes he thought that if anything happened between him and Joan, he would simply fall apart, disintegrate into fragments. Only a month before, a pilot had shot himself when the CO refused to transfer him off the station; unable to face the prospect of another night of screaming nerves and bowel-watering fear. It could happen to any of you. You did the job, and then suddenly you could do it no more. Something snapped.

As long as Joan was there to come back to, he knew he would not break like that. He might die from enemy action or from some mechanical fault which caused his aircraft to plunge into the sea; but he would not die from carelessness, or from his own hand; and if ever he needed her, Joan would be there to guide him back to safety.

When Patrick was flying, the nights seemed interminable. If she was not on duty, she could not sleep but lay awake imagining him in trouble – one engine out – caught in a storm – damaged by flak from an enemy ship – relying for help on one of the other girls, one of the

casual, slaphappy girls who spent their nights on duty flirting with the
officer or reading romantic magazines. She imagined the small green
blip appearing on the screen while the operator slipped out for a cigarette; imagined Patrick calling on the radio, repeating his call-sign
over and over, needing help and receiving nothing but the crackle of
interference in the empty ether. Saw Patrick's plane smashing into the
wave-tops and the little green dot fading out unnoticed on the cathode ray screen.

But if she herself was on duty it was scarcely better. Then every
minute seemed an hour as she spent the night half hoping, half dreading that she would hear his voice over the RT; and Fl Lt Dobbs's plat-
itudes were unbearable intrusions as her mind alternated obsessively
between praying that nothing would happen to him and fantasies in
which his aircraft suffered some near-fatal mishap and she guided him
to safety.

She would never tell him how she had suffered, or how afraid she
had been. How could you remain cool and clear-headed and follow
the prescribed procedures when the pilot linked to you by the fragile
invisible thread of the radio beams was your lover?

She was the first girl he had slept with. She had opened the treasure of
her body to him humbly and without reserve, and there was nothing
he would not give her in return.

Compared to the miracle of love with Joan, his previous gauche
fumblings were like the infant gibberish of a child that has not learnt
to talk – passionate embraces after dances with girls he had drunk
enough to believe fascinating; clumsy kisses and explorations in dark
corners, passion battling half-heartedly against stout stitching and
stiff morality. It was an absurd, beautiful paradox that the love he and
Joan made together should be so much more complete, yet so much
more innocent.

Flying just above the ever-heaving swell during the long hours of
the night, constantly searching, constantly tense, the ache for Joan's
body tugged at him like a physical pain. The thought that these hands,
now gloved and manipulating the machine of steel, petrol and
aluminium, had just a few hours before cupped the soft swell of Joan's

breast, traced the contours of her arms and explored the secret fast-
nesses of her body was almost too fantastic to bear. The knowledge
that he might not survive to cycle once more by Joan's side down some
honeysuckle-scented lane or lie hand in hand on a gorse-clad headland made what they had already known more wonderful; each day's
reprieve more precious.

When they finally made love, it was as if everything deep inside her
had been leading up to it; her whole life a preparation for that one
moment. She had expected disappointment, expected selfish male
roughness, expected something as crude as the other girls' bawdy
descriptions, as offensive as her mother's fastidious hints. Instead,
Patrick had been so gentle, the experience so wonderful that the brief
expected pain was ludicrously nothing in comparison. As he sank
exhausted on her breast she clasped him to her and could not believe
so much joy could be made so easily by two people who loved each
other.

She had given Patrick everything, glad to be able to prove how
much she loved him. She could easily end up pregnant – have to leave
the service, return home to the pained reproach of her parents; be
parted from him – and she embraced the risk gladly because it demon-
strated her love. There was nothing she did not want to give him, in
response to the wonderful gift of his love for her.

Losing Joan was unthinkable.
Which made his folly all the more stupid. How could he, who had
known the true gold of love, have been deceived by the base coin of
lust? How could he to whom Joan had gladly surrendered her inner-
most secrets, have traded them for ten minutes of smutty fumbling
with a practised little tramp?

Because he had been drunk, that's how. Beneath his flying mask,
Patrick groaned with self-disgust. He had been flattered to find
himself desired; and in his drunkenness he had believed he could go
just a little further without being unfaithful to Joan, then just a little
further still, until he had found himself in the MT park in the shadows
between two petrol bowsers with his trousers around his ankles and

the Harris girl kneeling before him, his fingers clenched in her dishev-
elled red hair.

Nobody had seen them together, that was one consolation. At
least, nothing had been said. Perhaps his friends had been too
disgusted by his unfaithfulness. Perhaps this was why his navigator
was being short with him tonight. He glanced sideways at the other
man's profile: perhaps they all knew.

His first instinct had been that Joan must never find out. How
could she understand how he could plead his love for her one day, and
barely twenty-four hours later – while Joan was on duty – let himself
make love to another? No woman would understand that. The trouble was, he had no confidence that Rita would keep their secret. She
was not a girl who would be held back by the finer scruples of
conscience. No doubt she'd boast to some friend or other, and that
friend would gossip to another; and sooner or later it would get back
to Joan.

He groaned a second time. How *could* he?


In the hut on the headland, the chink of Fl Lt Dobbs stirring his tea,
she grimaced in disgust.

Fool that she had been.

All the time she believed they had been exchanging their very
souls, the love had been all on one side.

On the other side had been nothing but the callous pursuit of a
scalp. The shared cycle rides, the endless talking, the intimate confes-
sions about her family and her growing up, the explorations of each
others' bodies – for her they had been beautiful and revelatory. For
Patrick, they had simply been a cynical campaign conducted to the
end of, as the other girls would put it, getting inside her knickers. She
was surprised he had thought her worth all that trouble. There were
plenty of girls on the station ready and willing to entertain a good-
looking officer. But no doubt that was part of the attraction: the
excitement of the chase. Being able to brag in the mess that one had
cracked a difficult case, laid siege to a particularly well defended
fortress and brought about its surrender. Got inside the knickers of
that silly virgin who works in the RDF hut.

Because yesterday, when Joan was on duty, Patrick had attended the Friday night dance. And there he had picked up Rita Harris, a freckled redhead who was billeted in Joan's hut, and after he had danced with her a little while, he had taken her to the MT park and there – but Rita had regaled the whole hut, her sly eyes edging all the while towards Joan, with her account of *exactly* what she and Patrick had done in the MT park the night before.

There was only one thing which might redeem him. He himself must tell Joan before anyone else did. There was just a possibility that a girl like Joan could – if not understand – then at least forgive. Even if she didn't it was what he must do. Even now someone might be dripping the poison into Joan's ears. It was all he could do not to turn the aircraft at once on to course for base and push the throttle through the gate.

He glanced at his watch for the umpteenth time. Two o'clock, just gone. In a couple of hours they would be safely down. He wouldn't wait until this afternoon. He would go straight from debriefing and seek her out. After that, it was up to her.

What she felt for Patrick now was at once burning and icy cold. He had made a fool of her. She had been so ready to believe his stories. All those lies men tell, all the plausible words that come so readily to their lips when they are after sex. And she had told herself he was different. She had been flattered by his interest. She believed it when he told her he loved her because she wanted to believe it – and now she despised herself for being such a fool.

He had duped her because she had been willing to be duped, and she had surrendered not just her body, though that felt soiled; but all the things deep inside her, things she had never shared, not with her mother, not with her dearest friend; things that had been stored away like a trousseau to share with the man she loved.

And he had thrown them back in her face. All that inner self of hers, he had taken and cast away, and now there was nothing inside her except a bitter emptiness and a cold, hard kernel of hate. And she nursed it, for it was all she had.

The other girls knew, of course. The concerned looks and the comforting remarks did not hide their pleasure. She thought she was better than them. Now she had had her comeuppance. She thought she had found love. Well, where had her love got her? It wasn't so different after all. Fine words butter no parsnips.

There was a scrape of wood as Dobbs opened the drawer in his desk, followed by the rustle of the newspaper. She glanced at the wall clock: twenty past two.

'Manage on your own for a moment, Joan?'

'Of course, sir.'

She heard his footsteps recede, followed by the distant bang of the lavatory door at the end of the corridor.

It happened in a moment, as these things always did. Flying so low in poor visibility, you were on something before you knew it. The navigator's yell was simultaneous with Patrick's jerk at the control column. They banked so violently that Patrick felt the flesh drawn back from his face, and then he was straightening out over the E-boat which he could just see wallowing in the trough of the waves. As he flicked the switch to select the bombs hung under the wings, a gun on the E-boat was already spitting fire.

There was a brief, terrible moment as they swept over the enemy ship, then he stabbed at the release and felt the aircraft leap as the bombs fell free. At once he put it into a second violent turn. Looking down past the navigator and the wing he saw the E-boat for brief moment silhouetted clearly in the track of the moon. It was picking up speed; he could see the white water foaming at bow and stern; and the lines of tracer reached up towards them. Then there were two violent explosions and the ship vanished behind a curtain of water.

The navigator started to say something and at that moment the aircraft staggered as if punched by a giant hand and the instrument panel in front of Patrick exploded. He felt a dull thump in his stomach and the navigator fell forward with a grunt.

For frantic moments which seemed like hours Patrick wrenched at the controls, trying desperately to fight the aircraft's determination to fall out of the sky. The E-boat had disappeared, lost in the darkness behind them. He had no time to spare to wonder whether he had sunk it. The death facing him now was his own.

Suddenly he found himself flying straight and level just above the heaving waves, both engines racing. Patrick throttled back and gulped a huge mouthful of air. There was a dull taste to it, a mixture of metal and burning. He saw at once that the navigator was dead. Where the back of his head had been was only mush. The instrument panel was a tangle of splintered glass and scorched wires. The altimeter seemed to be working, but that was all. Turn and bank, air speed, rpm, compass, fuel gauges – all so much junk.

There was a nagging ache in his stomach. He guessed a piece of the instrument panel had hit him, but his limbs were moving all right and his brain was clear, so he couldn't have been badly hurt.

He pondered his course of action. The obvious thing was to climb above the cloud and navigate by the moon and stars, but it would take him eight minutes to get above the cloud, and without instruments he would be disorientated in seconds. Even if he kept the plane right way up he could find when he emerged that he was flying in the wrong direction, without enough fuel to get back.

The wind had got up. He looked down at short, steep waves and knew that if he ditched, the plane would be smashed to bits in an instant. He would have no time to escape, but would sink to his watery grave. And Joan would be left to remember him as just another lying philanderer.

They had been heading roughly north-north-east when they met the E-boat. He had banked twice, each time turning through a hundred and eighty degrees, so in theory he was still heading in the same direction. Since being hit, he'd had no time to think of where his desperate attempts to regain control had taken him. Probably he was on a totally different heading. Without a compass, on a night like this, his chances of making a landfall, any landfall, were slim.

Which left just one hope. If, *if* he had not veered too far off course, then there was just a chance he had come within the reach of the RDF set.

He switched his microphone to R/T and began broadcasting his call-sign.

*

She watched the index line sweep round the empty display every eight seconds, regular and hypnotic, unconcerned with her troubles and tragedies.

At twenty-six minutes to three a faint, fuzzy dot appeared. Her hand moved swiftly and automatically to the dial, fine-tuning the transmitter.

After watching it for a few moments, she reached up and switched on the loudspeaker.

'Hello, Hearthrug. Hello Hearthrug. This is Grasshopper. Over.'

He thought of Joan's dark hair, its heavy richness in his hands.

'Hello Hearthrug. Hello Hearthrug, this is Grasshopper, over. Hello… '

The valley of her backbone, firm yet silken, deepening as his hand moved lower.

'Hello Hearthrug. Hello Hearthrug. This is Grasshopper. Over.'

The way she looked up at him, lying in the sheep-bitten grass, her eyes alight with mockery, as she reached up to pull him down.

'Hello Hearthrug, hello Hearthrug. This is Grasshopper. Over.'

Spinning down the narrow lanes to a rocky cove; Joan yelling to him; the sweet sharpness of anxiety as she lifted her hands from the handlebars; the relief as they tumbled off their bikes at the foot of the lane and into each other's embrace.

'Hello Hearthrug. Hello Hearthrug. This is Grasshopper. Over.'

Faint and distorted, a second voice came to him through his headphones: 'Grassho… is … ru… have you… '

Relief sandbagged him. He pictured the little hut on the wind-tossed headland, beside the slowly turning grid of the aerial; inside, the fug, the heads bent over the green displays, the calm voice of the duty WAAF repeating the readings, the green blip growing stronger on the screen, the calm authoritative voices.

And then the voice came once more, and this time it was clearer and there was no mistaking it.

'Hello Grasshopper, hello Grasshopper. This is Hearthrug. Over.'

And it was Joan.

*

Joan sat frozen at the cathode ray screen, as his voice issued from the loudspeaker. Then her hands moved over the switches and dials as she began automatically to follow the procedures which would enable her to guide her lover safely home.

'Grasshopper, this is Hearthrug. Turn port 60.'

She watched the screen. Next time the dial swept round, the fuzzy insect had veered off to the left.

After a few minutes she said: 'Thank you, Grasshopper. Turn starboard 60.'

The fuzzy insect tracked right again.

'Thank you, Grasshopper. We have you now.'

She read the figures off the scale.

'Hello Grasshopper. You are approximately two eighty, two eight zero, miles west-south-west of Lizard Point.'

'Hello, Hearthrug. Hello, Hearthrug. This is Grasshopper. My navigator is dead and cockpit instruments are u/s. I say again, cockpit instruments u/s. Over.'

'Roger, Grasshopper.'

She could guide him to safety. This was what she had been trained for. Automatically, she began to issue instructions.

'Hello, Grasshopper, this is Hearthrug. Grasshopper, this is Hearthrug, over.'

'Grasshopper, over.'

'Hello Grasshopper. Turn starboard 25 degrees. I say again, starboard two five degrees. Over.'

'Grasshopper, starboard two five. Roger.'

Joan watched the display steadily, her concentration not wavering for an instant.

Alone with his co-pilot's body in the cockpit with the wind roaring through the shattered Perspex, Patrick realised he was crying. He uttered a prayer of thanks that it was Joan in the RDF hut tonight. Now that he had so nearly lost the chance for ever, he was desperate to return to her, explain everything to her loving understanding, and lay his head on her soft breast.

He'd give her all she wanted – all his love, the best home, the best life he could make for them both. Even now, just knowing she was there gave him fresh energy. He would make it now. The storm and the E-boat had done their worst. He had almost died. He was alone with a dead navigator in a shot-up aircraft leaking fuel and with half the instruments unserviceable. But he had Joan, and her calm, lovely voice giving him directions. He pictured her bent over her display in the RDF hut, intent upon guiding him home. The speaker would be on; old Dobbs would be leaning over her shoulder, puffing his foul pipe. They'd have telephoned the airfield, and all the arrangements would have been made to receive him: the lights and the crash wagon with its firemen swathed in asbestos, the ambulance and the doctor. He was filled with a supreme confidence. He had been afraid – more afraid than he had thought possible. He had almost died. But Joan was there now, guiding him home. It was all right.

Patrick brought the aeroplane up another thousand feet. This was as high as he could go while staying below the cloud. Holding the aircraft steady was impossible. Rain lashed around him. From time to time, lightning split the black curtain, giving a glimpse of the heaving sea below. The aircraft was buffeted incessantly. Patrick fought it constantly, countering the storm's efforts to fling the aircraft on its back and toss it into the greedy sea below. The structure groaned and screeched with the strains upon it. He felt very weary.

He could tell her now, over the radio. What did it matter if old Dobbs or anyone else could hear? What did anything matter, except that Joan should know he loved her? The idea that he might have died before he could explain made him shiver. He could bear the thought of death better than the thought that Joan's only memory of him should be as a shit who had told her he loved her and then betrayed her.

But it didn't matter now. She would talk him back to the airfield and in a short while he would be back on the ground. He would meet her as she came off duty. He wouldn't waste a moment. He owed it to her to explain face to face.

The sea seemed to be getting steeper. He was very tired now. The ache in his stomach had turned into a throbbing pain. He put a hand to it, and his glove came away stained.

'Hello Hearthrug, this is Grasshopper. There's no sign of the coast. I say again, no sign of the coast.'

'Roger, Grasshopper. Maintain present course and speed.'

Once he was over the land he would pull the aircraft up and bale out. How much fuel did he have? The rain had eased and there seemed to be a lightening in the sky. Surely it should be ahead of him, not away to his right? He pushed his goggles up and rubbed his tired eyes. The pain in his belly had dulled, but his eyelids felt so damnably heavy. It was difficult to think. In a moment he'd see the land, and he would bale out, and Joan would be there.

Joan was lying in the grass. She was smiling up to him, reaching out her arms.

He jerked awake as one of the engines faltered. The aeroplane hesitated. Then it picked up its normal roar and the plane leapt forward once more. At all costs, he must stay awake.

Joan was looking up at him. She reached out and pulled him down, down, down to the softness of her breast.

The noise of the engines seemed to come from a great distance. When it stuttered and ceased, he was hardly aware of it. He felt only a sensation of great peace.

The green line swept round the display every eight seconds. The track of the aircraft edged slowly, so slowly across the screen. She felt the sweat damp on her skin. Her nails dug into the palms of her hands.

The green indicator line swept again. The pilot's voice was fainter now.

'Hello Hearthrug. Hello Hearthrug. This is Grasshopper. Hello Hearthrug. This is Grass...'

Lifting a hand, she flicked the loudspeaker off and the voice was silenced.

She watched the indicator line. Eight seconds. Flash. Eight seconds. Flash. The little green dot was nearing the edge of the display. Eight seconds. Flash. Flash. Flash.

The little green dot vanished from the display.

Distantly, the lavatory flushed. After a moment the door banged and Fl Lt Dobbs came through and peered over her shoulder.

'All quiet?'

'Yes, sir.'

'That's all right, then.' Dobbs looked up at the clock. 'Another night done.' He rubbed his hands. 'You'll be looking forward to spending the afternoon with that boyfriend of yours, I expect.'

'No, sir.'

'No?' He glanced at her. 'This bloody war,' he muttered at last.

'Yes, sir,' she said without emotion.

# Gum's Goer

## Amy Myers

*It seemed to me that an anthology with a theme of 'crime on the move' ought to have a story concerned with air flight. So what could be better than Amy Myers' amusing tale about intrepid pioneers? Like much of Amy's work, 'Gum's Goer' benefits from a historical setting, which is evoked credibly, economically and entertainingly.*

My name is Horatio Gum. You will have heard of me in connection with the extraordinary events at Trailing Edge House in Kent, where I was deliberately prevented from achieving the honour of being the first person to control a heavier-than-air flying machine in the heavens.

I was so stricken by this that I feel I owe it to the world to explain the happenings surrounding the unfortunate murder of Mr Tex Cotten that – through no fault of his – brought about my disaster.

First let me explain my Goer, which is still dear to my heart. It operates on the principle of the flight of birds, which I have studied for many years, devoting thirty minutes of each day in my garden to using my own arms and legs to get the feel of flight. As I circled round, head down, arms flung wide and the wind in my hair, my inspiration came to me, and the Goer was its result.

My dear wife quite understood and supported me in my ambition. So that I should not worry about her, she told me she would spend the time with her sister rather than accompany me to Trailing Edge House. Alas, she overestimated the time that I could have devoted to her. A man's dream must come first. In my case it was no dream. It was a certainty and one from which the world should now be benefiting.

There were four of us in this competition. It was to be held on the lawns on the day after our arrival and judged by three members of the Aeronautical Society. The prize was to be a silver duck. Such a presentation would of course be welcome, but the real honour would be that of being first to conquer the air. Such competitions are usually held in clement weather in the summer months, but for some reason best known to himself our host had chosen December – probably because the heavier construction of his own flying machine would give him an unfair advantage in the colder weather, while his competitors shivered.

I knew of my fellow competitors, though I had never met them in person, but I arrived at this delightful Kentish manor knowing I would sweep all before me. I was met by my host, Major Sir John Dale, who gave me an unwanted tour of his home, but at last I was reunited with my Goer. I was to be escorted by Charlie Thomas, who drove my host's motor car and coaches, to the converted barn allotted for the use of three of the competitors, including myself. The fourth, our host, had his own barn. That shows you the colour of the man.

Charlie took one look at my beloved Goer, then positioned on my handcart, and said: 'You for the flying machines? Sooner you than me.' Ignoring this comment, I followed him to the barn, outside which I met a gentleman – though I would dispute the word – clad in sporting attire of knickerbockers and Norfolk jacket more applicable to the golf course than the lawns of a country house. He had a most unfortunate air of overconfidence, as if he, not I, were about to change the world.

'You'll be Horatio Gum,' he greeted me. 'Joseph Mankelow at your service.' He pumped my hand up and down vigorously, but his eyes were enviously sizing up my Goer.

I glanced at the pile of firewood on Mr Mankelow's handcart standing just inside the barn with some amusement – which I trust I kept hidden. We inventors must always exercise courtesy towards those less intellectually endowed than ourselves.

'I am, sir. Can it be that I am in the presence of Mankelow's Marvel?'

'Indeed you are, sir. Isn't she a beauty?'

His mechanic was struggling to erect the firewood into a large diamond-shaped frame, consisting of wood and wire spokes and attached to what appeared to be a small tank and motor engine on two wheels. If anyone were rash enough to crawl inside it, there was just enough room for a human operator.

'It is indeed a marvel,' I replied truthfully. The marvel was that anybody could dare to bring such an idiotic contraption to this serious competition for heavier-than-air flight.

'You can pick my Marvel up and carry her with you,' its proud owner explained. 'She'll revolutionise warfare. Pop over and see what the enemy's doing and back in time for tea, eh? She'll even replace buses when everyone has their own Marvel to flit around the sky.'

I was about to modestly reveal my own machine when we were interrupted by what appeared to be an American cowboy, with a ridiculous large hat, red shirt and high boots. He had been watching us from the doorway at the far end of the barn.

'Expect this junk to get in the air?' he enquired of Mr Mankelow after a contemptuous inspection of the Marvel. It was a verdict with which I fully agreed, but would not be discourteous enough to voice.

'I do indeed, sir,' Joseph spat back at him. 'And who might you be?'

'Tex Cotten. Heard of me?'

'I have, sir. You fly kites, do you not? A schoolboy pastime. I'm most surprised to find you here.'

I was, I admit, intrigued, having heard about Mr Cotten's man-lifting kites, which had at least proved successful in that particular mission. This one had a small engine fitted too. I was inspecting the intricate arrangement of box-kites, coupled into an inverted pyramid, when I was aware of Mr Cotten and Mankelow behind him.

'They lift a man without an engine. Think what they'll do with one, tomorrow,' Cotten drawled.

'Drop him, no doubt.' Joseph burst into roars of laughter, looking at me for approval. I fear he did not receive it. The look on the cowboy's face did not invite laughter, and I was all too uncomfortably aware that however objective I am myself in judging others' contrivances, some inventors become all too personally involved.

'Listen, Buster.' Tex stopped admiring his childish kites and walked back to the Marvel, poking it with one enormous hand. He was showing every sign of wanting to crush it into even smaller firewood than had arrived on the cart. 'You'll laugh on the other side of your big mouth tomorrow. Collapsible, eh? Let's test it.'

'Keep your hands off my Marvel,' yelled Mankelow. 'And, yes, it is collapsible. It's meant for army officers to carry with them. Can't carry a bundle of kites.'

'This thing ever flown?' A push from Tex Cotten had the Marvel perilously rocking, and I was forced to rush to it to shore it up.

Meanwhile Joseph had hurled himself at Tex, shrieking defiance in defence of his paltry machine. 'Don't touch her. My baby, my Marvel. Take your kitey hands off her.'

'Sure, Buster.' Tex loomed over Joseph, holding him off as easily as he would a child. 'Let's see who's grinning tomorrow, eh?'

I began to edge out of the barn to be free of this violence. The air is for pure thoughts. We inventors have so much to give to the world in the sweet achievement of flight. But hardly was I breathing in its balm than I realised Tex Cotten was once again at my side.

'What is *that*?' he asked awed.

You will scarcely believe this, but he was gazing at Gum's Goer, and he began to shake with laughter. I could scarcely believe it myself. What could be amusing about my tall elegant Goer with its propellers, steam engine, and operating cords, supported on its two tiny wheels. There were no wings or ridiculous side appendages to laugh at. Did I need to explain the very fundamentals of flight to this idiot?

'It is a *bird*,' I replied to him in fury. 'Have you not the wit to appreciate that?'

'Guess not,' the fool chuckled.

I regret I was driven to stamp my foot. 'This machine is a bird. *I* am a bird.'

And to illustrate my point I ran round in circles with my arms flailing, head and forward, making brrh-brrh sounds. 'I am a rough-legged buzzard,' I emphasised. 'I am a sparrow-hawk. See, I dive. And why do I dive? Because my propellers force me forward and gravity drives me downward on an inclined plane.'

'Don't get your feathers ruffled, buddy,' was all Tex could find to say. And he called himself an inventor.

I appealed instead to Mr Mankelow, who at least was courteous. 'I shall be rising early tomorrow,' I said. 'I need inspiration for the contest. Do you know where might I observe flying ducks? There are some here, I suppose?'

Joseph Mankelow shrugged. 'On the dinner menu, according to our host.' He seemed to have some difficulty in controlling a quivering mouth. With dignity, I led my Goer into the barn to make it ready for the contest tomorrow. I bore in mind that we three were not the only competitors in this contest and that for our host's sake I should make some effort to treat my two companions here politely. Were it not for that, I should have had the greatest difficulty in refraining from fisticuffs. When my temper is roused, my dear wife tells me, I am a raging bull. However I owed it to my Goer to ensure its time of glory on the morrow should be unhindered by human frailties.

I tried my best. 'Tell me, Mr Cotten,' I asked, as he strolled past to his bundle of kites, 'what do you think of the Major's machine?' My two companions here must also have been treated – if that is the word – to the tour of Trailing Edge House. He is a most determined gentleman, is the Major. I was forced to admire his collection of memorabilia and photographs from earlier age of flying machines. I had duly praised a model of Stringfellow's monoplane and one of Phillips' absurd 'Venetian Blind' design, letters from Chanute – and chunks of metal from the flying machines of the Major's hero Hiram Maxim, who was the inspiration for the monster called Dale's Diver with which we would be called upon to share our limelight tomorrow. A most unfortunate name, in my opinion, for a machine destined to go upwards.

'Not a chance in hell,' Mr Cotten said dismissively. 'Steam's had its day and that goes for your pile of garbage too.'

Naturally that ended our conversation, and I occupied my time before dinner by walking round the grounds observing our feathered friends in flight in the happy knowledge that I would be joining them tomorrow. Across the lawns in front of the lake were rail tracks leading from the barn in which the Major kept his Dale's Diver and along which the poor man expected his flying machine to make its triumphant way tomorrow. Then – one should not laugh – he expected it to gather speed and leave the ground, just as Hiram Maxim's had by a pure fluke some years earlier; it had flown 600 feet before one of the screws was caught by a piece of broken track. Ever since then the Major, having retired, I imagine, from a not very glorious army career, had endeavoured to do the same.

I could not resist a slight detour from my path to look at the Dale Diver, and could hardly stop myself laughing when I saw it. It was about four times as tall as its operator, and of such substantial proportions in its three-tiered strung wingspans and steam engine that it would win my respect if it moved at all, let alone into the air.

'Everyone's going to see my triumph, Gum,' the Major had informed me on my arrival earlier. 'That's what it's about. Air has to be conquered and I'm the man.'

'Darling, you will be careful, won't you? Good afternoon,' the lady with him had then addressed me, 'I believe you must be Mr Gum.'

This I knew was the Dowager Lady Dale, the Major's mother. I fear she is less than affectionately known in our newspapers as Dotty Dorcas, since she is a prominent believer in women's suffrage.

Before I could bow over her hand, the Major forestalled me by beginning a family argument. 'Don't fuss, Mama,' he snapped. 'The competition is merely composed of children's toys. Mankelow's Marvel is a tin top, Gum's Goer… ' (he had clearly forgotten my presence) '…is a glorified jack-in-a-box, and Cotton is just a kid with a kite.'

I wondered if the Major really believed what he was saying. As for myself, I can take criticism well, but the two other competitors did not display any such balanced view of the world. It was fortunate, I thought, that we had a dinner to look forward to at which friendly relations might be restored. And so they might have been if the menu had not consisted largely of duck, which was most upsetting to me and a cause of great mirth to my fellow diners. What is more, it was very rich, and thus hardly conducive to sweet dreams. Somehow however I doubted whether any dreams under the roof of Trailing Bridge House would be sweet tonight, whatever the menu. I knew mine would not be.

'Not hurt, are you, sir?'

Charlie Thomas, the coachman, was peering anxiously at me, having just driven the Dale Diver from the Major's barn along the rails to the starting point, where the Major was all dressed up in his goggles and flying coat ready to climb into his hissing monster. Seeing my little mishap Charlie had come over to enquire after my health.

My anticipated triumph had proved a disaster. I had watched the expected demise of the Mankelow Marvel, with Joseph Mankelow rocking desperately within it as his machine lurched from side to side. It had hopped two feet upwards then fallen ignominiously on its nose, together with Mankelow who had to be rescued with wirecutters from this undignified position.

It had then been my turn. I had naturally expected to be last in the running order, since my Goer was clearly going to win the prize and I did not wish my fellow competitors to be humiliated by my superb performance. I was therefore somewhat flustered when at breakfast I was informed that I was to follow Joseph.

In the event my Goer was to be denied its moment of fame. I cannot be more explicit than that. It shot forward and up about four feet, but then I felt its power leave it, and within seconds it was falling, and though I flapped my arm and tugged the cord my gallant Goer slumped down on its rear leaving me wedged uncomfortably by its steam engine. My ear was extremely hot, but in my rage I took no notice of this. There had clearly been a plot to injure my machine. What other explanation could there be? My calculations had been lengthy, painstaking and accurate. It was clear to me a wire must have been cut, or perhaps a cord, or something put out of working order. Whatever it was could not now be determined since my gallant Goer had been wrecked. I did not know whom to accuse: Mankelow, the Major, or Tex. But one of them was my enemy. It could even have been Charlie, acting on behalf of his jealous master.

'I am well,' I told him in a fury. 'My Goer is not.'

'Ah well, sir,' he replied, no doubt thinking to cheer me, 'if God had meant us to fly he'd have given us wings.'

'One could argue,' I said viciously, 'that if he intended us to ride in De Dion Boutons… ' I believe that was the motor car I saw in the motor stable '…he'd have given us wheels.'

Charlie did not like this slur. 'It's a question of elements, sir. Land is land, and air is for the birds. I don't like it up there myself.'

'You?' I asked amazed. 'You are a flying machine operator?'

'Oh yes, sir. The Major usually sends me up in that contraption of his rather than risk it himself.'

And no wonder, I thought grimly, watching the Major clambering up into the monstrous thing that towered over him. Surely he had no expectation that the Dale Diver would fly?

I was aware of Charlie crying out at my side as with hissing and shudders the monster shot along the rails: 'Oh sir, twenty miles, thirty, forty miles an hour... .' To my astonishment there was space to be seen between the machine and the rails. It was floating, and, I hardly dare admit it, *flying*. And that honour was to have been mine, had it not been for the plot against me. Fortunately its brief burst of glory was soon over, and it sank heavily down on to the grass beside the track. The sound of splintering wood and rending metal could be heard among the cheers. The Major was emerging from the wreckage unhurt and judges and newspapermen crowded round.

I knew I must go over to congratulate him. I am a sportsman after all. As I reached the Dale Diver however the Major whipped off his goggles and helmet but to all our astonishments, instead of the Major's crusty face, that of Dotty Dorcas was revealed. A *woman*! I would not now admit that she flew, but she most certainly left the ground and travelled along. How great was my shame. How could I face my dear wife in such ignominy? It would be quite insupportable had I not known that I and my Goer had been cruelly robbed of the prize by some mischief-maker.

'I flew,' cried her ladyship. 'I have conquered the air, I demand the vote for women. Write that down, young man,' she ordered a journalist standing nearby and obediently he scribbled something on his pad.

'Here,' cried Charlie Thomas suddenly, 'where's Sir? Where's the Major?' Indeed this seemed odd indeed to me.

'My dear man, at this important moment for world history, I have no idea where my son is.' Dotty Dorcas continued to harangue the judges and demand the prize duck even though there was another competitor still to take his turn.

Charlie, however, was not to be deterred and ran across the lawn towards the Major's barn. Seeing Charlie emerge a moment later, I realised he could not have found his employer and so seized the excuse to leave the scene of my anguish to join him as he disappeared into our competitors' barn. As I reached it, I could see Cotten's box-kites still in position, and at that very moment I heard a shriek from Charlie.

I cannot think what possessed me but instead of turning and fleeing I went forward. Once I reached the box-kite machine, I could see the red stain of congealing blood on the concrete floor. My heart began to thud as I looked further and saw Charlie bent over the figure not of the Major but of Tex Cotten, sprawled out in his cowboy boots. His head had been obliterated by some heavy object – and then I saw what it was. It was the silver duck, which should have been awarded to me. Now it was covered in blood and lay by a murdered body.

'Hell and Tommy,' Charlie whispered. 'Go and get help from the house. I'll stay with the body.'

I did as he commanded, thankful he had not asked me to stay. My thanks were to be short-lived. As I burst into the house, the butler was running white-faced down the main staircase.

'The Major's dead. My gawd, he'd dead.'

A second body? Before I could move, the butler seized me by the arm and rushed me up the stairs. Why I do not know. Perhaps to verify what his own eyes saw. He pushed me into a large bedroom though remaining at the door himself, and I could see the Major's body sprawled out on the floor by the side of a day-bed.

'Dead. He's a gonner,' the butler moaned, creeping cautiously towards me.

I was frozen to the spot at all this horror, but fortunately this second nightmare was to be mitigated. A stertorous sound from the corpse reassured me that the Major, if not in the best of health, was at least alive.

'It ain't his usual time for a nap.' The butler sounded aggrieved that he had been so misled.

Fortunately I am a man of decision. 'Call the doctor,' I said imperiously. 'There is something gravely amiss with the Major.'

*

The following day we sat forlornly in the morning room, while Trailing Edge House was seemingly taken over by large policemen, who forbade us to leave or even to visit our flying machines. Normally never a day goes by without my visiting Gum's Goer at least six times.

Our mood was not helped by the fact that the Major had recovered from the laudanum with which he claimed he had been drugged by persons unknown and had been storming round Trailing Edge House threatening to murder his mother for flying in his stead. This was a threat the police were taking seriously in the circumstances, and he was therefore shut up with us under a constable's eye. The Major was furious at being baulked of his triumph and her ladyship's soothing words at breakfast had not been helpful.

'Darling, at least you can't be suspected of murdering that poor man.'

The Major had not been grateful for her consolation. Nor was he grateful for the fact that the police insisted on Charlie remaining in the morning room with us. The police were making it uncomfortably clear to the five of us that we were all under suspicion of having murdered Mr Cotton.

'Why?' her ladyship had asked with interest.

Because, so the flawed reasoning went, we all wanted the glory of being first in the air and therefore had reason to want to be rid of Mr Cotton who, so the police claimed, stood the best chance of achieving it. Even Charlie apparently came under this heading, either because he wanted the glory himself or on behalf of his master.

I have said the reasoning was flawed, and you will appreciate that this was the case when I tell you that it was based merely on the ridiculous evidence, so I ascertained, that the police had been discussing the matter with the judges.

'And who,' I asked earnestly, 'will judge the judges in this matter?'

But this logic was too much for the policemen who said that they would, thank you very much.

The Major protested in vain that as he was drugged with laudanum at the time he couldn't possible have murdered anyone. The policemen pointed out that he could have taken the laudanum as a bluff after killing Tex Cotton. This was an interesting theory, and in the circumstances one that Mankelow and I were keen that the police should adopt. Unfortunately her ladyship ruled this out.

'Oh no, inspector,' she said. 'You see, I put the laudanum in my son's breakfast coffee.'

It wasn't the police so much as the Major who took great exception to that. Indeed Mr Mankelow and myself found the uproar that followed quite amusing, as did her ladyship. 'I did it for The Cause, John,' she assured him earnestly, but the Major seemed to think his cause was higher than hers.

It was less amusing to realise that the suspects were now down to four, of which I was still one. I could not deny that in theory although Mankelow and I had left the barn together at ten o'clock, leaving Tex alive and well within, either Joseph or I could have hurried back to the barn to kill him either before or after our own *flights* (as at least mine could have been termed if there had been no deliberate meddling with it).

I saw Joseph looking at me, as doubtless he was thinking as I was. It would never have occurred to these policemen that our first duty was to The Skies, in other words our flying machines, from which both before our flights and in their hour of crashed need we would never have been parted. Indeed had it not been for Cotten's continual jibes and ill-informed criticisms, the Marvel and the Goer might well not have crashed. Perhaps Cotten in sheer jealousy was the person who carried out the mischief on my cherished flying machine. I decided not to dwell on this possibility to the police, however. Who knows what revenge they might imagine I took?

Joseph and I were beginning to see the merits of sticking together, and we assured each other that we had been together every moment of the time after ten o'clock and between the end of our flights and the discovery of Cotten's body.

'I see much merit in your Marvel,' I decided to tell Joseph graciously. 'The concentric design is a notion of sheer brilliance. If the angle of incidence remains constant of course—'

'A problem indeed, but a mere detail,' he smilingly acknowledged. 'And might I say, Mr Gum, that to use gravity in your Goer to point the machine downward in order to make it rise all the more powerfully when the stern is depressed is a concept of genius. Lateral control must of course be a problem... '

'What about the kites?' asked Charlie. 'They looked pretty good to me.'

A foolish man. 'You seemed to give up your chance of glory with the Diver very easily on this occasion,' I remarked.

'I told him I'd take it up,' growled the Major.

'And so did I,' said her ladyship.

'But I saw you in the breakfast-room yesterday, Charlie,' I persisted. 'Didn't the Major ask you to take the silver duck to the judges' table?'

Charlie looked at me in what can only be described as a withering manner. 'I did. And that's where I dumped it. Catch me wanting to go up in that iron coffin without having to.'

The situation was beginning to look distinctly ominous and the policeman guarding us looked as though he were sizing me up for handcuffs. Most unpleasant. I therefore applied the genius of my mind to considering what had actually happened here rather than to the ever present problem of flight. At least the Dale Diver and I were at one in choosing steam as the answer. The idea that kites could be used for serious flying was laughable and we all knew it, so why should any of us have feared Tex's contribution to the contest? Nevertheless as the Major could not have carried out the murder and I was doubtful if her ladyship would have the strength even if it had occurred to her, I realised that the police would be concentrating on Charlie, who really did not seem to have much of a motive and on Joseph or myself. It was time to apply my genius *quickly*.

Unfortunately my brain refused to act. Had I seen Joseph every minute of that time? Could I swear to it? I thought I could, but fear made me doubt whether he had seen me. Were his eyes not deflected from time to time to gaze at his beloved Marvel – as indeed had mine at the Goer?

And then I remembered something my dear wife had once said when I had been struggling with some particularly knotty problem over my Goer: 'The trouble with you, Horatio, is that you can't see the meat for the gravy.'

A typical woman's statement of course, but now I thought I saw what she meant. Above all, I wanted the Goer to fly – and it occurred to me that though I had made it simulate birds' flight I had not given it wings. Joyously I now saw the answer to the Goer's problem. World, I commanded, forget about box-kites. The Goer is on its way. I shall give it *wings*.

But to return to the murder. Perhaps gravy and meat might be applied here. I thought about them for some time, then I scraped the gravy (the drugging of the Major) off the meat (Tex Cotten's murder). And, behold, the truth. I went up to the police constable and demanded to speak to the inspector privately. There was some difficulty in that at first he assumed I wished to confess to the murder, but eventually he saw my point. I had achieved something in this doomed weekend. I had solved the murder, and I even more important I had solved the problem of flight for the world. The Goer was on its way to immortality.

Dotty Dorcas was very upset as she saw her son being led away by two stalwart policemen. The Major had been so set on achieving flight himself that he would let nothing stand in his way and he – stupidly – really believed that Tex Cotten's box-kites were a threat to the Dale Diver's success. He realised that his mother had drugged his coffee at breakfast and this put the idea in his mind. He waited until his mother left the room, then instead of drinking the coffee, took it away and hid it. He went to kill Tex after Joseph and I had left the barn, and then returned to take the laudanum to give himself an alibi.

I was distressed to see her ladyship's grief however and ventured to offer my commiserations. I need not have bothered.

'You stupid little man,' she informed me. 'I need my son here to build another Dale Diver. What use is he dead or in prison? Do you realise, Mr Gum, that thanks to you the world is now forever deprived of the benefits of flight? How foolish of my son ever to fear box-kites when the Dale Diver has now proved its power. Steam will reign for ever.'

Perhaps Charlie saw my misery at being spoken to so rudely, for he rose from his chair and thrust the morning's *Daily Mail* under her ladyship's nose.

'Take it away,' she ordered him impatiently. 'They've completely ignored my flight yesterday and only reported on this murder.'

'That's not what I wanted to show you, your ladyship,' Charlie said, pointing to a very short paragraph at the foot of a page.

I could not help being curious, as her ladyship looked at it, then flung the newspaper aside with a moan. I picked it up and read:

*Messrs Wilbur and Orville Wright yesterday successfully experimented with a flying machine at Kittyhawk, North Carolina… The idea of the box kite was used in the construction.*

Oh my Goer, my poor little Goer.

# The Lammergeier Vulture

## Christine Poulson

*When selecting stories for inclusion in the CWA anthology, I try to
ensure a balance between contributions from stars of the genre and
writers at an early stage of their careers, whose work seems sure to
appeal to a wide readership. Like Bill Kirton, Chris Simms and Sally
Spedding, Christine Poulson is a relative newcomer to the field, but
she is certainly one to watch for the future. This is her first published
short story.*

Anne was every inch the Englishwoman abroad: that in itself
wasn't a good enough reason to murder her, but it certainly
made the task more palatable. Gerald regarded his wife with
distaste. Her broad-brimmed straw hat had left a red rim on her forehead and her fair hair was lank and wispy. Her ankles were lumpy
with mosquito bites and her cotton shirt was creased.

They were in the shady construction above the throne room at
Knossos, where they had taken refuge from the heat and the crowds.
The swallows that nested in the corners of the roof darted and
wheeled above their heads. Gerald was well aware that Anne was
more interested in the birds than she was in the Minoan antiquities. In
the past this, too, would have been a source of irritation. But after all
it was bird-watching that had persuaded her to come to Crete and
bird-watching that would get him out of his fix.

Gerald had planned the accident for the last few days of the holiday, partly because he thought it would look less suspicious, but also
because he needed time to work himself up to it. The ten days they
had so far spent in Crete had certainly helped. The history of the
island was bloody and cruel. The Mycenaeans, the Romans, the
Venetians, the Turks, the Germans – they had all invaded and they
had all left their mark. Death was everywhere. The museums were
stuffed with sarcophagi the size and shape of hip-baths. At one

archaeological site there was even evidence of human sacrifice. One more corpse would be neither here nor there, Gerald told himself.

He smiled at his wife. 'All right, darling?'

Anne smiled back. 'Fine. I think I'll sit here a bit longer. I'm enjoying the shade. You go ahead and explore the palace.'

Gerald stepped out into the sun. It was as if a hot and heavy cloak had been dropped on his shoulders. He felt a prickling of sweat on his back and chest. It was always the same: at first the heat seemed intolerable but after a few moments one grew accustomed to it. The glare of sunlight off the stone hurt his eyes and he fumbled for his sunglasses in the leather shoulder bag that he always carried south of the Alps. As he made his way down the steps he was engulfed by a crowd of tourists coming up. He stood still and let them flow round him. It was like being jostled by a herd of cows. When he was at last alone, he walked over to the parapet. There was a fine view of the palace storeroom, open to the sky now, but still containing large earthenware jars for wine and oil. He stopped to admire the pots. Robust yet elegant. Ceramics were something he knew a lot about. In fact they were what had brought him and Anne together in the first place.

His thoughts drifted back to that day five years ago when he had gone to Lavender House to value its contents for insurance. As he sat there with Anne in the elegantly proportioned room, examining her father's fine collection of eighteenth century English cream ware, it dawned on him that he had found the love of his life. Not Anne, no, oh God, no! It was the house. Not very large, or very grand, just a little Regency villa in Greenwich, but it was perfect, inside and out. It was one of Gerald's profoundest beliefs that beautiful things belong by rights to the person who can most appreciate them. And no one appreciated beautiful things more than he did. Oh, Anne was fond of Lavender House, of course she was – it had belonged to her parents and she'd grown up there – but she didn't care for it the way he did. It was really just an accident of birth that she was living there instead of him. Luckily there was a way to rectify that. Anne was lonely. Both her parents had recently died within a few months of each other. She was nearly forty and her job as a biology teacher at a private girls' school in North London didn't provide many opportunities for meeting men. In her spare time she ran a local Girl Guide pack – Gerald suppressed a smile when she told him about that – and went bird-watching. He'd been able to let her make most of the running. Six months after that first meeting they were married.

It was unfortunate that Gerald's job at the auction house had come to an end so soon after that. The old lady had been sharper than she looked, hadn't believed his valuation, and he still felt that the director had been extraordinarily stuffy about what was, after all, just a bit of private enterprise. Anne had been very good about it – of course he hadn't told her everything – and had helped to set him up in the little antique shop in Kensington High Street. And now that had gone wrong, too, and this time he had to answer to Michael. He'd been running at a loss and Michael's proposition had seemed like the answer to a prayer. At first Gerald hadn't really understood. Michael looked and talked like any other prosperous businessman, a bit flash maybe with his black Mercedes and heavy gold cufflinks, but nothing out of the ordinary. That was before Michael had explained how recourse to the law wasn't really an option in his line of work. There were, however, other ways of making sure that no-one went back on a deal. And no-one ever had. 'At least... I tell a lie,' Michael said. He smiled at Gerald. 'There was someone once. Remember that bloke who was found in a burned-out car in Epping Forest last year? Never did identify the body, did they?' Gerald looked at him uncertainly, wondering if this was a joke. He saw that it wasn't. And now Michael was insisting that Gerald had abstracted one of those packets of white powder that he had agreed to bring over from Holland in a shipment of dodgy Delft vases. It was all a mistake, but he was demanding that Gerald pay him double its street value...

This was something Anne wouldn't be understanding about.

And yet in the end she herself had solved his problem by suggesting the holiday in Crete. He had jumped at the opportunity: it would at least get him out of the country. As he was flicking listlessly through the guidebook, he had come across the section on flora and fauna, and a more long-term solution had occurred to him. 'The Lammergeier vulture,' he read, 'wing-span up to three metres.

Habitat: remote mountain ranges. Nests in caves on precipices.'
Precipices! Remote! The words seemed to jump off the page. He could
see the towering, craggy cliff, hear the sea thundering below. The
eager ornithologist, trying to get a glimpse of one of these magnificent
creatures, leans out just a little too far and... Well, who was to say
that it was anything but a tragic accident.

Crete was the perfect place for it. In England there would have
been far too close a scrutiny. Not just from the police but from
Antony Evans, too. Just his luck that Anne's solicitor should have
been married to an old friend of Anne's. Since that friend had died a
couple of years ago, Evans had hanging around far too much for
Gerald's liking. Interfering bastard! Gerald was almost sure that if it
hadn't been for Evans he could have persuaded Anne to dip deeper
into her capital and then all this wouldn't have been necessary.

And now it was almost time to put the plan into action. Gerald had
been very careful. He had waited for Anne to suggest the excursion in
search of the Lammergeier vulture. He had known that she would. It
was one of the rarest birds in Europe.

A hand fell on Gerald's shoulder. He jerked as if he'd been electro-
cuted. He turned to see a man pointing something grey and metallic at
him. For a terrible moment, he thought one of Michael's men had
tracked him down. Then he saw the smiling Japanese faces, one male
and one female. It was a camera the man was offering to him. Now he
was gesturing to himself and his companion. He wanted Gerald to
take a photograph of them. Expansive with relief, Gerald gave them
his most charming smile, put his bag down, and took charge of the
camera. It was a big Nikon with a lot of attachments and it took the
man a minute or two of sign language to show Gerald how to use it.
Then another group of tourists arrived. It was a while before he could
get a clear shot of the honeymooning couple.

At last it was accomplished. They parted with nods and smiles.
Gerald picked up his bag and went to look for Anne.

It wasn't until late that evening when they arrived at their hotel on
the south-east coast that he realised his passport had been stolen.

The tourist police were adamant. Gerald would have to drive back to

Iraklion and get a temporary visa from the British Consul. Otherwise he would not be allowed to leave the country. There was nothing for it, Anne's accident would have to be delayed for a day. It would look strange if he didn't get this problem straightened out right away and anyway he didn't want to find himself stranded in Crete afterwards.

Normally, he would have persuaded Anne to share the driving, but she'd gone down with food-poisoning – those shrimps at lunch probably – and had spent the night throwing up in the bathroom. Gerald was furious with her. If anything further had been needed to harden his heart, this was it: a two and a half hour drive each way to Iraklion – much of it on winding mountain roads. And it wasn't as if he had a decent car. Anne was too mean to hire one of those sporty Suzuki Jeeps and he was stuck with a little Fiat without air-conditioning.

When Gerald got to the Embassy he spent the whole day being shunted from official to official. He didn't even have time for a proper lunch. By the time he arrived back at Makriyiolos at seven o'clock in the evening he felt like a wrung-out rag. His shirt was sticking to his back and he wanted nothing more than a long, cold beer.

Anne wasn't in their room and her handbag had gone, too. He looked around for a note. Nothing. Well, she couldn't have gone far without the car. He washed and changed his shirt. Then he went to reception to see if she'd left a message.

The proprietor explained that Madame Maitland had gone out around two o'clock. She had told the proprietor that she wanted to go bird-watching and had asked about the best place to hire a moped. Had she not returned? The proprietor looked grave. Perhaps Madame had sprained her ankle, or, God forbid, an accident on the road… His grandson would help Mr Maitland to search for her. He waved away Gerald's objections. No, no, he must insist. He turned and issued a peremptory command through the bead curtain that led to the family's living quarters. A swarthy youth appeared, wearing a white T-shirt with the sleeves cut off.

This, it seemed, was Yiorgos. He spoke just enough English to direct Gerald along the coast road and up into the mountains along a series of hairpin bends. This suited Gerald just fine. He didn't want to talk. He needed time to think. It hadn't occurred to him for a single

moment that the silly bitch would go on her own. Suppose she *had*
sprained her ankle. It would scupper all his plans. He wanted to
thump the steering wheel in frustration.

Higher and higher they climbed. The little hire car laboured as
Gerald nursed it up one in four gradients. He was beginning to feel
that he was welded to his seat when Yiorgos gave a grunt and indicated that Gerald was to turn right.

'Up here?' Gerald was incredulous. It was no more than a dirt
track.

Yiorgos nodded. Gerald shrugged and turned off the road. They
jolted and rattled over the rutted track, the wheels throwing up stones
that clanged alarmingly on the underside of the car.

'Madame,' Yiorgos said suddenly.

There by the side of the track stood a white moped. Beyond it a
footpath led up among rocky outcrops on to the headland.

Gerald pulled up behind it. Without a word he and Yiorgos got out
of the car. It was cooler up here and there was a stiff breeze.

'Anne!' Gerald shouted. 'Anne! Where are you?'

They stood and listened. There was no reply.

They struggled up the path, Gerald calling out Anne's name from
time to time, Yiorgos calling 'Madame'.

A spectacular sunset of dusty pink and coral and orange was blossoming in the west. The sky above them had darkened to that
wonderful blue that always made Gerald think of Bellini altarpieces.
As they got higher a series of headlands, each hazier than the last,
revealed itself. The vegetation grew sparser and scrubbier. They were
coming to the crest of the headland. The path wound round huge
rocks. The cliffs were steeper, sheer in places.

Gerald became aware of a faint whispering sound. It was a few
moments before he realised that it was surf breaking on rocks a long
way down. They reached the summit. There was a drop of about fifty
metres almost straight into the sea. As he stood looking down, Gerald
shivered. Even with the thought of Michael to spur him on, could he
really have pushed Anne off here? A flash of light caught his eye. The
setting sun was glinting on the lenses of a pair of binoculars lying far
below on a rock. Gerald had scarcely had time to take in the signifi-

cance of this, when Yiorgos gave a squeal of alarm and grabbed his arm. Startled, Gerald looked up. With his free hand Yiorgos was crossing himself. He was muttering something in Greek and looking up into the evening sky. Gerald followed his gaze. His stomach lurched. The hairs stood up on the back of his neck. About twenty feet up, floating towards them on motionless wings was the most enormous bird Gerald had ever seen. The creature had a wingspan of at least eight feet. As it drifted over their heads, its shadow fell on their upturned faces. He glimpsed a hooked beak and talons big enough to seize a child.

It was the Lammergeier vulture.

'I am desolated that your trip to our island has ended in this tragic mishap.'

It was not the first time Captain Michaelaki had said this, nor did he suppose that it would be the last. Every year there was at least one fatality. It was hardly surprising given the millions of tourists that visited Crete. Usually it was some young idiot without a helmet speeding around a mountain bend on a Vespa, occasionally an accident in the water. A fall from a cliff was rarer…

Behind him the ancient air-conditioning unit clattered and whirred. He looked thoughtfully across his mahogany desk at Gerald. The unfortunate lady's binoculars on the rocks, her straw hat caught in a bush halfway down the cliff, *A Field-Guide to the Birds of Europe* wedged in a crevice: the story they told could not be clearer. And what better alibi could Mr Maitland have? At the very moment his wife had been setting out on her moped, he had been sitting in the office of the vice-consul in the British Embassy in Iraklion. There were no gaps in his story and the hotel proprietor's grandson had accompanied him to the scene of the accident. And yet… and yet… why was the man so calm? The English were of course noted for their – what was the word? – yes, sangfroid. But still… he thought of other British holiday makers to whom he had broken bad news, the crumbled clothes, the faces bewildered and red from sunburn and tears. He noted Gerald's tailored shorts, the white linen shirt with the sleeves turned up to reveal tanned forearms, the expensive leather shoulder bag. He had met many middle-aged men like Gerald: Italian or French, or even, it had to be admitted, Greek: a little too dapper, a little too trim. There was probably another woman somewhere. But after all, why not... family was family, sex was, well, sex was something else. His thoughts strayed to a certain young widow in a flat near the harbour at Sitia...

With an effort Captain Michaelaki brought his thoughts back to the present. Gerald was looking expectantly at him.

The Captain cleared his throat. 'I am hopeful, but not, you understand, confident that we shall recover the poor lady's body.' He prided himself on the elegance and correctness of his English, better than many a native speaker he had often been told. 'Hopeful, but not confident,' he repeated. 'The currents – it could be days or... ' He frowned and shrugged his shoulders to indicate that the body might never be recovered.

'How long must I stay?' Gerald asked. 'There will be so much to sort out at home.'

Captain Michaelaki spread his hands. 'I see no need to detain you at present.'

'But won't you need me to identify the... to identify my wife.'

'The manager of the hotel has kindly offered to do to that. If it should be necessary.' Or possible, he thought, after the fish had done their work. But in truth identification wasn't likely to be much of a problem. There wouldn't be more than one blonde, middle-aged woman washed up on the beach or found tangled in a fishing-net.

'It only remains for me to extend my heartfelt condolences. Here is my card.' He pushed it across the desk. 'Please feel free to contact me at any time.'

As Gerald got to his feet, he said. 'If you should find her... '

Captain Michaelaki knew what he was going to say. 'We will of course co-operate fully with British Consul in arranging for the dear lady's remains to be sent home.'

The Captain opened the door for Gerald and watched him walk down the corridor. Something about the set of his shoulders revived his earlier suspicions. He felt a crazy impulse to call him back. All his instincts told him that there was something wrong here. But what exactly? He watched as Gerald became a dark shape against the light from the door on to the street, and then disappeared altogether. A formal report would be forwarded to the British authorities – that was always the case with the death of a holidaying British national – and they would hold an inquest. It might be worth having a quiet word with the vice-consul the next time they met for a glass of brandy and a game of backgammon...

Gerald paid off the taxi at the top of Croom's Hill so that he could walk the rest of the way and savour the anticipation of taking possession for just a little longer. During the winter the view from here took in the loop of river round the Isle of Dogs and you could see for miles across north London. Today the leaves obscured that view but through a gap in the trees he caught a glimpse of Canary Wharf looking surprisingly close in the afternoon sun.

Gerald took a firmer grip on his case and set off down the hill. On this warm Saturday in July Greenwich had a festive air. A silver Rolls Royce with ribbons on the bonnet was parked outside the Catholic Church of Our Ladye Star of the Sea. In Greenwich Park people were strolling with their children and lovers lay entwined on the grass. Somewhere nearby a wood-pigeon was cooing. Was it Henry James or Edith Wharton who said that 'summer afternoon' were the most beautiful words in the English language? How right they had been. Gerald felt a sense of well-being that was inseparable from the warmth of the sun.

Really things couldn't have worked out better. He was well aware that the Captain suspected him of murdering his wife. How ridiculous the man had been with his pedantically formal English! All the same there had been a shrewdness about him that would made Gerald uneasy if he really had murdered his wife. And that was delicious irony of it. He was completely in the clear. Good old Anne had done his dirty work for him.

A bend in the road and Lavender House came into view. His footsteps quickened. The house was set back a little and a laurel hedge screened it from the road. The late afternoon sun had transformed the upper windows into sheets of gold. He turned into the little circular drive and stood there just drinking it all in: the little portico with its fluted columns and cobweb fanlight, the glistening ivy clinging to the walls, the delicious contrast between red brick and white paint.

He frowned. Right in the middle of the little front lawn was a child's tricycle. Those brats from next door must have been making free with the garden again. The yellow and blue plastic jarred horribly. It was a small thing, but it had broken his mood. Anne had been too easy-going about lost balls and so on. That would have to change. He picked up his case and stepped briskly towards the house.

As he lifted his key to the lock he felt a thrill that was almost erotic. At last he was taking possession. He fumbled for a moment or two. The key wouldn't go in. He looked harder at the lock. It was a Banham. His key was a Yale.

He stepped back and looked up at the house. Something else was wrong. Now that the sun had left the windows the house had a blind, pained look. He saw that the chinoiserie curtains in the first floor drawing room had gone. In their place were the kind of curtains he thought of as tart's knickers, great drooping festoons of some ghastly chintz. He stepped over to the window of the little study on the left of the front door and cupped his hands around his eyes against the light. He saw polished floorboards, a small black leather sofa. Where were the little escritoire, the Persian rug?

He went back to the front door and leant on the door bell. Deep inside the house a child begin to bawl. Footsteps approached. There was the rattle of the safety chain being slotted into place. The door was opened and a woman of about thirty with abundant frizzy dark hair looked out. He had never seen her before in his life.

He heard himself stammer: 'Who are you? How long, how, that is, when you did you... ?'

'We moved in yesterday.'

A wave of dizziness swept over him. He put out a hand to the door jamb to support himself. The woman misinterpreted the gesture. A look of alarm appeared on her face and she began to close the door.

'Please,' Gerald said. 'It's all right. It's just that... I live here... I mean, used to... '

Something in the woman's face changed.

'Are you Mr Maitland?'

He nodded.

'Wait a minute.' She closed the door.

He heard her shoes clack-clacking away on the polished floor boards. A few moments later they returned. She opened the door and thrust a brown envelope through the gap.

'The solicitor left this for you.'

She closed the door.

Gerald's knees were trembling. He only just made it back to pavement. He sat down with his feet in the gutter and looked at the envelope. It was A5 size and stiff. The flap was stuck down with Sellotape. He fumbled with it for a moment or two, then tore it open. A passport slithered out and flopped on to the pavement. He opened it, and saw his own face staring back up at him. He felt inside the envelope and brought out a single sheet of paper.

Dear Gerald,

Did you really think I had no idea of what you've been up to? Long before you were so keen to go bird-watching with me, I decided it was time to hatch a plot of my own. A clean break is always best, don't you agree? By the time you read this Lavender House will have been sold, the furniture and ceramics auctioned off, and Antony and I will have started our new life together. It wouldn't be so very difficult for you to find us but I wouldn't bother if I were you. I think the police would be very interested in an account of your recent activities and in a sample of what I found under the spare bed. Both are lodged somewhere safe.

I never did get to see the Lammergeier vulture. But you can't have everything, can you?

Gerald was half aware of a car drawing up at the kerb. A shadow fell across the page. He felt a chill before he even looked up. Just for a second he thought it was the police.

When he saw who was standing over him, he wished that it was.

# Baba's Bites

## Chris Simms

*Here Chris Simms tackles the same social issue as John Harvey, but in a very different way. Such is the assurance of the writing that it is hard to credit that his debut novel,* Outside the White Lines, *was published as recently as a year ago. Judging by the quality of this sinister story, he also has a rare talent for the short form. Simms is a young writer whose reputation seems certain to go from strength to strength.*

Lamb rogan josh. My favourite curry and, once you've got the basic spices, one of the easiest to make. Brown off your lamb cubes and put to one side. Add a generous glug of oil to a wide pan, put the heat on medium high and throw in some cardamom pods, bay leaves, cloves, peppercorns, cinnamon, onions, ginger and garlic. Stir for thirty seconds. Add cumin, coriander, paprika and salt. Stir for another thirty seconds. Add the lamb, some yoghurt and a cup of water. Simmer for as long as you can resist.

I thought I had the curry sussed, until that night in Baba's Bites. Meat cooked until the strands barely hung together, yoghurt and spices perfectly balanced and some other ingredient that brought the dish springing to life. I thought of all the previous times I'd eaten it and knew I'd been stumbling around in the dark.

'Kaz,' I said, hunched over the shallow polystyrene tray, prodding towards the riot of flavours with a plastic fork, 'this is delicious. New cook or something?'

Kaz's brother usually prepared the curries, but I'd only had to smell this one to know it was in a different league. Kaz smiled as he sprinkled his home made chilli sauce over a doner kebab and held it out to the customer who stood swaying on my side of the little take-away's counter.

'No, no, mate. I mean loads of chilli sauce,' the young bloke said drunkenly, trying to speak slowly and clearly for the benefit of what he thought were foreign ears. In a larger version of the action I'd just made with my fork, the customer jerked his hand up and down to demonstrate that he wanted the kebab to be drowned. The smile didn't leave Kaz's face as he soaked the open pitta bread with gouts of fiery liquid.

'Cheers mate,' said the customer, grabbing the paper wrapped package and staggering out the door, leaving a trail of crimson drops behind him.

Kaz looked over at me and, with an accent that combined the nasal twang of Manchester with the thicker tones of the Middle East, said, 'Yeah mate. It's good then?'

My mouth was too full for any spoken reply. Holding up a thumb, I nodded vigorously. Kaz looked pleased as he turned back to the huge hunk of processed meat slowly revolving on the oil-soaked spike. Flourishing a long knife, he began carving away at its outer layer.

Once I'd swallowed my mouthful I said, 'So what's your brother doing then?'

'Oh, he's pursuing a new business interest. He won't be around so much from now on.'

The curry was too good for me to continue talking so, before tucking into it once more, I quickly said, 'Well, compliments to the chef.'

I'd dropped out of my chemical engineering degree half way through my second year. There was no way I could imagine a career in it. Life, I decided, was too short to spend doing something you didn't enjoy. I sat down and tried to imagine a job that I would enjoy. Twenty one years old, with a series of mind-numbing McJobs behind me and I was struggling. But during my gap year I went to Thailand (original choice, I know). Though I was far too much of a traveller to ever step inside Koh Samui's flashy tourist hotels full of mere holiday-makers, I watched the tour reps at work. I reckoned I could handle a life working in some of the most beautiful places on earth. Work it out for yourself: Manchester versus the Maldives. Britain versus Barbados. So a degree in Travel and Tourism it was.

Which left me with a new set of course fees rolled into almost two years of student debt. I got a night job in the bakers just down the road from my digs. 'Mr Wing's Chinese Bakers'. There can't be many of those in Britain. But you wouldn't believe the amount of stuff he churns out. During the day it's things like doughy rolls filled with sweet and sour pork, kung po chicken or special seafood mix or batches of little buns sprinkled with sesame seeds and filled with chestnut puree or honey paste. At five o'clock the day shift goes home, the front of shop shuts and the night shift appears round the back. While the rest of the country is slumped in front of the box, or enjoying themselves in pubs and restaurants, the output changes to speciality, or ethnic breads as they're classed on the supermarket shelves. Pittas, naans, raithas, chapattis, lavache, ciabatta – all that stuff. The monstrous silver ovens never get the chance to cool down. Staff scurry around them, transporting away the steady flow of produce like worker ants carrying off the stream of eggs laid by their queen.

My co-workers chat happily away in languages from India, Asia or Africa, but hardly any speak English. It's obvious most haven't got to Britain by legal means either. The cash changes hands just before dawn and, unlike my rate of pay, theirs reflects the twilight world they operate in. The minimum wage doesn't even come into it. It's probably because I'm an official British citizen with a clean driving licence that I got the job of doing drop-offs. And, seeing as working next to a furnace half the night wasn't my idea of fun, that was fine by me. I deliver to city centre takeaway joints that need more stock or the Indian restaurants on Manchester's curry mile that prefer to serve freshly baked produce. They all know Mr Wing's never shuts. The phone rings and I'm off in the little van with their order.

Baba's Bites called on my very first night. As soon as I wandered in with the tray of naans and pittas, Kaz spotted me for someone who was prepared to do a deal. And this is how it works: Kaz rings with an order, I pick what he wants from the racks of stuff in the storage room and swipe an extra tray or two. In return he gives me a free curry.

Baba's Bites – it's your typical late night, city centre takeaway place. A few stools and a narrow counter running along the plate glass window at the front. Overflowing bin by the door. Rear of the shop partitioned off by a counter with a glass case on top. Underneath the warm panels of glass are stainless steel dishes full of curry, lumps of sheek kebab on skewers, mounds of onion bhajis, saveloy sausages and pakoras. Above the counter is a huge back-lit menu. A panel of photos showing juicy morsels which generally bear no resemblance to what gets handed over. Along the back wall is the inevitable kebab turning in one corner, a couple of hot trays for the meat he skims off, a chip fryer, a hot plate for flipping burgers, a microwave for pizzas, a glass fronted fridge full of cans and a small sink, (never used). In the other corner is the tiny hatchway through to the kitchen. Although you can hear the clatter of pans in the kitchen, you can't actually see into it – a hanging screen of multicoloured plastic strips ensure that. Kaz shouts through and a short while later whoever is doing the cooking presses a buzzer. Kaz then reaches in and picks up the next batch of burgers, sheek kebabs or boiled rice. When I arrive Kaz always scoops me a portion of lamb rogan josh, then passes it through the hatch for the extra coriander and sliced tomatoes that I like to be added.

Where Kaz was lucky – and why Baba's Bites does so well while countless other similar places just scrape by – is that less than a year ago a massive late-night bar and club opened opposite. Now he's assured of a steady flow of revellers being drawn across the road to the glow of his shop like moths to a flame. Unlike the melting pot of ethnic foods on sale, the clientele are mostly white, mostly male, usually in their twenties. Eyes bright, they burst raucously through the door, vying with each other at the counter, sometimes loudly critical at what's on offer, sometimes reverently appreciative like kids in a sweet shop. Who knows which way alcohol will tip them. As they wait for their orders they discuss all manner of topics. The standard of women in the club they'd just left, how United or City are doing, the lack of black cabs. Sometimes it's stuff from the news – the state of the country's immigration system, scrounging asylum seekers, the flood of immigrants ruining the country. Even when they start to bitterly discuss Pakis or ragheads, Kaz's smile remains unchanged as he plays the dutiful patron, quietly carrying out their commands. Serving them food from the very countries they curse.

To the left of Baba's Bites is a Slow Boat Chinese takeaway, on the other side a 24 hour Spar complete with bouncers to stop shoplifters escaping. After that is a dive of a pub. The rest of the row of shops on his stretch of the street consists of daytime businesses – dry cleaners, a newsagent's and places like that. At the other end is a fish and chip shop which, for some reason, always shuts at around eight o'clock. The shutters are drawn down and padlocked long before I ever show up. Above the chip shop is a massage parlour. You'd miss it from the street, but in the alleyway round the back a discreet sign above the permanently open door leading up the stairs reads, 'Far Eastern Massage. Open 24 hours.' I only know this because, when I arrive with a delivery for Kaz, I have to carry it up the alleyway to his shop's rear door.

As you'd probably guess from the swell of my belly, I'm not too fussed about my food. As long as there's enough of it. But I'm sure plenty of people happily gorging themselves at the front would spit it out in disgust if they could see the state of things round the back. The alleyway is narrow and it stinks. While the food places are open for business, the extractor fans sound like a collection of giant vacuum cleaners left permanently on. The grills pump out warm, grease-laden fumes that mingle with the sickly sweet aroma of rotting food. The alleyway is littered with trays of all shapes and sizes dumped from the back doors of the shops. Most usually contain the remains of food: broken eggshells, mangled halves of oranges or overripe tomatoes with skins that are split and weeping. Discarded twenty-five litre drums of economy cooking oil sit piled next to empty beer barrels and crates of bottles from the pub. Industrial size wheelie bins seem permanently stuffed to the top, the lids unable to ever close properly. Crowding round them are broods of bulging bin-bags, haphazardly piled on to one another. Water, pooled in the pitted surface of the alley is either a foul smelling milky colour or tinged with a surface of glistening oil.

Kaz's door is like all the others – heavily metal plated. He's spray painted a large red 29 on it and I kick it twice to let whoever's in the kitchen know I've dropped off. I'm always back in the light cast by the lamps on the main road before the bolts go back and the cardboard trays vanish, dragged inside by, I presume, one of the kitchen assistants.

I found the note in about my eighth curry prepared by the new cook. Because I always have lamb rogan josh with extra coriander and freshly sliced tomatoes, she must have worked out it was the same customer asking for it each time. In fact, I was fairly certain that I was Kaz's only regular customer – the rest just stumble in because it's the first place they find serving food after coming out of the club. Most of them probably couldn't even remember what they'd eaten by the next day. I was halfway through my usual, watching with amusement as three lads attempted to cross the road. After about ten o'clock on a weekend it seemed pedestrians, vehicles and the watching police silently agree that daytime rules don't apply. Made impatient by booze, people would lurch out into the path of cars that instantly slow down or stop to allow them to cross. Similarly cab drivers pull up whenever they like or make U turns anywhere they fancy. The whole thing is a melee yet, apart from the occasional slanging match, it seems to work.

The three lads had made it through the door and were debating about whether to go for doner kebabs or quarter pounders when I bit on the strange object. At first I thought it was gristle – but it was too hard for that. An exploratory poke with my tongue revealed that it was something folded up. With a forefinger and thumb I extracted it from my mouth, sucking the remains of curry sauce from it as I did so. I held it up and saw that it was greaseproof paper, tightly folded. Carefully I opened it out and there, in the middle of the small square, were the words, 'Help me. I am prisoner here.'

I stared with puzzlement at the paper. Placing it carefully to one side, I decided to show it to Kaz once he'd finished serving the group at the counter. The first two had taken their burgers and wandered out on to the street. The third one waited at the counter, a twenty pound note dangling from his hand. But as he was handed his order, the customer whipped the money from Kaz's reach and spun around to run for the door. From the corner of my eye, I saw his two mates sprint away up the street. Until then I'd only ever seen Kaz from the chest up. He was of a thickset build and I didn't think particularly agile. But he vaulted across that counter in a flash. The lad had bumped against the door frame and lost a second as a result. Kaz sprang across the shop, grabbed him by the collar and dragged him back to the counter in one movement. With his other hand he reached behind it and produced a baseball bat. He shoved it hard up against the customer's lips, the wooden tip audibly catching on his teeth. A smear of blood ran appeared on his lips.

'Pay me,' Kaz demanded, aggression lowering his voice to a growl. All traces of the amiable kebab shop owner with a limited under-standing of English had vanished and I looked at the muscles bunched in his shoulders and arms, knowing that he meant it. The prospect of imminent violence hung menacingly in the air and I felt a surge of queasiness in my stomach. Thankfully the customer quickly produced the note from the breast pocket of his Ben Sherman shirt. Kaz snatched it, walked him back to the doorway and said, 'Night then.'

The lad walked shakily off up the street and Kaz returned behind the counter. He looked at me and said, 'Why do people have to be like that? I work hard all night, give him what he wanted and he tries to rob me.' He shook his head regretfully. 'It's a bad world Richard, a bad world out there.' His eyes turned to the street and he gazed with sadness at the procession of people flowing past. Then, with a smile and shrug of his shoulders, he picked up a ladle and began stirring the curries.

I couldn't believe how quickly he readopted his previous persona. It was like having a friendly dog snarl at you one moment, then wag its tail the next. Finding it hard to keep the same easy familiarity in my voice, I said, 'You're right there.' I looked at the piece of paper and, having witnessed this new side to him, decided against letting him see it.

Two nights later I was making a delivery at Baba's Bites again, but this time I had slipped my own note into the tray of naan breads. It read, 'Who are you? Why are you a prisoner?'

Not knowing if I would ever get a reply, I banged on the back door and then went round to the front and stepped inside. 'Same as usual?' asked Kaz, already spooning rogan josh on to a pile of rice.

'Yeah, cheers,' I replied and sat down on my favourite stool in the corner. He handed the tray through the hatch and a few minutes later it was returned with a garnish of coriander and tomato. Shielding the food from him with one forearm I sifted through the curry with my fork. A thrill of excitement shot through me when I found the little wedge of paper. Quickly I wrapped it in a serviette and slipped it into my pocket.

And so began a correspondence that would change my outlook on life forever. Over the next two weeks we exchanged a series of notes. Mine written on lined sheets, hers scrawled in a microscopic hand on lengths of greaseproof paper. She'd write them at night, sacrificing valuable sleep to describe to me her plight. Her name was Meera and she was a seventeen year old Hindu girl from the war-torn region of Kashmir sandwiched uncomfortably between India and Pakistan. Her father and both brothers had died in the crossfire between militants and government troops. That left her as the eldest of four remaining daughters. After a long and tearful talk, she had persuaded her mother that the only way to prevent the family from becoming destitute was for her to leave the war ravaged region and look for work. So they had paid almost all their savings to a man who promised to find Meera a well paid job as a cook in an Indian restaurant in London. Abandoning her dream of a university place in Jammu to read law, she had climbed into the back of a lorry with seventeen other people and begun the slow trek overland to Britain. The group was occasionally allowed to emerge at night for a few minutes. Twice they transferred to other lorries – the one taking them on the final leg of the journey was the newest. They sat at its end, crammed in on all sides by crates of tulips. Eventually they were all dropped off at a house, herded inside and the men and women separated. They were told they were in Britain, but certain arrangements still had to be made. After two days locked in a room with only a bucket for a toilet, some bottles of water and a few loaves of bread, a different man kicked open the door. Meera was dragged out by her hair and told the cost of her passage to England had gone up. Her passport was taken off her and she was told that, to repay her debt, she could work in a brothel or a kitchen. Of course she opted for the kitchen and was bundled into the back of a van and driven to Baba's Bites. When she asked me which city she was in, tears sprang to my eyes.

She arrived late at night and was led up the stinking alley, marched through the back door and chained to the sink pipes. She had enough slack to get around the kitchen and reach the toilet and sink in a tiny room at the back. She slept on a camp bed in the corner and hadn't seen daylight since arriving; the nearest she got to that was when the back door was opened up to take in deliveries. But she was made to hide in the toilet when that happened. After cooking from lunchtime to the early hours, she would clean the kitchen. Once Kaz had bolted the back door, he left by the front of the shop, padlocking the metal shutters behind him. Then he went round to the alley way and bolted the backdoor from the outside too. Once he was gone she was able to grab a few hours sleep before he or his brother returned late-morning. Then she would be preparing food – including my curries – until the shop raised its shutters once again at lunchtime.

In one of my first ever replies to her I offered to go straight to the police. But she wouldn't let me. If any officials were involved, she reasoned, deportation would inevitably follow. She needed to remain in Britain, working in a job that paid her cash to send home to her family. All she wanted to do was escape from Kaz's kitchen. She told me that the pipe she was chained to was old and flimsy; she was confident that she could bend or even break it. What she needed me to do was slide the bolts back on the outside of the back door, she would do the same to the ones on the inside of the door, and then she would be free. She didn't want any more help than that.

The situation she was in made me feel sick – and outraged at Kaz. I agreed to help her and we arranged that the next time Kaz rang, I was to put a note in the tray of breads confirming that tonight was the night. A previous note she sent me had stressed the importance of successfully getting her out; she was terrified of what Kaz would do if she tried to escape and failed. I wished she had room on the piece of paper to elaborate, but I reasoned we would soon have plenty of opportunity to talk face to face.

Friday night and I was sitting in the office, fan directed straight at my face, trying to learn the main aspects of insurance law relating to groups travelling abroad. (One of the less glamorous modules of my course.) At 10:43 the phone's ring put a welcome end to my study.

Pushing the door shut, I picked up the receiver and said, 'Mr Wing's Bakery.'

'Rick? It's Kaz here.'

By keeping to our established patter, I was able to hide the revulsion in my voice, 'Kaz, how's business mate?'

'Busy, my friend. Very busy. I need six dozen more pittas, two dozen naans and one dozen peshwari naans.'

'No problem. Any extras?'

'Just naans my friend. All you can get.'

'Coming right up. I'll be there in half an hour.'

Twenty-six minutes later I pulled up outside Baba's Bites. The place was heaving. A couple were sitting on the pavement outside, he finishing off a burger while she rested her head on her knees and moaned about how pissed she was. In the doorway four boisterous lads were struggling over a pizza, each one trying to grab the quarter with the most pepperoni on. I rapped on the window and once Kaz caught sight of me, I pointed to the trays of bread balanced on my other arm then set off round to the back door. As I picked my way between the debris in the alley I saw shadows moving in the glow of light shining from the massage parlour doorway. Keeping in the shadows, I watched as two men emerged in to the alley. Both smiling, they turned round to shake hands with the man who had escorted them to the bottom of the stairs and I realised with a shock that it was Kaz's brother. He patted each man on the shoulder and, as they disappeared round the corner, he headed back up the stairs. So that was the new business interest.

I banged twice on the door and as I leaned down to place the trays on the step, I noticed for the first time a bolt on the outside of the door. Looking up I saw another at the top. They hadn't been there a few weeks ago and, knowing the reason for their sudden appearance, anger surged through me – if a fire broke out at night Meera stood no chance of escape.

In Baba's Bites I stood silently in the far corner and waited for the skinny man sitting on my stool to finish his curry. I knew my presence by his shoulder was unsettling him, but I didn't back off. I even wanted him to say something; a confrontation might dissipate the ugly knot of aggression lodged in my chest. Alternatively it might aggravate it further: either way I didn't care. Hurriedly the man wiped up the remains of his curry sauce with a piece of naan bread and popped it into his mouth. Glancing at me from the corner of his eye, he left the shop. I sat down and scowled out the window at the people blundering past, all of their spirits lifted by the arrival of the weekend. I watched and wondered if any had the slightest concern for the army of anonymous workers slaving to keep them served with plentiful supplies of cheap takeaways and taxis. Sitting there I began to think about other parts of the economy that were kept running by illegal immigrants. The people who deliver our pizzas, clean our offices, pick our fruit and vegetables, iron our shirts and wash our soiled sheets. No-one on the street outside looked as if they could care less. A minute later Kaz called me over and handed me my curry. Hardly able to meet his eyes, I took it with a brief smile and reclaimed my seat.

Looking at the bright red curry I guessed that I'd put on a good half a stone over the past fortnight. It was as delicious as usual; Meera had explained in one note that it was Kashmiri rogan josh I was eating: she used fennel, cloves and a pungent resin called asafoetida. As I finished it off I saw the tiny scrap of greaseproof paper. Surreptitiously I unfolded it and saw she had just been able to scrawl the words, 'Please do not fail me.'

Raising my voice unnecessarily, I said goodnight to Kaz, hoping Meera was able to hear me in the back kitchen. The bakery night shift finished just after 4am and immediately I drove back to Baba's Bites.

Most of the clubs had shut around an hour before and now just a smattering of mini cabs roamed the streets searching for their last fare of the night. The shutters at Baba's Bites were drawn down and padlocked, the bin outside overflowing with the remains of that night's sales. Polystyrene trays were thrown into the doorways of the neighbouring shops, chips dotted the pavement like pale fat slugs. I pulled up at the corner and quietly made my way up the alley. The council bin lorry came round every Sunday and Thursday – which meant the refuse had been cleared from the alley only last night. However Friday was probably the week's busiest night and already the alleyway was piled with bags of rubbish, boxes and packaging hurled from the back doors of the shops. At the other end light shone from the massage parlour's open door. It spilled across the narrow passageway, helping me pick my way forward. Up ahead an enormous rat heard my approach. We looked at each other for a few seconds then, to my relief, it casually crept back into the overflow of a nearby drain. At the back door of Baba's Bites I put my ear up against the cool metal surface and listened. But there was nothing to hear. Tentatively I knocked twice. Instantly a knock was returned. She must have broken free of the pipe and was sitting on the other side of the door listening for my arrival.

Urgently I whispered, 'Meera, is that you?' Instantly I felt stupid: it could hardly have been anyone else.

Her voice was light and sonorous: and would have been beautiful to hear if it wasn't packed with so much fear. 'Yes Richard, it's me. I have broken the pipe, the kitchen is flooded.'

Looking down I saw water seeping out from the bottom of the door. Metal began to clunk and rattle as she started undoing the bolts on her side of the door. I stepped back to slide open the ones on my side – and to my dismay saw they were secured with two heavy-duty padlocks. I shut my eyes and silently swore. I didn't think Kaz would bother padlocking a door that was bolted shut from both the inside and out. But now it seemed an obvious precaution, especially considering the prisoner he kept inside. Meera's trembling voice sounded through the thick barrier separating us. 'I have done it. Can you open the door?'

'Meera,' I whispered. 'He's padlocked the bolts. I can't unlock them.'

'You must,' she cried, now panic-stricken. 'I must leave here!'

I needed a hacksaw; and nowhere would be open until morning. By then our chance would be gone. Even if Kaz turned up late, I couldn't stand there in broad daylight breaking into the back of a shop. 'I'm so sorry Meera, I need a hacksaw. I'll get one later and come back the same time tomorrow.'

'No!' she pleaded. 'I cannot be here when he comes. He will know what I have done.'

I looked at the tamperproof screws protecting the door hinges: there was no way I could free her. I slapped the palm of my hand against the wall in frustration. 'I'm sorry Meera. I promise to come back.'

She began to sob, 'He beat me for burning the rice. He said he will send me somewhere far worse than here if I do wrong again. Help me Richard.'

Desperately I whispered back, 'I will, tomorrow.'

I heard her slump against the door and start to cry. At the other end of the alley male voices were audible coming down the stairs of the massage parlour. Pressing my hands against the door, I could only whisper, 'I'll come back tomorrow night,' before quickly walking back out on to the street.

A soon as B&Q opened I was searching the place for hacksaws. An elderly assistant saw me scanning the aisles and took me to the correct section. 'It's a big padlock. The hasp is about a centimetre thick' I told him.

'Well,' he said, rubbing his chin with one hand. 'This will get through it in about five minutes.'

'Great,' I said, taking the saw from his hands and hurrying to the tills.

After that I went to the supermarket and bought a load of food, including a pile of fresh fruit and vegetables. I had already decided to insist that Meera stay at my place until she was sorted out with a job. I was confident I could get a place for her in Mr Wing's bakery, even if it would be for a pittance. Now, given what she had said about Kaz beating her, I wasn't sure what sort of a state she might be in when I finally got that door open. I had formed an image of her face – long dark hair, fragile features and large brown eyes. Picturing her now covered in bruises, I added bottles of ibuprofen and paracetamol to my trolley.

The rest of the day was spent dozing fitfully on my sofa. I kept waking up, my mind dwelling on what he'd do to her. He wouldn't hurt her too badly, I reasoned. After all, he needed her to cook. But I'd seen the flash of his temper and an uneasy feeling sat heavy in my mind. Flicking on the telly, I caught the lunchtime news. The presenter was describing how a major ring in peddling African children into the British sex trade had been broken up by the police. The implications of Kaz's brother's new business interest suddenly hit me like a slap in the face. Kaz himself had said she would end up somewhere far worse if she did anything wrong again. An image of a grimy bed in the Far Eastern Massage Parlour forced its way into my mind. Meera chained to it, a queue of punters at the door, pulses racing at the prospect of a new girl in her teens. I tried to push the thought away.

In Mr Wing's that night I sat staring at the Chinese calendar on the wall of his office. It was Year of the Monkey, judging by the number of primates adorning the pages. The relief I felt when the phone finally rang was instantly diminished when I heard Kaz's voice. Sounding unsettled, he asked for double quantities of just about everything. He hadn't time to make it to the cash 'n' carry, he explained. At least I now could make a delivery and then sit at the counter and observe him. Try and gauge by his behaviour just what he might have done to her.

So, after dumping the trays at the back door and kicking it twice, I marched round to the front of the shop. As soon as I stepped inside it was obvious something was wrong. For a start there was no lump of donor kebab turning on its vertical skewer in the corner. The fridge of canned drinks was almost empty – just cream soda and cans of shandy remained. People were waiting restlessly for their orders while Kaz hurried around behind the counter looking totally stressed out.

'Forget the chicken,' said one customer. 'I haven't got all night. How much are those things?' He pointed down at the skewers of sheek kebabs lined up under the counter.

'£2.50 each, including pitta bread and salad. How many?' asked Kaz, acknowledging me with a quick wave and passing a portion of lamb rogan josh through the hatch.

'Two,' the young man snapped, rapping a pound coin impatiently against the counter.

I took my corner seat and after a longer wait than usual, my curry arrived. 'You all right?' I asked as Kaz handed it to me over the counter.

'Yeah, staff problems that's all,' he replied distractedly. As I took the polystyrene tray I noticed a long scratch running across the back of his hand. Pretending I hadn't seen it, I took my curry and sat back down. With the first forkful I knew it hadn't been cooked by Meera. The sauce was watery, my extra garnish of coriander was missing, the lamb was burnt and the rice had been left in the pan until the grains were bloated and soft. A soon as it entered my mouth it turned into something that resembled semolina. I struggled through it, wondering what this meant. Was Meera beaten so badly that she couldn't cook? Or had she already been bundled up the alley and into the massage parlour?

Binning the container, I waited a few moments to try and ask Kaz where his usual cook was, but the shop had grown too busy again. Drunken men milled around at the counter, confused by the lack of donor kebab and settling reluctantly for the poorly prepared alternatives. Not wanting to arouse Kaz's suspicions by lingering for too long, I slipped back out and returned to Mr Wing's.

A soon as the bakery shut, I said my goodnights and hurried along the street to my car. Checking that the hacksaw was still safely stashed on the back seat, I set off straight back to Kaz's. In the alleyway I picked my way through the debris, nose wrinkling at the fruity smell being given off by a tray of rotten bananas.

At the door, I knocked twice and waited for a reply. Nothing. 'Meera?' I whispered loudly. 'Can you hear me?' From the other side of the door came only silence. Dark thoughts crowded my brain. Have they gagged her? Is her mouth so badly swollen she cannot speak? I raise up the hacksaw but, just as I start to saw, I realise that without her to unlock the inner bolts, the door will be impossible to open. Voices at the other end of the alley caused me to crouch behind a pile of bin-bags. Four men emerged from the massage parlour. They step out into the alley, laughing and patting each other's backs. One mimes a whipping motion as if he's urging a horse to the finish line and they all roar with laughter again. Holding up hands to slap each other's palms, they head back on to the street and disappear around the corner.

The image of Meera chained to the bed, legs spread, reappears in my mind and I throw down the hacksaw angrily. Looking at the entrance to the massage parlour, I consider barging my way up the stairs and demanding to see her. Two more men appear at the corner and disappear into the open doorway. Angrily I pull out my mobile phone and dial 999. Once connected to the operator I ask for the police. I'm put through to a tired sounding man and I explain that I have reason to believe there is an illegal female immigrant being held against her will in the Far Eastern Massage Parlour, just off Cross Street in central Manchester. The person asks how I know this for certain and when I reply that I don't, he says they'll try and arrange for a patrol car to call the next day.

'But you need to send someone now. She's probably up there being raped this very moment,' I almost shout.

The person at the other end of the line barely attempts to mask their boredom, assuring me that my report has been logged and will be dealt with at the earliest opportunity. But, he adds, with it being Friday night, that may well be some time.

Furiously I yell, 'Now! You must send someone now!' and kick out at the nearest bin bag. The thin plastic splits and among the scraps of shredded cabbage, tomato and cucumber that tumble out, is a human hand. Long feminine fingers, bone and gristle visible at the neatly severed wrist. I think of the rows and rows of sheek kebabs Kaz was so eager to sell and the lumps of crudely butchered meat in the curry I'd eaten earlier. As the vomit erupts from my mouth all I can hear is the officer saying, 'Sir, are you all right? Can you hear me, sir? Sir?'

# The Anniversary

## Sally Spedding

*Sally Spedding's first novel,* Wringland, *was published as recently as 2001 and attracted immediate attention as a distinctive and chilling contemporary ghost story. The follow-up,* Cloven, *was equally eerie. Her evocative writing has been much praised and, as 'The Anniversary' shows, her talents are not confined to the novel.*

A lifeboat rope slaps against the mildewed lounge window as the *Pride of Pompey* churns through the waves, leaving trails of meringue froth in its wake. The woman passenger tries to identify the colour of the water and decides on grey-green, but opaque, more like the inside of a pebble. However, as she's not a geologist, the name eludes her.

A gull hangs on the south-westerly breeze preparing for its target on C deck – an abandoned tuna and sweetcorn sandwich – while the woman's husband sleeps, an incipient snore in his throat. His head a red rock fissured by small cracks around the eyes.

This is the fourth spring of their Normandy purchase – a *fermette* in the typical *colombage* style, plus three sloping acres – and this trip, like all the others, has been planned with a military precision. They are now classified as regular users, with a discount on any meals taken in the Motorists' Bar and a free glass each of Vittel.

She sips coffee from her styrofoam cup, stares around at the funereal quiet of this floating coffin lined with eau-de-nil emulsion and slapdash watercolours in matching frames. Even the barman is motionless, his head bowed towards the cappuccino machine. A French couple saunter by, hands cupping each others' buttocks, until the woman's eye is caught by something else far more intriguing.

The ridged soles of a pair of boots. Not cheap, she can tell, and very new. Her curiosity aroused, she finishes her coffee and walks over to where their owner, a young man is lying down, spread out as if he'd just dropped from a great height. She sees pale blue cotton socks, two slivers of tanned leg. Then, from each stitched hem, her hungry eye travels upwards... .

She blinks. The fly zip is undone, exposing a V of dark blonde curls beneath. A small noise escapes from her lips. She feels she should move on, but cannot. That fault holds her, somehow urging her to pull the zip right down...

'Angela?' Her husband has woken up, his newspaper a crumpled tent on the floor. 'What are you doing?'

She turns. His redness needs only a pair of horns...

'Looking for the toilettes,' she replied, when in fact she was looking at the young man's neck, his Adam's apple jutting like the Mont St Michel which is visible from their fermette. His mouth is open as if he's singing and his teeth, like a sheep's, are small and white.

'Duty Free'll be closing soon. Are you coming?' Bellows the Ox, and she ignores him.

There'd been a blur of land and the usual announcements about docking and foot passengers. In twenty minutes, the boat would reach St Malo. She checks her watch. The beautiful creature is still in Morpheus' arms, his breathing slow and even.

She hovers like some guardian angel, the same as when her mother died, while his eyelids move to reveal irises the same green as the sea.

He's used to waking up just in time on these journeys, she thinks.

'I said, are you coming?' Her husband again.

The young traveller stirs, swings his legs to the floor, and a tanned hand smooths back his fall of hair.

'Well, are you?' He asks her.

'He's my husband,' she blurts as he attends to his fly. She sees the black canvas holdall he's used as a pillow Its side pockets bulge with bits of his life, and she wonders what they hide.

'Nice to have met you.' She backs away. 'Bon voyage.'

'Are you bloody deaf?' The Ox squeezes her arm. 'I wanted to get an underwater camera.'

*An underwater camera?*

She sees him sinking down to a bed of rocks, his white legs veined by weeds...

'And some Toblerones, *if* there's any left.'

She follows him to the Duty Free shop, aware of the stranger's eyes still on them. The sea, that bottomless sea...

It's deserted save for a schoolboy choosing a key ring, the till girl too bored to even check he might be shoplifting. The Ox picks an aquamarine affair decorated with tropical fish, but the Toblerone section is empty.

'Bloody gannets,' he snarls.

The schoolboy turns round. Acne and the smudge of a moustache. She feels an immense pity for him, even though unlike Jerome, their son, he still lives. Tomorrow would have been his birthday – always remembered somewhere other than home. When cards gather at the local sorting office waiting for collection. Every hour of her life she wonders what he'd look like, every fifteen year old boy a possibility. But not this one who pockets his change and farts as if he's alone.

The Ox sniffs, then lets rip about State schooling and the prevalence of pond life, as she spots the tall young man picking up a blue basket and disappearing behind the drink shelves.

The boat lolls, its engine cutting back and the bilingual PA system advises all car drivers to rejoin their vehicles. Her husband's skin turns magenta. He can't cope with deadlines any more, while formalities with police and customs officials change him altogether. She hopes they'll be stopped and searched, but never are.

'Yellow 5. Come on.' His hand manacles hers. She looks for the stranger, but the security grille in front of the Duty Free shop has unravelled to the floor with a bang and the young man has disappeared. The couple wait obediently at the top of the staircase as the *Pride of Pompey* turns into its berth. To her, that sleeper's presence grows ever more tangible, more real by the minute.

'There's no need to wait, sir. You can go straight down.' A passing crew member smirks at her husband. 'In fact, you're the last.'

'Didn't you want to buy that photo of us arriving?' She dares as he takes the lead.

'Waste of bloody money. Anyhow, we've got three already sitting in a drawer at home somewhere.'

'At least they make us look happy.'

'So you say.'

She watches the top of his head, the greying strands against the pink, but she cannot love him. Has never loved him and is only consoled by the terrible thought that Jerome might have grown up to be his replica.

'Hurry up, you!' He shouts, already at the car, flustering with the lock. A Renault Espace, in sober green. Too large now for just the two of them, but useful when they used to bring furniture over. People seem amused while they wait inside their vehicles ready to move off. He's making a performance of checking the headlight converters, the wing mirrors and then squats his huge frame by a wheel and appears to be kissing its valve.

At this painful point, she tries focusing on the chink of daylight at the far end of the car deck. Finally, the revving of engines and a honk of someone's horn from behind, makes him get in. He sniffs again. The car has a strange smell as if it belongs to someone else. She extracts her make-up mirror and tweezers to pluck a stray hair near her chin, but her mouth stays open, too shocked to close.

They're not alone. There's another face reflected behind hers – darker in shadow. Motionless. It's him. The tall fair stranger, but still she says nothing.

Their line disembarks first into the bright grey afternoon. The holiday farmer keeps his paperwork stuck to the windscreen even though they'll be waved through as usual. Both passports are already in his hand, fanned out, him on top as usual, hiding her shy smile.

She glances round. The back seat is empty.

'What's the matter?' He barks, once Customs have ignored them.

'Nothing. I was just wondering where I'd put our wellies.'

'In the John Lewis bag, stupid.'

Mercifully, he remembers to drive on the right.

A white van is being stopped, and a girl selling roses between the traffic is almost run over.

'Idiot.'

'Maybe she's hard up.'

'She deserves to be.'

Suddenly two hands grip his headrest from behind. Her husband swerves on to the hard shoulder and, thinking only of himself, tries to eject. But central locking has kicked in and the foreign finger stays on the button.

'I'm sorry, but I can't let either of you out.' The voice is Scandinavian, edged by ice. Her stomach folds in on itself, her hands in her lap feel hot as summer stones. 'I want Le Mans. Take the back road through Lazerne.' He said.

The Ox is obedient. She sees his red ear stuffed with hair, its lobe almost purple. There are other hitch hikers from an earlier boat. One holds a painted board saying 'CAEN'.

'Don't even think of it.' The young man snarls as her husband slows up. 'Keep moving.'

He is driving badly. Already he's missed a red light and on a round-about near Doncourt a rusty 306 nearly rams his sill.

'Concentrate.' Says the voice from the back. 'Or I'll take over.'

The thought of someone else at the wheel makes him slip into tricky cambers, way over the speed limit through one grim village after another. The passenger offers them each a wine-gum, black and soft from his pocket, and when they decline, tips the lot into his mouth. Then he tells them tales of his childhood. That he is Finnish, not French or German as most people think.

She listens as the road, no longer a dual carriageway, is now a single unmarked route between high spring hedges. By the time he's finished his story, she knows all about his father, holed up in some seedy boarding house near Helsinki, who spends his days listening to guests visiting the bathroom. Or wrapping his excrement in toffee papers and offering them round before dinner.

She listens, but, unlike the schoolboy in the shop, he engenders no sympathy, rather a growing apprehension close to fear. She thinks of the fermette, how it needs her tidy touch and two hours scrubbing away the winter's debris. What's in the larder? She finds herself wondering. Has Monsieur Lecroix got in some firewood?

'Next left, then stop.' The Finn's tone matches the brooding clouds. She tries to work out north south east and west, but the sun had been left behind in Hampshire.

'Why? Where are we going?'

'Do as you're told, Monsieur.'

Her husband checks his mirror. She can see anger creep above his collar. His chin juts out.

'Now look here, mate. We're bloody miles from where we want to go. What's your game?'

'It's not a game, I can assure you.'

'So how did you get in my car in the first place?'

'That is my business.' The Espace duly turns left. The young man leans over.

'Here.'

He is quick, agile, all the things her husband isn't, and before she can cry out, he winds something tight around her eyes. The Ox is next, she can tell. The cloth smells of horse. The engine dies.

'Get in the back. On the floor,' the stranger barks. He kicks them with his new boots and, clearly to make life easier for himself, ties their hands with ready-cut baler twine. He begins to drive. She remembers those pockets on his black travel bag. He's a proper boy scout all right. He's had this all planned. She is suddenly sick all over her husband's jacket, but he's more exercised by the chassis grazing the rough earth underneath, and the stones which crack against the new paint. The driver is crazy, pretending he's in a 4x4. She can sense it's a field sloping upwards, the gear dragging badly in third.

'Jesus Christ.'

The car stops. Its front wheels lodged fast in a rut. She hears the Finn get out, swearing.

'Where's the camera?' She hisses to The Ox.

'My pocket. Why?'

She doesn't answer. Instead, pulls it out with her mouth and props it up on the front seat. Click click she goes with her tongue. Click click. It's a futile exercise, but who knows? One has to try something. To get a record. She feels more sick snaking up inside her, but worse is the shame as she imagines opening that young man's fly, touching his cock. Lying upon him...

They hear a whistle, then another, with more swearing and blows to the car. Is this a signal? Some kind of warning? Suddenly the drum of boots and voices. The Finn must have got it wrong and it's punishment time because the Espace is buffeted to a hideous chorus of grunts and moaning, until a single shot shatters the air.

She waits, hearing a dragging noise fade away. Then silence.

Whoever they are have all gone, but she knows in her bones they'll be back. A British car in the middle of nowhere, and them helpless inside it. Besides, some greedy peasant would spot it a mile off…

'Come on. We've got to get out of here,' she urges.

But he's letting her down, sighing, as he's done all his life. 'Next thing is, they'll kill us.'

The doors are unlocked, so she pushes him out with all her frightened strength until he hits the ground. She severs her twine against the exhaust's edge then fetches nail scissors to set him free. She looks round, noticing blood spots dulling the earth and the ploughed field rearing up to the sky. Then she blinks, because below lies a lake as bright as a mirror amongst the trees. There's not a dwelling in sight, but at least they're both free.

'If we both push, the car'll veer to the left of it,' she suggests. But he shakes his head, inspecting the paintwork damage, the bruised hub caps. Her vomit has dried a strange yellow on his sleeve.

'This is my bloody car. My bloody money, and *I'm* driving.' He gets in.

She shrugs, noting how his weight sinks the chassis. There's nothing for it but to try and push the vehicle, with him in second gear. She fills her lungs, plants her feet as if on starting blocks and lets desperation do the rest.

At the third attempt the people carrier lurches over the ridge and runs with the furrows, downward, trapped in the only direction there is.

'George!' The first time she's used his name since that dreadful morning they found Jerome with a Tesco bag over his head. 'George?' But fainter now, as the mirror of water cracks upon impact, sending a spray of ducks into the trees.

She follows in silence, feeling the breeze which will later bring rain, sweep her hair across her face.

# Canal Blues

## Rebecca Tope

*In a relatively short time, Rebecca Tope has established herself as a skilful exponent of crime fiction with quintessentially English rural settings. Primarily a novelist, she is here contributing to a CWA anthology for the first time. A story with a canal boat trip setting fits ideally with the theme of 'crime on the move' and for readers who have not yet encountered Tope's work, 'Canal Blues' provides an enjoyable introduction to a writer whose reputation is steadily climbing.*

'Watch your wash!' Beryl screamed at Basil, as she hung over the back of the boat. 'You're making a wave.'

Basil ignored her, his eyes fixed dead ahead, neck stiff with tension. Whoever had described canal holidays as *relaxing* must be in need of psychiatric help. If you took your eyes off the water ahead, even for a couple of seconds, you were veering all over the place, running aground, hitting the side of a bridge. And oncoming boats seemed to appear out of nowhere, even at two miles an hour.

Beryl evidently wasn't very relaxed, either. She had listened all too attentively to the ten-minute run-through of the instructions, and now relayed them to him endlessly, as if he'd been somewhere else when they were issued. 'The *right*,' she bawled, when another boat came chugging towards them. 'You pass on the *right*.' He'd known that, of course, but if the bloody thing wouldn't respond in time, and you were already firmly on the left, then where was the harm? It wasn't as if they were on the M25.

At least they had good weather. Late afternoon sunshine came dappling through the waterside woodland, creating a picture worthy of the most artistic calendar. Reflections on the water, aquatic plants, semi-tame herons and pretty stone bridges all contributed to a scene that made Basil sigh.

Handling a sizeable narrowboat for a whole week with only Beryl to assist was going to be a serious challenge. He had said so all along, but his wife had dismissed his worries. 'There are only six locks on the entire canal,' she'd said. 'We can find somebody to help when we come to them. There are always people hanging about, wanting to lend a hand.' Basil didn't know how she knew this, but found himself almost believing her.

They puttered on, successfully negotiating another seven bridges before the sun began to disappear. 'Time we moored up for the night,' Beryl asserted. 'Can you remember what the man said?'

The man had said very little on that subject, in fact. Basil eyed the grassy edge thoughtfully. The water looked very shallow, with stones visible on the bed of the canal. Beryl would have to go up to the front and jump ashore with one of the ropes. Then he would have to try to keep the back end close in, and somehow kill the engine and jump off before it drifted out at right angles to the bank. His mind filled with all the things that could go wrong, and his courage failed him.

'We could wait for someone to pass by on the towpath and ask them to catch the rope,' he said with forced optimism.

'No need,' Beryl said briskly. 'I can do it. Look, there's a good stretch. All you have to do is go very *very* slowly, staying parallel to the bank. I'll jump off just as you put it into reverse to make it stop completely. Do you see?'

He had to admire her. How on earth did she know all this? She'd never been on a canal holiday, any more than he had. Had she forgotten she was sixty years old, thirteen stone, with a dodgy knee? At least he was relatively fit, and the bank did look fairly soft. Perhaps the worst that could happen was soaked feet, after all.

They accomplished it without any broken bones or even wet clothes. Beryl shouted a lot, and the boat's bottom scraped terribly on the stones, but they had it tied up securely and the gangplank just reaching from ship to shore, within five minutes. Basil inspected their work and told himself that it would all be much easier the next day, and the day after that. He looked at his wife, her face red and her hair in disarray and admitted to himself how much he disliked her. How in the world had he allowed her to persuade him to spend seven long days cooped up in this floating prison with nobody but her to talk to?

'You go off for a little walk while I get to grips with the cooker,' she ordered. 'There's an hour or two yet before it gets dark.'

Eagerly he obeyed.

He walked back the way they'd come, taking calming breaths and trying to savour the delights of his surroundings. There was a pretty Welsh mountain visible in one direction, the first of a promised series of scenic beauties. And perhaps Beryl wasn't going to be too ghastly, if she could let him escape like this every evening. It would be something to look forward to.

Another boat was mooring up around the bend from theirs. He paused and watched as four young people laughed and shrieked and made a dreadful hash of it. They made three attempts before the boat was properly tied up. One of the girls had curly red hair and wore one of those cut-off tops that left acres of smooth brown stomach naked to the world. When the boat was finally tied up, this girl grabbed one of the men and kissed him on the lips. He held her bare midriff for a second and then pushed her away.

Basil resumed his walk, catching the eye of the other man, standing in the well at the front of the boat. A dark fellow, in his mid-twenties, wearing a red singlet. 'Evening,' said Basil.

'Hi.' The chap seemed distracted, fiddling with the catch on the door leading into the cabin, head cocked rigidly. The red-haired girl was walking along the roof of the boat towards him and he turned away from her, looking directly at Basil, forcing a smile. 'Didn't I see you back at the starting place? Are you on one of these *Blues* as well?' Basil noted that the boat before him was considerably larger than his, and named *Blue Moonbeam*. Daft name.

'That's right. We've got the *Blue Feather*. We're tied up just a little way further on.'

'What a performance, eh! Thought we'd never manage to tie it up. S'pose we'll improve with practice.'

Basil laughed and nodded, and turned to watch a third narrow-boat chug past. It was the *Blue Kitten*. Had these hirer people just chosen nouns at random, to christen their blue fleet?

The *Kitten* was the same size as the *Feather*, and Basil noted that it appeared to be occupied by another middle-aged couple, much the same as himself and Beryl. The man was bald, and wore sand-coloured shorts. The woman was slender, with a bandana-thing wrapped round her head. Basil waved and the man waved back with a jerky irritable flip of his hand. *Not into the spirit of it yet, then*, Basil noted, with a little leap of complacency.

'Don't strain yerself, mate,' the man from *Blue Moonlight* muttered, earning himself a swift grin from Basil.

When he got back to Beryl and the *Blue Feather*, there were smells of frying onions and a sizzle of sausages. He hopped along the precarious gangplank, mouth watering.

'I haven't done any potatoes,' she said. 'Just bread.'

'No problem,' he smiled. 'It's a feast – I can see that already. Shall I open a bottle of wine?' He had made sure they brought along a caseful of mixed reds and whites, to see them through the longeurs. Beryl had already discovered that the television didn't work, due, she supposed, to poor reception amongst the mountains. Basil suspected deliberate sabotage by the boat owners, who nursed romantic hopes of weaning their customers on to simpler more immediate pleasures, along the lines of bird-watching, reading, and even possibly *conversing*.

'Did you see the *Blue Kitten* go past?' she asked him. 'Another couple like us. I think they've moored just round the next bend. I heard him giving instructions.'

'I did see them,' he nodded. 'Didn't much like the look of the bloke, I must say.'

Beryl did not reply, her attention on the sausages, lips puckered the way they went when she disagreed with Basil.

They slept in separate cabins, after a long embarrassing stand-off in which Beryl made reference to the narrowness of the so-called 'double bed'.

'It's barely four feet across,' she said. 'Nothing like wide enough for two.'

Basil made neutral noises, fighting to suppress any sign of his rising hopes that he could colonise the small cabin in the bows. Beryl might easily opt to sleep in there with him, since there were two single bunks, already provided with duvets and pillows. The double was in fact the dining table by day, requiring to be converted by means of a considerable rearrangement of legs, boards and cushions. His main ground for optimism was Beryl's need for ample space. A four-foot bed was just about the minimum she required.

She dithered for ages, moving between the cabins, assessing the facilities. 'I think I'd feel safer here,' she announced, in the main part of the boat. 'And warmer.'

Basil unobtrusively crossed his fingers. She could still change her mind.

'Yes, I've decided I'll sleep in here. Would you put it up for me?' She waved helplessly at the table.

'Of course. Now, you're sure, are you?'

'I'm sure.'

All of which left Basil with a snug single bunk the other side of the loo-and-shower area, a rear door he could leave open all night on to the water and woodlands, and a dawning sense of a sporting chance of peaceful enjoyment. Beryl clattered and thumped for a long time, and then fell silent. Basil read his book for another hour, savouring the soft outside sounds of night birds and faintly lapping water. The boat rocked almost imperceptibly. Perhaps it hadn't been such a daft idea to come on this holiday after all.

The next two days passed slowly. The weather was perfect, warm and cloudless. The sunshine filtered through the trees, never too intrusive, the handling of the boat became easier. But Beryl did not change. Beryl criticised and complained; she raged at the handbook for misinforming them about the proximity of shops; she bawled at Basil when he let the boat nudge the side of a bridge. When he pressed her into taking a turn at steering, she panicked and ran them into tall rushes when another boat came towards them. Basil began to tire of the long hours standing at the tiller, eyes fixed full ahead. Only the presence of other people, all of them friendly and interested, broke the monotony.

On the first day, *Blue Moonbeam* moored alongside them when they went to find somewhere to buy milk and bread. Beryl, Basil and two of the youngsters from *Moonbeam* all walked across the fields together. They exchanged the usual details – names, home towns, canal experience and comments on the weather. Basil permitted himself some modest banter with Caroline, the red-haired girl, while swarthy Paul tried to get a smile out of Beryl.

'Romantic, isn't it,' trilled the girl. 'Wonderful weather, lovely simple days, away from all the garbage that life usually is. I could get hooked on this.'

Paul glanced back at her, his expression anything but romantic. Basil found himself wondering about how the foursome were arranged. He'd seen Caroline kiss the other chap, but Paul had an air of proprietorship over her.

'It makes a change,' he said.

'And change is such a great thing,' said Paul, with some clear meaning for the girl that was lost on the older couple. 'Isn't it, Caro?'

'Sure is,' she grinned at him.

Basil's impression of their relationship seemed to be confirmed when Paul slung an arm around the girl's shoulders, on the walk back to the canal.

'Didn't think much of those two,' Beryl said, when they were back aboard the *Feather*. 'Such awful accents people have these days.'

They passed, and were passed by, the couple from the *Blue Kitten* three or four times, with small exchanges across the water each time. Basil met the eye of the wife, who threw him a delicious smile of complicity, just as Beryl was in midstream, complaining about the deficiencies of the shower, the television and the flow of tap water. The *Kitten's* master, steering cockily close to the bank, accelerated away from the *Feather*, eyes unswervingly on the canal ahead.

'Watch your wash!' Basil called after him, but there was no response.

'Don't be so rude!' Beryl hissed at him. 'It's none of your business how fast he goes.'

On the fifth night, the murders happened.

Detective Inspector Norris had some difficulty in taking the case seriously at first. Everything seemed so obvious, so tediously neat and clear, that there was little scope for initiative or ingenious detective work.

On the same night, a Mrs Beryl Roper and a Mr Daniel Graham had been murdered in their respective hired canal boats, within a mile of each other. The two boats had been moored up along a stretch of the canal well outside any settlements. No witnesses came forward to say they saw or heard anything. A third boat, the *Blue Moonbeam*, hired by two young couples, was half a mile further along the canal. Yes, they had seen the other two boats several times – in fact Caroline and Paul had gone to the shops with the Ropers from the *Blue Feather*, and Sharon and Frank had had a bit of a chat with the Grahams, only that morning. It was like that on these holidays – you kept seeing the same people, almost forming a little club for the week. It was one of the nice things about the whole exercise.

Firstly, he interviewed Mr Basil Roper, going over the whole story.

'You say you found your wife at eight-thirty this morning, when you went through to her cabin?'

'That's right. I wondered why she was so quiet. Usually she woke much earlier than that.'

'You heard nothing during the night?'

'Not a thing. I slept very soundly.'

'Could anybody have got on to the boat and into her cabin without your hearing them?'

'Obviously. That's what must have happened.'

'Did you not lock the door at the front of the boat, where your wife was sleeping?'

'I didn't. And clearly she didn't, either. She was generally rather safety-conscious, but I suppose she felt there was little to fear on a remote stretch of canal.'

'You didn't discuss it with her?'

'No.'

'Have you any thoughts as to a motive for killing her – anybody who would want her dead, or profit from her death?'

'None at all.'

'And can you offer any evidence that it was not your doing?'

'You know I can't. It's for you to prove that I did do it, unless I'm much mistaken.'

The man was calm and fluent in his answers, but his eyes betrayed real shock. Norris had seen this before – the way proven killers could manifest grief, trauma, rage – all of which came over as stunned amazement at what had happened. He had come to believe that they somehow partitioned themselves off from the self who'd done the deed. They could often come close to convincing themselves that they were as innocent as they claimed to be.

Then he interviewed Mrs Susan Graham, who told a story that differed only in the detail.

'Daniel and I had spent the first two nights together on the double bunk, made out of the dining table, in the cabin adjacent to the kitchen area. But it was really too narrow for us both, so Daniel decided we'd be better off in the cabin at the front, with the single bunks. They were really quite comfortable, and it saved making up the double every night. I don't know why we ever bothered with it, quite honestly, except that – well, it was a holiday, and I'd been hoping for a bit of romance, and… anyway, that's what we did.

'In the morning, at about eight, I woke up and looked across at him, and immediately saw the blood on his chest. It had soaked through the duvet and everything. I couldn't believe it. It seemed impossible. I hadn't woken up at all during the night. Somebody must have come silently through the door at the back of the boat into our cabin, and just stabbed him as he slept.' She shuddered. 'It could have been me!'

'Do you mean, it could have been you who killed him, or you who could have been killed?'

'I didn't kill him! What do you mean? Of course I didn't.'

'I'm sorry, Mrs Graham, but I'm sure you can see that that is not an unreasonable conclusion to draw from the facts.'

'Why would I kill him?'

'You were happily married?'

'Yes!'

'If we asked all your friends and family, they'd confirm that, would they?'

'Oh, well, they'd say he was a bit of a tyrant, a bit uptight. But nobody can see inside other people's marriages, can they? And why would I stay with him if we weren't happy? Women can manage quite well on their own, these days.'

'And what do you say to the fact that Mrs Beryl Roper was killed that same night, in an identical boat, half a mile along the canal?'

'I say somebody was on a killing spree, that the same person killed them both.'

'But why? Who knew them both?'

'Well, nobody, as far as I'm aware.'

'You had met Mr Roper?'

'The man from the *Blue Feather*? Yes. We'd chatted a little bit, and waved when we passed them. Nothing more than that.'

'And you didn't know him before this week?'

'No! Of course not. He comes from Leicester and we've lived for twenty years in Dorchester.'

'I'm afraid that doesn't go far towards proving an absence of acquaintance.'

'But surely it isn't possible to do that? Surely it's up to you to prove that we did? I mean, that I killed Daniel and Basil killed his wife?'

It was this echo of Roper's own line that clinched it for DI Norris. In his own mind, the case was sorted, settled and solved, from that moment on.

For form's sake, Norris interviewed the foursome from *Blue Moonlight* individually, starting with the young man named Paul. What had been his impression – in detail, please – of the people in the other boats?

'The people in the *Blue Feather* were snobby, especially her. They were making a reasonable job of handling the boat, or rather, *he* was. She just criticised and shouted at him all the time. Must have made his life hell. Don't know why the silly old fool ever came on a holiday like this, with only her for company.' A meaningful silence followed, in which they both heard the unspoken answer to the question.

'What about the others?'

'Well, it was a joke amongst us, them being in a boat called the

*Blue Kitten.* That bloke must have cringed every time he thought about it. A real retired colonel type, giving orders, expecting everyone to jump out of his way. Even the boat – you could see his neck going red when he tried to steer and it took half a minute to respond.'

'And his wife?'

'Nice lady. Determined to enjoy herself, in spite of him. Just let him get on with it, smiling calmly at us while he ranted about something.'

Norris was struck with an idea, an embellishment of his assumptions so far. 'Did you ever see Mr Roper and Mrs Graham together?'

'Once, yes. They were on the towpath, having a bit of a chat. I think it was Sharon who made some joke about them needing a wife-swop.'

The interviews with Frank, Caroline and Sharon went along much the same lines. For variety, DI Norris asked Sharon what had brought them to choose this sort of holiday.

'Oh, well,' she replied airily, 'it just seemed like a fun idea, you know? It made a change from the usual sand and sangria stuff.'

'Have you known Paul and Caroline long?'

'Oh, yeah, *ages*. Actually, I used to go out with Paul. Then I got friendly with Caroline, and Frank was in the local footie team with Paul, and so we just switched partners. It's loads better this way.'

'No stresses or strains? No uncomfortable memories?'

'Nope. We're all grown ups now. We know our own minds. And we think people should go for what they want.'

'Oh?'

'Yeah – like those poor bastards on the boats. You could see the bloke from the *Feather* had the hots for the woman from the *Kitten*. Good luck to him, we said.'

'Except they're not going to enjoy any time together, are they?'

Sharon frowned. 'Right. Pity they hung around to get caught, eh. Should have legged it when they had the chance.'

Norris scratched his head a little at this.

Norris charged Basil Roper and Susan Graham with murder of their respective spouses, carefully detailing his evidence. The autopsy reports had concluded that the same sharp knife had been used in both killings, dealing stab wounds to the heart in each case. This suggested complicity between the two survivors, and a possibility that the same hand had in fact dealt both blows. However, the motivation provided by an assumption that the two had formed a relationship meant they were equally culpable under the law. Although no proof was yet forthcoming, Norris harboured a strong suspicion that the whole exercise had been planned weeks or months earlier. All he needed was some demonstration that the two had known each other prior to embarking on their holiday.

Basil Roper and Susan Graham stared at him as he read out his formal charges against them. Then they stared at each other.

'We didn't kill them,' said Susan. 'I assure you we did not.'

Norris looked at her, with a flicker of regret. She was a nice-looking woman, patient and open-faced. Dreadful what love can make a person do, even in middle age and beyond.

'You're jumping to the wrong conclusion,' said Basil. 'But you can't prove we did it. There's no blood on our clothes, no murder weapon, no witnesses.'

'You read too many detective stories,' Norris told him. 'Who *else* could have done it?'

Basil shook his head. 'I'm not required to find an answer to that,' he said.

The trial was a long time coming. Norris had handed his case to the Crown Prosecution Service, and almost forgotten about it. When notified of the date, he jotted it in his diary and ran through his interview transcripts to refresh his memory.

The Defence was thorough. It extracted the facts very much as Basil Roper had originally listed them. No traces of blood on the accused persons' clothes. No weapon discovered. Nobody to help ascertain times of death, events prior to the killings, or any aftermath. Nobody, that is, except for Caroline, Frank, Sharon and Paul.

All four were called. They were asked to supply their names, addresses, employment and relationships. Caroline gave Frank as her fiancee, which sent DI Norris riffling quietly through his notes in puzzlement. The defence lawyer was ahead of him.

'But, Miss Spendlow, am I not right in thinking that Mr Paul Jones was your... um, partner... at the time of the fatalities under investigation?'

'That's right,' she nodded, with a rather forced giggle. 'Sharon's back with him, now.'

'Back?'

'Yeah. They were an item before. It just seemed...like, we had it right the first time. We should never have messed with it. Paul's not really my type, you see. He's manipulative, jealous. Likes to play God.'

Paul Jones looked older to Norris, and far from happy. He repeated his testimony about the two couples on the other boats, the clear indications that something was developing between Mrs Graham and Mr Roper, the obvious friendliness between them in the tableau on the towpath.

'But there's a very obvious flaw in this scenario, isn't there?' demanded the Defence. 'The two accused reported the deaths themselves, and made no attempts to escape the police. Isn't that rather strange?'

Paul shrugged. 'They must have thought they'd get away with it, blame it on some bloke from the local area. They probably assumed that's what the police would think.'

'Objection, your Honour!' said the Prosecution. 'This is all supposition.'

'Sustained,' said the Judge.

Norris sighed, and glanced quickly at Susan Graham, standing patiently in the dock, alongside Basil Roper. As he watched, she turned to look at Basil, no trace of affection on her face. Roper met her gaze, with a flat weary expression. In that moment, Norris's case imploded and he realised his mistake. He had not known the truth, unlikely though it might have been, when he heard it. He had not looked beyond the simple assumptions about a couple desperate to be together.

It had not occurred to him that somebody who liked to play God had tried to bring the couple together, tried to arrange a wife swop, to reflect his own situation. And Norris knew, in that moment, just who that person was.

# Another Man's Crime

## Alison White

*Alison White is most widely known as a writer of romantic fiction, but she has also carved a niche as an author of short mystery stories. 'The Bluebird' which appeared in the CWA's* Whydunit? *anthology was especially memorable. Occasionally, as with 'Plumage', which appeared in the* Past Crimes *collection in 1998, she utilises a historical setting, and she does so again in this tale of villainous cab drivers.*

### City of London, 1849

Mortlock Jangles would have sold his brother Benjamin for a few pennies. Or beaten him senseless and thrown him into the muddy and pestilent Thames without a moment's thought. But not yet. He had to bide his time.

Now, Mortlock was forced to work all hours, run his horses to death by pulling a cab that would surely never make it through the next inspection without money changing hands and live in absolute squalor with a whingeing woman around watching his every move. All because of Benjamin.

They'd travelled to London together from Ireland to make their fortune. A few little 'encounters' on the way had provided a start. Thieving was easy when there were two of you, one to distract, one to extract, and then they were gone. A bit of pick-pocketing from city to city, some selling off of their stolen goods here and there. But keeping on the move meant they hadn't been caught and they had made it to London with enough money to buy licences, a cab and two horses.

It had been Mortlock's idea. They couldn't live off pick-pocketing and driving cabs provided them with the excellent cover of earning a living (which, the way they ran it was not at all honest), and provided other means to ply their criminal trade.

Mortlock had always been the cleverer of the two brothers, but Benjamin was the one that most people liked. He was easier on the eye than Mortlock, who had a ruddy face with split veins and a bulbous nose which, in a certain light, made him look almost deformed. Certainly, Mortlock groomed himself just as well as Benjamin did, but he had never been blessed with the easy good looks, deep blue eyes and charming smile of his brother.

Somewhat slightly built, Benjamin always looked in the peak of health whereas Mortlock appeared on the brink of death. Even his own weight seemed a burden to him as his body strained at his clothes. He coughed and spluttered constantly, until his already red eyes watered and sometimes they matted around his eyelashes with a yellow crust. No-one looking at them would ever have dreamed they came from the same stock.

Although inside Mortlock there festered a resentment at this injustice, he did not worry about it sufficiently to disregard the benefits of Benjamin's charms. He did, after all, do as he was told.

The way they'd worked it in the beginning was that Benjamin would take the cab out during the day. With his pleasant manner and appearance, if anyone would be tipped, it would be him. Especially by the ladies. Whereas ladies tended to avoid Mortlock. Benjamin also picked up titbits of gossip from other cabmen, who found him easy to talk to. Benjamin thrived on the gossip, he'd take it back to Mortlock who could store it in his head until it might become of use. Mortlock followed the press too, keeping up with what the politicians and the gentry were doing. It paid to know who was who.

At night, the cab was Mortlock's, when the whole experience of cabbying was different. Once darkness fell and the fog descended, the yellow spots of light from gas lamps were all that lit the way; and the character of the city grew darker too. Through the narrow streets and alleyways of the slums and beyond, where all was not as it may appear and the city's gentlemen mixed with the chorus girls and theatre crowd. Or the ladies of the night.

Mortlock, with his memory for faces, names and places, was shrewd though, and cunning. Nothing that he saw on those dark nights shocked him. He sat there on his cab, in his customer's eyes, as impassive as the horse who pulled them through the streets. They felt their secrets were safe.

Like any man, Mortlock enjoyed a drink. But he saved his sessions for when he returned from work, preferring to keep his wits about him. Which was more than many of his customers did.

Drunkenness lead to foolishness, Mortlock observed, although this was not entirely the preserve of the drunk. There were many sober fools too, although there was no doubt that a drink could make a man more reckless. Perhaps it was that recklessness that lead so many to start to waver from the path.

Mortlock could understand why the men sought to visit the women of these areas. The chorus girls, who laughed at their jokes or those who offered a good time. They were warm and welcoming compared to many of their stiff little wives at home no doubt. But some didn't leave it at that.

Maybe to justify their behaviour to themselves, some men would develop an affection for some particular girl. They might pursue her madly if she was in the theatre, taking her flowers, then out to dinner, perhaps go somewhere where they could be alone, then a ride through the city streets in a cab. The men would pay Mortlock his cash in advance and leave first, requesting that he took the lady home.

'Goodbye my love, 'til next time,' they'd say, or some such nonsense. Invariably though she went on to some other gentleman. The fools never knew.

Mortlock always made a note of any interesting gentlemen he had as passengers. Where he had collected them from and where he had taken them to. Some were cautious enough to ask to be let out at the end of the street and chose to walk the final part of the way home but, on those occasions, Mortlock chose to stop for a moment, just to tend the horse. That way, he could see where they were going.

Those men deserved all they got.

Mortlock could judge the demeanour of a couple, the nature of their relationship and so decide how the gentleman – or even, in some cases, the lady – might respond to a little persuasion concerning the dangers should their liaison being exposed to wife or husband.

So far his instincts hadn't let him down. Not that he was ever the one to approach the victims regarding their foibles. For he was no fool and knew that one who looked as villainous as he did would not be trusted and so would risk staring a pistol in the face.

That was Benjamin's job. His innocent face and manner could convince the gentry that he was merely a messenger. Delivering a note from a fine gentleman with an instruction to take something back in return.

'Why, I have no name, sir,' he would respond when asked. 'But 'tis one of those reporters I believe. I often pick him up when he's been in the House of Commons listening to the debates and he's got to get his story to the paper. It's all too much for me,' he'd laugh. 'I don't even read myself, sir.'

The word 'reporter' usually did it. There would be a sealed envelope to hand over, often with a tremulous instruction to tell the gentleman 'there would be no more'.

They never did go back once someone had paid. Mortlock might be greedy but he was not foolish. When, on occasion, Benjamin was told someone had 'nothing to say to the gentleman reporter', then they left it at that too. There were enough easy pickings to be had without running unnecessary risks.

When they'd first arrived in London they'd taken rooms at a place that had been been full of villains, and they wanted somewhere better. Already their belongings had been ransacked by drunkards looking for easy cash, and when Benjamin had taken up with a lady friend who stayed at a less shabby inn nearby, they'd agreed to move.

Benjamin was to take what little they had, including their money, under cover of darkness, which he did, while Mortlock worked.

When Mortlock returned to their new home for the first time, he had worked most of the night and was in a foul mood. The people of London had been remarkably well-behaved that night. The fog, followed by heavy rain, had kept them indoors and business had been slow.

'No special jobs today,' Mortlock growled, ready for his bed.

'Sure, we'll see what turns up,' Benjamin said. 'We might get a bit of luck, you never know.'

But the only luck Benjamin had seen that day had been bad. The day itself was uneventful, until – just as he'd been on his way back to their rooms, on foot, having taken the cab to the yard – a young man had rushed by and dropped a wallet in the street.

Benjamin had picked it up. Only for another man to come around the corner shouting 'Stop thief!' followed by a policeman. This time, despite Ben's innocent face and his protestations, he was emptying the wallet and counting the money as they arrived, so he was caught red-handed.

The innkeeper's wife had witnessed the whole charade and came rushing inside to tell everybody, clearly enjoying the drama.

The innkeeper, very sternly took Mortlock to one side. 'We keep a respectable place here,' he sniffed.

Mortlock could have challenged that, but knew better. 'I know, sir,' he soothed. 'And I don't know what got into my brother. He was probably going to hand in that wallet, so he was. But no-one will believe him. He'll be tried for another man's crime!'

'I don't care whose crime it was,' the innkeeper hissed, 'I don't want the police on my doorstep, and if I have any trouble from you, you'll be out!'

It didn't help when policemen turned up to look in Benjamin's room. Mortlock's heart was in his mouth as they searched. He could murder the fool for him giving away their address. Why hadn't he told them his old lodgings? But they found nothing. No stash of money, not even the pocket-watch that one hapless victim had handed over. And Mortlock was as surprised as they were, though he couldn't show it.

'Maybe now, you'll believe my brother is innocent,' he said as they left. 'There's nothing to see here. I told you,' he added to the innkeeper, who had kept a watchful eye.

'I'm watching you, Jangles. And you can tell your brother not to bother coming back. That's if he ever gets out.'

But he would. Mortlock was going to make sure of that. Because, what in God's name had Benjamin done with their money? It was nowhere to be found. Mortlock even went back to their old rooms, forced the door and checked their old hiding place, but to no avail.

Mortlock had no alternative but to stay in this wretched place until that stupid brother of his got out of Newgate Prison. The boy was a fool. He wasn't going anywhere near the lock-up himself, it was way too risky, he didn't want the law getting to know his face.

With the loss of the daytime cab money – not to mention no Benjamin to ply their usual blackmail trade – earnings were way down. Mortlock struggled to make ends meet, overcharging where he knew he could get away with it, if his passengers were drunk or stupid or both, but at the same time he had to keep his nose clean in order to keep the roof over his head until he could get back his money.

He thought of it as *his* money now. Benjamin's stupidity having forfeited any rights he may have had to it. For Mortlock would not have been foolish enough to pick up that wallet as Benjamin did. Not unless it was dark and deserted without a footstep to be heard. And he would have pocketed it straightaway, not stood on the street counting the notes.

Mortlock had time to grow bitter with Benjamin and wonder what had become of their money. Had he gambled it? Spent it on a woman? Or stashed it away for himself. Could he even be planning to come straight out of Newgate and make off with it himself? But his brother wasn't there to ask or even to beat the answer out of.

To make matters worse, Mortlock had to put up with the weeping and wailing of the stupid woman Benjamin had taken up with. Rose worked as a seamstress but Mortlock felt sure she was not averse to taking on another sort of work when short of cash. That was no doubt how she'd met Benjamin, but now though, she swore she loved him and said that she was expecting his baby.

It was all Mortlock could do to be civil to her. But if it was Benjamin's child… and they had moved lodgings because he wanted to be near the damned woman… then he might not release their money to Mortlock if he found he had treated Rose badly. So Mortlock did what he had to do.

When her condition became apparent and the innkeeper threatened to throw her out, Mortlock promised that Benjamin would take her away on his return. In the meantime, she needed a roof over her head.

'You don't want to add to the waifs on the streets do you?' he reasoned with the innkeeper.

'What about when she can't work and pay her rent?' was the reply.

'Then I will pay for her, and recover it from my brother.' Mortlock sighed the weary sigh of the wronged. 'There's a lot he owes me now.'

Predictably, the feeble Rose did fall ill and unable to work, leaving Mortlock with the burden of her rent. It seemed that as fast as he brought money home each night it was eaten away. Then she lost her child and lay sick and weeping for weeks, still unable to work and pay her rent. When she finally did work again, she was not fit enough to earn as much as she had before.

'Benjamin will be out soon,' Mortlock said. To boost his own confidence as much as anyone else's.

'Newgate's a filthy place,' the innkeeper warned. 'I don't want him bringing the filthy pox here.'

'Just a couple of nights to settle and then he and his lady friend will be on their way,' Mortlock soothed. In truth, he didn't care what they did, for once he had his money he intended to be off himself. He'd buy another cab and work on the other side of town. Or even up North. Alone. He couldn't trust Benjamin again.

On the day of Benjamin's supposed release from Newgate, Mortlock had intended meeting him, but the wretched Rose was hysterical and begged him not to leave. Such had been the extent of her ramblings that the innkeeper had banged on the door to ask what the fuss was about.

Mortlock guessed she was scared in case Benjamin didn't want her any more. But he couldn't risk leaving her in that state for fear that the innkeeper might throw her on the streets and refuse to let any of them back in. So he did his best to calm her and together they waited. When Benjamin hadn't arrived by midday, Mortlock was pacing the floor. Where was he? And where was his money?

Finally, in the middle of the afternoon, he rolled up. The first Mortlock knew was when the innkeeper bellowed up the stairs, 'Jangles, come and take this fool away will you!'

Blind drunk, Benjamin had staggered into the inn, in love with the world and especially in love with his freedom.

'Sure would you begrudge a man a drink when he's not had the chance for all these months?' he said to no-one in particular, then: 'Mortlock, brother...' he held his arms open in an expansive gesture and in his rush to embrace Mortlock, stumbled over the leg of a chair and ended up face down on the floor.

'Stand up you damned fool,' Mortlock exploded, as he dragged Benjamin to his feet, his face growing purple with rage.

'Mortlock, what's the hurry?' Benjamin dusted himself down haphazardly, stumbling a little. 'Stay and have a drink. I've missed you – have you missed me?'

'For God's sake,' Mortlock hissed, throwing his arm around his brother and heaving him through the inn and towards the door at the back which lead to the stairs and their lodgings. He cast an apologetic glance at the innkeeper. 'I'll keep him out of your way don't worry.'

'Oi! What do you think you're doing?' Benjamin tried to struggle free of Mortlock and the drink had made him heavy and clumsy. He pushed him out of the way, but his eyes, blurred with alcohol now flashed with an anger that took Mortlock by surprise.

'Don't push me around, Mortlock,' Benjamin snapped. 'I've spent many months in a bad place. I'm free now and I've done nothing wrong and you know it. Where's the harm in that?' He flung his arm out again as Mortlock lunged at him.

'Listen to your brother, or you'll be out on the street and your woman with you,' the innkeeper growled. 'If he hadn't paid her way then she wouldn't be here now.'

Benjamin's face changed then, and he held his hands up in surrender.

'Any more of it and you're out,' the innkeeper snapped as he pushed them both through the door.

Benjamin sagged against his brother, 'Oh, Mortlock, it was a terrible place. I had to have a drink.'

Benjamin was heavier than he had been – which probably had more to do with a lack of exercise than with the richness of the food at Newgate – but what surprised Mortlock most was the change in his appearance. He looked altogether more worn and bedraggled. Gone were the sparkling blue eyes and the fresh skin. In its place a sickly pallor and yellowed eyes. There were sores on his face too and his hair was matted and unkempt. If he'd passed him in the street, Mortlock would not have known him at first glance.

He dragged his brother up the stairs towards their room, stopping on the landing. 'What did you do with the money, Benjamin? What did you do with my money?'

'What money?' Benjamin swayed on the top of the stairs. 'Mortlock, brother—'

Mortlock grabbed him by the scruff of the neck and pulled him close. He smelled of sweat and ale and his breath was rank. Mortlock stared into his eyes as he spoke: 'You think you've had it bad? I've been in this hell-hole for months, while you like a fool, served the time for another man's crime. Give me the money and you can get back to your miserable freedom.'

Another door opened and a timid, pale face with wispy blonde hair peeped out. Benjamin's eyes widened. 'Rosie! My Rosie.'

She called out to Benjamin and he flung out his arms to accept her into them, but Mortlock slammed him away from her and into the wall, just as the innkeeper appeared at the foot of the stairs. 'I've warned you.'

'Go away,' Mortlock yelled, barely controlling his anger. Then, 'I'm helping my brother. There won't be any trouble.'

With a glare, the innkeeper retreated.

'Let's go for a ride in the cab, Mortlock,' Benjamin was laughing, and dribble ran down his chin. 'Like the old days. Forget all this. How are the horses? Bessie? And Charlie?'

'You've had your last ride in that cab,' Mortlock growled. 'Get out of the way Rose.' He looked into Benjamin's face again. 'Where is the money?

Slowly, as though trying to make sense of something, Benjamin frowned as he thought through his alcoholic fug, 'Ah. Oh yes, the day we came here.' He put his finger to his lips. 'Shhh,' and giggled. 'We moved the money too. Well Rosie's got it. Rosie's got the treasure,' he said in a whisper.

Mortlock released him and spun round to face Rose who looked just as puzzled as he.

'You've had the money all this time?' he snapped, stepping towards her, snarling.

She trembled and stepped back, 'I don't know anything about any money. What do you mean Benjamin? You never gave me any money.'

'Rosie's got the treasure,' Benjamin was saying softly to himself, almost humming the words.

'You gave it to your whore? Who had another man's brat? And who bled me dry all these months too' Mortlock yelled, 'By God, I should kill you!'

'Benjamin no, I didn't – it was your baby and… I don't have any money, I don't…' Rose began to weep, as Benjamin stared at her, looking first horrified, then as he considered Mortlock's words, utterly betrayed.

'She's had every man in the land,' Mortlock yelled, his fists clenched tightly at his sides as he looked from one to the other. 'I wish to God I'd killed her before now. Where's my money, whore? What have you done with it?'

Rose tried to reach Benjamin, almost blinded by tears, her arms outstretched, then he flung his arm out to push her away. She was so light, she fell backwards at the force of the blow. And down the stairs. Bump… bump… bump… until she lay at the bottom like a rag doll.

Stunned, Benjamin wobbled, then passed out at the top of the stairs while Mortlock ran to the bottom, catching Rose up in his arms and shaking her brutally. 'My money! For God's sake, where's my money?' He was still shouting when the door opened and the innkeeper stood there staring.

The police sneered at Mortlock's insistence that Benjamin had killed her. When they arrived, he was still out cold, and they thought incapable of anything. Everyone in the inn said he'd been so drunk just minutes before he could barely stand.

'Mortlock threw that brother of his against the wall too. Saw it myself,' the innkeeper told them. He and several customers had restrained Mortlock while someone fetched the police. A fight was one thing. Murder something else.

'Threatened to kill them both,' his wife added with a shudder. 'Shouting terrible things at that poor mite.' She clutched her handkerchief and sniffed. 'We keep a respectable house here. And he had hold of her when we came out. Poor thing, he was shaking her till she rattled. As if she wasn't already dead enough.'

When Benjamin sobered up, he too said Mortlock had thrown Rose down the stairs, being jealous at Benjamin's return and of her

311 Another Man's Crime

love for him. Benjamin was so full of grief for the loss of Rose and the baby he had never known that even the police took pity on him. As did the innkeeper who agreed he could stay for a few days more.

Then, retrieving the money from where he'd secured it beneath Rose's mattress, within a matter of days, Benjamin had cleaned himself up, replaced the old cab with a new one and found himself better lodgings on the other side of town.

Weeks later, as the crowds gathered at Horsemonger Lane to enjoy a public hanging, Benjamin stopped his cab and watched for a while. He'd seen enough in Newgate Prison to know he never wanted to go back there and what had kept him going all that time was the thought of coming out and making a new life with Rose. But all he could see when he thought of her now, was her little frightened face as he'd pushed her away from him. Then the terrible bump, bump, bump, down the stairs.

What was it Mortlock had called him, 'A fool, serving the time for another man's crime?' Well now it was his turn.

Benjamin watched as they slipped the noose around Mortlock's neck. Then he cracked his whip and the horse pulled away, hooves clattering as they rode into the future.

# Seeing Off George

## David Williams

*Although I did not know David Williams well, I have enjoyed reading his novels and was very pleased when he approached me with a view to contributing a story to this book. An agreeable correspondence followed and David duly submitted 'Seeing Off George'. A few weeks later, I was shocked to learn of his sudden death and I am grateful to his widow Brenda for permitting me to include this urbanely told story, which was very possibly the last that he ever wrote.*

'George, it'll be the nicest birthday present you've ever given me. I can't imagine how you and Tristan have kept it a secret so long.' Laura leaned over from where she was standing behind her husband's chair and kissed him lightly on the cheek, her arms draped loosely around his neck. 'Thank you again, darling.' She kissed him once more, this time from the other side. He had looked up on each occasion, first into her eyes, and next, more fleetingly but just as appreciatively, into the inviting cleavage exposed below the opening of her pink negligee.

In a sensual way Laura Bodworski – maiden name Harrison – was an attractive woman, and proving to be enduringly so. Tallish, her figure, while not 'catwalk' slim, was firm and statuesque, her physical appeal enhanced by long, naturally blonde hair, almond-shaped brown eyes, high cheekbones and generous lips. Her whole persona was made the more engaging because her facial expression commonly exuded limitless intelligence and understanding. This last was an impression only, conveniently disguising an appallingly low intellectual acuity, matched in the same degree by some highly developed unsavoury instincts. She was selfish, manipulative, and ruthless beyond belief, though, above all, she was supremely practised at hiding manifestations of these baser characteristics from her intimates.

It was April 3rd, a Saturday, and exactly five weeks ahead of Laura's thirty-first birthday. The thought was going through her husband's mind as it did frequently that she was actually more comely to look upon now than when he had married her eight years before. She had been his secretary before deciding to become his wife. That she had no intention of ever being, into the bargain, mother to his children – she hated children – was resolved by her arranging never to become pregnant, and blaming the failure on her husband.

George Bodworski philosophically accepted the situation and counted what he took to be his blessings. 'I am hoping Tristan's able to build the pool before summer, like he's promised,' he said. His east-European grammatical constructions were now more detectable than the accent which he had very nearly lost. His gaze followed Laura's confident movements as she returned to her place at the table. 'I trust also, my dear, that it pleases you when it's done. It won't add anything to the value of the house, of course,' he completed, with a good-humoured pout and dismissive shrug.

'You've said that before, my darling, which makes it even sweeter of you to give in,' she answered. 'Tristan doesn't agree with you, does he?'

Tristan Gyder-Smith ran a swimming-pool business in the next village. Laura had met him at a Berkshire health club a year before this. Aged twenty-nine, he had been an only child who now lived alone in the modest home of his deceased parents. He had been married briefly but, after spending most of his inherited money, his wife had deserted him for the owner of a small chain of seafood restaurants who also played the accordion – not well so much as frequently. But, then, it takes all sorts.

Tristan was as ruggedly handsome as Laura was alluring, but where she was full of guile he was a malleable innocent. Leaving school at eighteen, after failing to enter university, he had subse-quently also failed to make a career in financial services, public rela-tions, as an advertising salesman, and finally, as a local government clerk. In desperation he had invested what little was left of his family money in a swimming pool construction and management course at a technical college, later hiring a young plumber called Ray Langford on a part-time basis, and turning the garage and toolshed of his house into a store and workshop. Since that time he had made a just passable living. He had recently been installed as Laura Bodworski's deeply enthralled secret lover, and, by the same hand, been made a friend of the unwitting George Bodworski, because Laura liked to have her paramours conveniently on tap, as it were.

George had waved a dismissive hand at his wife's last comment. 'So how should Tristan agree with me? He's in the swimming pool business, isn't he?' He paused, coffee cup halfway to his mouth. 'Not in a big way of business, come to that. I've given him the contract because you said we should help him.' His eyes had screwed up as if he wasn't totally sure that the reason for his largess had been a good one – excepting that the pool was to be outdoor and quite small.

'That was very generous of you, my sweet,' Laura responded. 'You're always insisting the country's future lies with start-up companies like Tristan's. I'm sure he'll do a good job. The plan's gorgeous.' She turned again to smooth the drawings that had been waiting beside her place, tied up with coloured ribbons when she had come down earlier. In fact the landscaping of her present had been based on a sketch she had made nearly two years before, when she had first decided it might be nice to have a pool. She hadn't pressed the whim at the time. It had been in the interim that Tristan had appeared and provided her with a fresh incentive.

The couple were breakfasting in the refurbished kitchen of their late-18th Century, ex-vicarage home in Farringly, a pretty village a few miles west of Windsor that offered views of the Royal castle. George had bought the house three years before this, its mellowed Georgian domesticity fitting harmoniously with the six-hundred-year-old, early Gothic church set beside it in the main village street. Nowadays the parish priest lived in a small modern vicarage a hundred yards away, leaving the old house to be sold to a rich commuter.

The heavily-built George was bald, wore an extravagantly large moustache, and was an inch shorter than his wife. He had not been married before. His parents had been impoverished political refugees from Poland who had come to Britain in the early 1960s when George had been a child. He was now a prosperous dealer in antique furniture, mostly acquired from countries in the old Eastern Communist Bloc. He owned a small retail establishment in nearby Eton, on the nearside of the ancient bridge over the Thames from Windsor. In addition to being the home of a famous English school, Eton was peppered with high-class antique emporia of which George's establishment was one of the most celebrated. He had another shop on West 54th Street in New York, and a network of contacts in Eastern Europe, where he travelled regularly.

The pickings for George were not as good now as they had been in the seventies and eighties, and his buying prices had rocketed, though not nearly so much as his selling prices. Any restoration work that was needed was done in the countries of origin, which preserved authenticity as well as George's costs. One of the reasons for his visits was to watch the progress of such labours. In his early days he had made the trips in a Ford Transit van and brought the goods back with him. Now he flew from nearby Heathrow Airport and employed specialist international carriers to transport the merchandise.

'If Tristan starts work on Monday, and the whole thing takes four weeks, it should be finished before you get back from your next trip,' said Laura. 'You're leaving two weeks today, aren't you?' she added casually.

'That's right.' George gave a mischievous smile. 'I planned it that way so I wouldn't be here when the garden's in a mess from the digging.'

'Naughty you,' she humoured him. 'So if you're away two weeks, I should be swimming by the time you get back.'

'Let's hope so.' He frowned. 'May isn't too early for swimming out of doors?'

'Not in a heated pool, it isn't. Oh, I'm so looking forward to it.'

'You are clever, Tristan. The poor dear's bought the whole deal,' purred Laura. It was later that morning. She and Tristan had been making love at his house. Her compliment had been a specious one. The plot they were involved in had been entirely her invention – only she praised him to bolster his courage. She wasn't yet entirely sure that he was capable of cold-blooded murder.

Otherwise the plan was a very simple one.

Tristan took a deep breath, expanding his well developed and presently naked, bronzed and hairy chest. Like George, he was solidly built, but taller than the other man, and a good deal slimmer. Facially, the two were very similar, even in the shape of their hairless heads. Because Tristan was balding prematurely he had taken to shaving off what hair he still had. He didn't wear a moustache, but that was a deficiency easily overcome. His experiments with false moustaches had made him look very like his lover's husband, and, as he and Laura had agreed, would certainly do so to a preconditioned observer. This had once prompted Tristan to remark that Laura kept falling for the same man – except he'd thought better of it.

'And the site'll be all prepared for us a week Friday?' She asked as they lay together on the bed, tracing her fingers down across his stomach.

'As far as it needs to be, yes. Four-foot-deep excavation with concrete-block side-walls ready for the plastic-liner to go in the following Monday. That last bit's a job for the two of us. I mean Ray Langford as well as me,' he answered earnestly. 'The boiler and filter will be in by then as well, but not running.' There was an existing, small outhouse in which both devices were to be housed.

'But only you'll be around at... at the critical time? Friday night, and Saturday morning?'

'Of course.' He grinned. 'We'll put the water in the following week.'

'I see.' Laura nodded her approval. 'What about the pool bottom?'

'I'll put in the sand and cement screed Saturday morning after... after...'

'After you've topped and buried George on Friday night. You won't be digging his grave till you've done the deed,' she volunteered coolly.

'Yes, and filled it in again when he's in it to match the rest of the bottom.' They had agreed he should leave spreading the final foundation layer of the whole pool bottom until the following morning. This was partly to avoid his needing to use outside lights late into the night, but mostly because he would need to see that George's 'plot' had time to settle properly. 'Well I can't dig the hole till he's dead, can I?' he added because of her earlier uncertain look. 'I mean what would I say if he asked what it was for? He's not stupid.'

She smirked, relieved to have him joke about his intended crime. It was Laura who had brought him to understand that, much as they adored each other, they had to eliminate George before they could live together on his money – and without Tristan ever having to work again. Laura had no fortune of her own, and Tristan was well aware that he could scarcely expect early retirement in the business he was in, let alone keep Laura in the style to which she was now accustomed. Put that way, committing a murder was the lesser of two evils for him. He hated work almost as much as he worshipped Laura, and she knew it. 'No, darling, my poor old George certainly isn't stupid, but he's not nearly such a good lover as you.' She moved closer to him. 'I can't wait to have you to myself for ever,' she whispered in his ear, before biting it.

There was no doubt that flattery had helped a good deal in making a villain out of Tristan.

'It'll be just light enough after supper on the Friday when I take George to look at the hole,' he said. 'I'll show him the piping for the water outlets, and how we'll fit the liner. It seems to cheer him up when I explain technical stuff to him. Probably because he needs convincing I know what I'm doing,' he completed in a self-deprecating tone, implying that George's attitude was understandable.

'And you'll dig the hole straight after you've dealt with him?' She watched his eyes after her pointed reiteration of events.

'Mm. It won't take long,' he answered, confidently.

He had passed her test.

The section of the south-facing, acre-sized garden where the pool was to be sited was screened from outside view by the house to the north, by tall hedging to the south and east, and was bordered, to the west, by a centuries old, six-foot-high redbrick wall that separated the vicarage from the church graveyard. Earlier on, they had considered slipping George into a substantial, flat topped Victorian tomb on the other side of the wall, over the remains of the couple lawfully occupying it. There was access to the graveyard through a nearby gate, but

Laura had abandoned this notion as too risky. Also, interring George in the same spot as he would meet his end avoided the possibility of incriminating evidence surviving where it could ever be found.

George had chosen a shallow pool, of the same depth all around, because it would save on costs. In the ordinary way it wouldn't save Tristan money, of course. But for him the job had long since ceased to be an end in itself. It was purely a means for providing a permanent, undetectable resting place for affluent George Bodworski

Disposing of the body was so often the undoing of conspirators like Tristan and Laura, and she knew it. But not only had she lighted upon the perfect solution to their problem, she had also devised a credible story to account for George's disappearance which would purportedly take place more than a thousand miles away from Farringly.

'Before I put George in… in his plot, I'll concrete it, then pack the soil around him. It'll all be well enough settled by morning,' said Tristan, now with the merest hesitation over naming the ownership of the extra cavity.

'And you're sure the faithful Ray won't suddenly show up to help you on the Saturday morning?' Laura questioned, running a finger across his lips.

'Absolutely sure. He'll be too busy catching up with his weekly pool maintenance work.'

'And George won't start sinking later?'

'Not a chance,' replied Tristan who had never buried anyone before. In the event he was lucky that his expectation proved to be right, at least on this occasion.

'And you're up to schedule, Tristan, are you?' George enquired. It was nine o'clock on the Friday evening, the night before he was due to fly to Poland. Tristan had joined the couple for supper as Laura had arranged he should. She was busy in the kitchen. Tristan and her husband were at the far end of the thirty-foot long, twelve-foot wide excavation beyond the terrace on the south-west corner of the house, the sides sustained by close set, parallel walls of concrete blocks. George was studying the plastic pipe-work for the lower water-outlet that ran out into a trench from the south end of the pool and then along the west side of it toward the outhouse, other piping joining it on the route. Tristan was standing immediately behind the other man. Nearby there was a pile of tools next to the temporary wooden steps the two men had used to descend.

'Yes, we'll be dead on time for putting in the pool-liner Monday morning,' Tristan replied, too tense now to be conscious of his unfortunate phrasing. He took a step backwards. Grasping the heavy duty hammer he had lifted from the pile, with a measured, two-handed swing he brought it down with all his strength and devastating effect on to the back of his victim's glistening head.

The rest of the plan unfolded exactly as intended, as well.

Tristan had returned at eight the next morning and laid the screed, covering what little visible evidence there had been of any disturbance to the previously wellraked and levelled earth-floor of the pool.

By not stopping for lunch, Tristan had completed the job just before two o'clock. He left immediately afterwards, calling a loud farewell to the Bodworskis, only one of whom was actually now alive to hear him, of course. It happened, though, that another widow laying flowers at her husband's grave beyond the churchyard wall attested later that she had heard Tristan well enough.

After returning to his own house two miles away, Tristan departed again an hour later for what he had previously told a neighbour would be an overnight birdwatching session in the New Forest, an hour-and-a-half's journey to the south-west, close to the Hampshire coast. Ornithology was Tristan's hobby, and a night's camping in pursuit of it was a common event for him in the springtime.

In fact Tristan altered course when clear of his own village, turning toward Heathrow. Once parked there, he had taken the courtesy bus to Terminal One, changing out of a padded anorak and heavy slacks into a grey check suit and lightweight raincoat in the men's room. In one significant respect he altered his facial appearance as well by attaching an ebullient false moustache to his upper lip, before checking in at the Club Class desk for British Airways Flight 852 to Warsaw. The plane left, on time, at 17:20, arriving at the Polish

Capital's Okecie Airport two hours and twenty minutes later at 20:40 local time, which was one hour ahead of London.

Laura had gone through the motions of driving her now non-existent husband to the airport to catch the same flight. Heavy showers had been predicted for the afternoon and she had waited for one of these before setting out, confident that the Farringley main street would be empty of pedestrians as a consequence, with no-one to notice that the passenger seat of her white, soft-topped Jaguar had been empty. She had, nevertheless, flashed her lights in greeting at the Reverend Adrian Ingran and his worthy if lacklustre wife, whose ancient Volvo station-wagon had been drawing out of the New Vicarage as she passed. The vicar recalled as much later without prompting, confirming her word that George had been with her, and volunteering that though his wife had been beside him, he thought that she had been cleaning her glasses at the time. In truth, while the cleric had recognised the car, he hadn't been able to see too clearly who had been in it. He'd only caught a side-on glimpse through its low-slung, rain splattered windows. What he had said about his wife had been uncorroborated and subjective wishful-thinking.

A passport-examiner at Heathrow had endorsed Laura's contention that Tristan would pass for her moustached husband once the distinguishing device was donned. The corresponding check at Okecie Airport was even more casual, with the uniformed official involved not even troubling to open George's passport. From there Tristan caught a domestic flight west to Poznan at 21:10, for which George had also had a ticket and a seat reservation. Tristan was delivered to Poznan forty minutes later – conveniently now already halfway back to the German border, by exactly following George's original travel arrangements.

Tristan next telephoned Laura to confirm her husband's safe arrival, using George's mobile for the purpose, ahead of dropping the instrument into the centre of a large clump of evergreens where it would no doubt soon be found, but not too soon. Then, instead of using George's guaranteed reservation at the airport's National Hotel, he changed back into his bird-watching gear in the men's room. He peeled off and flushed away the false moustache before packing his other clothes into the nylon backpack he had been carrying inside George's sole piece of luggage, a cabin-bag which he left hanging on the back of a cubicle door. The bag carried no owner's or manufacturer's identification. He then took the bus to the newly rebuilt main railway station on the outskirts of Poznan's old town, and bought a ticket for the 23:15 express train to Frankfurt, arriving there at 00:45. He had presented his own passport for checking when he boarded the train in Poland and when he left it again in Germany. Both examinations had been cursory, with no written notations involved.

Public transport to Frankfurt airport had stopped for the night. Since, on Laura's continuing instructions, Tristan was to avoid using taxis in his new guise as a budget-orientated tourist, he slept for several hours in a corner of the railway station's warm booking-hall. He shaved and showered in the men's room there at six, before taking the subway out to the airport. As he was well aware, there were any number of Sunday flights to London, all of them half-empty. In the belief that a foreign airline would be even less interested in his existence than a British one, either now or in the unlikely event of any enquiries being made in the future, he bought a standby ticket on the 09:20 Lufthansa flight to Heathrow. He collected his car on arrival and was back at his home by mid-morning, his ornithological trip abandoned early, he later took the trouble to explain to his neighbour, because of the now persistent rain.

The memorial service to George Bodworski was held in St Mary's church, next to his house, two years after it was accepted he left for the journey from which he was never to return. Most of the villagers attended. He had been well-liked locally and people were deeply sympathetic toward his wife who had borne her loss with great fortitude.

'Of course we must go on hoping, Adrian.' She had sighed, wide-eyed, as she and the Reverend Ingran, seated together on her drawing-room sofa, had been preparing the contents of the service sheet the week before. 'But in my heart I know he's... he's gone. Otherwise he'd have got in touch with me somehow, no matter how difficult it was, I know he would.' She paused, eyes now glistening as they lifted to gaze through the open window toward the placid surface of the swimming pool, the foundations of which gave solid assurance to the truth of her words. It consoled her to think that being buried in a vicarage garden was nearly as good as being in consecrated ground. Not that she was in any sense religious; only superstitious. She had never really cared to swim in that pool.

'I'm certain he was killed by thieves,' she went on, as it happened, again with perfect accuracy. 'He carried so much cash with him on those trips. That's the way in the antiques business, of course. A seller expects the money on the spot.'

'And you feel that someone saw how much—?' the middle-aged, athletic cleric had been supportive from the beginning toward his wealthiest and most glamorous parishioner. She had been a quite regular and generous member of the congregation since what nearly everyone now referred to as her bereavement.

'What else, Adrian?' she had broken in. 'I told you before, he always took £25,000 with him, in a mixture of sterling and Euros. Hard currencies. I used to plead with him at least to take travellers' cheques, but he wouldn't listen. So somewhere between leaving the arrival building in... in Poznan Airport, after he'd called me, as he always did, but before he could reach his hotel there, someone attacked him, or possibly abducted him. I'm sure of it.'

'And that time when you went to Poznan yourself, you learned nothing?'

'Nothing. The police theory is that after calling me, he decided to walk to the hotel and was set upon before he got there. He only had a light bag, and he liked to exercise after a flight. It was dark, of course.' She paused. 'Twenty-five thousand is a lot of money to most people, especially crooked people. If it was a gang of thugs that started out meaning to hold him for ransom, the money he had might have been enough. I mean to satisfy them without their needing to take more risks.'

'Indeed,' replied the clergyman. 'And, of course, he'd have put up a fight.'

'Oh, no doubt at all. I only wish I knew what they did with his body.' Slowly she turned her eyes from the pool, as a single tear ran down her cheek. 'I just hope he didn't suffer a painful or lengthy death.' On this, at least, she knew her hopes had long since been fulfilled.

'I've prayed for that often, my dear,' the vicar consoled her, stretching out a hand to squeeze one of hers. 'And you know you can count on me for anything I can do to help in the future?' Because of her warm response, he kept the hand where it was for longer than he'd intended before adding with a guilty primness: 'That applies to Charlotte and the children as well as me, of course.'

This is the life,' exclaimed Tristan Gyder-Smith, his feet dangling in the pool but not the pool he had built for the Bodworskis in Farringly. It was the pool that had come with the pretty, bougainvillea-draped villa Laura had bought in the hills behind Cannes on the French Riviera.

The South of France had suited them both – she because it was more *chic* than Spain, and he because wherever Laura wanted to live was fine with Tristan.

It hadn't all been plain sailing for the two of them since they had seen off George. Although for a pair with limited inventive brainpower between them, they had managed to bring off the perfect crime, there had been irritating surprises in the follow-up – the absence of a body being one. To date, this major deficiency had severely curtailed their freedom of action.

Fortunately George's business had been registered for tax purposes as a joint undertaking with his wife, with only one of their signatures required on cheques or contracts. This meant that while she had been free to dispose of the whole concern, the law demanded that half the proceeds of the sale had to be frozen for seven years against the possibility of George reappearing. Only after the statutory period was up would Laura be able to start proceedings to declare her husband legally dead, allowing her to claim all his assets, as specified in his will. Since the total valuation of their joint estate, including the Farringly house, was over £8 million (George had been a shrewd investor), Laura had accepted that she could rub along on half that until she became entitled to the lot. In addition, there was an insurance policy on George's life for £2 million. This too would not be honoured until he was legally dead, so that Laura reluctantly came to regard it as the delayed icing on the cake. It had been taken out by George at the time of their marriage far too long before his disappearance to suggest to charitable folk that it might have offered a reason for his wife to have murdered him. Since the insurance company was not a charitable institution, of course, its managers had, as a matter of routine, made discreet enquiries into the possibility of foul play before dismissing the abhorrent notion with a certain amount of entirely professional regret.

Laura had also been making discreet enquiries, but on her own behalf, about divorcing George for desertion, only to discover that such proceedings could not begin until five years had elapsed since the event. Her adviser had also warned that her ceasing to be George's wife might further delay her eventual outright entitlement to all his worldly wealth – including the life insurance money. She had thus decided not to pursue the course any further, on balance figuring that divorce might tarnish her nicely developing image as a chaste and grieving widow, while doing little or nothing to improve her existing material situation.

For Laura to continue as George's wife did, of course, elongate the conventionally 'decent interval' after which, and in the ordinary way, it would be socially acceptable for her to marry Tristan. This was the eventual, and in a sense precautionary course she had decided upon, after an objective appraisal of its merits, not the least of these being that a husband could not be obliged to bear witness against his wife.

Tristan had been strongly against a divorce, fearing it might still suggest a motive for Laura having been somehow involved in her husband's death – which was only a step away from the possibility of Tristan being involved in it with her. Altogether, while he was anxious to marry Laura for the purest of reasons, he rated their continuing status as innocents to be more important for the time being.

Over the two years, the pair had publicly acted out a friendly relationship that slowly and beguilingly had developed into something much more intimate. It was the Reverend Ingran who, by openly (and in a double sense vicariously) encouraging the liaison, by extension gave this mutual blossoming of affection the blessing of the church, and with it a moral status beyond challenge within the community, which included the regional constabulary. So it had not been for nothing that Laura had nurtured her association with the cleric whom she knew quietly idolised her. Certainly at the end of the second year, the holy imprimatur on the budding romance would have underwritten general approval of Tristan and Laura cohabiting if they had so chosen except that while they had both worked for this, it had never been their intention to activate it in the Farringly environment.

This was why Laura sold the house and moved to France.

Shortly afterwards Tristan sold his place for a good price. At the same time he gave the goodwill of his business to Ray Langford, the industrious young plumber. This was partly out of conscience, but equally because no-one except Ray would have bought it, and he had no money. In any event, the generous action was good for Tristan's image. It was clear to everyone that he was quitting the area to join Laura, but the matter was never the subject of malicious gossip. They both left the community with unblemished characters exactly as planned.

Laura too had found an instant taker for the Old Vicarage. The American buyer, Charles Pearce, was a high-flying partner in an international investment bank. He and his wife Janet, with their three boys, had been searching for just such a place for over a year. 'These days, you know,' Charles had remarked to Laura, after agreeing to pay her full and substantial asking price, 'a heated pool really does add value to a property.'

'My late husband never believed that,' she answered with a moving sadness, then added, 'but he still built this one for my pleasure. It... it was his last birthday present to me.' She now invariably referred to George as her late husband, and very nearly all the village people did the same.

'I'm so very sorry,' the young banker's pretty wife had offered at the time in a bonding, deeply sympathetic tone.

Tristan pulled his feet from the pool at the sound of a motor engine. 'I think that was the postman,' he said, striding into the house. He reappeared a moment later with a small clutch of envelopes. 'One hand-written letter for you with an English stamp. Can't read the post-mark,' he offered, passing the envelope to Laura who was sunning herself on a yellow-cushioned lounger at the pool's edge.

'Oh, it's from Janet Pearce,' she remarked with surprise. 'Funny, she's never written before. Always telephones.'

Janet, the new *chatelaine* of Farringly's Old Vicarage, had further warmed toward her predecessor when she had been making frequent visits to the house, deciding on new fabrics and furniture, before Laura had moved out.

'You should tell her email's cheaper than steam mail. Quicker too,' offered Tristan, settling beside her on a matching chair.

'She's not computer literate,' Laura went on, scanning the letter. 'Oh, and the poor thing's got laryngitis, says she has no voice at all and...' She stopped suddenly with a gasp, one hand leaping to her mouth. A moment later she uttered: 'Oh my God, Tristan, listen to this.' She began reading aloud. ' "You know how crazy our three boys were about the pool from the first time they saw it? Well all through the Easter holidays they've practically lived for their swimming, Andrew, our oldest, in particular. Now they're all back at boarding school and he's been put in as a reserve member of the senior swim-ming team. He's the youngest member but will very likely be captain next year, only the master who runs the swimming wants him to concentrate on diving, says he's a natural. Andrew is over the moon but, yes, you've guessed it, he wants to know if we can have our pool deepened to eight feet at the far end, with a diving board, of course, so he can practice when he's at home. As you'd expect, our other two are just as keen on the idea. We've told them it would all be too expensive to do, but Charles is so chuffed for Andrew he's got your nice Ray Langford on to the job straight away. Ray's promised to have the whole thing ready by half-term which is only five weeks away, so it's all hands on deck. Really it means starting again with virtually a new pool with a sloping bottom. Ray's suggested we have what's called a gunite base this time, with a blue ceramic finish. It should last for ever. Charles agreed, and work starts tomorrow—"'

'What's the date on the letter,' Tristan put in tensely.

'April twenty-third,' she answered looking up, her face drained of colour.

'That's six days ago.' He let out a deep breath. 'On the first day Ray will have torn out the pool-liner. He'll have had a drill and excavator in on the second, which is when he'll have struck the grave.'

'Tristan, we'll have to—' she began.

'It's probably too late for us to do anything,' he interrupted despondently. 'Even for me to do a bunk.'

'No it isn't, and there's plenty of cash upstairs.' Laura looked at the time before continuing rapidly. 'If the police come, I'll swear for ever I know nothing about what happened to George. That's what we've always said, isn't it… if the worst happened?'

'That I'd take all the blame? Of course,' Tristan completed for her, with total resignation. 'Stick to that and—' But he was cut short by a long, insistent ringing on the door bell.

A black Citroen saloon was drawn up in the villa's driveway. Three men had alighted. One was a uniformed French policeman, the others were detectives from the Thames Valley Police in England. There were a dozen more French officers, flak-jacketed and heavily armed, deployed around the fenced perimeter of the building in the street on the sloping, garden boundary to the south, and in the grounds of the two neighbouring villas.

It was the fence on to the lower road that Tristan had been scaling when he was overpowered, though he subsequently put up no resistance.

The English detectives were carrying something metaphorically quite as explosive as guns, in the warrants for the arrest of both Tristan Gyder-Smith and Laura Emily Bodworski on charges of murder and conspiracy to murder George Stanislaw Bodworski, plus a formal request for their prompt extradition to Britain.

At the subsequent trial, Tristan pleaded guilty, partly because the evidence against him had been overwhelming once the body was unearthed. After admitting his impersonation of George, Tristan's further story, invented for him by Laura, had been just about credible. He confessed to murdering George for his money in a deserted part of a Heathrow car park, tricking him into going there after check-in.

That he had left the body in the trunk of his car, and buried it in the pool after returning next day, all without Laura's knowledge, had been very nearly swallowed by the court. He had hoped his plea might shorten the length of his sentence – but he was still jailed for life.

So was Laura.

Her insistence that she'd later become Tristan's innocent dupe and lover might have held up, including that he had fooled her by imitating George's voice on the telephone from Poznan. But it was the evidence of an unexpected witness that had finally spoiled Laura's case.

The Reverend Ingran had agreed that he couldn't swear absolutely he had seen George being driven off that Saturday afternoon and it was the pressure from his faithful wife that had brought the admission. The lady had endured enough of her husband's incessant counselling of the Widow Bodworski when she had lived in the village, and during her months on remand before the trial. So when Mrs Ingran herself had then robustly testified under oath that the only occupant of that car had been Laura, the game was over.

Charlotte Ingran had never intended to allow the rich and guilty harlot to be freed, ready to seduce her besotted Adrian away from his sacred vocation, as well as from his deserving family.

And she might well have been right.

# AUTHORS' BIOGRAPHIES

**Ann Cleeves** is best known for her Inspector Ramsay novels set in Northumberland, but she has recently turned to non-series novels of psychological suspense. *The Crow Trap, The Sleeping and the Dead,* and *Burial of Ghosts* have earned considerable critical acclaim. As a member and bookings secretary of the Murder Squad collective, she works with other Northern writers to promote crime fiction.

**Mat Coward** was born in 1960 and became a full time freelance writer and broadcaster in 1986. Having written all manner of material for all manner of markets, he currently specialises in book reviews, magazine columns and short stories – crime, SF, humour, horror and children's. His first crime story was shortlisted for a CWA Dagger and he has also published two novels: *Up and Down,* and *In and Out.*

**Judith Cutler**, now based in rural Kent, draws on the murkier depths of Birmingham for her two acclaimed series of crime novels and for many of her short stories. Sophie Rivers, her feisty amateur sleuth, made her debut in *Dying Fall* and has been Dying to right wrongs ever since. Police officer Kate Power burst on to the scene in *Power on her Own,* and has continued to live up to her surname. Judith has also published romantic fiction set in Devon. Until recently the Secretary of the Crime Writers' Association, she has now turned her attentions to organic vegetables.

**Carol Anne Davis** writes both crime fact and fiction. Four reviewers chose her mortuary-based novel *Shrouded* as their debut of the year in 1997 and its successors include *Safe As Houses* and *Kiss it Away* She has published three non-fiction books, *Women Who Kill, Children Who Kill,* and *Couples Who Kill.* Carol's short stories have appeared in anthologies and magazines and have been placed in national competitions.

**Martin Edwards** has written seven novels about Liverpool lawyer Harry Devlin, published a collection of his short fiction, *Where Do You Find Your Ideas? and other crime stories*, and edited fourteen crime anthologies. His eight non-fiction books include *Urge To Kill*, a study of homicide investigation. In 1999 he was commissioned to complete the late Bill Knox's *The Lazarus Widow*. His latest books are a psychological suspense novel, *Take My Breath Away*, and *The Coffin Trail*, the first in a new series set in the Lake District.

**Jürgen Ehlers** works as a geologist at Hamburg State Geological Survey. Since his graduation from Hamburg University, he has published more than fifty articles in scientific journals as well as five books about Ice Age geology. In addition, he has contributed to a number of anthologies published in German.

**Kate Ellis** was born and brought up in Liverpool and studied drama in Manchester. She has worked in teaching, marketing and accountancy, and first enjoyed literary success as a winner of the North West Playwright competition. Keenly interested in medieval history and 'amateur' archaeology, she lives in North Cheshire with her family. Her novels featuring Detective Sergeant Wesley Peterson began with *The Merchant's House*, and the most recent is *The Plague Maiden*.

**Michael Gilbert,** born in 1912, was one of the first writers whom John Creasey approached when proposing to establish the CWA. Gilbert has edited a number of CWA anthologies and was awarded the CWA Cartier Diamond Dagger. The range of his work is extremely wide and includes thrillers, spy novels, plays for stage, radio and television, as well as non-fiction books. His short story collections include *Stay Of Execution*, *Game Without Rules* and *Petrella at Q*.

**Lesley Grant Adamson** worked on provincial newspapers before becoming a staff writer with *The Guardian*. Her first novel was *Patterns in the Dust* and her most recent, *Undertow*. Her other publications include *Teach Yourself Writing Crime Fiction*, currently in its second edition.

**John Harvey** is a poet and dramatist, as well as a novelist. He is best known for the series of crime novels featuring world-weary cop Charlie Resnick, which began with *Lonely Hearts* and was televised with Tom Wilkinson playing Resnick. His latest book is *Flesh and Blood*.

**Reginald Hill** is the author of over forty books, including the internationally acclaimed Dalziel and Pascoe series, which has been successfully adapted for BBC television. His other series character is the Luton private eye Joe Sixsmith. His many awards include the CWA Cartier Diamond Dagger and the CWA Gold Dagger for *Bones and Silence*. His latest book is *Good Morning, Midnight*.

**Edward D Hoch** is a past president of Mystery Writers of America and a winner of its Edgar award for best short story. In 2001 he was honoured with MWA's Grand Master Award. He has been guest of honour at the annual Bouchercon mystery convention, two-time winner of its Anthony Award, and 2001 recipient of its Lifetime Achievement Award. He has contributed to every issue of *Ellery Queen's Mystery Magazine* over a period of more than thirty years.

**Bill Kirton** was a university lecturer before taking early retirement to become a full-time writer. He has written and performed in revues at the Edinburgh Festival, written, directed and acted in stage and radio plays, presented programmes on Grampian Television and written and directed countless commercial videos. He has published two crime novels, *Material Evidence* and *Rough Justice*. He was one of the Royal Literary Fund's first Writing Fellows in Scotland and will be taking up a second Fellowship at Dundee University in 2004.

**Keith Miles** was born in Wales and educated at Oxford; he has written over forty plays for radio, television and the theatre. His published work includes biography, literary criticism, short stories, children's fiction and sports books. The majority of his crime novels are historical mysteries, written under the pseudonym of Edward Marston – the Domesday Books; the Nicholas Bracewell series, set in the Elizabethan theatre; and the Redmayne Mysteries, featuring an architect who is helping to rebuild London after the Great Fire of 1666. His latest book, set in the Victorian era, is *The Railway Detective*. He is a former Chairman of the Crime Writers' Association.

**Stephen Murray** is the author of seven crime novels, and his short stories have appeared in magazine and anthologies in the UK and USA. He lives in mid Wales and breeds Alpacas.

**Amy Myers** has had short crime stories published in many anthologies and in *Ellery Queen's Mystery Magazine*; a collection of them is shortly to appear under the title *Murder 'Orrible Murder*. She is also the author of a series of eleven crime novels featuring the Victorian chef-sleuth Auguste Didier and – under the pseudonym of Harriet Hudson – historical sagas and romances. Before becoming a full time author in 1988, she worked in publishing, editing fiction and non-fiction. Married to an American car-buff, she lives in Kent.

**Christine Poulson** was a lecturer in artistry before she began writing fiction. Her first novel, *Dead Letters*, features literary historian and accidental sleuth Cassandra James and is set in Cambridge. The second in the series, *Stage Fright*, appeared last year. Christine has also written widely on nineteenth century art and literature and she is a research fellow at the Centre for Nineteenth Century Studies.

**Chris Simms** has worked in airports, nightclubs, post offices and tele-sales centres. After travelling throughout the world, he settled near Manchester. Married with two young children, he works as a free-lance copywriter. His debut novel, *Outside The White Lines*, is followed by *Pecking Order*, another dark psychological thriller that builds towards an edge-of-the-seat finale in a grotesque and horrific battery farm.

Born in Wales, **Sally Spedding** studied sculpture at college, and is still a practising and exhibiting artist. She has won awards for her poems and short stories and her novels have also earned critical acclaim. She is married to a painter and lives in Northamptonshire, but writes in their home in the Pyrenees.

**Rebecca Tope** is the author of eight crime novels, mostly set in the farms and villages of the West Country. The first of a new series, *A Cotswold Killing*, was published in 2004. Rebecca is a member of the Secrets of Crime Writing collective and lives on a small-holding in Herefordshire. She is the Membership Secretary of the CWA.

**Alison White** was born and bred in Liverpool and returned to the North West after some time living and working in London. She has published many stories in magazines and her work has also been broadcast on BBC radio. Her short crime stories have appeared in a number of anthologies as well as in *Ellery Queen's Mystery Magazine*.

**David Williams** was a Welshman who founded a successful advertising agency before leaving commerce, following a serious illness, to start a fresh career as a full-time crime novelist. He created two detective series, featuring respectively Mark Treasurer and Merlin Parry, and two of his titles were shortlisted for the CWA Gold Dagger. He died in 2003.

# The Do-Not Press
## Fiercely Independent Publishing

# www.thedonotpress.com

All our books are available in good bookshops or – in the
event of difficulty – direct from us at the cover price (UK
and Europe only):
The Do-Not Press Ltd, Dept CotM,
16 The Woodlands
London
SE13 6TY
(UK)

If you do not have Internet access you can write to us at
the above address in order to join our mailing list and
receive fairly regular news on new books and offers. Please
mark your card 'No Internet' or 'Luddite'.